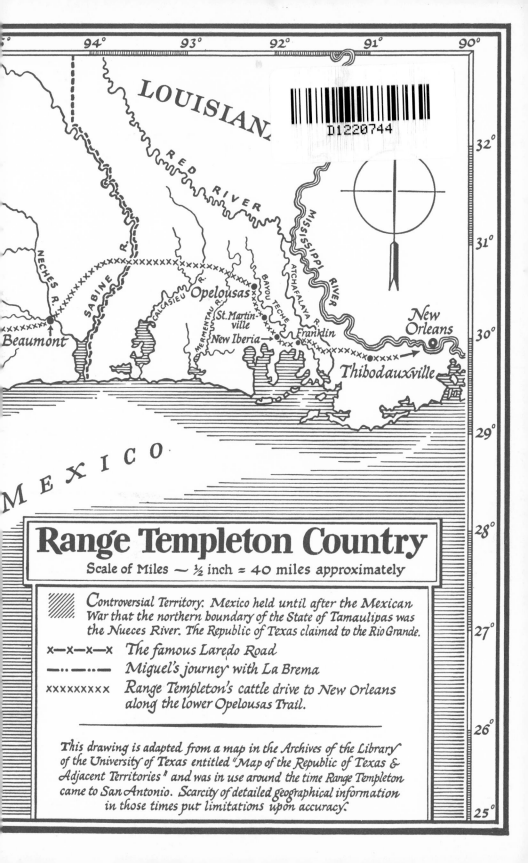

Range Templeton Country

Scale of Miles — ½ inch ≈ 40 miles approximately

▨ *Controversial Territory. Mexico held until after the Mexican War that the northern boundary of the State of Tamaulipas was the Nueces River. The Republic of Texas claimed to the Rio Grande.*

x—x—x—x *The famous Laredo Road*

—..—..— *Miguel's journey with La Brema*

xxxxxxxxx *Range Templeton's cattle drive to New Orleans along the lower Opelousas Trail.*

This drawing is adapted from a map in the Archives of the Library of the University of Texas entitled "Map of the Republic of Texas & Adjacent Territories" and was in use around the time Range Templeton came to San Antonio. Scarcity of detailed geographical information in those times put limitations upon accuracy.

ELITHE HAMILTON KIRKLAND

DIVINE AVERAGE

A HISTORICAL NOVEL ON THAT

PERIOD OF TEXAS HISTORY

WHEN "COW BOY" WAS A PHRASE

WITH A CONTROVERSIAL MEANING

AND "TEXIANS" A NATIONALITY

Shearer Publishing · Bryan

F
KIR

WB RG

Published in 1984 by

Shearer Publishing
3208 Turtle Grove
Bryan, Texas 77801

Copyright © 1952, 1984 by ELITHE HAMILTON KIRKLAND

First edition published in 1952 by Little, Brown
and Company, Boston

Library of Congress Catalog Card No. 52-6787
ISBN 0-94067-219-7
Reprint of the 1952 edition published by
Little, Brown and Company, Boston

Printed in the United States of America

APOSTROPH

O Master! O fils!
O brook continental!
O flowers of the prairies!
O space boundless! . . .
O race of the future! O women!
O fathers! O you men of passion and the storm!
O native power only! O beauty!
O yourself! O God! O divine average! . . .
O to promulgate our own! O to build for that which
    builds for all mankind! . . .

                        —WALT WHITMAN

To my father Free Hamilton
as kindly and tolerant a man as ever lived
and my mother Eva Hamilton
who loved him dearly

DIVINE AVERAGE

CHAPTER I

Luvisa Templeton's Account

BEGUN ON APRIL 21, 1858
AT SAN ANTONIO, TEXAS

I, LUVISA TEMPLETON, age 36, a consumptive soon to die (and I look upon the condition as a path of deliverance), have just recently, on April 15, 1858, given birth to my third child, a stillborn, conceived in a moment of violence and abuse as intense as the sweet passion of young love out of which I bore my precious twins, Luke and Laska, some twenty years ago.

I feel compelled at this time by the spirit of the Holy Mother and the force of God to leave an account of the things that have happened to me and mine. It all lies on my heart like a confession that must be made before I can die in peace . . . a confession not only for myself but for my husband, Range Templeton, who despises me now after twenty years of loving me; for my daughter Laska, lost to us and to herself, a companion to outlaws in the wilds of Mexico; and for my beloved son, Luke Templeton, so bold of mind and pure in heart.

I have returned to my grandfather's home in San Antonio and shall die here on the very bed where I was born. I have said good-by to the great ranch house across the Nueces. I saw my husband for the last time standing on the wide upstairs porch looking out in bitter contemplation upon his possessions, giving no sign to me in the departing coach, somehow balancing the loss of me, the loss of his

3

whole family, against the land out there, the land that for miles to the south, every inch and grain, every thorn and blade of grass, belongs to him alone: to Range Templeton! O Merciful God in Heaven, why was it never given unto me to understand him completely? If ever a man is to be understood, it should be by the one woman he has loved devotedly and lived with constantly for twenty years — a wife whose mind and heart, whose very soul, were always open to receive him. But it must be confessed at the very beginning of this account that I have found many locked doors as I walked down the corridors of my husband's mind. And yet these things I am so pressed to record are mostly about him. It is a shameful thing to relate and yet I must say it: that I have understood the character and actions of Miguel Sándivar (to whom my husband was hostile) oftentimes much better than his own. Perhaps it is because I want so much for someone to understand him that I leave behind me this account to be preserved and read and studied. If it cannot be understood in this generation, perhaps it will be in the one to follow, or the one after that.

If I am to die in peace, although despised and put aside by the one I love, I must believe, in spite of all mistakes and suffering, in the divine purpose of the life span . . . the gradual accumulation of goodness in the consciousness of the human race until pain and ignorance and greed are all crowded out, and somewhere down the passages of time the way cleared for more joyous living on earth. Now that I am about to die, I find it necessary not only to believe in a better life after death, but also to believe in the possibility that those who come after me may have a better life here on earth than I have known. My friend, Mr. Bryson, smiles a little as I say this and, I'm sure, considers me a little childish and fanciful in my illness. But he will write it all down. He has promised, and he is a man of his word — a man of mystery and much learning, Mr. Bryson, and the only tie I have left, you might say, with my husband. For Mr. Bryson is a friend, a very close friend, to every member of the Templeton family, a sort of guardian angel for these past

4

twenty years. He smiles again at the word "angel," and I'll admit the expression hardly fits him. But I'll tell more about Mr. Bryson in the proper order. I simply want you to understand why he is here with me in San Antonio and not with my husband at the ranch. My husband had him bring me here and instructed him to stay by me until the end. And now Mr. Bryson is humoring me in my resolution to have these things written down. It is fortunate for me that he writes such a fine hand and is so well equipped by education and experience to express the things I sometimes find difficult to give a clear meaning. Then, too, it matters not to him if I speak in English or the soft Spanish I love and have so denied myself in the presence of my husband who despises the sound of it.

Mr. Bryson has promised me too that when all this is done and I am gone, he will place it in proper hands with instructions that it be preserved until such time as it might seem fitting to give out for reading, in a book perhaps. I wonder when that time will be? How many generations before these things I have to tell may cease to be commonplace and become significant? Is it too much to hope that in some future generation these events may stir the minds and warm the hearts of men and women destined to know more and see further than those of us here now? Perhaps I attach too much importance to the life I have lived and the lives of which my living has been a part. But I yield completely to the compulsion that I must leave such a documentation. What becomes of it is in the hands of God.

Twenty-two years ago today, the great Sam Houston was victorious at the Battle of San Jacinto and many Texans consider this date the most important in our history thus far. But I have a much more personal reason for holding April 21 in cherished and sacred memory. It was twenty years ago today in Dr. Weideman's study that Range Templeton kissed me for the first time and I recognized that it was my destiny to love this man to the end of my natural life.

So I'll begin with that spring of 1838 when Range Templeton came to San Antonio and took board and room at the house of my grandfather, Ed Olson. Spring comes early in San Antonio and that

5

year the bluebonnets were blooming by St. Patrick's Day. Life in this settlement twenty years ago was an excitement to all the senses, and I can call back that excitement without the slightest effort: how colorful and confusing were the mixed garbs and languages of the Indian, the Mexican, and the American . . . the savage, desperate with the intrusion of the white man; the Mexican, uncertain and uneasy in the new republic so recently wrested from Mexico; and the American stranger so bold and possessive. I remember hearing my grandfather say there were about two thousand persons in San Antonio that spring, two years after the fall of the Alamo; and among that two thousand, the only ones who bore themselves with dignity and aloofness as though they belonged to the place and it to them were the aristocratic Spaniards whose roots were a hundred years deep in this settlement, for they were descendants of hidalgos and settlers of a king's colony. Over the Rio Grande was the threat of Mexican armies who still coveted San Antonio, and over the western hills was the threat of the Comanches who coveted the scalps and horses of every inhabitant. But dangers and fears could not erase the beauties of springtime nor hold back the caress of the soft winds. The plaza, often so dusty and warlike with things military, wore for a while a mantle of deceptive calm. The plaza, then as now, was the heart of the settlement and the San Antonio River its main artery. East of the plaza, willows waved dreamily and cottonwoods rustled an invitation to sit on the riverbank and drowse in the deep shade or lose one's thoughts in the placid movement of the blue-green waters.

But Range Templeton was not the dreamy type to slow his step to the pace of a climate or pause for the fragrance of a flower. I'm sure that first spring in San Antonio he observed few of the natural beauties. But he saw and learned the meaning of the ax set down with purpose by the door, the knife carefully placed at the belt, rifles and pistols primed and never put away, and all good horses under heavy padlocks in their stalls — for the Indians around San Antonio next to lifting a red-haired scalp had rather steal a good horse.

6

My grandfather was responsible for this preference. His nickname was "Firebush" because his hair was a fiery red and his beard only a shade darker. He trimmed his beard not at all and his hair only when Grandmother's threats became unbearable. When Grandfather became angry, his face and neck would flush to match his hair and his whole head would seem aflame. Range Templeton hadn't been in San Antonio three days before he heard the stories about Grandfather; I could tell the difference in the way he acted. Most young men when they first heard about Grandfather would get awfully curious and excited and try to set him talking about his Indian fights. I was surprised that Range Templeton didn't act that way. He just became more respectful and attentive. That caused Grandfather to talk to him more than he ever had to any other young man. Grandfather's passionate hatred for Indians was a decided influence on Range; and so I must put the reasons for it in the record, although it is not easy for me to do.

What hate made of my grandfather is as sad as the event which caused him to hate. My father was Ed Olson's only son and my mother loved as a true daughter. One evening (I was five years old at the time), they senselessly strolled up the river a ways, hand in hand, never having recovered from being in love, too happy to be alert to danger. When my grandfather went to search for them, he found their butchered bodies. He buried them in the pink shadows of the flowering queen's-crown vine that is still spread like a canopy across the corner of the high rock walls enclosing the back yard. He would not allow Grandmother or a single friend to look on or help. What prayers he said, what revenge he swore was his secret with God, or the devil. But it was not long until he had killed more Indians than any man in the settlement. Those who fought with him soon learned of his methodical mutilation of the bodies after battle, and forgave him the barbarity, for they realized it was a duplication of what he had found up the river that day.

My grandfather never scalped an Indian — he beheaded him. He collected the heads in a rawhide bag always tied to his saddle. What

7

he did with the gruesome trophies was also a ceremony of his own. In returning with a fighting party, he always left them before arriving at the settlement and came in several hours later with the fateful bag empty. The Indians, it was generally believed, knew about the ceremony and the indignities it implied.

It was not in the bold nature of Range Templeton to be repelled by the stories about Grandfather. Quite the contrary; he felt awe and a certain admiration, I am sure. Grandfather sensed this and it pleased him. His obsession had cankered his true nature and he was beginning to feel a certain vanity in his vicious exploits. He and Range began to have long talks, and that was how it came that Range was so well prepared in mind and method for fighting Comanches at seventeen though a greenhorn in Indian country.   .

He had come to San Antonio from Tennessee, traveling overland with a family moving here all the way from North Carolina. His parents had died in a plague when he was just a baby and he'd lived with his Uncle Jesse Templeton. When he made up his mind to leave his uncle and come to the Republic of Texas, the old man must have been greatly saddened, for he had no children of his own and he knew better than Range the uncertainties of life on a frontier. But I don't think he protested, for he bought the piece of land Range had inherited from his parents, making it possible for him to get a fine horse, proper equipage for travel, and still carry a money belt with enough coin to meet his needs for some time.

My grandparents were rather strict with me. I did not eat with the boarders and only occasionally passed polite conversation with them. For a week or so after Range Templeton arrived, our acquaintance was limited to several long looks and a few brief remarks. I learned that he liked the Republic of Texas better than the United States of America, that he liked brush country better than hill country, that he liked to wear buckskin better than homespun, and that he liked Range Templeton better than anybody else in the world.

Although Range was only seventeen when he came to Texas, he had a length of stride and a breadth of confidence that pro-

8

nounced him a man. Indian Toego, the horse that brought him to Texas, and Eli Dawson, the man who gave him a job soon after he got here, were both instrumental in getting him accepted around San Antonio as a man full grown. A copper chestnut lean of flank and long of limb, Indian Toego was fleet as a mustang and brainy as a blueblood, a strong man's horse, a tall man's horse of such height that he could be mounted with dignity only by a man of Range Templeton's proportions. And Toego was partially responsible for the job Range got with Eli Dawson. Dawson freighted from San Antonio to the border country, and sometimes beyond. He hired riders to protect the goods in his wagons from marauding Indians and robber bands. He picked men fearless enough to relish a fight with the Comanches and well mounted enough to escape or pursue as the conditions of battle required. Dawson had made a rule not to hire a man who hadn't killed at least ten Indians. His first exception to this rule was Range Templeton. He told Grandfather that he thought the boy was a natural born Indian fighter and Grandfather said he felt the same way. Eli said he considered the boy a good risk as a rider on another count too: that the animal he owned had the longest neck and the longest legs he'd ever seen on a horse, and, furthermore, if he, Eli Dawson, ever had a chance he'd lay his money down and be as sure as come-Christmas that Templeton's horse could outrun anything that Indian, Mexican, or white man was astraddle of in Texas. I overheard what they said and knew Eli was hiring horse as well as man. But it was a man's job by any measurement, and I felt proud and excited in a way I was certain my grandmother wouldn't approve of. I had never sought a young man's attention before, but I set out to do so now, and did it very cleverly, I think, considering how careful my grandmother was of my conduct and how shy Range was of women. After siesta time, he'd usually be sitting on the porch and I'd come out to make my daily visit to the church. . . .

*　　　　　*　　　　　*

9

Range was waiting for Luvisa, and any minute now she'd open the door and pretend surprise at finding him there on the front porch. Then he'd walk with her across the plaza to the church entrance and wait while she went inside with flowers for her saint, a candle for her prayers, or some gift for the parish priest. Range had no feeling about religion. He figured it was for women and old folks.

Toego's head came up and his ears pricked forward sharply. Range let his chair clop to the floor and jumped to his feet, removing with courtesy the big-brimmed hat he wore with bravado, the tilt of it to the back in a cavalier flourish, the top crushed flat. Luvisa was standing there. The door must have been unlatched, and she always moved with an easy quietness.

Her bright blond hair was done in loose braids and fashioned into a neckline knot that was more of a natural gesture than a style. Her dress was one of severe modesty with full skirt, long sleeves, and high neck, but its color gave her a kinship with the flowering huisache tree in the patio — the same cool, inviting green of the fernlike leaves of the huisache — her head the rich, soft gold of its blossoms. A creamy bit of shawl loose about her shoulders would be used to cover her head when she entered the church.

She smiled at Range.

"Miss Luvisa, you come on a feller quiet as an Indian."

The smile left. The dark centers of her wide gray eyes expanded. The startling dark-brown eyebrows raised just a little.

Range had said the wrong thing. Luvisa nourished a memory as bitter, though not as vicious, as her grandfather's. In her expression the emotional scar left by severing childhood from adoring parenthood at the age of five was plain and harsh. Range shared the painful instant with her. He even indulged in an undefined yearning for his own parents, lost to him in an epidemic when he was too young to be caught in memory's clutches.

Range spoke no word of remorse for his clumsy remark. They simply looked at each other and reached an understanding. In this understanding they were discovering strange new compensations for old losses. They felt the stir of inner certainties and strength, but neither was able as yet to express them. Range helped Luvisa down the front steps and they walked slowly and silently toward the church. It pleased them to be together.

Range was a little more than a year older and a little more than a foot taller than Luvisa. There was something of swagger, something of sureness, in the way he walked, wearing fringed buckskin with youthful elegance, carrying with ease around his hard-muscled waistline the belt that held two heavy pistols and a knife. The slight figure of Luvisa moving at his side, green skirt swishing, further emphasized the confidence of his carriage, added a certain dignity and rhythm to their movement across the plaza.

An old Mexican crone, dressed all in black, stopped and muttered to herself as she watched them pass — a prayer for youth or a curse for old age. A Mexican wood-hauler let his burro make its own way while he openly stared at the couple. A group of roughly clad soldiers looked and remarked in undertones among themselves. A flashy stranger, black-booted and black-hatted, paused indifferently but allowed himself a raised eyebrow and a cynical smile a moment later. They walked on down an aisle of attention to the very door of the church where Luvisa quickly disappeared and Range remained standing outside as if on guard.

When they left the church together, their steps were slower still and they turned to that side of the plaza which would make the way longest to the Olson House. Range had to mention his job with Eli Dawson. With the men he had pretended indifference about it, but here was a chance to brag without exposing youth or inexperience.

"I'm riding with Eli Dawson's wagons, pulling out next week."

Luvisa didn't comment at once. As he waited for her answer, Range felt a physical surge of pleasure that cut short his breath for he knew she would call him "Mr. Templeton." Luvisa was the first person ever to address him in this full-grown fashion.

"When did you ever do any fighting, Mr. Templeton?"

11

"I never. Unless you'd count the bear hunts I been on in Tennessee as fighting."

"How did you make Eli Dawson think you had?"

"I didn't. I wouldn't lie to get a job, Miss Luvisa."

"He doesn't hire men who aren't Indian fighters, Mr. Templeton. My grandfather says a man must kill ten Indians before he can ride with Eli."

"He thinks I'm a born Indian fighter, Miss Luvisa. He wants to see me kill my first Indian, I reckon."

It was four measured steps before she had anything more to say. Her lips moved in a "Madre de Dios!" without a sound.

"And is it something you can hardly wait to do — kill an Indian?" was the quiet inquiry she turned back to him.

His answer was not quick but there was nothing uncertain in the sound of it. "I aim to live in this part of the country and I reckon that means the Indians got to die."

"Oh, I see. You expect to kill them all, Mr. Templeton?"

Range was unabashed. "I expect to get my share, Miss Luvisa."

"And when there are no more Indians, what will you do?"

"I'll get me some land — all the land I want — thousands of acres of it!"

Luvisa didn't register any surprise at his intensity.

"Then what, Mr. Templeton?"

"I'll build me the biggest house in the whole Republic of Texas!"

They were back at the Olson porch. Range, with dreams wild in his eyes, reached out and absent-mindedly patted Toego and let his hand rest on the horse's neck.

"And who will live with you in your biggest house?"

Luvisa's question startled Range a little and his reply was made with instinctive male caution. "I'll figure that out later, I reckon." He looked away from her, wishing he'd said something else.

She was at the door ready to leave him.

"I am sure that you and your beautiful horse will be very happy in the biggest house in the Republic of Texas."

The door closed behind her and he thought he heard laughter. That confused him more. He hadn't said anything funny nor, by his estimate, had she.

Range was baffled and uneasy. Luvisa had left him with feelings he couldn't account for. His breath was short as if he'd been running. He felt the same excitement he had when Old Man Dickson, who'd been his companion in the overland trip from the States, announced they were on the soil of the Republic of Texas, "Where a man can have what he can take."

He felt the same fear his Uncle Jesse had told him about that time when he knew he was going to kill a full-grown bear without any help. "You'll feel a tremble and a sweat," Uncle Jesse explained, "a sort of torture of the senses. But it'll pass and your strength will flow and you'll know what to do."

Well, it had been like that and he hadn't felt any less manly because of the fear. But that was a bear and a contest of life and death. He couldn't complete the analogy. He only knew he felt the "torture of the senses" and he wished the mist would clear and his strength would flow.

Luvisa had walked into his fantastic Texas dream house and he wasn't at all sure he knew what to do about it. Uncle Jesse had told him exactly how to take care of himself in the hunt or the fight. But nobody had instructed him about women.

He started to put his foot in the stirrup, and then realized he hadn't untied his horse. Toego turned his head and gave his master a pitying look.

Range headed for the river road to give Toego a workout. Here the men of the settlement came in the late afternoon to exercise and train their horses. For about two miles the road stretched out among the cautiously placed agricultural plots extending south from the plaza along the river. The horses that pranced and paced and reared and ran along this road every day were some of the fleetest in America.

Their common characteristic was speed. Their breeds and strains were as diverse as San Antonio's population. Some were of the finest bloodlines from the deep green pastures of the Southern states. Some were the wild mixtures of the Texas plains whose last orthodox ancestors were the pride of nomadic Arabians centuries ago.

In the Republic of Texas in 1838 a fast horse was the best guarantee a man had of staying alive. So the best horses, used for escape and pursuit, were kept carefully in their stalls, as protected as a man's family.

Today the first rider to greet Range was Dr. Weideman on his bad-tempered little filly Nightmare. Dark brown in coloring, with flowing black tail and mane and a black stripe down her back, she was dangerous as a tiger under anybody's hand but the doctor's. Her kicks were vicious, especially styled for surprise, and she would fight man or beast with the abandon of a rat terrier and the tenacity of a bulldog. The doctor made no attempt to alter Nightmare's natural inclination to violence. Her viciousness served him well during Indian raids and gave her an immunity from horse thieves.

She reared up, snorted, and rolled her eyes, displaying insult and fury at the very sight of Toego who shied a little and looked shocked that one of his own kind could be like this. It was Range's first meeting on horseback with the doctor.

"What do you think of my little black devil, young man?" the doctor asked gaily, pulling Nightmare to a reluctant dancing stand, her nostrils flared, her ears back just a little.

"I'd like to buy her from you if'n I was hell-bent on suicide."

"I see you understand character in the horse-flesh. I only sell her to my most unworthy enemies — the ones I don't want to take the trouble to kill myself."

The doctor laughed and left it up to Range to decide whether to take him literally or not. He was twice the age of Range Templeton. He had been born a century or two before his time, realized it, and considered the matter a huge joke on himself. He had seen much of the world, spoke many of its languages. He was a Russian scholar, trained as a physician and surgeon in the czar's household. He was

14

also a naturalist and was on a government mission in this field, making a study of the vegetable and animal kingdom of the region, collecting birds, snakes, and wild animals. Most of all he was having fun, fighting Indians and studying them . . . moving in the society of the best families, being amusing, giving them occasionally of his excellent services as a doctor . . . and continually playing pranks on the ignorant and the prejudiced. This doctor with the spirit of an adventurous, aggressive American, the viewpoint of a world citizen, and the humor of a misguided adolescent, was probably less of a misfit in San Antonio de Bexar than he would have been anywhere else in the world.

With a hand on Toego's neck to quiet him, Range sat silent in the saddle watching the doctor and the ferocious little beast under him. He was willing to talk but had nothing to say. He never approached new experiences with words and he'd never met up with nor heard about anybody like Dr. Weideman. The doctor realized this and was enjoying it.

"If I were an artist, young man from Tennessee, I would here and now dismount from my demonita and do a virile sketch of you, sitting so quiet on that quiet steed of yours, ready to take off into the violence and the madness of the future."

Range sat even more quiet.

"Oh, you New World gladiator! You do not know how violent!"

Range did not know what gladiator meant. He stopped looking in front of him and looked straight at the doctor. And waited.

"Do you know what I would call my sketch? 'Lusting for Land.' But I'd have to be careful about the eyes, for there's where I see it strongest, in the steady, flat, uncompromising gray of your eyes. It is not an easy thing to detect in a man, this lust for virgin soil — not so easily discerned as the more physical passions. But you have it, and I should like to be witness to what it makes of you."

Range shifted a little in the saddle.

"Shall I continue my analysis?"

Range appeared to nod.

15

"You are shamefully strong and amazingly temperate in your habits. You will need only one woman if you are well matched. Drink and evil companions are not your kind of trouble, but violence and intolerance will draw you close if you don't beware. And allow me to caution you, Hercules, rawboned and unawakened as you are, against a certain narrowness in your mind that could worm-eat the nobility within you. As you come upon this new land and possess it, you must fight and hate. To fight better than the Indian or Mexican is necessary . . . to hate wisely is also necessary — an important character development. Can you understand that?"

"Some . . ."

"Do I mystify you?"

"I never met your kind of man before."

The doctor threw back his head and laughed. Nightmare reared up high, and he jerked her to her four feet again.

"Do I frighten you?"

The expression on Range's face was a mild sneer.

"I am known widely among the populace here as 'El Demonio.' It is a belief firmly held by many that I am in close league with the devil."

Range showed some amusement for the first time. "Are you?"

"There are times in dealing with the godless when one needs the devil's aid."

"Like when you fight the Indians?"

"That is one example."

"I hear next to Firebush you're the best fighter in these parts."

"That's a reputation I nourish carefully."

"Maybe you and the devil could give me a few pointers."

The doctor laughed again. His black eyes sparkled with high merriment. "Maybe we could. In the name of His Satanic Majesty, I accept your offer."

"What offer was that?"

"To learn . . . It is as important that a man offer to learn as another offer to teach."

16

"I already know a few things. I can throw two knives from my two hands and hit two different marks quicker'n a bear can blink, and I can set my ball and powder for a shot before you can say 'honey in a holler log!'"

"Let me add that before I can say 'honey in a holler log' an Indian could release three arrows from his bow and throw his lance with remarkable accuracy. And as for the time it takes a bear to blink, a Mexican skillful with the blade could plant a knife in each eye while the impulse to blink is being formed."

Range accepted this information in silence.

The doctor was thoughtful for a moment. "You have been in this newborn republic for only a few weeks, and yet you consider yourself a Texian?"

"I like it well enough to stay, if that's what you mean. And I aim to take root."

"And spread out?"

"That's it — spread out."

"You realize, don't you, that your identity as a Texian is still strongly contested. The Mexican Congress denies the very existence of the republic — Texians are rebels and heretics."

"I heard the war was over."

"Then open your ears wider and hear again. The war has only begun."

"That's all right with me."

"It will be all right with you only when as a warrior you can excel both the Mexican and the Indian. Here in this area I see a triangular conflict of cultures hemispheric in its significance. Right now the triangle is equilateral, but soon — " The doctor broke off. "Do my mathematical terms elude you?"

Range was not easily confused. "I never had much trouble with arithmetic," he said, looking the doctor straight in the eye. "I can add, and I can take from, and I know my times tables through the twelves."

The doctor's mouth twitched with suppressed amusement.

17

"That is entirely sufficient. If you take from and add to an adequate number of times the result will no doubt be astonishing."

Range ignored the implication.

"I'm pulling out with Eli Dawson before long."

"Allow me to congratulate you. You know, of course, heavy betting is being made."

"On what?"

"On you. I myself have up a token fee in your favor."

Range felt a current of excitement rise up heavy in him bringing a small flushed spot to each cheekbone. "I wouldn't want you to lose anything."

"Then get back here from Laredo with your hair on your head and the same horse under you."

"I aim to."

"That's the reason I'm betting. I think you're destined to do what you aim to. But that horse of yours will be coveted by every Comanche that rides a lesser one . . . and you as a fighter are a babe in the brush. I must offset that some way. I must give you some special instruction. If the Indians do not accommodate us with a raid soon, perhaps we can take a little ride too far out some afternoon and invite them in."

"Suits me."

"As a teacher I have no peer. I adapt my methods to my pupil." He bowed slightly to Range. "Until we meet again then . . ."

The doctor made a sweeping gesture with a black-gloved hand that put Nightmare in a dancing frenzy to be off. When he released the bit, she twisted and struck out with a vicious back kick that neatly sliced a bit of hide from Toego's rump, and then was off down the road in a dead run. The cape the doctor affected swept out behind like a small black cloud.

Toego lashed out with a return kick much too late, almost unseating Range. He jerked the reins with a quick harsh hand.

"Devils!" he muttered between clinched teeth. "Devils, both of them! Horse and rider, hell's henchmen!"

Toego trembled under him. Range became conscious of the horse's alarm, spoke softly and relaxed in the saddle, reining the sensitive, excited animal into an easy canter that took the tension from both of them.

In the next half mile they met no other riders, and Range was about to turn back when he heard hilarious whooping and yelling just ahead and came out upon an improvised race track. The run forked out of the main road to the left and extended in a wide curve down to the river's edge and back into the main road. Most of the riders, about a dozen in all, were scattered along the track waiting for two others getting in place at the main road for a dash between a scrawny, long-haired, shabby pony and a classy, well-cared-for, blooded animal. A heavy-set Mexican of Indian visage, his coarse black hair tied down with a kerchief, sat the pony indifferently. The other rider was one of the adventure-clad young Americans who had become a class unto themselves since recruited from the States during the Texas Revolution. Bold, undisciplined, cocksure, they sat their horses with vanity and a challenge. Definitely, this one considered the competition beneath him. They were waiting for a signal from some point down the track. When it came it was a piercing "Yi-eee!" from someone astride a paint pony stationed at the halfway point. The horses and riders picked up the signal at the same instant and were off. Toego insisted on a similar response but Range held a tight rein and continued to ride along the main road. He believed Toego could outrun any horse in San Antonio, but he wasn't ready to show off. He wasn't shy, but he was careful about timing — and it was no time for calling attention to himself. He didn't feel easy about the betting on his ability to fight Indians. He liked to win and brag. But he didn't like to brag before winning.

He noticed to his surprise that the scrawny pony carrying the heavy Mexican was going to win the race by a length. He put his astonishment aside for future reference. Toego's excitement as the racing pair approached him was almost exploding in Range's hands, so he said "Let's go then, boy," and gave Toego's long limbs their

19

freedom through the reins. They were off up the road and out of sight from the race track in a copper-colored flash, and Range left Toego in the long streaking run for another mile.

Only one person on the track had been conscious of the streak of dust and color that was Toego disappearing down the river road, and that was Firebush Olson. He screamed, "Stop, you damn young fool, stop!" before he realized that his warning could not carry beyond the frenzied yelling of his companions as the race approached its climax with the shaggy Indian pony in the lead.

The Indians were an ever-present and constant menace on all sides of the settlement. In the two years since the Revolution, the Comanches had taken more than a hundred women and children captive and killed double that number of men. No man ever traveled alone beyond well-defined limits. Efforts at farming small fields just outside the settlement had been repeatedly abandoned because the Indians were so adept at scalping the labor and stealing the horses. Time and again sad parties had gone out from the city to recover the bodies of those who traveled too carelessly along the roads at the edge of town. This was the reason for Ed Olson's frantic call to Range. Beyond the race track the road was dangerous for a single rider. But Olson did not strike out after Range nor organize a group to overtake him. He was somewhat of a fatalist. He shook his head slightly, pursed his lips in concentration as if making up his mind what would happen, then dismissed it all in a big bellow of laughter at the outcome of the race.

Range and Toego were enjoying themselves. After the thrill of the run, Toego was calm again and had settled into a rocking-chair gait that gave Range time to consider the scenic side show that was the San Antonio River. After a while, he turned off on a side trail where he could approach the water and let Toego drink. In the middle of long thirsty swallows, Toego raised his head and pricked his ears inquiringly toward the riverbank on the right. He started to finish drinking but instead raised his head again. It was then that Range realized he had come too far. He knew, for Toego had told him plainly, that something was nearby and moving toward them.

Since in the brush and timber near the river there was no chance of locating an enemy, he realized for the first time in his life what it was like to feel no protection in gun or knife. The fleetness of his horse, with some trick movement and maneuvering on his part, was the only chance if Indians were watching him. If they were only on one side of him, and he believed they were . . . He tightened the reins . . . alerted Toego with his heels and was just ready to jerk him into a quick turn when a hoarse voice so close that his very flesh felt the sound of it cried out to him.

"Wait! Please God, wait!" And a dry strangling sound punctuated the cry.

Range could not locate the body to the sound . . . it was from his immediate right hand. His spine tingled. His throat felt tight. He said nothing.

There was a silence, then another dry strangling sound.

"I need help! I am a woman. . . . Say something to me! O Merciful God, can't you speak English?"

"Sure, I can speak English. What's your trouble? Is anyone with you?"

She began to sob, rough, dry, gasping sobs. She was still completely hidden from view, but very close by. No doubt it was a woman, Range thought, with all that crying, but the voice was peculiarly hoarse. Was it a trick or trap of some kind? Why didn't she come out of cover? If he dismounted to see, he would be at a disadvantage — maybe that was the trick.

"It's gettin' a little late. . . . I got to be movin' on back. . . . Come on out and talk to me straight, or I'll have to get along."

There was a rustle of movement, some branches were pushed aside and Range saw the head and shoulders of the woman. He gazed at her in a fixed stare of horror that drew the muscles tight in his stomach with a retching sensation and caused the palms of his hands and the soles of his feet to burn and sting painfully. The woman stared in terror lest the horror she must cast upon him drive him away.

She wore a ragged buckskin blouse. Her hair hung in matted shreds a few inches long over her forehead and around her head as if chopped off with a dull knife. Her face was covered with open filthy sores, and the nose was not there, only two heavy scabs where it might have been. One ear was gone and the other hung as if the blow intended to sever it had fallen a little short. Her disfigured, toothless mouth hung open for breathing and for the words that would not articulate now that she must reveal herself.

Range was the first to speak. "What's your trouble?" he asked again.

Her tortured lips moved but no sound came.

"You're — you're not an Indian?"

She shook her head. "White woman . . . Jeannie Dodson."

"Are you by yourself?"

"My boy . . . hidden back there."

"No Indians around?"

She shook her head.

"You got away from 'em?"

She nodded.

"How long they had you?"

The pain in her eyes was an additional horror to behold. She held up a hand. It had only three fingers on it. He supposed she meant three years.

Range couldn't think of anything else to say so he said, "Get the boy."

The leaves were a curtain between them again, and only by listening intently could he detect her movements as she went for the child. Range's face was beaded with sweat. He still looked at the spot where she had appeared, waiting for her to reappear not looking as ghastly as his mind still pictured her.

She came back out into the trail above him and called, "Here." She was holding a boy, probably five years old, by the hand. He

22

was scratched and thin, ragged and sad, but not matching the utter wretchedness of his mother. Range rode up close and dismounted. In full view the woman's misery was ultimate for she was heavy with child.

"Take the boy to his father," the woman said. Her concern with the child gave her more composure. "Do you know Pete?"

"Pete who, ma'm?"

"Pete Dodson. . . . I said back there I was Jeannie Dodson."

"I haven't been around here long. I don't know many people."

"I'll tell you where to find Pete. . . . It's a house on Acequia Street. . . ."

It dawned on Range that the woman was talking as if she weren't going into town with him.

"You can tell me after we get there, Mrs. Dodson. It's nearly sundown. We won't have time for me to take the boy in and send back for you. My horse carries double and he's easy gaited. I'll help you up behind and take the boy in the saddle."

"I'm not going back. You take the boy."

"I won't do it that way, Mrs. Dodson. You'll be killed if I leave you here after dark."

"I've stayed alive seventeen nights after dark since I got away. I could stay alive another one, if I wanted to."

Range realized the woman had no intention of going back with him, and yet to leave her alone was unthinkable.

"You let me help you on now. . . . I won't take the boy back without you go along."

"I can't ride a horse . . . the way I am," and then she lashed out in her strange hoarse voice, "unless you want to midwife an Indian bastard along the road somewheres."

The realization of the full measure of Jeannie Dodson's torment and tragedy hit him like a slap. Fury coursed through him. This woman degraded and mangled by savage hands and bodies might have been as young and lovely as Luvisa . . . might have been as loved by her husband as he could love Luvisa. Manhood in all its

23

cherished idealism rose up so strong in rebellion within him that his body was racked with a passion and a storm. And he hated violently for the first time.

Mechanically he lifted the boy up behind his saddle and climbed on himself. Mechanically he said, "Stay around here. I'll send a cart back," knowing all the time that she wouldn't stay around.

"Take the boy to the Olsons . . . they'll take him to Pete."

"I stay at the Olson House."

"Ella'll know what to do."

They looked at each other. Was she trying to tell him something more . . . give him some message for Pete . . . ask him to fashion a story about finding the boy alone? He never knew. He could find no words. And her lips moved soundlessly again as when she had first exposed her hideousness to him. The boy gazed at his mother in apathy. He had not said a word since he had appeared with her on the trail. He said nothing now.

Range prodded Toego and they set off in a fast trot. The woman stood gazing after them, her misshapen figure grotesquely in silhouette against the dark-green trees.

CHAPTER II

JEANNIE DODSON who had wanted to die so many times during the last three years still wanted to die, but she was not quite ready. She had thought she would be ready when her son was rescued from savagery and restored alive to his father, and she was fixed in her purpose that the hateful, forced life within her broken and befouled body should never know existence outside her womb. Yet she was not ready to die.

She knew an intensive search would not be started for her until the next morning. The sun was down and the afterglow was dim.

She turned back down the trail, moved into the woods along the riverbank, and with animal-like caution began to make her way toward the settlement. Her destination was a house on Acequia Street.

Range had dismounted at the stables where Firebush was finishing his evening chores. "Whatcha got there?" Olson inquired good-naturedly, pulling his bushy eyebrows together as he squinted at the boy, clothing a leaping curiosity with a kindly smile for the hungry-eyed child.

"Could Luvisa and Mrs. Olson clean him up and feed him while I kinda have a talk with you?"

"Sure could. Come along, son."

Range lifted the bony, silent little figure from the saddle, and then stood very still leaning against his horse until Olson returned. He recounted what had happened in choppy unemotional phrases. Firebush listened, standing like a wrathful thunder-god: his fists clinched, his legs wide apart, his head thrown back, his breath slightly hissing between his teeth. The story brought the lines of his whole body into a pose of majestic hate.

Range stopped talking, waited a minute, then said flatly, "What do we do?"

Firebush had no answer. Finally he spoke another question, "What'll Pete do?"

"We better go find out what he'll want to do. He'll be glad to get his boy, and he'll want to find his wife . . . I reckon. If you'll go with me and show me where he lives — "

"Don't get back on your horse till I tell you some things. We got to take this slow."

"But that woman out there — "

"Now see here, that woman won't be out there if we go. Even if she wanted to be found, it would be a risky business unless we roused the town and took plenty of riders. You tried to bring her. She wouldn't come. That's got to be the end of that until we clear things up at this end."

"Clear what things up?"

"Like I said — there's some more to the story. Stable your horse. He's tired. And I'll tell you about it."

After Toego was fed and the stable door carefully locked, the two men sat on the edge of the water trough . . . and a radiant moon, not quite full, rose and shone brightly on them. Haltingly, for Ed Olson was not a man of eloquence, the story of Jeannie Dodson was told to Range Templeton.

Pete Dodson had built a new house on Acequia Street. He had a little mercantile business and had done well — well enough to order some furniture from New Orleans. He'd gone to the coast with some trusted Mexican cartmen to haul the stuff back to San Antonio. His wife, a lovely energetic little woman he'd brought with him from South Carolina, had stayed in their new home during his absence with the two children, Molly, five years old, and David two. There were two Negro servants, Russell and Annie, given to Jeannie by her father when she married and came to the Mexican province of Texas, and she felt no need for further protection when her husband was away.

On the fatal night when Jeannie was made captive, Comanches had crawled and snaked their way through back yards and lots until they had collected a herd of good horses on the edge of town. No one had been aroused until Jeannie, disturbed at the restlessness of one of the children, was wakened. As she rearranged the cover, she glanced out the window in time to see one of Pete's best horses being led from the stall. She was more infuriated than fearful. Quietly and quickly she rushed downstairs and into her servants' room off the kitchen and roused Russell. He must slip out the side door, she insisted, and rush to Dr. Weideman's a few doors away and tell him to sound the alarm. Russell was reluctant, but she pointed out he couldn't be in much danger since the Indians were at the back raiding stalls and stables. She opened the door to let him out and stood for a moment watching him — stood a moment too long, for two Indians who'd made themselves invisible against the outside wall near

26

the door let the Negro pass unmolested. A woman would be a better prize. They snatched Jeannie from the doorway and stopped her scream before it left her lips. Then to their own surprise, there was David the toddler just behind her; he had been awake and following her around unnoticed. So they took him too. The thieves were well out of town and on their way with the horses and two captives before any pursuit was organized. The men who finally took up the vain chase were seriously handicapped because their best horses had been stolen. To make the story easier to tell Pete Dodson, when he returned a month later, the friend who bore the message related how the bodies of the mother and the boy had been found far to the west weeks later by a rider who passed through San Antonio. The rider had carefully buried the bodies, Pete was assured. Nobody could ever tell him who the rider was or give him any clue as to where the grave might be. The myth was perpetuated so that Pete wouldn't go out of his mind thinking about what was happening to his wife among the Indians. All the men knew too well what usually happened to captive women. Olson didn't enlighten Range on this point; he just went on to tell how Pete decided to take little Molly back to South Carolina to live with Jeannie's aunt. Jeannie's mother was dead and this aunt was almost as young as Jeannie, looked a lot like her even. When Pete got back to South Carolina, he stayed several months. It was hard to leave Molly, and Jeannie's aunt was a sweet, good woman. So she and Pete were married and came back to San Antonio. They had a baby boy. A lot can happen in three years.

Now what could he tell Pete, Olson wondered.

"Tell him the truth," Range said.

"It'll be hard on Pete . . . and hard on his wife . . . makes their marriage unlawful."

"That's easy compared to what happened to Jeannie."

"Yeah . . . but we got to take more thought for the living than the dead."

"Jeannie's not dead yet."

27

"Likely she is."

"She wasn't ready to die."

"How could you tell?"

"Just the way she was standing there when I left — like she had something else to do."

"What would it be?"

"I don't know. I just felt that way."

"Hmm . . . let's go talk to Weideman before we see Pete . . . he likes to figure things out."

Pete Dodson and his wife Julia were late retiring that night. Neighbors had visited until almost midnight. When they were gone, Pete felt restless and unwilling to go to bed. Julia watched him anxiously.

"Are you worried about something, Pete?"

"Just kind of wide-awake — feel like I ought to be doing something."

"I think you've done enough for one day. Let's go to bed."

"Not yet, Julia. I'll read a little. You run along. Don't fret. I'm all right. I just want to sit up awhile."

Julia didn't protest. She kissed him lightly, sighed a little and turned to leave the room. At the door, he called to her.

"Turn around and let me look at you."

She turned and smiled gravely.

"You are very beautiful."

"Thank you, my dear. Good night."

When she had gone, Pete's face reflected the utter sadness in his eyes. It hurt him sometimes to the very marrow of his bones when Julia looked so frighteningly like Jeannie — as she did tonight. It put madness into him. He wanted to run out into the night screaming for Jeannie.

He relighted his pipe, walked around the room without purpose, blew out all the candles except the one he'd take upstairs, and finally stopped before a window opening on a small, well-kept flower garden.

He propped his foot on the casement, took a few puffs on his pipe, and studied the outline of the flowers in the bright moonlight. Their perfume was deep and rich and somehow discomfiting to him. His sadness deepened into misery . . . into desperation. God help him, was his reason fleeing his body? Why was his very spirit being squeezed and twisted in this nameless torment. "O God," he groaned aloud, "O God!"

There was movement near the garden gate, just behind the white oleander. Pete caught it, even in his distraction. Someone was in the garden. Someone who knew the place well. The entrance to it was too intricate for a stranger. There was none from the front, and the one from the back he and Jeannie had called the secret passage. The garden was very small and very private and had been Jeannie's idea when they built the new house — even the latch on the gate was a trick one. Someone was in the garden.

Pete did not know what to do about it. He decided it must be just his nerves, after all. But again there was movement and some slight sound that told him nothing but panicked all his senses. He had to get out of the room. He had to get into the garden. The window was heavily barred. The way around through the house and the side yard was further than he could possibly go. He didn't want to leave the window. "Don't go away!" he panted, "Don't go away!" and went stumbling through the house like a blind man. Julia came running down the stairs.

"Pete!" She was frightened. "What is it, Pete?"

"Don't get in my way!" She was delaying him. The hall was dark and he hadn't picked up the candle. He was breathing like a man wounded unto death. "I've got — to — get — to — the — garden."

He bruised himself against chairs and table corners until finally he stumbled through the back door and into the moonlight. He fell to his knees once on the trail around the house and crawled a few steps before he could find the strength to rise. And just as he got to his feet, the figure collided with him on the narrow path. It was a hideous figure, made even more hideous by moonlight, and the

29

stench of it suffocated him. It was past him and gone, and he leaned against the house heaving with a violence that tore at the very roots and core of him.

Jeannie Dodson stumbled on out into the deep shadows without identity.

Range and Olson visited late with Dr. Weideman. He had insisted that they eat with him, that they seat themselves comfortably and smoke and discuss the Dodson case calmly and in detail. Pete was his neighbor, and a good one, he said, and his life must not be ruined. Also, they must decide what to do about Jeannie; her part in the drama of life was not finished, he said. She had one more entrance to make.

Firebush didn't understand what he meant by that.

Range understood a little. He said again, "She was not quite ready to die."

"Would you like for me to tell you what she is doing now?" the doctor asked.

Olson thought the doctor was joking and it was no time to joke.

Range was looking at the doctor, and felt the power of the man. "Sure," he challenged, "tell us."

"This is diagnosis, my friends, not black magic. I knew the woman once — the lovely, lively Jeannie Dodson. You have told me her condition, now I will tell you what she will do. After she has been relieved of the suspense about the safety of her child, she will have one last thought for herself, one last generosity to herself before she takes her life. She will return to look on her home and her husband in secret."

The doctor's diagnosis was accepted by both his listeners.

"She may even be there now," he added.

"Shouldn't we go see?" Range asked. "Maybe we could save her."

"For what?" Olson countered gruffly. "For who?"

"I guess it's too late," Range said, thinking how she looked when he left her.

30

The doctor, suddenly feeling the full conviction of his own pronouncement, jumped to his feet in anger. "Who do we think we are?" he blazed. "God's three wise men? The Holy Trinity? Sitting here like judges on the bench of destiny! I shall go out and find Jeannie Dodson. I will cleanse her wounds — heal her sores — deliver her child as a doctor should! I loved a wife once!" He shouted at them. "And in spite of all my fool's artistry, she died — died in youth and beauty — untouched by hands other than my own!" The doctor raised his hands and shook them in a wild gesture before his face. "But had she met Jeannie Dodson's fate, I would have loved her still. I would have wanted her ministered to, not shunned and left to seek death alone, as we are leaving Jeannie Dodson!" He ended his outburst with a heavy foreign expletive that tore at his throat, and in complete agitation grabbed his hat and slammed it on backwards. Range and Olson, disturbed, were ready to follow him. The three men made a confused exit at the back of the house.

But they didn't have to go hunt Jeannie Dodson. She was there, at the very doorstep where she had fallen after her flight from the garden. She had tried to get up. She was on her hands and knees, rocked back and forth by convulsive jerks. Her wheezing gasps for breath were punctuated with hardly audible whimpers.

The men moved at the doctor's command. Jeannie's filthy heaving body was carried with difficulty and placed on a clean high bed. José and Carlota were wakened and issued rapid orders in Spanish that sent them scurrying from room to room bringing what he demanded. As the doctor started cutting and ripping the ragged, rotten buckskin she'd worn so long, revealing the white skin of her naked body and the scars it bore, Olson turned away and said, "I better fetch Ella."

The doctor snapped at him, "Spare Ella. Remove your coats, both of you, and if you are men enough, stay on your feet." As if to complement this statement, Carlota at that moment set a basin of soapy water on a table near the bed, and slid quietly to the floor in a dead faint.

31

"Drag her out of here," the doctor instructed the horrified José. "Leave her flat on the floor. Then bring me more water."

The next three hours were a sweating, harrowing struggle in the fetid fumes that rose from the writhing anguish of Jeannie Dodson, lacerating the emotions of the two men who must hold her while the doctor cleansed her sores, time and again sponged blood-flecked foam from the corners of her mouth, and used every skill he knew to induce the childbirth that would release her from the rack of pain. Life's protest against the long torment of this woman's mind and body was expressed in an extremity of pain and a fetor of decay that defied control or diminution. Yet the doctor did not yield before this defiance, and the old man and the young man working with him poured their strength in with his, measuring out a triple portion of male sweat and stamina to match the single portion of female blood and agony.

The sounds in the room were the old man's labored breathing and occasional mutterings . . . José's barefooted scuttle out of the room and back again, out and back again, automaton to the doctor . . . and the doctor's low-voiced constant stream of talk to himself, to Jeannie, to his servant and the men at the bedside with him. But no sound from Range, for the needle of experience was cutting deep and etching strong into the very fiber of him a complete sensory picture — a picture that was to flash clear before him time and again as the years made manifest the pattern of his destiny. He met Jeannie Dodson's frantic and uncontrolled responses to pain with a certainty of movement and strength of grip that followed exactly the doctor's instructions. But not a single sound from Range Templeton: hands steady, pupils dilated, nostrils flared, neck cords drawn taut, sweat pops on brow and cheek hollows rolling off when he'd shake his head a little after matching his strength with that of the pain-crazed woman. From Jeannie Dodson all sound was involuntary: choking gasps for breath before the stab of each labor pain and dry wheezing pants after, and sometimes the inhuman whimper; but no screaming or crying, for that had been erased from Jeannie's reflexes

32

three years ago on that first night of capture when she had endured countless savage perversions and debaucheries — endured them silently that her child might not be terrorized, endured them that night and many more, kept alive only by the will to live that she might rescue her child. And now Jeannie Dodson could not scream or cry. Neither could she give birth to the symbol of vicious lust housed in her womb. Again Jeannie's will was performing unnaturally.

"She has been delivered of two children normally and yet for this one the womb will not open," the doctor was saying to himself, "the resistance is psychological and absolute. I once attended another woman who wanted life so much within her sterile body that she developed in all her functions as a pregnant woman develops although no life had been conceived . . . and now here is this woman whose mind denies the actual life within her so conclusively that no labor pain is strong enough, no physician's manipulation skillful enough to cause it to be born." Then he added, almost matter-of-factly, "The pains are now so hard and so frequent that she will die within the hour, the child still clutched tight in her womb."

The two men looked across the bed at the doctor, Olson's eyes frankly prayerful that she might be dead this instant, frankly grateful to God that the child could not be born; Range, however, was inquisitive, seeking, expecting something more this side of death, looking to the doctor for some new instruction.

The doctor met the look, and a slight twitch at the side of his mouth indicated that he acknowledged the demand reflected there. He gave José specific instructions for bringing more instruments.

Jeannie's pains were now less than two minutes apart. In the few seconds while she lay limp and still, her body accumulating some final dregs of strength to meet the ever-increasing violence of labor striking with all of nature's fury at the wall of her will, the doctor said strange things to Range and Olson.

"It is in such extremity as this I am inclined to indulge in the weakness of self-pity, for it is a sad thing, in the nature of a deformity

33

or an affliction, to be born out of one's time. You, Ed Olson, with your courage and intolerance, twisted by events as you are, fit well into the colors and rhythms of your time . . . and you, Range Templeton, compounded of strength and nobility, of passion and the storm, are an example of exact timing, carefully selected and designed for the here and now. I, on the other hand, prove that in the eternal power must reside a sense of humor, for in me have been placed thoughts without outlet and skills without tools. So I laugh with the gods at myself and occasionally turn a trick that I think pleases them and somehow fits into the mysterious and unrevealed pattern of all life. I am about to turn such a trick now. I would be a surgeon in any age, but in this one I have at my command none of the potions or compounds, injections or inhalations, that a century from now will ease the pain of the patient and enhance the skill of the surgeon. So I will leap beyond that time into the centuries still further ahead when the mental skills may surpass the physical, when misnomered black magic may become applied wisdom for the greater man. And you shall help me make the leap. You must not distract me or the woman by thought or touch. All right now, let us see her through this one . . . then you must stand quietly . . . believing simply that she will sleep."

Jeannie's anguish rose and subsided again in the awful swirl and tangle of pain. This time there would be scarcely more than sixty seconds of release, and soon within the quarter hour, would start the final relentless tempo of pain from which death alone could furnish release.

Range and Olson stood, their hands not touching Jeannie or the bed, trying to subdue the sound of their heavy breathing, trying to believe she would not have to meet the implacable force of pain again.

Jeannie's eyes remained constantly open . . . in the excesses of pain they were rolling and darting about expressing a trapped-animal terror, seeking an escape that was impossible — expressing, too, all the agony that should have come forth in shrieks and cries. When

34

the pain would recede, her open eyes would fasten on a cut-glass paperweight that flashed gaudily on the table among the doctor's paraphernalia of dressings and bottles and basins. In a desperate visual concentration on the object, she was trying to sidetrack pain from her consciousness. The doctor had observed this.

He was holding Jeannie's hand. He leaned over the bed until his face was on a level with hers, blotting out the vision of the bright paperweight. Her eyes began darting again, seeking the object, seeking a way around the face to the brightness beyond. Then he began talking, quietly, clearly, and with conviction.

"Jeannie . . . look at me . . . listen to me . . ; I have something to tell you . . . it is important . . . it will pull back the curtains of your pain and leave you in a place of cool and fragrant quietness. There this agony will be stripped from you . . . for I shall take it and carry it away with me . . . and your body will rest in this place . . . in all purity and slenderness it will rest. To get to this place of peace, Jeannie, you must look at me . . . look deeply into my eyes and I can take you there. It will take so little time . . . but you must be very still and look at me steadily . . . then you can close your eyes and see the place, Jeannie. It is a place blue and green and silent and without presence . . . a place of such cleanness that only love can touch it, a place of such beauty that only the spirit can know it . . . Jeannie . . . let me take you there . . . we have so little time . . . we must go now, Jeannie . . . steady . . . look now . . . think . . . think of the sweet rest in the blue-green silence."

Jeannie's eyes focused and cleared. Looking directly into the doctor's eyes, they took on a coloring of mad brilliant blue. For an instant her body tensed as if to leap out against the doctor in a wild abandon to pain. Then her gaze reached further into the dark intensity of his, and the madness passed, and the color became tranquil, and a veil dropped. The lids closed slowly, softly. And a deep, heavy, hypnotic slumber reached out to the tips of all her senses and beyond into the place of blue-green silence.

35

The doctor's face was very pale, drawn into strange, unnatural lines. He motioned with his hand for Range to come stand beside him. He placed the instruments José had brought on the bed close at hand, and in a time so brief that his witnesses could not believe what he had done, his knife made the Caesarean incision, deep and long, and there was a high gush of blood, and the doctor reached into the great gash with precision and brought forth by its heels a plump boy baby, lusty for life, breathing and yelling on the instant, and all those in the room shared an inexplicable moment of undiluted exhilaration at this manifestation of the triumph of life over death. The doctor lay the baby nearby, not taking time to sever it from the placenta until he had stopped the dangerous flow of blood. Then he turned to the child, performed the final surgery that gave it freedom from its mother's womb, wrapped it in a towel and placed it in the arms of a bewildered José.

"Is Carlota revived?"

José nodded.

"Take the child to her, and as she values her own life tell her so to value this one."

Then he looked at Ed Olson . . . saw the conflict rising . . . saw the hatred gathering in him . . . felt the accusations to come. "Sit down, Ed," he said kindly. "Sit down and rest."

He gave all of his attention to Jeannie again, and the only things he said were the things necessary to co-ordinate the steady hands of Range Templeton with his own. Range brought him the things needed to complete the operation. The doctor closed the abdomen with careful sutures and dressings, and brought clean, white order to the bed on which she lay. Then tenderly, almost cautiously as if she might be easily awakened, he arranged a sheet to cover her, tucked a large white napkin around her head to hide the matted ugly tangle of her hair and the mutilation of her ears, and placed a dressing across the maimed remnant of her nose. Her face in complete repose was less hideous now.

Olson, who was watching the doctor's every movement, spoke to

36

him heavily, chokingly for the first time since the ordeal had begun.

"She still alive?"

"Yes . . . still alive."

"Can you wake her when you want to?"

"Yes . . . I can wake her . . . she must rest a little more."

"You know how the Indians waked her up, don't you?"

The doctor didn't answer. He seemed remote, detached.

"They stuck a live coal of fire to her nose . . . that always woke her up quick."

The doctor appeared not to hear him. He said to Range, "You and Ed go to the kitchen and drink something."

Olson got to his feet. His thoughts were not easily deflected. "You done a wicked thing . . . goin' ag'in nature . . . givin' life to a half-breed nobody wants. Whatcha gonna do with it, drown it or give it back to the Indians?"

"Why no, Ed, I shall keep it myself," the doctor said calmly, and then knowing he would shock and baffle the old man into complete silence, added, "You know that is my official business here, collecting wild-life specimens of this region."

Olson was stunned, uncomprehending, for cynicism was as foreign to him as the Russian language itself. His rage submerged in bewilderment, he left the room with stiff awkwardness. Range followed.

The baby was crying continuously in the servants' room off the kitchen where José and Carlota were occupied with its care. Its voice had the vigorous healthy sound of new life discovering the satisfaction of lung expansion combined with the instinctive plaintive appeal that brings adult subservience to a baby's demands. Range and Olson tried to ignore the sound. José had hastily set out food for them before running to Carlota's assistance. Neither of them reached for the food. Instead, Olson rummaged in the cupboard until he found brandy. He didn't bother to pour a drink but lifted the bottle for several heavy swallows before sitting down at the table, his hand still tight on the bottle. Range poured strong thick coffee from the pot that sat on the back of the stove, its flavor the bitterness from

37

long accumulation of grounds. Then he drank the scalding liquid as if it were lukewarm.

Still the baby's cry played high discordant tunes along the edges of their nerves . . . and the sound of it mixed with the brandy to rouse the tired fury of Firebush Olson to a new fierceness. In harsh snatches he told Range Templeton the full horrors of Comanche cruelty as he had learned of it in more than twenty years of frontier warfare, and he felt stimulated by the high response to hatred he could feel emanating from the young man. He told of a Mexican captive whom the Comanches had carried with them for several days' journey, showing him the kindest treatment and even deference and admiration, but when he helped them dig a deep and narrow hole for what he thought was to be a religious ceremony, it turned out to be his own grave into which they thrust him alive in a vertical position, tightly bound from neck to ankles. His head was left sticking above ground; and to accent the torture in which he must die, the warriors before leaving him lifted his scalp in such a manner that his ears, eyelids, and nose were cut off. Thus he was left exposed to the cloudless heat of the desert day and the relentless cold of the plains night. It was a matter for much jovial betting around Indian camp-fires, Firebush said, as to the number of days it would take the unfortunate man to die — the favored number was eight.

Then Firebush told how captive women were treated — why so few of them lived through the ordeals — how if they were pretty women, like Jeannie Dodson, for instance, the abuse would stop just short of death in order that the defenseless body might be revived to abuse again. Range Templeton's fingers were so tight around the coffee cup that it shattered in his hand. The coffee ran onto the table and dripped down the edges. Neither of the men noticed. Olson added to his story by explaining that night after night as the raiders made camp on their return to the tribal encampment, the captive woman was the object of their revelries — as long as she had strength to resist she was staked by her hands and feet. If she died, her body was left behind mutilated and scalped.

Range stood up. Sweat was standing out on his face again as when he'd held Jeannie Dodson through her pain.

The baby's cry rose to a higher pitch. Olson stood up too.

"I can kill it," was all he said.

"But you won't." The doctor had come in, his face white, his hair awry, his clothes bloody, his step slow and very quiet. He took a chair and pulled it to the side of the table where the coffee wasn't dripping.

"Pour me a drink," he said to Olson, "in a glass."

Olson had to move to the cupboard to get the glass.

The baby's cry slid down the scale and whimpered to a stop.

Range stood looking at the mess on the table.

"Sit down," the doctor said, and Range sat again.

José came as if the very sound of the doctor's voice had brought him. He moved silently cleaning the table and pouring three cups of coffee while Olson, shaky and clumsy, managed to pour out the brandy for the doctor.

"How is Mac?" the doctor asked José.

"Bueno," was José's all-inclusive reply.

"The baby's name is Macduff," the doctor announced in a commonplace tone, "who, according to Shakespeare, was from his mother's womb untimely ripp'd, as this one was." He took a sip of the brandy and then licked his lips several times savoring the taste and strength of it. The two other men drank some of the coffee because it was there.

Range questioned in a strange, flat voice, "How's she doing now?"

"She's resting."

"Sleep of the dead or still in that — "

"In natural slumber. I awoke her. She had no strength for saying anything. She did whisper Pete's name. She'll sleep for many hours now."

"She'll live then?" Olson asked accusingly.

"For a while — not long, I think. But it will be time enough to bring Pete here in the morning, when we've had some rest and she may have accumulated enough strength to talk to him."

39

The silence was heavy, three-dimensional. The doctor realized he must push back the fog of weariness and try to deal with his old friend and his new friend before the hatred they were generating, the fight-and-kill feeling they were nurturing, should spew forth some new violence or disaster into the burdened night. They must, if he could manage it, understand that the sleep he had induced and the operation he had performed were not of evil origin, and that the life he had brought and the life he had prolonged were not actions based on a personal whim of his own but a spiritual responsibility to the life cycle. He started talking, easily, utterly without emotion.

"The operation you saw me perform has been done hundreds of times through hundreds of years — history admits of it before the time of Christ. There was a Roman law in the time of Caesar that a child should be so taken if the mother died in childbirth leaving the baby still unborn. The law and the legend that Caesar himself was born by such an operation has given it the name of Caesarean. Ed, you are Swedish" — Olson nodded in confirmation — "so you'll no doubt take satisfaction in learning that it was a Swedish pig-gelder who performed the first such operation on a live woman. The woman was his wife, the operation was successful, and the time was some three hundred years ago."

Olson's red face took on a deeper flush.

"Performing such an operation in our time still does not give a woman a chance to live, my friend. I was not as generous as you thought. I gave her only half a chance or less, and she will probably not take that."

Range didn't appear to be listening, but Olson had been shocked into attention by the mention of the Swedish pig-gelder.

"The sleep I induced was a performance a little more rare," the doctor continued, "but also a very ancient technique. I learned it from my father, physician to the czar. It is practiced some among court physicians, those who have the gift for it. I suspect some ancient civilizations knew it well. Strangely enough, some primitive tribes now know more of its power and use than those of us who pursue progress. It is a power like all other forces in nature — it can be directed in the good or the evil way."

"What do you call your way, you black-brained devil?" Range shoved his chair back and it overturned with a crash. "To my notion your way is about as *good* as an Indian way — they caused it and you finished the job for them." When he stood up a sharp flashing knife was in his hand. His sudden transition from inertia to violence was so unexpected that neither of the men at the table could for the moment make a move or a sound in response.

"You took a knife and give life and breath to a curse when you coulda let it be. . . . I gotta knife too. . . ."

Range was lost in a flood of passionate feeling completely out of control — a feeling that had constantly built up since he'd first seen the hideous tortured face of Jeannie Dodson on the river path. Now his brain was seething with all the pictures Olson's horror stories had conjured up — a baby picked up by its heels and its brains dashed out against a stone wall . . . a girl with the soles of her feet burned so she couldn't run away . . . a boy with splinters stuck like a porcupine's quills all over his body while squaws lighted fire to each splinter . . . a woman, Jeannie Dodson, staked out for attack . . . and over and over the writhings of Jeannie Dodson unwilling to bear a life so viciously conceived. The doctor had opposed Jeannie Dodson's will, Jeannie Dodson's desire that no such life be admitted through her into the world. And he and Olson, like witless fools under his spell, had helped. It seemed to Range Templeton now, in the confusion of his fury and his urge to do something that would still make things right for Jeannie Dodson, that what the three of them had done at the doctor's command had only made things worse, had only added to her misery, consummated her disgrace.

The baby started crying again. Range's whole expression and posture took on a mood of ominous quiet. Then he turned, the knife halfway poised, and started walking slowly and stealthily on the balls of his feet, as if he were stalking an animal. He was moving directly toward the small, insistent wail. The cry kept sharpening the imagery of the babies Olson had told him about — babies of captive mothers . . . babies swinging by their heels in the hands of savages . . . babies about to have their life beat out against a tree or a rock . . . or, like Olson said, just thrown in the river to drown. He'd put a stop to that crying and things would be evened up a little. They'd all feel better — Jeannie would rest better.

The doctor still hadn't moved. He said, almost to himself, "Reason has left him. . . . In that rage he can kill. . . ."

Then to Olson, "You have given him an overdose of your own poison."

Olson hunched down over the table a little more, his hand clinching the brandy bottle tighter, "Let 'im alone. No harm in killin' a varmint . . . no harm in killin' half a varmint."

"You could have selected a better time to tell him hate and horror stories, Ed." The doctor rose, making a decision.

"Good a time as any, I'd say — better'n most." Olson started drumming the fingers of one hand on the table top.

The doctor moved directly after Range, no hurry in his stride, just a deliberate following with no attempt at stealth.

Carlota was holding the baby on her lap, not quite sure what to do to quiet it. She was so concerned, and Range had entered so quietly, she didn't see him until he was beside her chair.

"Jesús!" She was startled and scared and clutched the child to her.

Range was startled too — Carlota's presence and her possessive, protective gesture was a stumbling block to his rage, a signal to his sanity — but the wildness was strong in him. With the knife still poised in his right hand, he reached out with the other as if to strike at Carlota or snatch at the bundle she held. But the doctor's voice halted his movement.

He spoke in Spanish, and Range was immediately at a disadvantage, uncertain, trying to understand what he could not understand. The doctor was talking to Carlota, calmly, specifically. When she arose from her chair and moved over to the bed to lay the baby far out in the center of the big white counterpane, Range did not

42

make a move. And as Carlota moved around and back of him going out to the kitchen with a muttered "Ay Dios mío!" he still did not move.

The baby, lying flat on its back, its arms and head out of the wrappings Carlota had snugly arranged around it, whimpered and snuffled a little, flayed its arms a few times in feeble protest, and then let the wrinkled redness of its face relax into slumber. The doctor was standing by the bed; Range came a little closer, placing himself at the foot of the bed. He looked at the doctor, seeking a challenge, preferably a physical one, wanting to spur his overwrought feelings into actions. The doctor did not meet the look; he kept gazing at the baby. Then he began talking a thoughtful stream of words that Range felt powerless to interrupt.

"New life from the womb is the expression of a natural law that man can neither fully comprehend nor abrogate . . . its derivation is not of race or nationality . . . its restrictions are neither of the civilized nor the primitive . . . its demands not so simple as love or hate, desire or aversion . . . its classifications not limited to son, bastard, or half-breed. It is life itself rooted in a plan still far removed from us, where the mind cannot reach and the spirit gropes about in semidarkness — a plan for the achievement of the divine average somewhere down the eons of time." He paused for an instant or two and then went on, "To kill, to slay, to do battle unto the death in a contest for survival is a destiny we must accept for a while, but to reject the hope and triumph that is inherent with the act of being born is a spiritual denunciation man cannot afford.

"Since I am chiefly responsible for the admission of this life into the cycle of our living experience — and you helped me, with calm and able hands . . ." He paused again, and this time looked at Range, "I venture to predict there will come a time, far distant and painful though it may be, when you will understand what I have said, see purpose in it, and even have cause to agree with me in some measure. . . . You resent that, don't you?"

What Range might have answered, what he might have done, was

43

erased by the hurried entrance of Luvisa, shawl over her head and shoulders, breathless from running, worry dark in her eyes. Carlota had let her in the back way. Her ghost could have made an entrance no more surprising.

"Luvisa, child . . . you didn't come out alone?" The doctor exclaimed.

"Oh, Dr. Weideman, I had to. Granny and I were frantic. Range and Grandad have been gone so long, and we didn't want to spread the alarm . . . Grandad said keep quiet about Pete's little boy — not let anybody know till he came back. And now — now — it's nearly morning, and I couldn't stand it any longer, especially with the little boy suffering so. You — you must tell me what to do, doctor." She looked from the doctor to Range and at the baby on the bed, and she felt the sharp currents of conflict in the room charged with a desperation that prefaces tragedy. She was frightened. "Where is Grandad?" She clutched the shawl a little tighter around her shoulders in a gesture of self-protection.

"Your grandfather is in the kitchen, safe enough. The baby is Jeannie Dodson's, just born. She came here. Don't be frightened, Luvisa. Tell me, what is wrong with the boy?"

She looked at Range. Her lips trembled a little. But she told the doctor about the boy. "He was so starved. He ate too much. We couldn't stop him. He fought us, and bit us. Then he vomited so hard, he had no strength left, and we put him to bed and he slept. But the last two hours or longer he has been awake and he has been crying — he must have had an awful dream or something. It is a crying of little noise and without tears. It hurts him so. I believe he will die unless you do something, doctor." Her own eyes filled with tears of fatigue and pity for the child.

The doctor reached deep within himself for more strength and it came easily because of his thankfulness that one crisis could prevent another. "I will go see him at once, Luvisa, but you will have to take charge here. I will take Ed home as I go. See that Carlota minds the baby. See that this tired boarder of yours finds a couch and gets

44

some rest. Make the house yours until I return." He smiled gallantly at her. She smiled back. He hurried from the room with a doctor's natural urgency.

Range and Luvisa stood looking at each other. Time stretched out, all length and no depth. Finally, she seemed to understand. She came to him and placed her hands on the hard unrelaxed muscles of his arms. Then she leaned against him, her cheek against his chest.

"I'm so weary," she murmured. His free arm held her and with the other he sheathed his knife. If her softness and sudden dependence were being used as a device, there'd never be need for her to admit it or him to know it. At any rate, it brought magic. The quiet house seemed to hold only Luvisa and him. His emotions, so compounded of youth and vigor and unexplored passion, spiraled and swirled from cones of darkness into peaks of light. He held her closer. Her breathing was faster than when she had come running into the room. "I — I feel a little faint. I — must rest a bit, I think, Range." She had forgotten, or did not see the wisdom in remembering, that the doctor had prescribed rest for Range. He had forgotten too. She was the one who needed tending, leaning against him so weakly, breathing in little gasps. He took her up tenderly in his arms. The house was strange to him, but he recalled the fur-covered couch in the doctor's study where he and Firebush had sat talking about Jeannie Dodson. He carried her there. Then he sat by her side, holding her hands, saying nothing for long moments. Her eyes would close for composure's sake and then open to meet his steady gaze for a long time. It was first love, complete in all its wonder, silently admitted and accepted . . . discovered in the dawn of a day emerging from a night of despair. The first kiss, and it was the first for either of them, was a long time in coming. It was also a long time in coming to an end.

Jeannie Dodson remained quiet, her eyes closed, her breath short and irregular, evidencing no pain or consciousness of any kind. Luvisa and Range stood by her bedside, holding hands tightly, each

45

of them wishing silently that Dr. Weideman would return. It was almost sunrise and a faint light showed Jeannie's scarred face in such complete repose that the hideousness seemed somehow removed from it, and the doctor's careful bandaging had been done with the thought of Pete Dodson's arrival as well as Jeannie's comfort. Their own newly discovered and admitted love made Range and Luvisa especially sensitive to the tragedy of Pete and Jeannie Dodson. Between them they created a suspense that sharpened with Jeannie's every breath.

Luvisa prayed silently, then whispered audibly, "Dear Mother of Jesus, let Pete come."

Jeannie stirred. "Pete," she echoed the name.

There was a sound at the front door. Luvisa hurried to open it. It was Pete Dodson. Luvisa expected the doctor to be with him but he was alone. She asked urgently, "Where's Dr. Weideman?"

"With Davy. He sent me on. He was afraid I might not — " He couldn't go on. He asked the question with his eyes. The nightmare illness he had known after the scene in the garden, the wild restlessness that had possessed him until Ed Olson had come for him and told him about Davy, and then the doctor's shocking news that Jeannie was at his house and alive, but would not be for long, had together packed an emotional strain now almost beyond endurance. If Jeannie were not alive, there would be no strength he could call upon for another step or another word.

"You're in time, Pete."

He followed Luvisa. There was no hesitation, no evidence of shock when he reached the bedside. It was Jeannie. His hands gently grasped her shoulders. His face rested against hers.

"Jeannie, my dear."

"Pete . . . I waited for you."

"I've been trying to get to you."

"I brought Davy back."

"Yes, Jeannie."

"He's all right?"

46

"Yes, Jeannie."

"I can't stay . . . much longer . . . Pete."

"Please don't go just yet, Jeannie. . . . Look at me, Jeannie. . . . Please look at me."

Jeannie opened her eyes. They were clear and tranquil and very blue. All the love she had ever known for Pete Dodson was there . . . but that was all . . . no recognition that Luvisa and Range were in the room . . . no memory of pain.

"I'm going now," she said, "into the blue-green quietness. Won't you come with me, Pete?"

"I can't, Jeannie."

"Why?"

"There's Davy."

"Oh, yes, Davy . . . and Molly . . . there's Molly, too, Pete?"

"Yes."

"And Julia?"

"Yes."

"Then I'll just rest until you all come." She closed her eyes again. "Pete?"

"Yes, dear."

"Carry me there."

"All right." He placed his arm under her shoulders and drew her close to him.

"To my garden."

"Yes, Jeannie."

"Near the white oleander."

"Yes . . . it's almost in bloom."

"I know. . . ." She sighed in deep contentment and breathed no more.

When Dr. Weideman, Ed Olson, and Range Templeton had prepared the grave in the garden near the white oleander bush, Pete Dodson carried Jeannie in his arms and laid her there. It was the following night — the moon's radiance was a soft glow in the garden.

47

Jeannie's funeral was for these four men and two women: Luvisa and Julia, Jeannie's aunt and now Pete's wife again. The death would go unrecorded, Jeannie Dodson's return unknown. It was best that way, they all agreed — best that the story end with Range's rescue of Davy.

There was no weeping, only the sounds of the earth filling the grave and Julia quoting from memory: "Peace I leave with you; my peace I give unto you. . . . He maketh me to lie down in green pastures. . . . He leadeth me beside the still waters . . ." and praying: "Our Father which art in Heaven . . . Thy will be done . . ."

In the calm of Julia's sweet voice Range caught for the first time the real significance and power of a religious faith, but he erased it with the bitter reflection, "If such as this is God's will . . ."

CHAPTER III

XAVIER MIGUEL SÁNDIVAR bore his name with pride and his fifteen years with dignity, and it was not beneath his pride or dignity to have made a decision to follow a cow — especially La Brema, for she was a beautiful cow with a dignity all her own. Miguel knew little of bloodlines but was more impressed with what his father told of La Brema's German lineage which included a prize bull of Bremen than of his own which took into account a grandee of Spain.

In the state of Tamaulipas in far-northern Mexico on a spring evening of 1838, both the boy and the cow were so far removed from their origins by geography and circumstances that no trace of responsibility for pedigree or nobility could be placed upon them. And they were preparing to shed further responsibilities by leaving home and owner. The cow was focusing such faculties as she had on a certain broken place in the rock fence which enclosed the

48

Sándivar acres, a place strategically concealed by heavy clumps of thorny brush. It had served as her secret exit on several previous excursions. The boy was trying to control a pounding inner excitement as he planned how to execute the ruse of sound slumber until all his family slept, then to slip undetected from his straw pallet, pick up the hidden carga of supplies he had so carefully collected, and follow La Brema on a mysterious trail northward.

La Brema was an unusual cow with an individualism rarely exhibited by a member of the bovine family. Her coloring was also unusual — the burnished red of maize dead-ripe, relieved here and there by rather carelessly placed white splotches. One white marking in the center of her forehead, somewhat in the shape of an inverted question-mark, upset the calmness so characteristic of the face of a cow and put into her expression something that searched for grazing grounds afar off, where water flowed ever clear and grasses grew tender, tall and green.

It had not been in La Brema's plan of existence, however, to cause her owners trouble or anxiety by straying from the home pastures. She liked the comforts of her dilapidated stall on the Sándivar ranch, the attention and affection of Miguel, and the respect and awe with which she was attended each season when she augmented the waning fortunes of the family with a large, husky calf. Most of all she liked the feeling of good flesh and good milk that came from having her several stomachs well filled at regular intervals. But in recent times she had been deprived of this feeling. The grass was dry and crisp and unsatisfying. The small portion of corn at evening feeding time was only enough to make her feel restless and a little mean.

So the drouth had finally sent La Brema on a realistic search for those grazing grounds afar off. Her disappearance had grieved the Sándivars, Miguel most of all. Then she had returned, several weeks later, fatter than she had ever been, beautiful to behold, and they were delighted with her sleekness and her resourcefulness in these dry and barren times. As the drouth continued to hold back spring

49

grasses and the landscape became more lifeless, La Brema's repeated sojourns into a better land took on an aspect of awe and mystery. Miguel came to recognize her departure moods and on one night had followed to the passage in the fence. The urge to go on and on had been almost too strong to resist, but he was unprepared; for so long a journey on foot he must have food and a weapon. Now he was ready; this time he would not turn back. La Brema would be leaving tonight, and he would go with her. His mother and father must not know. They would not permit it. The land to the north held many dangers, they said. But La Brema had ventured out to return unharmed, so why be afraid? Then too, she was soon to calve and he should be with her to see that all went well; so he reasoned to quiet his conscience, for ordinarily Miguel was an obedient and thoughtful son.

Emilio Sándivar seldom found it difficult to sense what was in his son's mind; and on the evening before the cow and the boy left together, he knew it would happen. The cow's restlessness, the boy's bright eyes that avoided his father's questioning looks, and his over-eagerness to help his mother about the house made clear sign language to the older man. Yet he could not bring himself to speak of it directly. He talked vaguely about wars beyond the Rio Grande and of raids on the ranches to the north by the fierce and far-riding Comanches. He added hastily that as he had heard it, these Indians cared more for horses than any other loot and they would hardly trouble to harm anyone traveling on foot.

Then he thought bitterly to himself, "That is poor consolation for you, Emilio Sándivar, who must send your oldest son forth on his first journey from home with nothing more than worn sandals under him, when his blood and his bearing deserve a prancing steed, a bright serape, fine leather, and the jingle of silver spurs. Poor consolation indeed that on foot he may go unnoticed and unharmed."

Except for the strain of good Spanish blood, Emilio Sándivar felt that the heritage he offered his son was a bleak and barren one: family prestige and fortune lost with the fall of Iturbide's empire, his own flight to northern Mexico to an abandoned ranch once operated by a distant relative, the impulse that caused him to let Francisca, devoted Indian servant of the Sándivar household, accompany him on his flight; these things left his heart and hands empty of the things a man like Emilio Sándivar would care to offer his son. Francisca was Miguel's mother and had become Emilio's wife through the offices of an itinerant priest soon after the boy's birth. Four other sons were born in the fifteen years to follow, but Miguel remained his father's favorite. The other children reflected clearly the strong Indian blood of their mother, while Miguel stood alone in the family as a symbol of Spanish aristocracy lost and a bit of wild Irish long dormant for it was only in the strange dark-blue coloring of their eyes that any resemblance between mother and son could be found — a bright and rather startling remnant from an Irish-Indian union several generations removed.

Emilio Sándivar, born into the confusion that marked the end of the Spanish colonial period in Mexico, could no more control his emotions and attitudes about caste than he could repudiate hunger or thirst. At the end of the eighteenth century, there had been four distinct divisions of caste in Mexico: the gachupines, natives of Spain who held all the power in government and business; the creoles, pure-blooded Spaniards but Mexican-born, who aped the habits of the gachupines and lived in luxury off the wealth of mines and haciendas; the mestizos, the mixed race, considered lower class, despised and underprivileged but destined to create the Mexican nation; and the Indians who lived as peons on the haciendas or in villages too remote to be disturbed.

The Sándivars of Mexico City were among those creole families who wanted independence from Spain in order that power might be taken from the gachupines and placed in the hands of the creoles. The only freedom they wanted was freedom from Spanish rule; their philosophy included nothing of equality or social reform — the mestizo would still be distinctly lower class and the Indian still a peon.

51

Independence from Spain in 1821 meant many things to many people. To Agustín de Iturbide, hero of the brief but decisive campaign that brought independence, it meant a chance to be emperor. To the Sándivars and other wealthy creole families it meant a chance for long-delayed assumption of power through a native monarchy. The father of Emilio was honored with high office and young Emilio was made a knight of the Order of Guadalupe. It was a little while before the empty treasury, the unpaid army, and the million creoles who expected some share in the bureaucracy became a problem — but only a little while. In less than ten months the Sándivars had lost a family fortune in trying to help Iturbide prove he could be emperor. When the Congress sentenced him to perpetual banishment and put him on a boat for Europe, there was no place for the Sándivars in Mexico; it was understood that they should accompany Iturbide. And they did, all except the proud Emilio who felt he could not bear the shame of proceeding with the banished party to the boat. Then too, he found himself possessed with an altogether unexpected desire to cleave to the soil of Mexico. This spontaneous surge of devotion to his native land surprised and amazed him. So with two good horses, a small bag of gold and silver coins, and Francisca, he fled to the north.

Because of the emotion that carried him along, Emilio expected something great and good to happen to him. But his resourcefulness was meager and his skills limited to those acquired in a society devoted almost wholly to luxury and amusement. It was Francisca who met and overcame the hazards of the long and perilous journey out across the mountainous backbone of Mexico into the uncharted and almost unknown regions of the Far North; but for her he would have perished.

His disillusionment was complete when they reached their destination in the state of Tamaulipas. On the land records at Mexico City he had found the ranch in Tamaulipas listed as one of the Sándivar holdings, but unreported on for profit or taxes for a number of years. He had imagined it a place of fertile acreage, widespread buildings, and peon villages, for that was the way he wanted it. He found it completely deserted, spiders and stinging scorpions the only occupants of the crumbling buildings. Due to some change in rainfall or underground currents, the wells were dry; and so there was not even a bird about the grounds to make living there seem feasible. The acreage was extensive, but Emilio was too disheartened to check the boundaries. The soil seemed fertile enough and there were signs of fields once irrigated from the wells. But without labor or water, it offered little more than a desert. Emilio was in despair, but Francisca accepted it all with Indian passivity and settled down to take care of him. She discovered a covered well in the kitchen of the old main house that yielded enough water for cooking use, a few animals, and a garden. The adobe structure was still secure enough for shelter. She rode out alone for long distances until she discovered a neighbor within a day's ride. He was an energetic and successful mestizo rancher. Then she persuaded Emilio to take the fine horse she rode and trade it for two good cows and six goats. Their small supply of coin went for seed and blankets and enough corn and beans to last until the garden could yield.

And thus the son of the noble family of Sándivar, an ex-knight of the Order of Guadalupe, lived from the years 1823 to 1838, with the Indian woman Francisca — strong, adequate to the environment, a devoted servant — bearing his children. Morose and withdrawn, Emilio was somewhat useful at tending the vegetables and flowers. He rode his horse daily, without destination, and found some consolation in the animal's proud gaits, even though age had begun to subtract speed and alertness. He taught his son to ride in the manner of a Spanish gentleman, although he was unable to provide him with a horse of his own. He also taught Miguel with much patience and precision to read and write and speak a fine Castilian Spanish, but he did not trouble with the other children. For what reason had he tried to perpetuate this semblance of culture and aristocracy, he wondered . . . that his son might follow a cow?

He knew why Miguel was not telling him of his resolution to

53

follow La Brema. He would have to forbid his going — his own parental anxiety and Francisca would see to that. It was only with regard to the children that Francisca was emotional and dominating. When the boy was gone she would blame him and give him some hard times. But, Mother of God, what difference did it make where the boy went and when? His father had nothing to offer him at home, nothing but some papers in a pouch, all of dubious value. He had brought the pouch from Mexico City. At the ranch it had hung on the peg with his saddle, and had not been removed or opened since he had arrived there. Francisca and the children obeyed implicitly his order never to touch it. He felt a little foolish sometimes for cherishing it so. The papers were proof of a wealth and prestige now vanished. There were copies of land grants awarded the Sándivars by the King of Spain, vast properties acquired through several generations of loyalty to the Spanish crown and lost in a few months of frantic fervor for a Mexican monarch. In the suddenness of the sacrifice, a few of the distant properties had been passed over, their worth unknown; the abandoned property on which Emilio resided was one of these. There was another, unsettled and unclaimed as far as he knew, its location somewhere between the Rio Grande and the river called Nueces. But how could it be found? What could it mean now to him or his son? More disappointment, perhaps . . . worse than the land they were on, most likely. Governments changed so fast in these times, a man could hardly know or claim anything for sure. This land to the north of the Rio Grande had been granted to the Sándivars by a king that was no more, and Mexico no longer belonged to the country he had ruled. Moreover, the grant had been located in the state of Tamaulipas which had extended to the Nueces River until the Texas rebels defeated Santa Anna and set the boundary of their new republic at the Rio Grande. Now, Emilio supposed, the land granted his family so long ago by the King of Spain would be in the Republic of Texas. And yet the priest on his last visit had said the Mexican Congress had refused to recognize Santa Anna's treaty

54

with the Texians, and that, strictly speaking, Texas was still a part of Mexico, and the Nueces River was still the northern boundary of the state of Tamaulipas. It was all very confusing and he gave up the idea of trying to explain it to Miguel.

The priest had brought another item of news that further emphasized for Emilio the futility and irony of all life and the events that fashioned it. The news concerned Agustín de Iturbide's bones which had been resting in the state of Tamaulipas almost as long as Emilio had resided there. In less than a year after banishment, the impetuous ex-emperor had decided to return to Mexico. He sent word ahead that Spain was planning to reconquer Mexico and he was returning to fight again for independence. He didn't wait for the Mexican government's answer that he would be put to death if he came back. When he landed on the coast of Tamaulipas, he was arrested and shot. That, Emilio had thought, was the last sardonic twist of events in the Iturbide-Sándivar tragedy, that Agustín I should be executed almost in the shadow of an impoverished Sándivar. And now fate's last fantastic touch in the year 1838: according to the story the priest brought, the bones of Iturbide had recently been moved with great ceremony and high honor to the Cathedral of Mexico. Such were the caprices of government and time.

Yes, indeed, concluded Emilio in dark reverie, it was easy enough to honor the bones of the dead, but the lost fortunes of the living could not be restored. No need to tell Miguel of the papers in the pouch.

He sighed deeply. The boy and the cow would be gone in the morning. What final admonition should he give his son? As he passed through the room where Miguel slept with his four brothers, he paused and watched the boy self-consciously feign the usual preparations for bed. He felt weak and helpless and sad to the core of his heart. The fine flourishes of speech which he often exchanged with his son lay heavy and unspoken. At last, he found voice.

"Watch the rattlesnake this season, my son. Francisca says his poison is more deadly in the dry times."

55

As he closed the door securely behind him to shut out from Francisca any sound of Miguel's departure, his despondency was unrelieved by any hope that his son might be able to rise above the misfortunes of his birth. From the confines of his frustrations and the uncertainties of his times, he was wholly unable to recognize in his son the manifestation of a new nationality in which the Spaniard and the Indian along with fragments of other races would be absorbed into a distinctive Mexican compound. For Emilio Sándivar there was only the degrading evidence that circumstances had made him, a pure-blooded creole, father to a brood of mestizos.

But in the pattern of Miguel's destiny, there was to be something more than the reflection of a new and highly picturesque nationality: a forecasting, even a microscopic contribution, to the creation of the brood continental, the blending of all races into the race of the future — a part in the inevitable movement through the grand arches of time toward the attainment of the divine average.

La Brema, the cow, was the instrument of destiny used to remove Xavier Miguel Sándivar from the placid stream of his childhood into the turbulent current of his future.

The boy and the cow traveled easily and without weariness during the cool of the night, and by dawn they were well beyond the boundaries of Sándivar property. La Brema had shown no uneasiness at being followed, and as she made her way with purpose along the narrow trail winding northward, Miguel was close at her heels dreaming of the strange, faraway land into which her deliberate pace would lead them.

He was comfortably clad in a white homespun suit; his pants held up by a drawstring were in length several seasons above his ankles; he had the loose ends of the blouse opening tied carelessly at his middle. His knife, carefully encased in leather and convenient to his right hand, was hidden in a trick fold of his blouse near the knot at the front; it was his only weapon, sharp, long, and light in weight. On his back he carried a small carga of food and water which included dried corn and meat and some goat cheese; rawhide loops

56

for his arms supported the bundle, and there was also a loop for his head, to be worn Indian-fashion about his forehead in case his shoulders tired. A worn straw hat, rather small and perched high on his head, and crude, homemade sandals completed his equipage for travel with La Brema.

Miguel's soft, dark hair was long on his neck, and the shadows of fuzz on his upper lip and high along his cheekbones placed the shadings of manhood on his delicate and well-formed features. In the way he walked there was a motion both graceful and fearless. His Irish-Indian eyes of an odd dark-blue brilliancy carried a certain firmness of expression, suggesting a quality that composes dreams into reality. Following La Brema to an unknown destination was an expression of this quality.

La Brema's respect for siesta time was a great relief to Miguel for by noon the heat of the sun was pitiless, he was tired to the marrow of his bones, and the bottoms of his feet were burning almost beyond endurance. He was especially grateful when she made her way into a cavelike clump of brush and lay down to cud-chewing as if she might spend the whole afternoon. After drinking sparingly from his water jug and chewing a few grains of corn, he worried about staying awake. If he slept, La Brema might leave without him. He tried sitting propped against her. She offered no protest and instantly he was asleep.

When he awoke with a thud as La Brema moved and stood up, it was dark, the stars were bright, and his body stiff and chilled. For a moment he was deeply frightened and wished with all his heart that he was at home in bed with his four brothers. But he had no time to dwell on these things. La Brema was moving out of the brush. He was entirely dependent on her instincts and must follow wherever she went. It was evident now that their longest treks were to be at night. That way La Brema could last longer without water. So far she had had nothing to eat or drink. On the second day out she stopped for a while to strip new leaves from a mesquite thicket. Here Miguel came upon a rattlesnake, teased it for a while to study the angry music it made, then from a safe distance threw his knife with a stroke that neatly severed its head. He thought of his father's warning and then came the realization that after all his father had known and had not disapproved. He felt immensely better after this and the carga on his back seemed lighter.

Late in the evening of the second day La Brema found water, a low stagnant pool in a creek bed where some ranchero had dug out a watering hole. The animal tracks about the place revived Miguel's spirits. Having been in the company of his family every day and night since he was born, his present condition of complete aloneness began to press in upon him as something that might be endless. To add to the immense solitude of his journey, most animal life had migrated before the drouth, and there seemed to be not even a rabbit or coyote to enliven the earth with sound or movement. But there were always rattlesnakes; he decided to kill one for each day of the journey and save the rattles as a sort of calendar.

Heavy with calf, La Brema was not traveling as fast as on previous trips, but on the night after Miguel had added the fourth rattle to his carga, her pace seemed to quicken. A little after dawn, Miguel smelled the blessed odor of mesquite smoke. He gave La Brema a slap on the flank and for the first time since they had left home, he ran ahead of her.

"Come on, La Brema! Smell the sweetness of the smoke! Hurry! Hurry! Follow me! We have arrived somewhere! It is the end of our journey perhaps! Oh, how I wish you could speak! Hurry yourself, you heavy old goat! Oh, please me, and hurry along!"

In the early morning light the hut of sticks and clay before which the breakfast fire was burning seemed nothing less than a sanctuary to the breathless, haggard boy who stopped before it. He called a hoarse greeting and trembled with excitement as he waited for an answer. A grizzled vaquero came to the door of the jacal and stood gaping in utter astonishment.

"By the Blessed Virgin," he finally muttered, "it is the visiting cow again, and this time she has an escort."

It was Miguel's turn to be astonished. "You know my cow?"

"It is better said that she knows me and my soft heart. Look at her now, fixing her corn-hungry eyes on me. I must give her the tortilla ready for my empty stomach and the few grains from the nose bag of my poor Si-Bueno."

While Miguel protested excitedly with all the fine Castilian phrases his father had ever taught him and which the old vaquero hardly understood, La Brema's needs were cared for. She actually accepted the tortillas that lay on the stone by the fire, emptied the bucket time and again that her benefactor drew up from the well, and finally sunk her nose gratefully into Si-Bueno's feed bag, suspended ridiculously from her short curved horns, while the puzzled horse from whose head the bag had been removed watched enviously.

Before the silence of the old man, Miguel became embarrassed, realizing that the elaborate manner of his speech was out of place and there was too much of it. He submitted to a quiet, intense scrutiny as the squinted, sun-wary eyes of La Brema's friend not only studied his outward appearance but also seemed to probe behind his eyes in search of his thoughts.

"You may address me as Apollonius," he finally instructed. "Also, compose yourself, and address your thirst to whatever water remains in the well, and your hunger to the stew of bull meat here that the cow has so graciously left for us."

"Your name is a fine-sounding one," Miguel said, repeating it carefully, "Señor Apollonius."

"It is indeed," the old man agreed. "And does yours sound as well?"

Miguel gave his name and was ready to explain its proud origins, but Apollonius said, "Bueno," with a finality that dismissed further details. Then with his knife he began deftly to prepare two ladles from the stalk of a Spanish dagger while Miguel quenched his thirst at the well.

In all his life Miguel had never been so hungry, and the pure pleasure he found in eating the tough, peppery meat scooped from the caldera with the ingenious ladles Apollonius had prepared was an experience he would never be able to repeat or forget.

Belly-full and heart-content they sat in the cool morning shadows, knowing the time was brief before the heat of the sun would confirm the realities of the day. A few whirring insect sounds and the far, yearning cry of a mourning dove were the only breaks in absolute silence. Si-Bueno stood, head down and saddled, still as a statue, waiting for bridle and rider to animate him. La Brema had finished the corn, shaken off the nose bag, and stood in complete comfort and repose, almost as if she slept standing.

The shrill complaint of the cicadas started, as if to break the harmony of the moment. Discomfort and uneasiness began to rise in Miguel. Was this to be the end of his journey — this lowly jacal and this barren ground no better watered or grassed than his father's acres? Had La Brema grown so fat during each absence on the tortillas and raw corn fed her by this ancient vaquero?

Apollonius sensed it was time for words. "Your eyes are full of searching, young gentleman. What it is you would find?"

Miguel told of La Brema's strange journeys during the time of the drouth and his own resolution to find the place of thick green grasses and flowing spring waters that he had visualized.

Then he inquired timidly, "Is it here that she comes to fatten and beg corn from the kindness of your heart?"

Apollonius startled Miguel with a sharp snort of sound that crossed contempt with laughter and distorted his wrinkled, leathery face into an outlandish grimace.

"You fool yourself if you detect in Apollonius enough kindness to fatten anything big enough for the eye to see, much less your mountain of a pet cow."

"But my eyes saw you feed her the tortillas prepared for yourself, and my ears heard you speak of the softness of your own heart."

"I jested with you and with myself, young gentleman. I am a vaquero as mean and as old as El Diablo himself, as tough as the rawhide in the riata I swing, as fiendish as the wild cattle I round up for my chief along the Río Bravo. Those who do not know my name call me 'El Vaquero Diablo.' The softness in my heart is equal to the tameness in the heart of a mustang bull."

"Yet you fed my cow," Miguel insisted, "on this morning and at other times when she has come here."

"Yes, I feed your cow," Apollonius admitted. "Each time she comes, I feed her. When she arrives from the south, she drinks the feeble well dry and takes the corn from the bony Si-Bueno and me until we scarcely can live until our next allotment from the store-house. When she returns from the north, she requires little. . . . Sí, each time I feed your cow, but not from kindness."

"What other reason then?"

"Because of the portento."

"The portento?"

"Sí. The cow is more than a cow. She is the going-before . . . the sign of something-intended-to-be. In feeding her I show a regard for the Order of Things, which is unrelated to kindness. I live by the portent, and it is why I live so long, the understanding I have of the trails leading into the brushy darkness of the future."

Apollonius looked to the north. His voice became soft and monotonous in tone. "We are all as birds . . . even as I am the paisano, a common one, without caste, staying close to the earth, running here and there along the trails and in the brush, going nowhere in particular . . . even as you are the eagle, a noble one, born to the upper reaches of the air, seeking the heights, soaring to your perch on the topmost crag. But there comes a challenge from another eagle, a bird of larger and bolder breed. The great birds struggle for the pinnacle . . . one eagle falls wounded by the sharp claws of the other . . . falls to the lower regions of the air . . . and there a hawk, savage and ruthless . . ."

Apollonius broke off. Miguel, pale, breathless, his eyes wide and his lips parted in an effort to miss not a word, waited for him to go on.

But Apollonius did not finish the story of the birds. He spoke again directly to Miguel.

"You come behind the cow and are a part of the portento. For that reason I have shared with you the strength and vigor that comes to me through the stew of bull meat. Across the Río Bravo the cow has a gift for you . . . and now do not sit there like an aimless grasshopper. Follow her on!" For emphasis, Apollonius slapped his rawhide leggins with the quirt that hung at his wrist and the pop of it jerked Miguel to his feet.

Apollonius turned from Miguel's astonishment and began to prepare for his day's work, bridling Si-Bueno, tightening the girth of plaited horsehair, arranging his riata and long cow-whip, giving a special hitch to his leggins before mounting. The old vaquero and his tough, dun-colored horse merged into a cow-hunting unit, all the color of old leather, the riggings and encasements of rawhide matching hair and hide of man and mount.

From his superior position, Apollonius turned to Miguel, and his parting words were like an effort to prove his unkindness.

"A man on foot is without dignity or defense," he said. "You will soon meet an enemy, a well-mounted one. See that you have a horse. In this country of wild horses, only a fool goes on foot." As if to demonstrate the advantages of being mounted, Apollonius gave some signal to Si-Bueno that caused him to leap and disappear into the brush behind the jacal so quickly that Miguel could hardly fix his eyes on the action.

La Brema seemed to come to life at the same time, and Miguel, dazed and wondering, found himself trailing her north again, the visions and admonitions of Apollonius keeping him close company.

As they approached the valley of the Rio Grande, animal life was more frequent and animated, and he felt a buoyant kinship with it all. The road runner darting about seemed to tease him and invite him to hurry on down the trail; like Apollonius there seemed something sardonic and wise about this erratic, earth-bound bird. The armadillo, bouncing and scooting along, aware of something unusual but harmless, paused to look askance. In his fancy, Miguel imagined they were all expressing amazement that he was unmounted; that perhaps

62

they had seen in this country only riding men, none ever walking. The long-eared jack rabbit that reared up at a distance to look him over better seemed to Miguel to be sympathetic, pitying him possibly for having only two legs and no leap. At this idea he laughed aloud and then jumped aside in sudden caution for there was the familiar whirr of warning before deadly attack . . . the rattlesnake . . . laughter and grim danger wrapped in the same moment. His knife flashed out. Miguel laughed again. He cut the rattle from the tail and counted eight buttons.

"Thank you, Señor Rattlesnake. Three times you have given me the rattle with eight buttons. I choose to believe that on the eighth day of our journeying, La Brema will take me into the land of sweet grasses."

It was late evening, almost dark, when La Brema picked her way carefully across the river bed of the Rio Grande. Miguel thought the Río Bravo looked very dead and powerless, not at all the great and grand river he had heard so much about. He removed his sandals and trousers quickly and waded across in the shallow murky trail that La Brema defined.

There had been no siesta that day, and Miguel had not slept since the early part of the night before. His excitement had spent itself in the morning hours through the meeting with Apollonius; so, even if he had realized that he was crossing a border of continental significance and entering the Republic of Texas, his weariness would have snuffed out any further emotion. If only La Brema would stop and rest this night!

But La Brema merely slowed down to graze along a rather clearly defined cattle trail. Miguel staggered after her, not daring to stop, fearful of sleeping while she traveled on without him. It was amazing how continuous was the movement of a grazing cow and how great the distance she could cover moving slowly and with direction.

The next forty-eight hours were woven into a walking nightmare for Miguel — fighting fatigue, waking stiff and frightened from the short naps he had leaning against La Brema the few times she bedded

63

down. In the early part of the third night after the river crossing, Miguel began to reach the very limits of his endurance. He staggered along until it seemed a full night had passed but it had really just begun. Several times he stumbled and fell, until finally he hadn't the strength to rise again. La Brema paused, missing his footsteps. He crawled forward, begging her to wait. She hesitated, but he realized she had no intention of bedding down. She was going on.

Not far away a coyote yelped and then let out a long and lonely wail; it was answered by a chorus that increased the cry until Miguel felt he couldn't bear the peak of unearthly agony it seemed to express. But the fright of it stimulated him to crawl desperately after La Brema. She had paused to give attention to the coyotes' howl, and Miguel was able finally to reach the bushy end of her tail; he pulled himself up and stood propped against her; tears of weariness and shame at his own weakness fell on her back. She moved with impatience, and he realized what he must try to do. He must ride La Brema. It was an indignity he would never have considered except in extremity, to ride a fine domestic cow, almost ready to calve. But even with his carga, he was a light weight, and La Brema seemed unconscious of either insult or imposition as he managed to climb up and stretch himself out almost at full length along her strong, meaty backbone.

When Miguel awoke, he was lying face downward in fragrant grass. There was the sweet sound of flowing waters. For a moment he dared not open his eyes. He tried to think back. Had he killed that seventh rattlesnake or had it struck him? Was he in paradise, or was this . . . ?

The varietal melody of a mockingbird filled his ears; he rolled over and opened his eyes. He was in the shade of a wide-branched, lacy willow tree. La Brema lay nearby, placidly chewing her cud, her contentment crowned with an expression of extreme self-satisfaction. Spring waters were flowing cool and clear within reach of his hand. He pulled himself to the water's edge, let his carga fall from his shoulders, and drank deeply. Then he lay with his hands in the

64

water feeling its goodness and cleanness, splashing it against his face.

For a time unmeasured Miguel was still, lying in a trance of utter physical enjoyment of the beauty and wonder of the place. Long roots of his earth-loving Indian forebears seemed to reach through him and attach themselves firmly to this piece of ground. Apollonius had said the cow had a gift for him. . . . He would call the place "Regalo de la Vaca," the gift of the cow.

A hawk flew over and its shadow fell across him for an instant. Apollonius had also said he would soon meet an enemy. . . .

Apollonius had said a man should be mounted for dignity and defense. . . .

Apollonius had said an eagle must seek the heights.

CHAPTER IV

ON THE DAY that Miguel and his cow arrived at the springs, Eli Dawson pulled out of San Antonio with freight wagons bound for Laredo. . . . Eli Dawson fitted the times in which he lived as a well-turned boot holds firm the lean ankle of an active man. He had patience, tolerance, endurance, courage; men respected him. There was no meanness or smallness in him, and yet he could handle mean men and overlook small vices. He was rough of garb and sometimes crude in manner; he fought, even killed when necessary; he could handle a drink or a deck of cards skillfully but without undue excitement; and he freighted with more success than any man hauling out of San Antonio — success to him meant keeping his men alive and getting the goods most needed in and out of the settlement for he was not one to profit overly much on the needs and desires of the people.

His wagon train of twelve two-wheeled ox-carts, each with its Mexican driver, assembled on the plaza. Twelve riders, including

Dawson, well mounted and equipped to fight for the supplies piled high on the carts, were ready for the trail. The youngest and most inexperienced of these was Range Templeton, and yet on the prancing, long-legged Indian Toego, he sat almost a head's height above the others and proclaimed in his very bearing that he was the type most likely to survive exigencies of war and frontier.

The dusty air of the whole plaza was charged with the high excitement of last-minute preparations and the suspense that precedes departure upon a hazardous journey. High-pitched voices in two languages called out jests and warnings, made dares and bets, and exacted repeated promises about purchases to be made, news to be noted, and letters to be delivered.

There were many stimulants to the senses: much color and gaiety, the noise of jesting and shouting and general hilarity, vendors with delicacies sold only on special occasions, pungent odors from gunpowder and dust and the sweat of spirited, restless horses, and an exciting display of costume and equipment for both man and mount. The Mexicans were arrayed in the fanciest trappings, going in for braid and silver, much decoration of leather, and lavish use of bright color (with the exception of a certain type of vaquero from the brush country who seemed to encase himself and mount in rawhide so that against his own landscape he blended like a quail or coyote — Eli Dawson had two such men for this trip). The Americans, however, were not without their vanities too, expressed in fringed buckskins, red shirts, and hats of endless variety, from beaver and coonskin to wide felt and oriental straw; what they wore, however, was not as important as the weapons they carried. When they purchased rigging for a trip, the quality of gun came first, then hat, then belt (wide, strong, and sometimes ornate for holding two guns and a knife), then boots, and with what was left something to cover the body.

Drivers, as well as riders, were well armed, giving the train a total of twenty-four fighters in case of raids. The driver on the end cart was the highest paid for he was equally good at cooking and bullwhacking; and Eli Dawson fed his men well, stocking the cook's cart

66

with the best camp fare available. He paid his men well too — if the freight got through.

Freighting was a highly lucrative and proportionately dangerous business. And riding for a freighter, guarding his supplies, did not mean dragging along beside the train at the pace of the oxen pulling the carts. Eli's riders fanned out from the train and scouted the country. They brought in game. They collected a fund of information about the country through which they passed. At night they rode herd on the oxen and kept careful watch against surprise attacks by the Indians; for somehow the Indians would learn of the fine horses with the train and the supplies of calico, tobacco, and hardware stored in the carts and would covet all these things every ox-track of the way.

When the supplies were delivered in Laredo, the success of the freighting venture would be only half assured because trading would not be complete or the profit determined until the carts were safely back on the main plaza at San Antonio loaded to capacity with such necessaries as beans, sugar, flour, leather, shoes, and saddles.

As Indian Toego pranced back and forth beside the carts, making Range Templeton the most conspicuous of the riders, Range felt stimulated to a peak of enthusiasm and recklessness so strong he could hardly restrain himself from shouting, shooting, or just letting Toego out to race like mad around the center of the plaza. A small Mexican boy, son of one of the bullwhackers, riding a young filly bareback, seemed to feel the same way, and, having no cause for restraint, started cutting a violent circle of dust round and round the string of carts and their indifferent oxen, at the same time shouting unintelligible tributes to the bravery of his father and the accomplishments of bullwhackers in general.

As departure became more imminent, Range looked about for the specific faces of his friends. He had visited them, he had told them good-by, but he wanted to see them once more — Luvisa, Firebush, Pete Dodson and Davy, and Dr. Weideman.

The experiences with each of them were as much a part of him

67

as the garb he wore: Luvisa, whose promises were held as a close, sweet secret between them; Firebush, whose stories of Indian atrocities had touched off such a passionate response during the grim realities of Jeannie Dodson's agony; Pete Dodson, whose son David he had restored and whose beloved first wife he had helped to bury by the white oleander in the little private garden of the house on Acequia Street; Dr. Weideman, whose strange teachings and extraordinary actions shocked and stimulated.

"Don't shoot, don't yell, and don't let that magnificent piece of horseflesh wear himself out reflecting your own spirits." It was the doctor's voice, calm and slightly derisive. "Save yourselves for the Indians."

Range turned in the saddle and looked behind him. The doctor, attended by his servant José, stood a little apart and under the shade of a low-trunked palm tree that spread over him like a huge umbrella.

"Let the Indians save theirselves for us," Range said, becoming quiet under the doctor's steady gaze. He pulled Toego around and came nearer.

Dr. Weideman had discarded the black, satanic outfit with cape and gloves that he often affected in public and looked very cool and remote in a costume all white — even the wide-brimmed hat of some imported tropical weave was an unrelieved white. To Range every meeting with the doctor was a surprise. On their first encounter when Dr. Weideman had been riding Nightmare, it had seemed to Range that he'd met the devil on horseback. In the ordeal with Jeannie Dodson his actions had taken on godlike proportions; then a few nights later he had turned fighting man through and through, and in a successful skirmish with Indians who'd made off with two Mexican children and some horses had given Range the promised instruction in outwitting and outriding a Comanche.

Today the doctor's presence put a damper on Range's high spirits and filled him with disquietude. He suddenly felt oppressed with the secrets he carried, especially about the baby Macduff. There were

68

only six people who knew that Jeannie Dodson was his mother: he and Luvisa, the doctor and Firebush, and José and Carlota. They were all committed to silence for the sake of Pete Dodson and his family. But what if Pete should find out? What about José and Carlota? They would be sure to gossip.

"You would be interested, I suspect," the doctor broke in on his thoughts, "to know that my staff of servants has been augmented by one Macduff Martinez, approximately one week old, nephew to José and Carlota. His mother died. I let them have the child to keep at my house. They love it as their own."

José nodded and smiled proudly.

Range did not smile. He felt a dull anger. But he had no time to stir the embers of the dark passion that had possessed him when Dr. Weideman had saved and protected the baby. Luvisa and her grandfather, and Pete Dodson with Davy in his arms, were coming across the plaza to join the doctor and José. Range did have time, however, to look at José and say with unmistakable threat, "If Pete Dodson ever finds out, I'll know who to — "

It was the doctor's turn to be resentful. The pointed anger in his eyes startled Range a little. His voice was even but his inflections bordered on insult.

"There is only one danger. I state it deviously in a quotation from an English man of letters: 'Young men are very apt to tell what secrets they know from the vanity of having been trusted.'"

Range's face flushed a deep red.

Luvisa hadn't heard but she read the emotion Range couldn't hide. She placed her hand reprovingly on the doctor's arm. "You haven't started some unpleasant argument for Mr. Templeton to remember us by, have you?"

The doctor laughed, his anger turned to teasing. "His blush should please you, Miss Luvisa, not disturb you. A young man who blushes is much to be preferred over the pale, bloodless type. Any young lady about to choose her mate — "

"Dr. Weideman!" Luvisa's blush was high too.

69

"You are well matched!" The doctor laughed again. The others joined him. Range and Luvisa looked at each other helplessly. They hadn't said a thing to anyone about their feeling for each other; they had intended to keep the knowledge of it a close personal secret. Now they were betrayed by a blush and a look.

Luvisa looked at her grandfather; he didn't seem in any way displeased. José was grinning widely. The doctor raised his eyebrows at her expectantly. Pete Dodson smiled at her quietly, encouragingly. She knew exactly what Pete meant, because he knew about love and the limits that time places upon it. She was more of a woman now, less of a girl. That she was to be parted from this man so newly and completely loved brought on a destitution of spirit she had never known before. She was to be his wife — if he didn't meet Indian arrow or bandit's bullet on this trip — and she faced the months of not knowing if he were dead or alive. She walked with careful step, appeared calm, acted demure, but her mood bordered on hysteria, and to save herself from an exhibition of tears and protest, she decided on what she knew her grandmother would consider forward and unbecoming behavior. She would kiss Range Templeton good-by before all these people. It would make the parting more endurable, give her a stronger reassurance of possession. She looked at him with such love and anxiety, such an intensity of longing, that he was to feel a constant awareness of her on his journey, and to be made stronger and more alert by the power of her devotion.

She took the few steps that brought her close to Indian Toego; the horse was so high and Range so tall, and what she was about to do was so bold, that for a moment she felt small and scared.

"Mr. Templeton?"

"Yes, Miss Luvisa, what is it?"

"Tell them. I think it will be better. Then — then it will be all right — I think — if you kiss me good-by."

Awkwardness and embarrassment left Range. He hadn't known until now that this was exactly the kind of leave-taking he wanted. He dismounted easily and took her hand.

70

"Mr. Olson, your granddaughter has promised to marry me when I get something for us to start on and get my piece of land. I aim to — " He hesitated. "What I aim to do's no matter. I'll take care of her when the time comes."

He didn't wait for comment or approval. He took her in his arms, kissed her several times, and then without a word got back on his horse.

Eli Dawson gave the signal up ahead. The first cart in the train moved. Whips popped, the yells of the drivers were positive, the crowd quieted, and the oxen lurched ahead. Six of the riders dashed to the head of the train and on out of the plaza. The others moved forward. Toego pranced excitedly. But no one could think of the final words.

"The stage is set and the actors in their places. Too bad we've all forgotten our lines," the doctor said.

Then Pete Dodson said the truly appropriate thing to Range. "We'll take care of her, don't worry."

"Thank you, Pete, and take care of Davy, too."

The quiet, thin little boy almost smiled at him.

Firebush Olson stepped up to Toego and slipped the strings of a leather pouch over the saddle horn. "Look this thing over when you camp tonight. Might help you out. Got no use for it myself. Got my own system with the redskins. Won this off a stranger that had more rum in 'im than money on 'im and inclined to bet higher than the cards showed."

"Thanks, Mr. Olson."

Eli Dawson signaled for Range to join him. Range raised his hat in a wordless gesture of farewell and followed his boss into the long day ahead that with good luck would end at a campsite on the Medina River . . . and onto a trail that with exceptional good fortune would end with their safe arrival at Laredo within two or three weeks' time. Without bad weather, or breakdowns, or Indian attacks the carts could average ten or twelve miles a day.

Among the eleven men Eli Dawson had hired for riders, there

71

was no uniformity of garb, equipment, or mounts and small compatibility of temperament. They could not even share a common language. Of the six Mexican riders, only three spoke a little English: Señor Batres, the Laredo merchant; Luis Martíniano, gay caballero who lived for ornamentation; and Juan Elizondo, nephew to the alcalde at Laredo. Juan had traveled the road more times than any other member of the party and considered himself irreplaceable as scout and weather prophet. The two vaqueros and close compadres, Pedro and Pablo, neither spoke nor understood English; Manuel Rodriguez, the quiet hunter, understood the two languages but spoke only one. Eli Dawson himself and old Flaco Davis, the oldest rider of them all, could use as they needed it a rude and highly ungrammatical, but thoroughly adequate form of Spanish they called "meskin." Of the other three Americans — Range, Silver Bryson, and Jesse Faze — only one could communicate with the Mexican drivers and riders, and that was the young man with the old look, white-haired Silver Bryson, whose careful, scholarly speech in either language never failed to shock his more rugged companions; but the shock usually went unvoiced because Silver's handling of the polished old dueling pieces he carried was as careful and scholarly as his speech. Mudo, the Tarahumare Indian from Chihuahua, could speak no language at all.

The only uniformity Eli Dawson tried to achieve in the selection of his riders was that the horses be fast and the men on them daring with certain skills in fighting that would be effective not only against Indians but against freebooters operating out of Laredo. It didn't matter to him whether the Comanche met his end by the grace of Silver's dueling piece, Flaco's rifle, Manuel or Mudo's bow and arrow, or a knife well placed at close quarters; and a robber was just as dead jerked from his horse by Pablo's cow-whip wrapped around his neck or Pedro's riata flashed out in a deadly circle as he would be if caught in the range of Eli's own horse pistol.

And there were other talents besides riding and fighting that could add to a man's value on the trail. There was Luis Martíniano, for

72

example. Luis was a dandy and dressed himself and his horse accordingly. His sombrero was broad and gaily tasseled, his trousers braided, his serape very bright, and his saddle heavily embossed and inlaid. Large silver spurs, and silver on stirrup shields and bridle were accents in the brightness of his regalia. His horse, a beautiful rusbayo, light dun with a dash of gold, carried his gaudy trappings with a vanity that matched his master's.

Range viewed Luis with open distaste from the start of the trip.

Eli rode with a different one of his riders each day. On the first day he rode near the train and kept Range at his side. He sent Mudo and Manuel Rodriguez, both good hunters with bow and arrow, and Juan Elizondo to scout ahead of the train, hunt game for the evening meal, and prepare the campsite on the Medina River. Five riders were deployed at some distance to the right of the wagons, from which direction attack was most likely to come. Luis and Señor Batres scouted not far to the left.

As Range watched Luis ride away giving the appearance of leading a grand parade, Eli did not find it hard to read the disapproval in the stern gray eyes.

"I guess you're wonderin' if he can fight as pretty as he can look," Eli drawled. "Well, he can't, as a matter of fact. With that fancy pearl-handled gun of his, he couldn't hit a bear hide on a barn door. But he's just as good in a fight as if he could. He's as reckless as all sin on the loose. And he feels as good in a fight as a horned toad does in a red-ant bed, and comes out of it just as full and satisfied. He's got a fool's pure luck . . . no more sense about gamblin' than about fightin' but comes out of it the same way — winnin'. That's how come all the silver trimmin's. Luck like that means a short life. I don't think he'll live much longer. But as a decoy, he's worth the risk."

Range had nothing to say. Eli was silent for a minute, not expecting comment from Range or even approval of his motives in hiring Luis, but just letting his description soak in.

"Then again," he continued, "Luis is a musician. I always try to

73

have somebody in the train who can entertain a little. Breaks the strains at the end of the day. Some wild feelin's get to stirrin' around my campfires sometimes, and the music most times will soothe 'em down and keep us from cuttin' each other's throats. Except in case of necessity, a'course. Now I got one rider on this trip I may have to kill or see that he gets killed before we get to Laredo. Luis's music won't help him none."

Range was startled out of his sullen attention to Eli's remarks on Luis. Instinctively, in spite of himself, he reacted physically. His body jerked slightly, and his hand glided to the handle of his pistol and rested there.

Eli smiled. "I'll tell you about it later. Don't let it bother you none. He's a spy for the freebooter bunch headquarterin' now in Laredo. He'll be mighty loyal and useful to me till about ten or fifteen miles this side of Laredo, only we won't take him that far. Let me know when you make up your mind which one he is. See what kind of judgment you got."

They rode on in silence, separating after a while, Range riding on an entire circle of the train, scouting the inside area between the train and the other riders. In the meantime, Eli checked each cart, to see that the freight was riding securely, water kegs still tight in their frames on the back, oxen and horses showing no signs of being footsore. In addition to the twelve teams of oxen pulling the carts, there were six teams for replacements being led behind the carts, and six extra horses in case any rider should cripple or lose his mount.

There were no stops for midday meal or siesta. The day, cool and partially cloudy, made pleasant traveling for man and beast. There was no need to rest or feed the animals until evening. Most of the drivers carried food prepared by family and friends as a parting gift. Bread and cheese were handed out from the supply wagon in pocket-size packages to the riders as they left on Eli's scouting assignments. Some of the riders carried water canteens; others had drinking shells made from gourds tied to the pommel of their saddles and took drinking luck with their horses at whatever watering places they found.

74

With the drinking shells, it was not even necessary to dismount in order to scoop up a drink. No one working for Eli Dawson was allowed to carry whiskey or rum on the trail. There was whiskey in the supply cart but it would be distributed only in such amounts and at such times as he designated.

They were making good time for an ox-cart train, almost ten miles by midafternoon. They'd make the Medina River by sundown. The springtime beauty of the country through which they traveled seemed to mock at precautions against danger, so incompatible was any form of violence with the loveliness of the landscape.

When Eli and Range were riding side by side again, Range inquired, "Why do you use oxen and these carts for your freighting? Why not mules and wagons? Wouldn't it be faster, save you time and money?"

"Lots of reasons," Eli said. "First place, Indians don't steal oxen, hardly ever — hard to handle 'em and hard to sell 'em, so they just leave 'em alone. Second place, oxen hold out better. Don't take so much feed or water or attention, got more endurance, and not liable to stampede with a bunch of wild horses like mules do sometimes, and this is wild-horse country. Third place, I'm using Mexican drivers, and these ox-carts are the Mexican pace and the Mexican way of hauling. It works out better this way."

"Do you have to use Mexican drivers?"

"Well, not exactly. But San Antonio is mostly Mexican, and this country to the south is so Mexican that we're not even trying to claim it beyond the Nueces River yet. Deaf Smith and some of his friends took a little jaunt down to Laredo last year and tried to plant the flag of independence down there, but they come back with it unplanted. When working in Rome, work the Romans, I always say."

"But no matter how many Mexicans are still around, you're not working in Mexico. You're working in the Republic of Texas."

"Some folks think so. Some still think different. We'll see. This is just a lull. Mexico's not through trying."

"If we keep acting like this part of the country is still Mexico, won't that make it easier for 'em? Aren't there enough Americans in Texas to run the Mexicans back across the Rio Grande where they belong?"

"I picked you for a smart one. Don't make me feel stupid."

"What do you mean?"

"I mean it would be just about as easy to uproot all this mesquite and cactus and put it on the other side of the Rio Grande as it would be to clean out the Mexicans and make 'em stay out."

"How many Americans in Texas now?"

"Nobody knows for sure, I reckon. I've heard tell, some thirty thousand, maybe forty or fifty thousand; anyways about twice as many as there are Mexicans, I'd say; and more of us than Mexicans and Indians combined for sure."

"That ought to be enough."

"Enough for what?"

"To get rid of the Indians and Mexicans both."

"The country's too big and we're all too scattered, and like I said the Mexicans are planted in these parts. They got several hundred years of roots down, and I'm thinking they're liable to stay, republic or otherwise. And if you're gonna operate this side of San Antonio any time in the next hundred years or so, you'll get along better if you speak a little Spanish and get wise to their ways."

"I'll get along."

"I reckon you will, one way or another. But there's the hard way, and other ways."

"Looks like with the Indians you figure the hard way is the best way. Trying to kill 'em out in these parts, aren't you?"

"Just the thievin', butcherin' ones like the Comanches; not all Indians. Not good Indians, like my rider Mudo."

"You call him a good Indian?" Range considered Mudo, trying to anticipate how Eli would defend him. . . . Mudo, seated on his dwarfish mustang, his saddle a crude wooden framework, no hat over his flowing, jet-black hair; his only dress the scanty, homespun, woolen breechclout and a short much-worn poncho of the same ma-

76

terial; his only weapon the bow and arrow of craftsmanship as crude as his saddle. What good could be in this Mudo? Yet, he respected Dawson's judgment, and felt an eagerness to understand everything that would in any way help him to possess this land. He might not be able to think like Dawson, any more than he could think like Dr. Weideman, but if you could get to the bedrock of a man's thoughts you could measure him better for the things he'd do and say. That doctor, now, was a strange one on the subject of Indians: Kill the dirty, marauding dogs with zest, he'd said, but don't lose your perspective on Indians in general. Well, maybe there were different kinds of Indians, maybe Mudo was a different kind, but personally he didn't like the sight or smell of him, gave him a bristly feeling, like a dog with his hackles up.

"You call him a good Indian?" he repeated, prodding Eli to explain. "How's he any different? Looks worse'n some and smells worse'n most I've ever seen."

Eli guffawed. "So you don't like the way he smells. Well, he don't like the way we smell either; says some of us smell like pigs and some like coffee, and both are plenty bad smells far's he's concerned."

"I didn't know he could say anything. Somebody was saying he was dumb as a post — couldn't talk."

"Mudo and me got a sign language. We can talk like a house afire when we want to. But he is dumb when it comes to speakin' for he's got no tongue to speak with."

"Born that way?"

"Hell no. The reason he hasn't got one is the reason I'd trust him to the jumping-off place." Eli didn't hurry with his story. He broke a twig off a hackberry tree and stuck it in the corner of his mouth to chew on and slumped to one side of his saddle in a restful position.

"I picked him up in Chihuahua City on my last freight trip there. Got the story of him off a man I trade with some. There's silver and gold mines and buried treasure in the state of Chihuahua from before the Spanish times that's not been located till yet. Once in a while an Indian shows up with some chunks of gold or bars of silver, but

77

nobody's ever found out any way to make 'em talk, and plenty of ways has been tried.

"Mudo's a Tarahumare, pure-blood. They're the greatest runners in the world. A young, healthy one could run from San Antonio to Laredo without stopping. I figure if we got in a tight spot and lost our horses, Mudo could take off on foot and bring us help. Tarahumares are good hunters too. Mudo and Rodriguez make a fine pair to get in the game on a trip like this." Eli digressed from his story a little. "They're both mighty handy with bow and arrow, and on the little stuff like rabbits Mudo has a boomerang he knocks them out with. No guns poppin' around to give away our whereabouts. If they've had their usual luck we'll have turkey, venison, and rabbit at camp tonight."

Eli chewed the hackberry stem for a while. Range rode along in an attentive silence.

"Well, this Mudo some years ago gets caught with some of this treasure stuff he's been taking in to an Indian family in Chihuahua City. The two men who catch him want to find out where he got the gold. They know from experience that the torture business won't work. So they decide to try something new.

"There's an old half-breed called Sleepy Eyes that claims he can cast a spell and make a man talk. These two men take their captive Indian to Sleepy Eyes who's about half medicine man and has quite a reputation among the Indians for his mumbo-jumbo. Mudo knew what he was in for and it never entered his head that Sleepy Eyes couldn't make him talk. No kind of pain could make him talk, but spell-binding was something else. So when they untied him he just stood quiet, thinking out some way to defeat Sleepy Eyes. The old witch doctor got right in his face and went through the sounds and gyrations that would mesmerize him. In a slow movement, so's not to excite anybody, Mudo turned his back. This pleased the two men. They thought he was in a trance and would start out in a minute and lead 'em to the treasure. But he didn't take any steps, just moved his arm up to the side of his face. Sleepy Eyes kept giving him the works. All of a sudden, Mudo turned and threw something at the feet of the old wizard. Know what it was?"

"By this time I got an idea," Range said.

Eli brushed the chewed bushy end of the hackberry stem across his teeth reflectively, threw it away, and concluded his story. "Yeah, that's right. He'd torn out his own tongue by the roots!"

The camp on the Medina River that night was such as the adventurer dreams of when he longs for the open road. There was no campfire. Its warmth was not needed and its light might be revealing. There had been a sunset of riotous brilliance, its colors ranging from softest pinks and golds to burnished reds caught up in the great rolls of clouds that had made the day's traveling so pleasant. A few reluctant streaks of light hung long and low in the west, lengthening the twilight. Fireflies, unbelievably large this season, lazily flashed their lights off and on, competing with the glows at fingertips and lips as the men sprawled and sat in comfort at their smoking.

There had been plenty of meat provided by Mudo and Manuel, as Dawson had predicted; and Juan Elizondo had prepared it in a large rock-lined pit that after the initial firing acted as a fireless cooker for several hours before the arrival of the train. Mudo had eaten to sufficiency before the arrival of the carts and was ready to take charge of the oxen and the horses for the first watch. Two others would be assigned to guard duty after a brief rest. There were four watches of three men each. The drivers were not expected to be on guard duty out from the train. Each man bedded down by his cart and in case of attack was expected to defend its contents against the intended pillage. But it wasn't time for bedding down yet. The moon would be up before long, the boss would pass a drink around, Luis would sing a little, and one of the vaqueros would likely tell a story. Until then, matters rested, and a man could absorb the mild night air along with his smoke and feel a contentment that needed no definition.

The whole group of men, although not widely scattered, were sep-

79

arated into natural segments, the drivers the largest closely knit circle. Pedro and Pablo, the only vaqueros, were slightly withdrawn and carrying on a desultory, soft-spoken conversation. Luis had Manuel and Juan for his immediate audience and was sharing with them in secretive tones some of the exciting details of the baile the night before and the conquests he had made.

Range and Silver Bryson, discovering a pleasant congeniality, sat, backs to a live-oak tree, listening, saying little, thinking, seeking an understanding of each other and of the things about them.

Flaco Davis, Señor Batres and Eli Dawson had age and trade in common at least and sat together in the "hunkered" position of buttocks supported by one heel and the other foot flat, Eli and Flaco chewing their tobacco, Señor Batres smoking rather fastidiously and a little nervously, the position he had assumed not quite comfortable, not nearly so much at ease as the men he aped. Señor Batres had reason to be nervous. He and four companions had made the trip to San Antonio several months previously, only to be waylaid by Indians shortly after they had started on their return trip to Laredo; pack animals and horses were taken and his four companions killed. Somehow Señor Batres had managed to escape. He had no difficulty in signing on with Dawson. Laredo, as subject to Indian depredations as San Antonio, gave its inhabitants plenty of experience in fighting the Indians. Dawson didn't mind that Batres was a one-way rider; he wouldn't have any trouble picking up somebody in Laredo just as eager to travel in good company on a return trip to San Antonio.

Jesse Faze, squat and bearded, his mannerisms jerky, was the only man entirely apart from his fellows. There was Mudo, of course, but his aloofness was of his own choosing; he didn't like pig and coffee smells, oxen and horses were better. But Jesse Faze resented his isolation and blamed others for it. He sat cross-legged not far from Range and Silver and aside from Dawson.

Dawson said, "A couple of you better get on guard. Anybody want to go now?"

Flaco, skinny and stiff in his joints, rose to his feet with a moan. "My belly aches when I eat, no matter what I eat, but it hurts worser when I set still than when I'm on the move. So if you don't mind, I'll go on lookout now."

Flaco's complaints were endless. He'd had many a ride with Eli Dawson, and if he'd stopped complaining, Eli would have worried about him. His digestion seemed to improve only after a successful skirmish with the Indians.

"Go ahead, Flaco," Eli said. "Your belly'll git better as we go along. We've had too much good luck today. It's a bad sign."

As Flaco walked away, Eli explained, "Funny thing about how an Indian fight affects him. Stirs him up some way so he gits along with his food for a while. Never has the bellyache after a fight. Eats hearty and goes right to sleep."

"Maybe he's part Tonkawa," Jesse Faze put in. "Maybe he eats hisself a hunk of Comanche on the sly."

The remark brought no comment. Jesse seemed pleased to have said something disagreeable. "I knew about a Comanche once that got caught by a Tonkawa. . . ."

Señor Batres rose with a grunt that indicated he shared Flaco's ailment. "Perhaps Señor Davis should have company in the lookout," he addressed Dawson.

"Bueno, señor, gracias," Dawson agreed, releasing him from the unpleasantness that seemed imminent.

"I knew about a Comanche once," Jesse repeated, in a tone that dared anyone else to leave until his story was finished, "that got caught by a Tonkawa. . . ." He had his audience now. Eli turned a little more in his direction, Silver Bryson and Range were very much aware of him, and Luis ceased his chatter so that he and Juan and Manuel could listen.

"The Tonks are cannibals, you know." He began by emphasizing what everybody listening already knew.

"They got this Comanche and they staked him good. They built up a fire and got ready for a meal. Then they started cutting off the meat where it was the thickest. Not troublin' to kill the Comanche, o' course. Jest the other way round. They took pains to keep him alive, searing the places where they took the meat with live coals. And what do you think that Comanche did?"

Nobody offered to tell him what the Comanche did, though most of them knew.

"Why he took it just as calm as that white-haired feller sittin' up against that tree there. That is, until the Tonks cooked the meat and started saying how delicate it was and how flavorable, and eatin' it right in front of him, even offerin' him a bite now and then. That was too much, even for a Comanche. But did he start screamin' and cryin'? Oh no."

No man ever had listeners more attentive but at the same time less appreciative than Jesse Faze. It was not the condition of the Comanche that was provoking questions in their minds, but the condition of Jesse Faze himself.

"He remembered his Indian manners. He said, 'No thank you. Never mind passin' the meat.' Then he told 'em off. He said his flesh was poison as rattlesnake spit and would be a curse to them and their sons and all the sons after that till finally he got some of 'em a little uneasy and they lost their appetites just a little and maybe got the bellyache like old Flaco did here after his supper. But was that all he did, just tell 'em off? Oh no."

Jesse paused to spit with a whistling sound through his teeth.

"He had to sing a little to finish things off . . . had to sing 'em his death song in his best voice before takin' off to his happy huntin' ground."

Jesse spit again, and concluded, "So you can't say a Comanche ain't got guts when that's about all he has got by the time a Tonk finishes with him."

He dropped his last line expectantly, hoping someone would pick it up, confident his disgusting details would arouse some kind of response, certain that the contamination he had thrown into the quiet pool of congeniality and repose would spread. But it surprised

Jesse that Silver Bryson's cultured voice was the one to take over.

"Your story has a well-placed point, Mr. Faze. It makes us realize that the Indian has not invented his debaucheries in cruelty for the white man alone. He can practice them with equal skill on enemies taken in conflict between warring tribes. Also he can endure as well as administer cruelty, and that makes him at least a consistent sort of creature."

Jesse had not intended his story as an educational lecture and Bryson's interpretation annoyed him. He would have liked to return to the possible cannibalistic tendencies of Flaco Davis. He was totally unprepared for Bryson's next remark.

"Mr. Faze, I observe that your face is heavily bearded. The indication is that your body might also be heavily suited with hair, since the open neck of your shirt shows the hairy covering extending to the chest. Have you never feared such proud exposure of hairy surface might in an Indian fight make your scalp coveted above those of other men in the party?" The question was asked with cool objectivity, but Jesse Faze could understand it only as personal insult. He jumped as if he'd been struck and was instantly on his feet, standing in a brutal crouch, his gun leveled on Bryson's white hair. Range made a movement to rise but Bryson placed a restraining hand on his leg.

"Please, Mr. Faze," Bryson spoke with the smoothest patience. "I mean no offense, no offense at all. We're all learning together about Indians and their ways. Every little contribution adds to our store of knowledge and strengthens us in our stands against them. You were kind enough to favor us with something from your fund of experience, now I want to return the favor. My remark to you was no more intended for an insult than your jest about Mr. Davis being part Tonkawa. I happen to know something about the art of scalping, the Comanche way, that must be unknown to you, else you would shave occasionally, cut your hair, and button up your shirt. Do you want to hear what I have to say, or shall I keep quiet?"

Eli Dawson answered the question. "Speak up, Bryson. Jesse had his say. Nobody stopped him. Go right ahead."

"When I came to the frontier — " Bryson started easily and Jesse Faze relaxed from his threatening position but did not sit down — "I thought all scalping was a flourish of the tomahawk and a hank of hair. Now I am better informed. The characteristic weapon of the Comanche is not the tomahawk but the knife, and his reverence for hair, having none on his face or body, naturally leads him to broaden the scope of scalping, shall we say. So a scalp that is merely a crown of hair from the head carries not nearly the prestige for a warrior when he returns to camp as a scalp that includes the bearded cheek flesh. And a really magnificent scalp, that puts the warrior's trophy in top-rank classification, is one that includes the flesh peeled from a body carrying heavy hair growth in the armpits, on the chest, the belly, and the crotch."

Before Bryson finished his sentence, Jesse Faze stalked away, river gravel crunching noisily under his angry steps. Eli Dawson allowed himself to smile in the semidarkness. Range drew a deep breath of satisfaction in Bryson's victory. There was silence in the camp. The moon began to show its great orange disk through the trees. A mockingbird welcomed it in a solo of jubilant song.

"Sing for us, Luis," Eli requested in Spanish.

"I have not the mood for singing," Luis replied. "I can sing only when my heart wills it."

"We need your singing," Eli insisted. "It will make us all feel better."

"I know," Luis replied, "my singing is good, but it must wait until the heart wills it."

Pedro said quietly, "Let Luis be quiet. The voice of the mockingbird is sweeter."

Pablo said, "Perhaps Luis should hear the story of the mockingbird and its vanities."

"Tell him the story," Pedro invited.

So the voice of Pablo mixed with the mockingbird's song and he told a story. There was a soothing cadence in the vaquero's voice. Bryson leaned close to Range and interpreted the story for him.

84

"He is telling how the mockingbird came to have white feathers in its wings. . . . In the long ago, when El Zenzontle, the mockingbird, sang, all things were still and listened. . . . The singer became conceited and began to brag of his greatness to his wife. . . . 'All nature obeys me,' he said. 'When I sing, spring comes, flowers bloom, birds mate, and even man takes notice and dances for joy.' . . . His wife told him all these things were responsive only to the voice of God. . . . So he invited her to a concert he was giving for the flowers that she might see how they swayed and danced at the sound of his voice. . . . Her reply was, 'You sing "Con el favor de Dios," ' which means 'If God wills it.' . . . This devoutness of his wife angered El Zenzontle and he said he would sing whether God willed it or not. . . . Perched high on the limb of a huisache next morning, he made ready for his concert. But before he could make a sound, a hawk swooped down and carried him away. . . . El Zenzontle thought of the wisdom of his wife and repented with all his heart. . . . 'O God,' he cried, 'it is You who cause the flowers to bloom and the birds to sing, not I!' . . . He felt himself slipping, and fell far, far down onto a plowed field where he lay bruised and tattered. . . . A white dove found him and mended his wings with three of her feathers which he has worn ever after as a reminder of his foolish pride and conceit. . . . And to this day, Pablo assures us, the mockingbird never sings without first saying, 'Con el favor de Dios.' "

Pablo had finished his story. The silence of his listeners was a fine tribute. The mockingbird sang on. After a while Luis went to the supply wagon and brought back his guitar.

"Luis Martíniano will now sing for you," he said. "Con el favor de Dios." Luis, like El Zenzontle, had some ground for his conceit, for the rich, sweet quality of his voice reached out and possessed the beauty of the night, and those around him felt their senses submerged in whatever mood he chose to reflect.

"What's he singing about now, Bryson?" Range asked.

"About the beauty of first love, the sweetness of the first kiss, and the promises, the dreams and the yearnings that come after."

85

CHAPTER V

RANGE and Silver Bryson were riding together for the first time. It was the fourth day out and there hadn't been another camp like the one on the Medina River. A small band of Comanches had been sighted on the afternoon of the second day, but they were moving to the west away from the train; caution and watchfulness had filled every man's mind and made the night to follow an uneasy one.

Thunderstorms had added discomfort to suspense throughout the third day, and camping for the night was again a dreary interval merely to be endured. But tonight, Juan assured them, there would be clear skies and a beautiful campsite on the bank of a small stream called La Parrita. If their luck held, and the afternoon passed without further sign of Indians, they could relax for the evening while the cook prepared something special and Luis tuned up his guitar.

Dawson was soon aware of the current of congeniality between Range and Bryson, and, deciding it was a good thing, hadn't lost much time in making it possible for them to become better acquainted. Now they had been riding together for half a day and had paused in a shady, rock-bottomed creek bed where their horses could drink at a clear seep while they ate noon rations of bread and meat. There had been little conversation between them and no personal questions. There was no need for talk just yet. They felt a partnership, yet intangible, in the future, and each wanted to examine this feeling further, turn it over in his mind. They felt an intimacy with the land over which they traveled, as if their future lay right around them, a setting to be animated with their own lives. It was certainly not the kind of land the average settler would consider desirable; and, with every mile southward, it was becoming more undesirable, more stubborn and unwelcome in aspect, daring man to wrestle it for profit. Woods and grass were thinning out, sand pulled more tenaciously at wheel and hoof, brush seemed to clutch the earth

86

more fiercely, prickly pear and Spanish dagger asserted an ever-increasing boldness on the landscape, and the lacy leaves of the mesquites became more deceitful, hiding longer and sharper thorns.

Range, not quite as tall as Bryson and a possible ten years younger, felt neither deference for the cultural attainments of his new friend nor curiosity about whatever experience had given him white hair so prematurely. It was enough that here was a man he could trust. Not that it would be altogether safe for any man to trust Silver Bryson, but simply that mutual trust was a natural component of friendship so quickly recognized and firmly established. Range was acknowledging this trust when he went to his saddle and untied the pouch that Firebush Olson had given him on the main plaza at San Antonio.

"Bryson, I got something I want to show you." He opened the pouch and took out a pistol, a weapon of strange line and dimension, unlike any of the popular arms of the times. "Never saw or heard tell of anything like it." Range said. "Tell me if you ever did."

Bryson took the gun Range offered him and examined it; his sharp amber-colored eyes, his long thin fingers missed no detail. "I've heard of it, but never had one in my hands before," he said. The pistol was hardly ten inches long, had a blued finish, an octagonal-shaped barrel without a ramrod, and an ornamentally engraved revolving cylinder containing five chambers.

"It's the revolving pistol, invented by Samuel Colt . . . shoots five times without reloading . . . if it works . . . and I presume it does. . . . It seems to have been handled and used." Bryson was removing the cylinder and observing the five loaded chambers, each containing its measured charge of powder and a .31 caliber rounded bullet.

"I guess you could call it a five-shooter," Range commented, "or maybe a ten-shooter, for here's another cylinder that goes along with it, making ten shots in all before you have to get out powder and ball to reload."

"Have you tried this gun yet?" Bryson inquired.

87

"No. Didn't want to stir up a noise and didn't want to waste ammunition."

"Stir up a noise, did you say? Don't you realize that this weapon distributed in proper quantity could stir up a noise that would reverberate down the corridors of history! With enough of these, we could rout the Indian, defeat the Mexican, and literally become lords of all we survey."

"How do you figure that?"

"It's easy. You've been here long enough already to see that except for our expert marksmanship and maneuvering, we are at a disadvantage in this country. Right now the Indians have us stopped and the Mexicans have us worried. Our mounted Indian adversary carries forty or fifty arrows. We carry at the most only three shots, each in a separate weapon bulky and unwieldy — two heavy pistols and a rifle — all designed for shooting when a man's feet are planted firmly on solid ground — all requiring that fatal extra minute for reloading. And during that meticulous and time-consuming task of measuring and pouring powder, ramming ball and priming, the Indian rides three hundred yards and shoots twenty arrows."

"You got it down to a gnat's bristle, Bryson. But you make it sound like we hardly got a chance."

"We have a chance, all right. Our range is longer, our accuracy more deadly. But to have the advantage that counts, we need to be able to remain mounted throughout combat as the Indian does and send bullets at him faster than he sends arrows at us. This weapon could give us that advantage — if it works — and if we had enough of them."

"Why can't we have enough of them?"

"Mainly because the citizens of the Republic of Texas do not have two hundred dollars apiece to spend for a weapon and the impoverished government itself is no better off. The manufacture of arms is a poor business unless the government becomes a purchaser. A gunsmith who had seen the patent on Colt's repeating carbines and pistols told me of its wonders but wasn't very hopeful about supply-

88

ing them since the United States government had declined to adopt the Colt arms. If the ordnance board had tried out the new weapon in frontier warfare rather than in testing rooms, it might be a different story."

"Wish we had some good reason for trying it out now."

"Don't be giving signals to fate. The chance will come soon enough."

But Range had spoken the comment that makes coincidence.

They were riding on the west side of the train; so were Juan Elizondo and Luis Martíniano. Juan and Luis were riding in advance of the train as Juan was usually given one of the chief scouting positions. Range and Bryson were riding further to the west, scouting in an arc from the rear to the head of the slow-moving procession of loaded carts.

As Bryson handed the pistol back to Range, they heard two shots up ahead. Then came two answering shots a little closer. They were almost instantly on their horses, no word exchanged between them, heading straight for the trouble now four days overdue.

Sounds told the story before they came in sight of the desperate chase. Savage yells . . . another shot . . . a high-pitched, exuberant, taunting yell that answered the Indians and was undoubtedly the voice of Luis. . . . Then Range and Bryson were up over a slight rise and in plain view of as deadly a race as man could run, exhibiting as primitive a joy as man could show. There was no doubt about it, Luis was enjoying himself, and he had given the six Comanches after him the advantage they craved in battle: the pursued in retreat ahead of them while horses ran full speed and bows snapped, releasing arrow after arrow, seeking the fatal strike that would bring down the rider and leave his good mount unharmed.

The streak of bright colors and the flashing of silver ornaments that marked Luis and his horse excited the savages to a positive frenzy which was further accentuated by the impotency of their arrows sliding under his big, fancy sombrero and even under his arms, but leaving him untouched. That he was utterly without fear

89

and would even turn and yell to them in unmistakable challenge gave to the chase on both sides a fantastic abandonment of even the most instinctive cautions. Luis must know, however, that he was leading toward Range and Bryson and a possible rescue from his predicament. But before they could ride in on the chase, he swerved his horse abruptly, dashed through some heavy brush and down a gully that soon resolved into a small, narrow canyon.

Range and Bryson both surmised that Luis had seen them and now expected them to follow and surprise the Indians in a rear attack. Their horses seemed to realize what was expected. Indian Toego stretched out in a long leaping run as if the rock and sand and low brush were a clear race track. Silver Bryson's white stallion acted as if the whole thing were a private race between him and Toego.

Juan Elizondo was missing from the race, Range was thinking. The early exchange of shots meant the Indians had a gun or two. Had Juan been hit or killed; or, would he be warning the train? Were these six Indians a part of a general attack on the whole outfit, or just a small hunting party on their own?

Luis and his pursuers disappeared around a sharp curve in the gorge and the echoing of wild yells and clattering hoofs in a mad race over rough bottom and brittle driftwood magnified the deadly little seven-place game out of all proportion. Certainly the Comanches were yet unaware that they in turn were pursued and that two more players were sitting in on the end of the game.

There was a single shot fired up ahead and by the time Range and Bryson could round the curve, all sound had ceased and momentarily the scene before them was in pantomime. The Indians had been very close on Luis and the rifle shot that had caught him between the shoulders could hardly have missed. He lay sprawled, face downward, arms and legs flung out to full length, blood spreading in a quick wide pattern over the white embroidery of his jacket. His horse stood, head drooped almost to the ground, feet still braced from the impact of a sudden stop. The Indian who had fired the shot sat immobile, his rifle still held in one hand halfway aloft, surprised at the completeness of his success; his five companions were in various poses with bows and arrows and shields.

The chase had been action so completely intoxicating that it took this instant of stillness to realize it had come to an end and the prize in all its glitter and brilliant colors lay before them for the taking. In that instant, time betrayed them, for the two riders were upon them. If the inert body of Luis had materialized into two live men before their eyes, their astonishment could not have been more complete. Bryson's dueling pistol and Range's gift from Firebush Olson sounded together. Two Indians sprawled on the ground in positions almost identical with that of Luis. Then, as Bryson's second gun spoke, there were four more shots in quick succession from the Colt weapon. The Indian ponies raced riderless on down the ravine. Luis's horse looked after them, made a restless turn, sniffed at Luis's sombrero, and decided to stay.

"It works," Range said, turning the weapon over in his hand.

"Yes, it does," Bryson agreed.

They examined Luis. He had died as instantly as the Indians who followed him.

"Con el favor de Dios," Bryson muttered as they tied Luis across his saddle so beautifully embossed and inlaid with silver and brass, using the fine, horsehair stake rope that he always carried.

Then they carefully reloaded their guns, spending some time over the revolving pistol. As Range removed the barrel in order to replace the empty cylinder with a full one, he was conscious of the awkwardness of having the gun in three pieces for reloading.

"What if I'm riding hell-for-leather trying to reload this contraption with Indians on my tail, and I drop a piece of it — it would be good-by scalp, wouldn't it?"

"So it would."

"And this business of the trigger folding up and disappearing when the hammer falls and coming in sight again when you cock the thing — I managed all right this time, but I got scared-like, waiting for it to come back out, and thinking what if it didn't."

91

Bryson grinned wryly, kicked a dead Indian lightly with the toe of his well-made boot, and remarked, "Your aim did not seem to reflect the uncertainty of your thoughts. Too bad Mr. Colt can't have the benefit of your experience today. It would instruct and inspire."

They both realized without discussing it that the party of Indians they had just wiped out might be only a small contingent of a band out to raid the train. They took the three rifles and all ammunition found on the Indians with the conviction that the guns had not long ago belonged to men not so fortunate as they had just been.

"I've got a feeling that one of these guns belonged to Juan," Range said.

"I think you're right."

"Rodriguez and Mudo might could use some of these arrows and stuff for their hunting." Range quickly gathered up the three best-looking bows and a supply of arrows, and they tied these with the rifles on the rusbayo to make a rather fierce and gaudy funeral cargo for the beautiful horse.

"I notice you picked out three bows," Bryson said.

"One's for me," Range admitted. Then he felt a flush rising from his neck to his cheeks as he waited for some light remark from Silver about playing Indians. He wanted to explain that getting the bow and arrows for himself was not a childish impulse for a souvenir or plaything but something to use for his own instruction. But he couldn't say anything more.

It was the last time he was ever to worry about his thoughts or actions being interpreted as immature, for to his intense surprise and relief, Bryson only remarked, "Good. It is not always necessary to have a better weapon than the enemy in order to defeat him; sometimes the matter is resolved merely by being able to use the weapon of your opponent better than he himself can use it."

As they left the place, Range looked back once and reflected for the first time: These Indians are the first Indians I ever killed. There were no particular emotions accompanying the thought. He wondered if he should have taken scalps as a sort of tally or proof, but the idea of grasping the coarse hair and slitting the skin was repulsive to him. Silver hadn't bothered, so why should he? To his own surprise, he found himself voicing a rather intimate thought to Bryson.

"Killing Indians is different than killing bears," he said. "Did you ever kill a bear, a big man-size one?"

"No," Bryson said, "I've never killed a bear."

"Well, when you come against a big one, the excitement is something terrible. And when you've finished him off, you feel like you've got all your own strength and the bear's too. And you want to put your foot on 'im and yell loud enough to make all creation tremble. I did that the second time I killed one — I was too paralyzed the first time — and it did seem like things around me shook a little."

Bryson was very attentive.

"You don't hate the bear — you're sort of thankful to him for making you feel older and stronger. And unless you want the skin and the meat, you'd just as soon he was alive again so's you could give him another tussle sometime. But you don't want to hurry right out and fight another bear. There's something in you that's satisfied for a spell."

They were making their way directly to the train to report to Dawson, but they couldn't travel fast because of the loaded horse they must lead. Range was silent for a while and Bryson studied him closely. He saw in his young friend's very expression an acknowledgment of inner tensions and the effort to understand them. It was usually like that, he knew, the first time a sane, healthy man killed human beings, regardless of compulsions or motives. And the conclusions he drew or evasions he set up would affect him ever after.

Range was talking again, as much to himself as to Bryson. "It's different, killing those Indians, different from anything else. I feel more power in me maybe, but I'm not satisfied. I'd like to kill some more of 'em. I feel a tuggin' way down deep in my guts and it won't stop till I've killed —" he hesitated, his hand holding the reins

93

clinched so tightly the knuckles were white — "till I've killed I don't know how many."

Bryson said quietly, "When killing is purposeful and a man considers that he has no moral cause for regret, the power that he feels afterward can be a dangerous thing, a disastrous illusion. But whether the power of the thing killed is added to or subtracted from a man's inner stature depends on what he has killed and for what purpose."

"Do you like to kill Indians?"

"It is easy when the need arises, but I feel no tugging at the guts, as you call it."

"Maybe you don't know — "

"About Indian atrocities? I believe I do. On the Day of Judgment if there is any doubt about their qualifications as demons in hell, I shall probably be called as the first witness."

There was no reproval in Bryson's tone, but Range realized that here was a man who had actually seen the things he had only heard about, and, because of the obvious difference between them, he reached a clarity of reasoning about himself that was to have a continuous bearing on the rigorous circumstances that would shape his fortunes in the Republic of Texas.

"I hate 'em for what they are and for what they got. To let savages like them hold the land is like — " he thought of Jeannie Dodson — "is like letting them hold on to all the women they capture and use them like they want to."

Bryson, hardly realizing the full implication of his words, replied, "Strangely enough, the nature of the Indian is slightly akin to your own in that they think more of the land than they do womankind."

Hate and anger were strong physical passions with Range Templeton that raged through his body on high accents of pain. His love for Luvisa Olson was so acutely and keenly in his consciousness and welcomed there, and his desire for power through possession of land so much more subtle and hidden a passion that Bryson's remark sent a hot arrow of anger through him piercing him from crown to groin.

Bryson realized instinctively what he had done. In the violence of some people's emotions there is a powerful influence, akin to a vibration, that can be felt by the person arousing it. Bryson hadn't known when he made the remark that Range Templeton had the love of a woman fresh in his mind and heart and, at the moment, recognized as the most important thing in his life. He knew it now. And he felt lonelier for the knowledge. I should have made that remark twenty years from now, he thought. But the harm was done, and it was not in the nature of Silver Bryson to utter an apology.

Juan Elizondo had arrived at the train ahead of Range and Bryson, his right arm hanging loosely, a trail of blood marking the path he had come. The first shot by the Indians had caught him and caused him to drop his rifle; two shots from Luis and his usual play for starting the chase had diverted the savages and allowed Juan to escape. Luis had evidently planned to allow Juan to return to the train with warnings while he led the Indians into a trap where Bryson and Range could pick them off. Luis had planned well — he just hadn't counted on his luck running out.

There were no other signs of Indians reported from the riders. But Eli was certain now that a bigger raid was in store somewhere down the trail, probably beyond the Nueces, because by that time men and animals would be more travel-weary and the conditions of the country more inimical to survival.

They buried Luis at once, stopping the train, putting the drivers to digging the grave, working in relays. A well-concealed spot, a small clearing in a clump of brush, was selected; it was so small in fact that there was hardly room for the grave and the men who gathered around it. It was a quick and awkward business, burial on the trail. There was no formality even of wrapping the body in a blanket. Nothing was removed, not even the money belt under the shirt, for nothing was known about the family of Luis Martíniano. There was no ceremony, but religious gestures were not entirely absent. While the grave was being dug and the body lay unwatched, Mudo furtively removed the sombrero from the face and with some difficulty managed to get a slick, round, red pebble into the mouth. Pablo, too, had an offering. He snapped two twigs from a mesquite and with some horse-hair tied the two pieces in the form of a cross and placed the object in the stiff hand that had moved with melody across the guitar strings.

Eli, Señor Batres, Range, and Silver placed the body in the grave. As the sand quickly covered the tasseled sombrero, the gay serape, and the silver spurs, Bryson, looking on, hands on hips, white hair tousled on his forehead, quoted audibly, " 'Who knows but life be that which men call death. And death what men call life.' "

Señor Batres, mopping great drops of sweat from his brow, murmured that he would have prayers said at Laredo. Eli Dawson looked at him strangely.

Range caught the look and concluded, "This is the man Eli may have to kill before we get to Laredo."

But maybe he was wrong, for Eli said to Batres, "I wouldn't worry about praying Luis out of purgatory if I was you. He'll sing his way out."

The campsite at La Parrita was indeed a beautiful one, as Juan had predicted — on a quiet, clear stream bordered by large oak trees, a profusion of willows, and occasional huisache in heavy blossom — a lavish setting designed by nature for peace and serenity. But the design of circumstance was stronger and the composite mood of the men was fraught with uneasiness and memories of pain. Juan Elizondo, in agony after the long afternoon ride in a jolting cart, suffered in grim silence until darkness came and swept away his courage. Then his cries were blended with the wailing of the screech owls and the coyotes' call which carried through the night like a last entreaty from lost souls; and the pauses were filled with the melancholy croaking of frogs and the restless rustling of leaves caught in an uncertain breeze.

Juan was finally quiet, his pain saturated in brandy from Eli's private pack. A late moon brought a radiance that seemed more malignant than kindly, and for a brief period nature seemed to match the stupor in which Juan lay with a portentous stillness. Then a sound like distant thunder pierced the consciousness of every man in the company, rider and driver, with the single exception of Juan Elizondo. Each man, his weapon in hand and his mind on Indians, was in readiness beside horse or cart before he came to realize that in the tempo of the approaching roar was something unhampered and unguided by human hand.

Eli was the first to realize fully what was about to happen and yelled, "Mustangs on the rampage. Shoot if you have to. Watch the loose horses."

The horses in camp were excited almost beyond control. Their high squealing whinnies pierced the night. They were frantic to join their untamed kind now exhibiting the ultimate in freedom as they began a circling of the camp, curious and concerned about the domestic animals, as if deliberately planning to free the captives held there. Finally, before the circle came too close, the riders on guard began yelling and firing, causing the leaders of the wild horses to wheel and take their herds thundering away.

Range was part of the guard and added his shots and shouts to the bewildering mélange of sounds. So this was wild-horse country! He had never imagined the herds were so immense, their movement so exhilarating! There were thousands of horses in this perfectly organized mass of speed charging across the country. Why, the whole night seemed to be running and trembling with excitement! Indian Toego was almost beyond control — never had he exhib- ited such reluctance to obey, such a desire for freedom, and his call to the departing mustangs was a scream of disappointment and rage.

When the sound of the great wild movement was only a faint roar to the south, and the guards came in to check up, it was learned that no man had lost his horse . . . that is, no man alive . . . but Luis's rusbayo had escaped and Juan's good gray mare also, fleeing perhaps as Juan's spirit had fled to a wider range and an unfettered existence. For Juan Elizondo was dead, the loss of blood and the endurance of pain too much for his weary heart.

The train arrived at the Nueces River crossing on the tenth day, six days after the skirmish with the Indians — days uneventful, monotonous, tiring with too much watchfulness. The San Miguel and the Rio Frio had been crossed. Large herds of deer, wild cattle, and more wild horses were encountered, although not in as large droves as had encircled the campsite at La Parrita. They were well into brush and cactus country now. Flaco said anybody going through this part of the country was following the devil's tracks. Pablo agreed and said surely God had never passed this way, otherwise the jonco bush, all thorn and leafless, from which Christ's crown of thorns was made, could not flourish so.

On the trail between the Frio and Nueces rivers, Range riding with Flaco had observed some massive petrified tree trunks and had asked the older man the meaning of this.

"Well, it proves that what is hell now was once paradise," Flaco answered.

"Might be that way again sometime," Range commented with a strange deep thoughtfulness that measured the possible richness of the earth.

"Hah!" Flaco snorted, "that's like expectin' my pore, wore-out, sore belly in its old age to be like it was when I was a kid enjoyin' my ma's cookin', the best in Missouri. No, I reckon it was when the devil got kicked out of heaven that he stopped off here on earth to make a mess of things before goin' on and creatin' a private hell of his own. I guess he turned all the purty trees into stone around here and kicked up a lot of dust and left all this devilish thorny stuff to remember him by."

"You talk crazy as a Mexican."

Flaco squinted at Range but took no offense. "Reckon I do at that. Been around here long enough," was all he said.

Range had eliminated Flaco as the possible member of the freebooter's band that Eli had challenged him to spot among the ten

98

riders. Flaco had been with Eli too long. There was a congeniality between them that flowed as easily as between himself and Bryson. And Silver Bryson simply was not in the running; his sense of honor, Range knew, was such that he would not prey upon other than a declared enemy. He thought upon each of the others: There were Luis and Juan, of course, and had it been either of them, Eli's job would be done; but Juan had carried with such genuine and burdensome pride his reputation as a guide and his relationship to the alcalde at Laredo that to suspect him of serving two masters was hardly possible; Luis, too, seemed far removed from intrigue with his love of show and song. Mudo, along with the two vaqueros, Pedro and Pablo, and the hunter Rodriguez were all unlikely tools for a robbers' raid, Range reasoned. The natures of these four men were alien to duplicity, and a core of wisdom in Range recognized this, but from the top layer of his reasoning he dismissed them as too stupid.

So it had to be Jesse Faze or Señor Batres, Range believed. He would like to know for sure which one, and then let Eli know he knew. It was important to Range to perform for Eli.

Jesse Faze was mean and lonely. Señor Batres was friendly and afraid. Range despised both men, repelled alike by coarse brutality and unctuous mannerisms. He didn't allow himself the satisfaction of deciding which he'd rather it would be, but he did realize that he and Bryson would be better off if Jesse were disposed of; but maybe they would want to do that themselves in their own good time. Jesse included Range in his hatred for Bryson, and Range was aware of the sullen, ferocious nature of the man turned against them since the first night out when Bryson had elaborated on the Comanche's respect for hair on the human body. Range noticed that after Luis was killed, Jesse wore his shirt buttoned all the way up. Jesse Faze would be bad business, once they got to Laredo, he felt sure, but now each man's survival depended on the combined strength of them all, and any personal grudges or antipathies must be held closely in check.

Eli declared a day of rest at the Nueces River; the most difficult,

99

dangerous section of the trail was still to be covered. And besides, Eli had a hunch. The Comanches were around. They'd attack within the next day or so. Flaco thought so too.

He said to Eli, "I smell Indians."

"Me too," Eli said, and made up his mind they'd stay in camp where they'd be rested and watered until the attack. But he said nothing to the men; on the contrary, he planned to do everything possible to make the stop a pleasant one. Several of the men fished and brought in long strings of a small, delicious catfish the Mexicans called "bagre." Mudo and Rodriguez provided wild turkey. Pedro and Pablo found a bush of chiltipiquin peppers on a scouting ride they made for Eli, a few miles to the south, and the cook seasoned the great pulpy paste of frijoles to suit the toughened, fiery palates of the Mexicans.

Range had had little experience with true Mexican foods, having taken most of his meals at the Olson boarding house in San Antonio. The mashed beans smelled delicious. He had a big helping and had taken several mouthfuls before the fire took hold of him. He ate on, apparently unperturbed, but great drops of sweat formed on his face and forehead and dropped down into his plate. He felt that not only his mouth but his entire head was filled with live coals of fire. Bryson observed his agony; he did not smile or comment, sensing that Range's suffering was a deep embarrassment. Eli would not have been so considerate. The men needed a big laugh.

But it was fortunate there was no laughter, for even when the heat of the chiltipiquin had subsided and his skin was dry again, humiliation raged within him, the violence of his emotions out of all proportion to the experience. . . . The cursed Mexicans! Range was not prone to flights of fancy, but under the physical punishment of the potent little peppers so loved by the Mexican, he had a vision of the dominions of hell heavily populated with Mexicans, the hair of their heads on fire, burning with a bright blaze, sweat pouring from their faces. The picture pleased him mightily. He held on to it until the fire was gone from both his mouth and his brain.

CHAPTER VI

BETWEEN the Nueces River and the Rio Grande lies the Great Brasada, a concentrate of thorny brush and cactus growth both sinister and grand. During the ten-year period of the Texas Republic, the Brasada was a sort of Satan's sanctuary for the outcast and an open range for the marauder.

When Santa Anna was defeated at San Jacinto in 1836, he agreed that the boundary between the new Republic of Texas and his own country would be set at the Rio Grande. The Texas government, however, was too weak financially to extend its claims beyond the Nueces River; and, in the meantime, the Mexican Congress repudiated Santa Anna's treaty with Sam Houston and refused to recognize any boundary whatsoever. But the Mexican government, like the rebel republic it denied, was in a condition of chronic financial crisis and unable to actually reclaim any territory north of the Rio Grande. So, for the decade from 1836 to 1846, the area between the Nueces and the Rio Grande, claimed by two countries and defended by neither, was any-man's-land; and the outlaws who roamed its desolate but protective acres had to fear only the rattlesnakes, the Indians, and each other.

The Mexican town of Laredo was the only town south of the Nueces and north of the Rio Grande. Located on the southern edge of this land-without-law, a tenacious and important settlement of Spanish origin, Laredo, with its roots thrust almost a century deep into the north bank of the Rio Grande, ignored the existence of the Republic of Texas and continued to function as if it were still a town of the State of Tamaulipas, Mexico. The government of Mexico, in turn, ignored the loyalty of Laredo whose alcaldes had been pleading with the central government since 1828 for more protection against "the bullets, lances, and arrows of barbarous Comanches." During the year 1835, Laredo had been preyed upon so continuously by Indians and stripped so mercilessly of grain and horses by Mexico's invading armies that her town officials protested they did not feel an integral part of Mexico. Alcalde Don Bacilio Benavides in 1836 sent a final desperate appeal to the supreme government, of which Santa Anna was the head, to help the people of Laredo or they would abandon the town so filled with "the grieving widow, disconsolate father, and the wails of abandoned orphans," its cattle industry destroyed, its fields desolated. This plea to the "Beloved President" was printed with ironic timing the day Santa Anna was taken prisoner at San Jacinto, there to acknowledge a boundary that placed Laredo in the Republic of Texas.

In the two years that followed, Laredo existed in a despairing isolation. Captain Agatón Quiñones, head of a robber band, and other freebooters made the town their headquarters. Located at a point about halfway between San Antonio and Saltillo, Laredo was a strategic outpost along the barren trail that freighters must travel in the exchange of goods carried on in spite of revolutions and robbers.

It was a natural thing that this town, so neglected by the two countries claiming her, should become the center of a movement to establish a "Republic of the Rio Grande" with Laredo as the capital; and equally natural that Benavides, the alcalde, should cast his lot with the Federalists of northern Mexico who were seeking to bring this about.

Eli Dawson, aware of all these things, felt more uneasy at his present crossing of the Nueces than on any previous trip. He had declared a day of rest for the camp but found it impossible to rest himself. A hunch was prodding him hard. He tried to ignore it, tried to tell himself that the pressure of fear and danger was nothing more than the complaints of an overloaded stomach. After the heavy, early afternoon meal, most of the men had let the siesta habit have its way with them.

"Ought to catch a wink myself," Eli thought, "instead of actin' like an old woman seein' a bear in every bush." But the tension on his nerves tightened, and he looked with resentment at Flaco, who slept so little, now dozing and cat-napping, a cigarette stub about to drop from his fingers as he sat with his hat pulled low over his eyes, hiding his indiscretion. Only the ever-wakeful Señor Batres, and Bryson and Range in quiet conversation, were awake to keep Eli company.

Mudo was with the stock. Maybe he was asleep too, Eli thought distrustfully. Jesse Faze, stretched out full length on his back in a clump of thick shade — as usual, somewhat removed from the others — was snoring with a windy gusto that Eli found unreasonably annoying.

"We're ripe for pickin'," he said disgustedly, standing up, jerking his hat hard on his head. "That's where Houston got Santa Anna, in his siesta. Rodriguez!" He bellowed so fiercely that Rodriguez leaped to his feet and started stumbling about before he was fully awake. Several others, disturbed in their sleep, turned over or raised up to look. "Get the hell out there to Mudo and send him to me on the double. If he's asleep, wallop him where it'll wake him the quickest. Quita! Get a move on!"

Señor Batres seemed disturbed with Eli's display of nerves. Silver and Range were mildly curious, but said nothing, since Eli seemed to be expecting no comments. He looked at them with something like apology and kicked at a stone.

"Well, here we are, fellers, all nice and cozy on the south side of the Nueces . . . on our own in a land that's owned by nobody . . . making ourselves at home where nothing civilized is making a home. . . . President Houston or President Bustamante — or even God — can't help what happens between here and Laredo. Texas *claims* to the Rio Grande, and Mexico *claims* Texas has got no claims; but it takes spondulics to cinch anybody's claim, and Sam Houston is as busted as Bustamante."

"And God likewise?" Silver inquired. "Is He, too, without resources for extending His claims to this area?"

" 'Pears that way with Indians and outlaws ridin' as high and wide as they do in these parts, preyin' on honest freighters." Eli's irritation was rising again. "Señor Batres!" His tone was aggressive.

Batres started self-consciously.

"I hear that pore ole Benavides is having one devil of a time down at Laredo, what with Indians on the one hand and robbers on the other and the Mexican government turning a deaf ear to his cries for help. Is that right?"

Batres swallowed. "Sí, sí . . . things are bad . . . very bad."

Eli thought that over. Batres made aimless little movements. Range kept very still and attentive. Batres was surely the man Eli intended to kill. Was he about to do it now?

"I hear too," Eli continued, "that folks in northern Mexico are hatchin' up a little fracas kinda like we did up here in Texas, and there may be another republic sproutin' down that way with Laredo as the capital. You heard anything about a 'Republic of the Rio Grande,' Batres?"

Batres's eyes rolled in surprise. "That is a very strange thing you say, Señor Dawson. You speak serious?"

"Dead serious."

"I have hear of it, yes." Señor Batres spread his hands and tried to smile broadly in explanation. "It is on the streets of Laredo a joke . . . funny talk, that is all."

"There is much funny talk on the streets of Laredo," Eli spoke bluntly. "Juan Elizondo passed some of it along to me. I laughed real hard when he told me about Quiñones and his funny robber men making Laredo their headquarters. Mighty handy. Nobody to protect trade. Makes freighters easy pickin's. How about that, Batres? Same kind of joke?"

Batres's face grayed. He made an anguished gesture or two before he stammered, "I know no Quiñones, señor."

"I didn't know you was a stutterer, Batres," Eli chuckled. He appeared to relax. His eyes crinkled with pleasure. But his enjoyment of Batres's agitation was interrupted by Rodriguez, who came running and panting with startling news.

"Por Dios, Señor! Mudo no está ahí! Ay Dios mío! No Mudo! En ninguna parte, no Mudo! Ay! Ay!"

Rodriguez was mourning as well as announcing, for he was fond of Mudo.

Flaco roused enough to pull out his knife and start whittling on the calluses in his hands. "Ah, grassburrs, Rodriguez! Shut up! Mudo's not gone! He's just out on a little business trip, ain't he, Eli?"

Eli was very still, as if listening to distant sounds and weighing implications.

"Yeah," he answered Flaco, "a little business trip."

Eli couldn't explain to the others about Mudo and his unauthorized side trips, or rather, he was afraid to try. A man at the head of a train couldn't risk his men tagging him as loco. And yet, he knew as sure as he had ten fingers and ten toes that Mudo was out to gather bad news. It had happened before, and each occasion had brought hell on a toot right into camp, but with warning enough from Mudo to prevent annihilation. He hadn't ever been able to figure what it was that sent Mudo on a prowl to ferret out the danger he sensed.

"The sign is in the earth under my feet," Mudo had tried to explain one time, "and I follow the sign. I cannot stop to tell you that I follow or the sign goes without me."

What was the sign like, Eli had inquired. Mudo had looked disturbed as he searched his mind for some descriptive conveyance. Finally, he had drawn a wavy, jagged line in the sand and indicated it was such a line that he followed. Eli never troubled too much about interpreting Mudo's sign; he simply respected it and believed in it.

Now his annoyance and irritation were gone. He became quiet and efficient. He calmed Rodriguez and sent him back to watch the stock. He asked Flaco to wake the drivers and check their weapons and ammunition supply. He instructed the riders to prepare for mounted combat. He asked Batres, politely, to pass the jug; told him where to find it, and suggested each man have a pull "strong enough to wake him up good." He sent Pablo and Pedro to hide the extra horses as

105

best they could in a thicket down river. Then he took Silver Bryson aside for some orders no one overheard.

While Range stood somewhat apart, checking his riding gear, speaking to his horse in confidential tone, quieting Toego and himself at the same time, Batres was suddenly beside him, offering a drink from the jug.

"No, thanks, I'm plenty wide awake as it is," he gave the jug that Batres held up a gentle push away.

But Batres spoke to him in a tormented rush of words, harsh whispers that weren't audible to anyone except Range. Jesse Faze had taken his horse to water and Eli was standing apart still talking to Bryson.

"Pretend — pretend you take a drink, and listen to me. I am in trouble — Ay Dios mío — such trouble!"

Range pretended. "Tell me something I don't know already."

"It is what you don't know already that I tell you. You think like Señor Dawson I am a Quiñones man. Válgame Dios! It is not so! That animal down by the river is the one — un ladron! un cochino!"

"Talk so I can tell what you're sayin'. You mean Jesse — he's the one spyin' for the robbers?"

"Sí — yes — yes. He is the one!"

"Why don't you tell Dawson?"

"The hairy one, he will kill me when I do. That is why I tell you, so you can tell Señor Dawson who may kill me if you do not help me. Faze, he is safe for as long as Señor Dawson is thinking I am the one."

"Maybe Dawson knows about Faze. Maybe he's pickin' on you just to keep Jesse fooled for a while."

This possibility bewildered Batres for a moment, but he quickly rejected it. "It could not be that way. Señor Dawson does not know of the gold I carry."

It was Range's turn to be taken aback. "What gold is that?"

"It is gold I help Juan Elizondo get in San Antonio from friends of his uncle, the alcalde at Laredo."

"Benavides? What does he want with gold?"

"It takes the gold, señor, to pay the men to fight and to get started the Republic of the Rio Grande. Juan and I, we come together to San Antonio from Laredo to get the gold."

"And you need protection on the way back, so you line up with Eli's train?"

"Sí."

"How about that story you gave Eli about the Indian fight you had on the way into San Antonio? As I remember it, you lost four friends and all your supplies, but I never did get it straight just how you got away."

"That is just a story for hiding behind. The business of gold we must keep a secret. To carry gold for the Federalists might not be a pleasure to the Señor Dawson."

"Was Juan carrying any of this gold?"

"Until he died . . . sí."

"Then you managed to get it off him before we buried him?"

"No." Señor Batres looked disturbed. Range was sure he had tried to get the gold Juan carried and had failed, had found it already removed. "I believe the Señor Dawson has it, and that is well, for he will take the things of Juan to his Uncle Benavides and will not ask him questions. But if I tell him of the gold I carry, it is very mix up."

"I can see that."

"But I tell you so that for sure you can believe me. Then you tell Dawson Faze is with Quiñones, but you do not tell of the gold I carry, do you?"

"No tellin' what I'll tell."

Batres looked crafty. "Some of the gold, it could be in your pockets at Laredo, señor."

"Plenty room in my pockets," Range said, impassively. "Keep passin' the drinks, and settle down. I'll talk to Dawson."

But the first person Range talked to was Bryson. "What's all the commotion about?" he asked. "What's Dawson gettin' set for?"

"He hasn't confided in me about that," Silver replied. "But it looks as if he's playing a hunch and waiting for a message from Mudo which he expects to be the opposite of glad tidings."

"I got the same kind of message for him."

"Batres?"

"Yeah."

"Then you better get it delivered for when business begins to pick up around here, messages may be a little hard to get across unless you can code with that five-shooter of yours."

Leading Toego, Range walked purposefully toward Eli Dawson. Before he reached him, however, Dawson mounted his own horse and rode up to Range.

"Get on and ride with me a little ways," he told Range. . . . "Flaco, Templeton and me's gonna ride on a quick, short scout to the south. Keep the water hot. May want to scald a pig." With this facetious instruction, he rode out of the camp with Range.

"Keep your eyes skinned for Mudo," was all he said for a while. When they were about a mile from camp and on a slight rise, he pulled up and scanned the country to the south carefully. Then he slid to the side of his saddle, one foot out of the stirrup, resting, listening. "Spill it," he said.

Range didn't start talking on the instant. He assembled his thoughts carefully. He had to divide Batres's talk into the true parts and the false parts and present some definite conclusions.

"Batres is for sure the man you want to get rid of," he said.

Dawson just looked at him and didn't show whether he agreed or not.

"He told me Jesse Faze was a Quiñones man," Range continued. "He knows Bryson and me got no use for Faze, so he figured I'd fall for that and pass it along to you. He says Faze has threatened him, and that's about right. Somehow or other, Faze has got on to it that Batres is carryin' gold for Benavides but workin' for Quiñones. So he tells Batres to give him the gold or he'll spill the beans to you. I figure he was tellin' the truth about him and Juan gettin' up

108

some money to take to Benavides, only Juan didn't know about the double cross: that Quiñones was in on the gold deal too — that he'd take the train and the gold with it, cuttin' Batres in on it heavy when everything was worked out. I figure Batres planned it so's when Quiñones held us up, he'd be handy to throw a few bullets into Juan and anybody else close around. But he's gettin' cold feet now thinkin' what if the bullets get goin' the wrong way."

Range paused for Eli's approval. He got it.

"That's the way it is, all right. Juan got worried before we pulled out of San Antonio and told me how the land lay. I told him to go ahead and carry the gold to Benavides and I'd help him keep an eye on Batres. Didn't take long for me to get the goods on him. And he figured me wrong on that gold deal. I want the alcalde to have it, and I want him to have his little republic too if he can get it. . . . Plenty of country down that way. . . more than Texas or Mexico can take care of. . . . Maybe a little more dividin' up is what we need. If they'd get organized down there on the Rio Grande, maybe we'd have a little protection of some kind in this part of the country and trade'd get better. Yes siree, I'm dead set on Benavides gettin' that gold, and that's more than Batres bargained for — a sight more! . . . Mr. Templeton," he added gravely, "a man who can listen and divide what he hears into truth and lies, and divide it right, can do some mighty big things. It's a power. You can raise men up or beat 'em down with it. Be careful you don't lose it before you learn how to use it. Sometimes it's a lot easier to listen for what you want to hear than for what's truth and what isn't. . . . Yonder's Mudo."

Range couldn't see or hear any signs of Mudo. Eli sat very still, waiting. When Range finally saw Mudo, he was less than a hundred yards away, running easily, swiftly. Eli got off his horse and Range followed his example. In a moment Mudo and Eli were looking into each other's eyes with swift greeting; then Mudo dropped to his knees and began with drawings and gestures to tell his story. It did not take long.

Eli said, "Get to camp," and climbed on his horse. Mudo slid on behind.

Range knew that time was, for some reason, too precious for repetitions, and felt no resentment that he was momentarily denied the news.

The two horses raced straight for the campsite on the Nueces where restive fighting men were waiting for release from uncertainty and suspense.

There were no preliminaries. Eli did not dismount. "We are about to have some company ,we didn't expect, along with what we been expectin' all along. About fifty Comanches crossed higher up and was due to cut our trail a ways out from the river today. But since we didn't come along, they're movin' back to check up. The other party, the unexpected one, is not so numerous, 'bout fifteen or twenty of 'em, and they got a little off schedule too maybe, thinkin' we'd be further out in the brush. But this surprise party's takin' no chances." He began to speak more deliberately, more pointedly. "They had to get ahead of Quiñones — way ahead."

He paused slightly, then snapped, "You got it! Another bunch of freebooters."

His next words reached and caught Batres like a slap. "Never figured on that, did you, Batres? Well, the only way you can save your hide now is to hang up about six of their'n for me. If I don't feel like we've done well enough on killin' thieves when we're through, I'll just throw you in for good measure!"

Batres stood shocked into a stonelike stillness.

"Now then," Eli continued, "the Comanches are movin' in almost side by side with the border gang, but they haven't been travelin' that way long and they aren't on to each other yet. Our best chance is to move in between and cause a mix-up. And we got to do it quick, right now, pronto!"

He waited while Flaco finished a rapid translation of what he had said for the benefit of the Mexican drivers.

"Alberto!" Eli called to one of the drivers and told him in

Spanish to take Rodriguez' place with the stock and send him in.

"Alfonso!" This driver was to stay with the horses and see that they came to no harm.

"That evens things up now: ten drivers to defend the freight, ten riders to go out and stir up things."

He turned to Range. "Templeton, you and Bryson with Flaco and Faze will give the Comanches something to run after. You're to lead 'em cross country to where — " Eli slipped out his gun and turned it with deadly purpose on Faze — "to where we're shooin' Faze's friends and relations out to meet you. Two thieves in the crowd is one more than I had on the books. I reckon I didn't keep close enough tab on you, Faze. I got a kind of one-track mind and for a while Quiñones was travelin' on it. I'd sort of neglected to realize that this country is openin' up, gettin' more and more habitable and comfortable for coyotes and cutthroats. You got a knack for killin', Faze, specially Indians, which is what I hired you for. So you'll ride with Flaco, and I'm dealin' out to you the same medicine that Batres gets. Kill enough Indians to make it worth while for me to let you live a little longer. Flaco here has my permission to eat you raw or make stew meat out of you any time it suits his fancy."

Faze accepted his sentence without threat of resistance by word or movement. His eyes showed more hate than defeat.

Flaco gave Faze a malicious grin. "Buzzard's meat," he muttered.

"Rodriguez and Mudo," Eli continued, "will move in between the parties we're bringin' together and pick off whatever comes their way. Me and Batres and Pedro and Pablo'll pull something out of the bag to head Faze's boss and buddies into the Comanches. Flaco, it looks like I'm dividin' things a little one-sided, sendin' just the four of you to spot the Comanches, but that gun of Templeton's will turn the trick. I don't want you to wade in fightin' — I want you to get 'em to chase ya — the horses you're ridin' are good bait. Give 'em the Martíniano treatment, but tone it down, and by the time they've chased you a mile or so, we'll all be mixin' it up together."

He shouted positive, brief orders to the drivers guarding the carts, consulted with Mudo in a few flashes of sign language, and said, "We'll follow Mudo a ways." He motioned Batres to his side, Flaco moved in close to Jesse Faze, and they left camp in pairs: Mudo and Rodriguez in the lead, Range and Bryson together, Pedro and Pablo bringing up the rear.

They rode together for about half a mile before Mudo gave the signals that he and Rodriguez would go ahead and the rest of the party should split. Eli translated Mudo's instructions as to how far they should move, and in what direction.

"That's it. Spin your spurs!" And the horsemen divided.

Flaco and Faze rode ahead. Range and Bryson followed. Range was surprised that Faze had kept his temper and withdrawn without any commotion into his shell of sullen silence. There must have been some guesswork in Eli's accusations, but he had hit the mark so well that for a while at least Jesse would be concentrating only on the importance of staying alive. Once he turned and looked at Range and Silver, and something of satisfaction in his glance brought an uneasiness to Range. Silver felt it too.

"He's thinking what a pleasure it would be to him if we wind up without our scalps," he said to Range.

Jesse was thinking that, and something more; he was thinking how very good the chances were that he'd have this pleasure.

It was Flaco who spotted the Indians, moving leisurely but with a certain caution back toward the Nueces, headed for the trade route crossing.

"We'll ambush 'em," he decided. "Take us a good rifle shot from on foot, leave 'em minus four, then ride like hell's behind us. We'll head easterly, and we'll locate Eli by whatever shootin' he turns on in that direction. We better pair off a little when the chase starts so we can divide 'em. . . . Wind's blowin' from southeast. That's good."

No other word was spoken until they were settled in the brushy ambush and the Indians well within their sights. "Let's don't all shoot the same Injun. . . . Eeny, meeny, miney, mo, I'll take the one with the big red bow moving to one side and a little to the back."

"I don't like the one holding his lance so high, located about center," Silver made his choice.

"I want the pretty one with all the feathers," Jesse spoke almost companionably, "right out front."

"That leaves me plenty," Range said. "I'll keep my pick a secret."

"No use puttin' off the fun," Flaco said. "When I say *now*, make it like one shot and take to the horses."

"NOW!"

The four rifles exploded in a single funnel of sound and created an effect among the savages like buckshot in a hornets' nest. Their confusion, however, was not prolonged; and soon they surged after the riders, screeching their fury, yelling their mad pleasure at having the advantage in the chase with the enemy fleeing before them. They let loose their arrows and a few random shots along with their wild cries, but brush and fast horses gave the riders a fair margin of safety.

Range and Bryson were taking the chase as a game in which they were on the winning side, trusting their horses, assured somehow that whatever luck was needed would be forthcoming. Eli's promised shots came, spotting his location, but at the same time, putting the Indians on guard and scattering them in more cautious pursuit. A full dozen of the warriors, however, kept in full pursuit of Range and Silver, for the fine white stallion and the long-legged sorrel were trophies more desirable than the scalps of the men who rode them.

But misfortune in an unexpected guise overtook Silver Bryson and Range Templeton while they still had a good lead on the Comanches. Suddenly, Silver's white stallion was running riderless and he had landed in a brush patch, his saddle still clutched between his legs. Range swerved Toego and rode at full speed back to meet the Indians. The brushy terrain was some protection and kept the action from being suicidal. It was a surprise attack with the effect doubled when at fairly close range he emptied the five chambers from the revolving cylinder of his pistol. He didn't know how successful his shots were, but paused just long enough to turn the chase upon himself, in a direction away from Silver.

His challenge was taken up, and they were after him. It was a relief. Silver's stallion wouldn't go far, Range reasoned, and Silver could make it in bareback if he couldn't fix his saddle . . . cinch strap must have broken . . . he probably wasn't bad hurt because he'd landed in a thicket.

Range headed Toego in a direction that was generally southeast and let him pick his own way while he tried to replace the empty cylinder of his gun with a loaded one. As the cylinder snapped into place, he heard a tearing sound under his right knee, and the next three movements he made were the difference between life and death. His right hand which held the gun let it drop into his big jacket pocket, and his arm reached out to encircle Toego's neck, while his left hand took a firm grip in the horse's mane. In the next instant his knees were gripping the horse's shoulders and the saddle was gone.

Jesse's satisfied look flashed big across his mind, and the cause of his and Silver's predicament was clear. He didn't slacken Toego's speed. As far as the horse was concerned, he was better off with the weight of the saddle gone.

The Indians would know of his handicap and would follow now with more assurance. If he could be sure there weren't more than six or seven after him, he'd take a chance on dismounting and picking them off, for he had five shots in the gun in his pocket and two in the pistols at his belt. But there was no way to be sure. So he set out to outdistance and lose them.

The Comanches proved stubborn and tireless. They knew that he was alone and stripped of his saddle and the gear that went with it. They wanted the horse and the scalp. They wanted revenge for their slain comrades. They were curious about the manner of man and weapon that could shoot so fast and kill so many. They could follow wherever he could lead.

Range had long since passed out of hearing distance of the shots and shouts that went with whatever confused battle Eli had worked out. He dared not turn back to the north for fear of meeting more Indians. So he continued southward, hoping he had not strayed too far from the trade route trail. But distinctive landmarks were few, and the country took on a sameness that was bewildering. He began to be concerned for his horse. He'd as soon be dead himself as wind Toego. Time and again he'd stop or slow down, thinking his trailers had given up; but small, telltale clouds of dust or the bobbing heads above the brush would appear again. He realized he'd have to do something different before night or the advantage would be all theirs.

His deliverance came unexpectedly and made it unnecessary to match wit or skill with the savages. A dark, swift-moving cloud out of the northwest announced its approach with a flash and a rumble. It was nearly sundown and Range hadn't noticed the quick gathering of thunderheads to the back of him. It seemed only a matter of moments before the lightning and the roar were continuous. The wind struck and Toego ran ahead of it as if its lash were a signal he'd been waiting for; then they were caught in a whipping sheet of rain, and Range was thankful that the strong downpour would wash out all tracks. To make sure of this, he jerked Toego up and headed him down a gully that would soon be flooded with high water. Later he pulled out of the wash and headed straight before the wind and rain.

As the energies of the cloud subsided and the rain stopped as suddenly as it had struck, Range found that his energies too were depleted and that Toego was lagging with head low. The horse seemed to know that his master's anxieties had quieted down; the body that had clutched him so fiercely during the past hour was relaxed and loose on his back. There was no tug on the reins, no movement to urge him on; so he stopped and let his own long limbs relax from the strain. There was a faint, red glow of twilight in the west, and Range was sure of his directions, but he had no idea how far he had come since rushing to Silver Bryson's rescue; he knew only that it was by far the longest bareback ride he'd ever taken and that he was too stiff and tired to plan for tomorrow. He simply slid off his horse and onto the ground, thinking that he never knew before how soft the ground was, and slid just as quickly and easily into deepest slumber.

Eli Dawson's camp that night was a place of contained violence and desperation, of victory turned sour with the loss of Range Templeton and the conditions that made extensive search impossible. The Comanches not slain or trailing Range had withdrawn to remain an undetermined threat. The robber band, drawn into the fight with the Comanches, had been almost wiped out. Four of them, wounded or surrounded, had begged Eli's protection to Laredo. He said he ought to string them up on the spot, but agreed to turn them over to the Laredo authorities instead if they proved useful when Quiñones attacked. He made a similar limited concession to Batres and Faze who had come through unscathed. Bryson further limited this reprieve by taking Faze into his personal custody with the understanding that unless Range Templeton rejoined the train by journey's end in Laredo he, Silver Bryson, without benefit of authority, would fittingly bring to a close Faze's career as cutter of throats and saddle girths.

Range Templeton awoke with a strange and exalted feeling. It was not as if he were lost, but rather as if he had found something. Near him was the print of Toego's body where he had lain and rested too. Now he browsed nearby, nibbling at the brushy growth and mesquite. His sorrel coat was roughed and scratched, but his ears were pointed and his eyes alert as Range spoke to him. The sun was not quite up, and the brush was alive with birdcalls and scurryings on the ground. The rain had seasoned the earth and brought renewed fragrance to summer leaves and blossoms.

As the brilliant sunlight began to play on the vigorous greens of the thickets, the fantastic, slablike structures of prickly pears, and the clear, washed colors of flowering bush and tree, Range slid onto Toego's back so that his vision could reach further out into this wild array of beauty, concealing everywhere the contradiction of fragrant blossom and poison thorn.

A huisache tree dominated a small clearing not far away, and Range urged Toego forward to this spot. The beautiful aromatic tree in full bloom, its graceful spined branches almost sweeping the ground, brought somehow an urgent memory of Luvisa. And with the memory came a young man's vision of acquiring and conquering an immensity of this land that seemed to attract a man while it repelled him, offer while it withheld. And across this vision streamed herds of wild cattle and wild horses, and a woman's calm gray eyes looked with approval upon him, and her golden hair, like the burning gold of the huisache blossoms, was soft to the touch of his hand and fragrant against his face.

It was the pangs of hunger and the sun's early heat that put an end to his daydreaming. He considered meat and a fire, but caution was stronger than hunger. The sound of a shot or a line of smoke might put the savages on his trail again. He could not be sure how far Toego had brought him in the storm. He was completely lost from the train and the trail. He could strike out to the north until he hit the Nueces and then head up to the crossing and try to overtake the train, hoping to avoid the Comanches. Or, he could continue south to the Rio Grande and up the river to Laredo to rejoin the train there. It would be a hard ride either way. Going south, he reasoned, he'd at least not have so far to ride, whereas going north he'd be backtracking and taking more chances with his own and Toego's endurance.

So they headed south through the heart of the Brasada: man and horse, both of unusual stamina but unprepared for the ordeals that awaited the uninitiated in this wilderness of spike and thorn where every growing thing reached out to tear and scratch, and claw and prick, and poison and bruise. There was meat for a man and browsing for a horse; but a man can't eat when poison from the thrust of a black thorn sends cold chills down his back and makes him sick at his stomach, and a horse can't carry his rider with speed and dignity irritated by the continuous snagging in his hide and hair and made lame by the cushions of thorns underfoot. And the nerves of a man and his mount are soon raw with listening for the vicious buzz of the deadly rattlesnake. . . .

His first meeting with javelinas cost Range the five shots in his revolver. He was on foot, leading Toego, and the fierce, monster-like appearance of the wild hog startled him into emptying the cylinder. He had meat, but the gun was of no further use since the ammunition for it had been on his saddle. The powder in his horn, the few balls in the pouch at his waist for the two heavy pistols he still carried were all the defense against hunger and attack left to him when he emerged from the big thicket five days later trailing a herd of mustangs on their way to water.

Range had heard Flaco remark once that the wild horses usually came to water about eleven o'clock in the morning. His luck in spotting water holes had run out the day before; coming upon the fresh tracks of the mustangs early in the morning, he'd deviated from his plan to keep directly south and followed the meanderings of the horses. He knew now that he'd done the right thing for the horses had led him, not to another skimpy water hole tightly guarded by chaparral and prickly pear, but to a beautiful grassy clearing dominated by huisache and willow and the thick shade of hackberry and elm.

Exhausted and desperately thirsty, the tall, stubborn man and proud, sorrel horse limped painfully across the clearing toward the springs. The mustangs, for some reason Range did not understand, had continued in the edge of the thicket and drank far down from the center of the clearing. Too tired for extreme wariness, since he'd been walking most of the morning in an effort to relieve

Toego's lameness, Range took the shortest rather than the most protected route to the water.

Suddenly Toego raised his head and whinnied in high, friendly fashion. There was an eager answer from under the trees. A domestic horse . . . a camp . . . maybe Indians . . . it was too late to turn back into the thicket without being seen . . . might as well go ahead as be shot in the back. Range tried not to limp as he walked straight ahead toward the sound of running waters. The horses called to each other again.

There seemed to be no one around. Then he saw the horse and stopped in amazement. It was the rusbayo that had belonged to Luis Martíniano; the horse was staked on the far side of the stream that flowed with such pleasant sound from the mother springs a short distance away. Still no one appeared. Toego trotted to the water's edge and buried his nose deeply in the cool clearness. Range didn't look down at the water, but removed his hat and dipped the brim of it, drinking a few swallows while he searched for some sign of the horse's captor.

He decided whoever was around was no Indian. The rusbayo had been cleaned, brushed, and shined like a circus horse. He was staked with a long piece of rawhide and on his feet wore something that looked like leather coverings drawn up over the hoof; moreover, the lower joints of all four legs were heavily bandaged. But the most astonishing thing that had been done to the horse was the decoration of the long heavy golden hair of mane and tail. By plaiting tiny strands of hair here and there, flowers had been woven in until the appearance was that the golden strands themselves were in blossom. The finishing touch was two clusters of bright blue blossoms at each ear, so that as the horse turned toward Range and Toego, ears pricked forward, and whinnied softly, the effect was so utterly ludicrous that Range laughed aloud. The sight of the flowered horse and his own laughter were both so shocking to him that he wondered if he weren't feverish and seeing things. But the horse remained very much before him, tilting his head to one side

119

in curiosity at the man's laughter and sending Range into another guffaw that exploded into greater laughter he couldn't control — laughter that shook him until his knees were weak and water poured from his eyes. He sank to his knees finally, threw his hat on the ground, slid onto his stomach and buried his face in the flowing water, drinking, sloshing the coolness over his head. When he finally raised his head to look again and make out for sure that the funny horse was still there, he found himself staring into the eyes of Miguel Sándivar. What he saw there was the dark fury of insult. Range measured the boy. He was not a man — not much more than half as big as himself. He was barefooted and dressed in some tight white stuff that looked like cotton underwear to Range Templeton. The boy's hair was pretty and soft like a girl's and looked as if it had never been cut. But his feet were firmly planted wide apart, and in one hand he grasped a knife. With a sense that seldom under- estimated an opponent, Range knew that the boy could throw the knife straight and sure and would not hesitate to do so, for he was primed and ready. He wanted the horse, Range figured, and would fight for it. He was also mad as blazes about the laughing. So Range didn't make a move. He didn't smile or show fear. He waited for the boy to measure him and his horse too and see how ragged and harmless they were.

Miguel was thinking as his fury at the laughter quieted a little: Is this the enemy? Is this the larger and bolder breed Apollonius spoke to me about? Can this be an eagle? I cannot think so. He is torn and bruised and weak. He is lost from somewhere. I have no fear of him. But I hate him! Miguel's eyes clouded again as he thought of the laughter, but the hold on his knife loosened. The desire to kill was new to Miguel. He had killed animals, of course, but only for food or protection; and now there was a sense of shock that his hand had been so eager to hurl the knife at the stranger. So he shrugged and replaced his knife, and went about unstaking his horse, ignoring the foreign one whose ridicule had burned him so sharply.

Range wondered if the boy could speak English and if he were alone. "Hey, where'd you get the horse?" he asked. Not even a glance was bestowed upon him for an answer.

So, as a test, to make sure he wasn't understood, he said things that would bring some response if the words carried any meaning to the boy.

"What makes you pet that horse up so? Don't you know he's not worth shooting? . . . He's not your horse . . . I know who the horse belongs to . . . if you keep him, you may get hung for a horse thief."

Miguel gave no sign of attention, finished unstaking his horse, and walked away leading him. The rusbayo limped slightly but seemed utterly content with the flowers, bandages, and rawhide shoes that had come to him with new ownership.

Range removed the bridle from Toego and turned him loose to graze. Then he stretched full length on the soft, sweet-smelling grass. He was too tired to hunt food and cook it, too weary to follow Miguel and investigate.

When he awoke, a late evening glow was upon the earth and a sense of unreality held him very still, listening to the sounds of moving water, birdcalls, and Toego hungrily pulling grass somewhere close to his head. Then an odor struck his senses with terrific reality — meat cooking! He stumbled to his feet, stiff with the soreness that relaxation brings after long strain and endurance. When he came to Miguel's campfire, he was surprised that the boy was still alone, and from the looks of his camp was traveling alone. He observed the large domestic cow and that she was about to calve, and decided the boy must be some Mexican rancher's son out with the stock.

Miguel, tending his meat at the fire, tried to ignore his visitor; but when Range moved up closer to the cow to satisfy his curiosity about her, Miguel moved quickly to her side, fiercely protective, speaking softly to her, smoothing her distended sides as if he feared she might become alarmed at the bold attention of the stranger.

121

Range felt a mounting resentment at the Mexican boy's advantages and humiliation at the appearance he must make before him, ragged and scratched and hungry. He wanted some of the meat at the campfire — craved it more than he'd ever craved food before in his life — and there was plenty there for them both, but his feeling was: be damned if he wouldn't eat a cactus before he'd ask for it and get beholden to the little cuss. His hunger intensified his feeling of ill will, and the bridge of speech over which he might have made some approach through explanation of his circumstances was closed to him. Miguel too might have made some talk about his cow and his trip to the springs that would have reduced the barrier between them. But prejudices grow easily from differences between people — differences misinterpreted — differences misunderstood — and the innate human quality of disliking that which cannot be understood or appreciated; and when the something not understood stands in the way of something desired, it is easy to move emotionally from dislike to the desire and intention to destroy.

Miguel reversed his decision of the night before. This was the enemy, so tall and insolently curious. The design of courtesy and hospitality in which his father had so carefully trained him failed him now in this situation where fine flourishes of speech were impossible and where convictions of enmity were so strong. Yet, the man had done him no actual harm; and, thinking of his father, he felt the compulsion of gentlemanly instinct urging him to offer the stranger meat. He tried to think that the big one might have spoken courteously to him had he known his language. Words had been spoken yesterday but somehow the tone of them had carried no courtesy. Yet it was possible perhaps that the tone as well as the words of the stranger was different from his own. The man was very hungry, he was sure of that. If he offered meat, he wanted to do it with a gesture that would imply he neither feared the man nor sympathized with his condition, but simply that he, Miguel, knew the proper thing to do in such circumstances. He kept brushing La Brema with the flat of his hand, struggling to decide how to express such an attitude and invitation. Before he could make up his mind, Range left him, turning his back abruptly, taking long, angry strides away. Had Miguel known the will power required of the famished man to walk away from the fumes of the roasting meat and how narrow was the margin of decision, his hand would have been closer to his knife, his mind less occupied with the problem of proper social behavior in the absence of verbal expressions and flourishes. For Range Templeton had held in check his impulse to walk to the fire, kick the meat out, grab it and eat his fill; and, if interrupted by the hateful little Mexican, knock him down, kill him if need be, just as he'd killed Indians a week ago. Mexicans were mostly Indians anyway. But sometimes an established code of conduct is stronger than a new-found prejudice. Range controlled his impulse only because the meat had been killed and cooked by the one who refused to share it with him.

Just at twilight, about a mile down the stream from the springs, Range killed a young deer, built his campfire on the spot, and ate ravenously of the tender venison, broiled just enough to drip with a succulent, bloody broth — ate with a deep and angry satisfaction.

The next morning he awoke as he had that first morning in the Brasada, exultant with a feeling of discovery; but this time there was something added to discovery — decision. Daydreams took on the outline of plan and purpose. As he went to the stream's edge and sought a hole of comfortable depth, removed his clothes and bathed long and lazily . . . as he rebuilt his campfire and cooked more of the luscious meat . . . as he meandered slowly back to Miguel's location, he added up in his mind the things he wanted and intended to have. He wanted land south of the Nueces, a world of it to make his world.

He'd beat the thicket, conquer it, and make its wildlife his livelihood: horses and cattle — mounts and hides and meat — men have to have 'em — and there ought to be ways of getting 'em to the places where they were scarce. Men made livings on farms and ranches they stocked themselves in protected places; if a man could protect himself and didn't mind a few thorns in his hide, Indians on his tail, and Mexicans underfoot, why couldn't he carve out just about what he wanted in a land where the only law in operation was nature's law of the survival of the fittest — a land in which he had seen for himself such countless herds of brush cattle and mustangs that he would not have believed another man's story of it. But a man didn't take a woman into the middle of such a land, not if he wanted her to look pretty and be happy and live a long time, not if he wanted just one woman all his life like he wanted Luvisa. But a spot like these beautiful springs: if a man could build a home here, big and thick-walled and cool, if a man had riders and guns to protect his home, then his woman and their children might have more than other women and children in other parts of the country. When he got back to San Antonio, he'd go to the land office and see exactly what land he'd have coming to him as a married settler in the Republic of Texas, and he'd get Eli to pay him off in land scrip. Maybe Silver Bryson had some land rights and would throw in with him. All in all, his chances were good. What was to keep him from having what he wanted? Nothing, he reasoned, out of an egoism that encased him as snugly as an armadillo's shell: not outlaws, or Indians, or Mexicans — not anything outside hell's high picket fence!

Miguel had his dreams that morning too. He tried to put aside the thought of the unwelcome visitor and succeeded partially, for he had his beautiful horse to attend. It had been only four days since the rusbayo, lame and sore, had come to the springs in a herd of mustangs, and, sensing the presence of a human being, had left the herd and sought Miguel, whinnying for attention. Each day thereafter, when Miguel awoke, the wonder seemed greater that he might possess this horse if no one came to claim him. "Lustre," Miguel called him, because now with coat glossy and clean, there was about him a glory and a splendor, a lustre grande.

This morning as he brushed the horse and allowed himself to feel the full thrill of ownership, there was, for the first time, reality in all the things his father had told him about the fine horses, grand houses, and gentlemen and ladies dressed in fine cloth and laces. He could see Lustre in full equipment of silver and tassel and fine leather prancing in Chapultepec Park where his father had loved to ride. But it was Miguel himself astride Lustre that paraded through the dreams he wove in the bright morning sunshine, his eyes wide open and his hands busy with the wad of stiff grass he was using to brush the horse. The dreams took a jump from Mexico City which existed for him only through his father's stories to the reality of the beauty around him at the springs, and he erected a great hacienda here where his mother was happy attending the borders and patches of flowers in the patio, and his father in a big room of books and pictures and polished furniture received important guests who were anxious to partake of his wisdom. His brothers, each equipped with fast horse and fanciest vaquero regalia, rode herd on his vast range, the Rancho Regalo. And there was someone else in his dream, someone he accepted but did not identify, moving through the cool corridors of the hacienda by his side — someone small and delicate as a butterfly and fragile as a rain flower.

The sound of Range Templeton approaching cut short his dreaming. He made a quick prayer to Our Lady, fervently beseeching that the stranger would soon go and without challenging his possession of Lustre, for he had realized the friendly calls between the horses on their meeting yesterday indicated that likely they had met before and the stranger was probably lost from the same place Lustre had come from. But since the man had a horse, perhaps he would not find it necessary to return this one to its owner. Miguel decided to practice a deceit upon the stranger to reduce chances of his taking the horse. As he thought of it, he murmured to Lustre to forgive him. When Range was quite near, Miguel forced a "Buenos días" that was so unmistakably an attempt to reduce animosity that Range grudgingly responded with a flat "Mornin'." Then Miguel became extremely busy with his horse in a manner to indicate that his duties were very urgent and that he didn't mind an audience. Range

125

watched with interest for he figured he might learn something to give relief to Toego's lameness before riding him on to Laredo. Miguel removed the poultices from Lustre's legs, wet the rawhide shoes to soften the stiffness and took them off. He rubbed all the joints briskly with armadillo oil. He applied new poultices made from the thick prickly pear leaf, its thorns burned off, the leaf split and the soft, gluey surface heated before application. When he removed the shoes, he managed to place a small stone in the tender hollow of the footpad where it would cause the horse to limp painfully. When he had finished with massage and poultice, and before replacing the shoes, he led the horse about apparently testing the condition of its lameness. One foot seemed to be much worse than the others, and the horse actually grunted when his weight struck it. Miguel in dramatic pantomime registered concern and then despair over the foot. Range wondered disdainfully if the boy was going to cry but did not suspect a trick. The horse would be in bad shape for a long time, he decided, maybe never any good for running again. This diminution of the Mexican's advantages made him feel better.

Toego was lame and stiff too but nothing that a little rest and some good shoes wouldn't cure. Range decided to get busy and provide some rawhide shoes for his horse like the ones Miguel had made for the rusbayo. He had to be getting along in a day or so. Maybe he'd better try to question the Mexican about the Rio Grande and Laredo and get his bearings a little better.

"Where's the Rio Grande?" he asked.

Miguel understood. He pointed and answered in such a way that Range concluded it was not far away and the shortest distance to it was a little west of south.

Then he asked, "Where is Laredo?"

Miguel understood this question too, but had not the vaguest idea in which direction to go from the springs to find Laredo. He had heard the visiting priest speak of the town in talking with his father, but his father had never been to Laredo. What could he answer? If he said he didn't know, the stranger might think he didn't want to tell and was being purposely discourteous, or, worse still, might think he actually didn't know. This man who might be the enemy, might be the eagle with whom he must struggle, must not think him lowly and ignorant.

"Laredo? Ciertamente! Sí, sí . . ." he responded. And drawing with his finger in the sand a winding line to represent the Rio Grande, indicated with a cross on the north bank of the river a point southwest of the springs.

"Aquí está Laredo."

In his heart he was hopeful that the stranger would get lost and never find his way to anywhere at all. This was another deception that Range never suspected, for with unwitting clairvoyance Miguel had mapped the way from the springs to Laredo.

Although unimpressed with the prickly pear poultices, since the Mexican's horse was still severely lame, Range decided it might be worth trying to take the stiffness out of Toego's joints. And the rawhide shoes, he realized, were a necessity. It was a day's work. He spent four hours perched in a cramped position high in a tree above a water hole much frequented by wild cattle. The wild bull he killed and skinned furnished hide not only for the horseshoes but also for a pad with girth and foot straps that would make his riding more comfortable. To make the shoes, he cut round pieces from the soft, wet hide, and punched holes around the edge; then using some pieces of leather trimmed from his bridle reins for drawstrings he carefully pulled them up around each hoof where they would harden and give protection from thorn and stone.

When he had finished with the shoes, he remarked to Toego, "Well, now, boy, all you need is some flowers in your hair." And he laughed again as he thought of his first look at the flowered rusbayo. Range Templeton's mind was closed to the tolerant thought that the flowers were an expression of adoration from an idealistic youth of artistic race and temperament who loved his horse no more or less than Range himself loved Toego.

Leading his horse, for he felt self-conscious on the rawhide saddle he had rigged up, Range passed Miguel's camp on the following morning ready to head out for Laredo and found the boy in acute distress.

La Brema was having her calf. It had delivered partially according to nature's plan, back feet first and parallel, in a straight line with the body, and then the main part of the torso; but the head refused to deliver, for a front foot, out of position for following the head, was bent to the back of the head and obstructing its passage.

Miguel, bloody and weeping, pouring out a torrent of sympathy and instruction to the cow, was a pitiable sight indeed. He looked at Range with a wild appeal that said plainly, "If you know what to do, for the love of God, do it! Help me save my cow!"

Range had a brief struggle with himself. He thought he knew the trick of releasing the foot and getting it back in position. Back in Tennessee, he'd been with his uncle a time or two when a cow needed help. But some perverseness arose within him, a desire to avoid the gratitude that would gush forth from the emotional Miguel if he gave assistance. So he shook his head, as if it looked hopeless to him, and struck out, the sounds of the heaving cow and the protesting boy stirring within him a heavy nausea — the marginal struggle between life and death bringing a burdened memory of Jeannie Dodson.

His conscience gave sharp accent to his misery as he hurried away; indicting him, however, far more for leaving the cow unattended than for lack of response to the suffering of Miguel.

La Brema and her calves were of great economic importance to the Sándivar family. Miguel realized this. Moreover, La Brema was dear to Miguel as a companion and a pet; she had shared her adventures and her discoveries with him; she trusted him. Her suffering was an agony to him and her possible loss a despair. For his highly emotional nature she had recently taken on a sacred aspect in his life — she was a symbol of dreams come true. Had she not brought him, as if under divine direction, to the beautiful springs? To lose her would be to lose also the dreams he had fashioned for the future here where she now suffered.

The fury and hatred that swept over him at Range Templeton's indifferent departure, when he felt so certain that the strength of the big one might have come to the aid of his cow, left him weak and silent. His face was white and bleak — the tears and the frenzied words gone. His hands opened in a gesture of hopelessness, he relaxed from a kneeling position sitting back onto his heels, his head bowed. La Brema bawled — a moaning appeal for release from pain, an animal sound of protest against pain beyond its knowledge of pain. Miguel's head jerked up, his arms spread out wide and he began to pray — he prayed without regard for ritual — he prayed to all forms of the deity that he had ever heard of or his imagination could conceive — a fervent stream — whispered, impassioned, his face lifted, and over and over again the plea for a miracle — milagro. "Un milagro, Dios mío, un milagro!"

It was thus Apollonius found him. Miguel remained on his knees, still as stone, as if any movement of his might take the vaquero away. Apollonius said no word as he dismounted and took full account of the condition of the cow. He spoke a few quieting phrases to the cow, and began the skillful manipulations that she seemed to know would mean relief. Miguel still did not move when the calf lay whole and breathing before him. The wonder of it was too much. But the wonder was only half done; La Brema was giving birth to another calf and this one pure white. When Apollonius had assisted La Brema with the swift and surprising delivery of the second calf, he turned to Miguel.

"Are you a stone or a living thing?"

"If the things I see are no dream, then I am alive and witness a miracle," Miguel said.

"You see what you see," Apollonius replied. "A prayer and a portent traveled together and this is what you have. The white calf is great good fortune to your house."

"I have heard my father say that in a double birth there is no fertility."

"Yes, but your father has never witnessed what you see, two she-calves, and one the sacred white, the mark of the miracle . . . there will be no barrenness in these two."

"I must hurry and tell my father."

"You must hurry to nowhere . . . the cow will decide when she is ready to go and you will follow."

CHAPTER VII

From Luvisa Templeton's Account —

. . . When Range Templeton came back to me in San Antonio after his trip with Eli Dawson, he was a man full grown. The dangers and hardships, the fighting and killing, the things he had learned of himself and other men had skimmed his nature of all boyishness. I had changed too. A girl of sixteen can become a woman quickly if she loves deeply and is disciplined by months of unrelieved anxiety. I was not a lovesick girl pining for her first beau . . . I was a woman waiting for a destiny as certain as God. I suffered during this first parting from Range Templeton with a maturity of agony that could seldom be relieved or distracted by those around me. There is no ardor so devastating, no attraction so demanding, as a strong, sure, virginal love striking at the very threshold of manhood and womanhood while the secrets of life are still unrevealed and the mysteries of creation through the unity of man and woman are yet unexplored. The senses become intoxicated, distorted, so that colors are too bright or too dim, sounds too sharp or too distant, odors and tastes too flat or too pungent, and in the sense of touch some new awareness . . . I wondered why the velvet on the rose petals felt so thick that summer and why the honeysuckle was so strong of sweetness that my head ached to smell it. I lived in emotional extremes: there was the ecstasy of daydreaming, when I relived the dawn in Dr. Weideman's study, our love declarations, the long kiss . . . there was the despair of imagined catastrophes wherein I saw him lying in the brush torn and bloody, his scalp gone, defenseless, deserted, a prey to buzzards and coyotes; or worse still, alive and tortured in a Comanche camp. I ate little and grew so thin that my grandparents demanded a tonic from Dr. Weideman. He had me come to see him. I sat with him in that same study. He placed me there for a purpose, I knew. But he was kindly and I didn't mind. I looked at the fur-covered couch. Memories possessed me. Tears came to my eyes and I trembled until my teeth chattered. He did not laugh at me or even smile.

"He will be back, Lu. Calm yourself," he said. "Frailty is unbecoming to you. A weak woman can be no match for Range Templeton."

"I am not weak," I protested with tears running down my cheeks.

"Then prove it by eating and resting as you should. I will give you a pretty pink tonic. It is merely to relieve your grandparents' anxiety. I have yet to discover the chemical combination that will offset or tone down the shock to the nervous system caused by such a stroke of acute love as you are experiencing. You must develop your own controls."

I felt better after that visit and went about eating and resting more sensibly, determined that I should be strong and well when Range returned; but I hardly had time to develop my controls, as the doctor had instructed, for only a few days later Mr. Dawson's train was back on the plaza. It rolled in at siesta time. I was sleeping more heavily than usual, and knew nothing about it until Toego skidded to a stop at the front porch and I heard the quick steps of the man I waited for. I rushed to the door, and, when I felt the tightness of his arms around me, I fainted dead away. I was ashamed of that weakness. It was the first and the last time I ever fainted.

There was wonderful talk in the patio that night. Eli Dawson was there and Mr. Bryson, and of course Range Templeton. It would not have been seemly to sit by his side and let him hold my hand as I yearned to do. So I sat by my grandmother and across from him where I could look at him every second, study every expression, watch every movement, and not miss a glance he might give me. I think my grandmother was a little embarrassed for me. She patted my hand from time to time. Range was intent on what the men had to say and on his own part in the conversation, but he was aware of me, happy that I was there, and I knew this. The sensations of that evening are as clear to me after twenty years as the things I can see and touch in this room right now. Wave after wave of happiness would wash over me as I watched him and listened to him, and ripples of pleasure would caress me when he looked into my eyes.

Strangely enough, I heard the things that were said too . . . about the fights, about Range saving Mr. Bryson's life, his wanderings in the Great Brasada, the beautiful springs and the Mexican boy there. I did not like the way he spoke of the Mexican boy — I felt a prick of fear or resentment but refused to let it intrude on my happy thoughts. As for Señor Batres and Jesse Faze — as I dwelt on the dangers they had brought to Range, I'll admit that some streak of hardness made me wish most heartily that they had not come into Laredo alive. But Mr. Dawson said he found more use for them alive than dead and that he had turned them over to the alcalde in Laredo for proper punishment as thieves and conspirators. He had done the same with several other members of the robber band who lived through the Indian fight in which Range was lost, after using them a second time to good advantage in a skirmish with Quiñones just outside Laredo.

"Didn't seem quite proper to string 'em up after usin' 'em for shields. Even the devil's got to have his dues," he said.

Grandfather said that according to his notion they all should have been properly hanged and that they were probably safe somewhere in Mexico at that very moment. Luis and Juan were the only men lost on the trip. One Mexican driver had been wounded when Quiñones attacked but he would recover.

Grandfather was in exceedingly high spirits as these stories were related. I could tell that he and Mr. Dawson both were proud of the showing Range had made; there was much speculation too about the future use of the Colt revolving pistol because of the one Grandfather had given Range to try out. Mr. Bryson insisted Range had killed five Indians with the five shots from this weapon, but Range was equally certain that Mr. Bryson's gun had accounted for one of the five. Anyway, they were all agreed that properly supplied with such arms, they could rout the savage in short order.

I was mightily surprised later in the evening when Range told my grandfather he had a private matter to discuss with him, and they excused themselves for a while. Mr. Bryson and I studied each other carefully and made light conversation, both of us realizing some-how that through Range Templeton our lives would be drawn close together.

When Range and Grandfather returned to the patio, Grandfather carried a tray with glasses and a bottle of his best brandy. I was not sure what had happened until Range came and stood beside my chair. Nothing was said while Grandfather set the tray on the table, poured the brandy, and solemnly passed it to everyone.

"Stand, gentlemen, close friends, and drink a toast to young love," he sang out with a flourish. "I have just given my permission for Range Templeton to wed my granddaughter, the fair Luvisa." He reached for my hand and pulled me to my feet. Range moved to my side. Grandfather gave us each a glass; we touched them and drank to each other. Then there was a toast to Grandmother and Grandfather and much laughter and well-wishing. The men moved out on the porch to smoke, Grandmother kissed us both and said "bless you" in a quiet, happy way and left us alone in the patio.

Range and I held hands tightly for a moment, and then there was our betrothal kiss, sweet enough to justify all existence. We planned our wedding to be soon; I would remain in San Antonio until he

133

had settled matters of land and money that would determine where our home would be. He and Silver Bryson were rounding up a crew to take into the country between the Nueces and Rio Grande, where they would collect wild horses and cattle and trail them to New Orleans. Some they might market to planters in East Texas and Louisiana on the way to New Orleans; on the other hand, they might buy domestic stock from these planters and drive it on to New Orleans for a profit. What they bought or sold along the way would be determined by the conditions prevailing in the settlements as they passed through — the heart of the venture must be the wild horses and cattle they could round up and drive to a market.

That night and many thereafter until their departure I heard endless talk about the "cow-boy" system, a term that had just come into use to describe the companies of hardy and adventurous young Texians who since the Revolution had been making expeditions into southwest Texas gathering up the semiwild cattle abounding in that region. The cattle were, for the most part, the offspring of herds originally belonging to Mexican ranchers who had abandoned their holdings both because of Indian raids and the defeat of the Mexican army. The first mounted men to go into the abandoned country to drive cattle out had been detachments sent out by General Rusk to supply the soldiers of Texas who were suffering for meat. The cattle-hunting trips were so successful that some of the soldiers when discharged made a business of collecting these cattle and selling them to the western settlers whose herds had disappeared during the invasion. Some of the settlers themselves went out to get these wild cattle to restock their grazing grounds. Sometimes they would come upon gentle cattle on a range not yet abandoned by the Mexican owners, and the "cow boys" seldom hesitated to include these cattle in their drives even if it meant conflict with the owners. There was much discussion of the right and wrong of this matter, but it was generally agreed that such raids were justified since the Mexicans had caused such suffering and damage during the conflict; then too, Filisola's army as it left Texas had taken all cattle found on its line of retreat. The Alamo and Goliad massacres were fresh memories and it was hard for the average Texian to think kindly of any Mexican, even though some of them, native to Texas, had supported the cause of independence. I was sensitive to the opinions I heard expressed by the menfolk around me and pondered them all, although I would never have ventured to express one of my own.

"A lot of 'em are part Indian, that's what makes 'em so mean," my grandfather said. "Unless they can prove they're pure Spanish, I got no use for 'em. I'd be in favor of scalpin' 'em same as Indians."

"Viciousness is a matter of condition and circumstance, not of race or race mixture," Mr. Bryson said quietly, but did not elaborate.

Eli Dawson was inclined to poke fun in a way that always made sense. "I'll bet a pound of bear grease to a coonskin cap that half of this crew you round up for your cow-boy venture is meskin. They been in the cow and horse business in Mexico and Texas for three hundred years. That gives 'em considerable edge on anybody in this crowd."

"We can use some of 'em for help but keep 'em in their place," Range said.

"Like Negroes?" Mr. Bryson asked, in a strange sort of way.

"Yeah. Something like that," Range agreed.

Dr. Weideman interrupted almost with anger. "Such a comparison is absurd. The Negro came to this side of the world unwillingly and as a slave . . . the Spaniard came as an adventurer and conqueror. The Negro mixed with the Anglo-Saxon, producing only more slaves; but when the Spaniard mixed with the Indian whose culture, though different, was as deep-rooted and complex, a new nation and almost a new race was produced — a race of independent character, the Mexican, with its own newly acquired Republic of Mexico."

"So newly acquired," Mr. Bryson put in, "that Mexico was still in a state of weakness and shock over independence from Spain and not prepared to deal with a revolution in its own realm such as we put on here in Texas. Our timing was as good as our fighting — better perhaps."

"Some of those poor devils with their ranchos this side of the Rio Grande who haven't been killed off or scared off by this time must find it a little hard to figure things out if they're tryin' to live by the law," Mr. Dawson said. "First they find out the jig's up with His Majesty the King of Spain which was as much a surprise to many of them as it would be to jerk the Catholic Church out from under them; then before they get used to a president instead of a king, they learn, the hard way mostly, they're in another republic with another president — and yet they haven't gone anywhere. They get no protection from anywhere, and if they don't watch out, the border bandits of their own race, the Comanches, or the cow boys will put them out of business."

Range would sit, listening and remote, seldom making a comment. Whatever his thoughts were during these discussions, no one knew exactly, and for some reason I cannot explain, I was thankful he did not express them.

"It would be amusing to be around for comparisons a hundred years from now," Dr. Weideman remarked. "I should like to watch the disease of prejudice run its course in this part of the world, for here it seems we are in the most affected area — a sort of continental border. But of course a hundred years is much too soon for a complete cycle of development. Attainment of the divine average, I have decided, must be measured in thousands or tens of thousands of years. Nevertheless, in a century the trends would be evident: the black man a free man, free of his actual chains, that is, and recognized by law as a human being; and the despised Mexican walking with pride in your business and social circles . . . and you, Mr. Templeton, if you are bold enough to make your home in the country between the Nueces and the Rio Grande, may hold a grandchild on your knee with Mexican blood coursing buoyantly through his veins."

Range's face grew almost as red as Grandfather's when he is in a

136

temper. His fists clenched, and he finally muttered, "You're joking, I guess."

"I'm always joking," the doctor said, and laughed heartily at Range's discomfort. My grandmother and I heard these things as we sat with our needlework in a room just off the patio.

"Such a strange man, the doctor," my grandmother mused, "with moods that shift and change so fast it is often hard to follow him. He seems angry and then you discover he is merry; he is so kindly and yet there is a certain cruelty about some of the things he says and does."

When Range and I were alone, he talked to me much about the wonders and the terrors of the country through which he had traveled alone — the great herds of wild horses, the cattle, the awful barricades of brush and thorn broken by clearings covered with fine grasses, some of these clearings so extensive as to be vast unsettled prairies where thousands of cattle could graze and fatten. He talked of the great house we'd build at the springs and the ranch that would spread out from it. He and Mr. Bryson were partners, he told me, in an odd sort of arrangement that suited them both. Mr. Bryson, for some reason he declined to explain, wanted to possess no land. He had forsworn all ownership of property outside of personal apparel and equipment, and although he didn't think much of his life, he said, he admired the way Range had saved it; so he'd stick around and help him make some money and get his land. Mr. Bryson wanted the privilege of living on the acreage he would help Range to acquire but not an acre in his own name ever.

I asked Range what about the Mexican ranchers who might have claims to some of the land he wanted. Maybe they wouldn't want to sell out.

"Sell out?" He laughed at me. "The few left won't be around long. They'll be glad to get out alive, if they do."

Then sensing some of my concern, he told me not to worry for he and Silver would go to the land office at the proper time and get papers that would make things legal. They both had settlers' rights,

137

and Mr. Bryson was entitled to some extra acreage because he had fought in the Revolution; then too they both had land scrip they had taken from Mr. Dawson in payment for their services on the freighting trip.

"That land down there is any man's land and I'm going to get my share," Range told me. "There's no government protection down that way, but there's no interference either. The Mexican garrisons have been withdrawn and Texas is still too poor to set up any. South of the Nueces may still be claimed for Mexico but it belongs to Texas, and all a man's got to do down there is take what he wants and hold on till Texas gets stronger."

I could tell that Range had learned a lot about Texas on his trip to Laredo and was excited about it, for he talked to me more than was natural for one of his disposition. Some of his talk sounded more selfish than patriotic, but I didn't dwell on that. I was happy just to listen and dream with him. I didn't even allow myself to worry about his disregard for Mexican ranchers and their claims. It was only important to me then that he loved me, and it was a long time yet before my conscience and my love would be in conflict.

The wedding was soon after my grandfather's announcement. The things that I wore, the festivities, the ceremonies at the church, were no different than other weddings at that time. I am sure now that for Range the Catholic ritual was something to endure for my sake and rather distasteful to his pagan sort of nature. But I did not care then to try the doors on his inner thoughts. There was no such thing as a quiet wedding, for we had few enough occasions for celebration in those days. There were many troubles and sorrows and hard times, but a wedding was the time to forget them all and make merry. I remember so few of the details, overcome as I was with happiness and excitement . . . there was a bright-faced child at the church steps when we came out whose smile was so sweet that it brought tears to my eyes . . . there was the beautiful quilt I had never seen, made of tiny strips of velvet and satin that my grandmother had made for my mother and father, the quilt that had covered the bed on their wedding night as it did on ours . . . then there was at last the rapturous realization of the true proportions of love. I have heard it said by some ladies of my acquaintance that a man must be experienced with careless women if he would initiate his good and lawful love into the true bliss of a wedded union. I know not how it is over the world with other women, but, for myself, I must contradict this . . . for me any awkwardness only made tenderness the sweeter, any hesitancy the feeling more ardent. Perhaps we should regret, Range Templeton and I, having loved so young and having experienced the man and woman intimacies only between each other. But we do not. I know him as I know myself there. He touched no other woman before me; he will take none after me. It is astonishing in a love like ours how much of character and conscience each will reveal to the other without willing it, as if the senses were linked together and the thoughts flowed through. If I had had forty years with him instead of only twenty, I think I might have understood him completely, might even have known how to grapple with the demon in him that has defeated me and made of him a man whose touch is feverish and harsh and much too painful to bear.

If love were a more orderly enslavement of the senses and the heart did not so constantly betray the mind, a woman of my heritage and disposition would have sought to match with a man of more tolerance and less ambition than Range Templeton. But perhaps there is a wisdom unapparent, an enforcement of some natural law through God's intent, in the blending of natures so diverse by an attraction so compelling. Perhaps unpredictable loves between men and women of different race and temperament, sad accidents of birth such as befell the boy Macduff, and such strangely mixed origins as those which produced Miguel Sándivar may be counted a part of that achievement generations hence, when the brotherhood of man will have progressed from idealistic doctrine to simple reality.

When Range left me a second time in San Antonio, several months

139

after our marriage, as spring came again to waken the willows and the huisache, the parting was different. There was an ache for the loneliness ahead, but with it all a sustaining contentment. The absence would be long and his fortunes uncertain, but complete separation was impossible, for new life was within me and if he delayed as long as six or seven months I would have the company of a son or daughter to divert me. So the good-by embrace was not a tearful one. I remembered that Dr. Weideman had said that frailty was unbecoming to me.

It was a reckless venture, seventeen men setting out to round up and drive wild cattle and horses over unknown trails to an uncertain market. As they gathered the herd they would be in constant danger of Indians, marauders, or Mexican invaders who might outnumber them many times. And the work of handling the horses and cattle would be equally dangerous. Then there would be the hardships of taking the cattle along a strange trail with many rivers and swampy lands to cross before reaching New Orleans. There had been cattle driven to New Orleans from the more settled eastern areas of Texas where cattle raising was practiced as a form of livelihood, but I am confident that Range and Mr. Bryson were among the first to gather wild horses south of the Nueces and take them all the way across Texas through Opelousas, Louisiana, and on to New Orleans.

It is the way of a woman, I suppose, to worry about the inconsequential things, and I must admit that it gave me a pang when I thought of Range and Mr. Bryson (who I was sure knew so much of the ways of the world) in New Orleans alone after months of hard work. I had never been there, but it was to all people who knew the name a most sinful and wonderful city with its grand hotels, its places of pleasure, and its beautiful quadroons. I trusted Range in these matters if he were left on his own, but under the influence of Mr. Bryson I was not so sure. Ah! Now that I know Mr. Bryson better, I realize there was no cause for alarm. He knew the great city well and but for him Range would not have had such success in his business dealings. . . . I have the feeling sometimes when we talk

140

of New Orleans that Mr. Bryson had some experience there before he came to Texas that would account for his peculiar slant on life and also perhaps for his hair so unnaturally white. It is a look of desolation far back in his eyes that makes me think so. . . .

*   *   *

A white moon, leaning far toward the west, cast a halfhearted radiance over the quiet plaza. It was a full hour before dawn. Two men sat on their horses, waiting, riders and mounts held in a stillness and beauty of posture like the statues that would immortalize their kind centuries later. It was the moment of long thought before movement that initiates a contest with the unknown. Range Templeton and Silver Bryson were waiting for the fifteen-man crew they had hired. They were early because they were the leaders and it would give the men a better feeling to find them there ahead of the rest. But no one would be late. Timing was too important. The seventeen riders would be well on their way before dawn, their departure unannounced.

The stillness was broken first by the clop of the supply mules in the charge of Wong, a Chinese who rode his mule with dignity and purpose and whose going was both an adventure and a sacrifice — an adventure for Wong himself who had been excited beyond all measure when Firebush Olson, prompted by his granddaughter, had suggested Wong become a part of the expedition — a sacrifice for the entire Olson household where Wong's services in kitchen, yard, and stable had over a period of many years become a part of the family life. Wong's loyalty, his good cooking, his skill in the presence of sickness or accident, his marksmanship on foot or muleback when he rode on Indian raids, all were a solace to Luvisa Templeton as she lay wide awake and hardly breathing, listening in the lonely dawn for the sounds that would tell her when the riders departed: the dogs barking their disturbance, the horses left in the stalls neighing their anxiety.

Flaco, guide and "wise man," entered the plaza from a point almost

141

opposite Wong. His horse, ignoring the mules, walked with quiet un-hurried gait toward the leaders. Even in the dimness of the moon's light, Flaco's mustang was an ugly animal; low and chunky in out-line, he showed dull-colored and shaggy like worn rawhide in the light of day. But like his rider, the horse had endurance and a certain wisdom in meeting emergencies that gave him a peculiar value; no man in the crew knew the country they would traverse as Flaco knew it, and no horse was better built to endure its rigors and dangers than the unsightly little mustang. It might have been the irony of coincidence or the affinity of mount for master, but never-theless Flaco's horse had the annoying habit of blowing through its nose and grunting as if in pain when tired or displeased with some-thing his master seemed intent on doing. Other riders usually became nervous or irritated to the point of violence when riding with Flaco listening to his complaints and the horse's grunts. So he usually rode alone. Eli Dawson had it figured out that Flaco liked it that way and even suspected he was proud of his own nuisance value and also that of his horse. Eli had released Flaco from his freighting crew with reluctance, but allowed that the "cow boys" would be just "babes in the brush" without a good scout who knew the country. More trails and more trade were needed to put lifeblood into the republic, Eli Dawson figured, and he'd like to see this cattle-marketing venture of Range Templeton's made the beginning of something big. He had the notion that strong men and sound trade could straighten things out.

The Negroes, Cicero and Caesar, rode onto the plaza after Wong as if he had given them the signal to follow. They rode close together, stirrup to stirrup, Siamese fashion, showing plainly from the be-ginning their desire to stick together, their realization that they were the only two of their kind in the company, their deep-down in-stinctive cautiousness. They were brothers and free Negroes and had a blacksmith shop in San Antonio. They had been persuaded to close their shop and go on the drive for they had grown up at Anahuac, at the mouth of the Trinity, and were the only men on the drive who knew something of driving cattle in swampy land. Silver Bryson had been the one to convince Range of their value; Range had agreed but didn't believe they'd go. He left it up to Silver to get them and was surprised when they actually closed shop and made preparations to leave. Range never knew how Silver made the venture so attractive to the Negroes but was irritated from time to time all during the drive at the manner in which the brothers looked to the white-haired Southerner as their sole boss. They would take orders from Range but look for an approving nod or smile from Bryson.

There were four Mexicans, all mustangers, experienced in catching and taming wild horses: Alfonso and his sons, Andrés and Armando, and their cousin Romaldo. These four, with a young Indian, Tomás, from the San José Mission, friendly to Alfonso's sons and Romaldo, entered from the far end of the plaza below Wong and the Negroes and moved into a loose group as they rode toward the men who had hired them. Tomás had asked to be included when he learned his friends were going. He too was an experienced mustanger, descended from a family of Mission Indians who for generations had been catching and training the horses used around the missions. Range Templeton would learn much from Tomás that would be turned into strength and wealth; they were about the same age. But there would never be an awareness of the giving or the taking, for a vast current of indifference lay between them, across which neither animosity nor admiration ever moved.

The six Americans who completed the company rode in from scattered points and gathered in a careless semicircle around the leaders. There was no urgency among them to hold together, no uneasiness, and a quality of listlessness. They were through with adventure, and going home. Their stomachs were turned against Indians and fighting. Their pockets were empty, their land scrip traded for supplies and their supplies gone. They had little to recommend them beyond the fact that they had survived, which, translated into the life of the times, meant that they could ride and shoot, knew something of the ways of Indians, and were accustomed to hard times and tough fights. Now they wanted to go home, back to the States, each to his own place for his own reasons. Range and Bryson figured they would make good hands because that would be the only way they could get home. The agreement with each of these six was that when the cattle were delivered in New Orleans and sold, he would be free to take the mount he rode, the equipment he carried, and fifty dollars in hard money and take out in any direction that suited him.

There was no need for greetings or questions. Range with a slight wave of his hand signaled Flaco to move out ahead. Range and Silver followed, and Wong came next for the importance of supplies was an accepted condition and the supplies must be protected. The Negroes rode along beside Wong prepared to help him keep the loaded mules in line; the white riders snaked along in pairs or singles; the Mexicans came last, and, wherever the trail allowed, rode abreast. Flaco would set the pace.

As they rode along and the light spread, Range dwelt long and solidly on the fact that when he returned to Bexar, he would be a family man. He was resolved to acquire before that time such means and prospects that the Olsons would regard him as the head of the family. He had left a proper amount of money for Luvisa's care, but Firebush, in turn, had invested more than that in the drive, insisting that Range might want to buy up some cattle from East Texas settlements as he made his way to the New Orleans market with his wild stock and thus pick up some extra profit for both of them.

Flaco thought the drive should originate at San Patricio, an abandoned Irish settlement about seven miles above the mouth of the Nueces; it was situated on the northeast bank and surrounded by a grassy prairie good for grazing while the herd was being collected. And along a woody fringe of the river a few miles up from San Patricio was another settlement, depopulated because of border warfare and Indians, which would prove useful as an outpost before crossing the river and where abandoned buildings and corrals could be converted into pens and a general headquarters for the drivers. As for Indians, Flaco advised, they would have to kill out any small bands that discovered them, and trust to luck that no bands too big to wipe out would find them. If they worked fast, they had a good chance, Flaco believed, to get together as many cattle and horses as the bunch could handle before being discovered. Wild horses, he said, were thick as fleas on a hound dog in Patricio County, which, according to a rough map Eli Dawson had copied for him, was about a hundred and thirty miles long and seventy or eighty wide.

"Them long-horned cattle born to the brush 'er wilder than Satan on a toot," Flaco explained, "but if we can mix 'em up with some of the ones left behind by the Mexican ranchers and those settlers around Patricio, things won't be so rough on the drivers." Range and Silver agreed that Flaco's plans and observations were reasonable and Range kept to himself his original plan of operating from the springs where he had met Miguel. By a glance at Flaco's crude map, he estimated that this spot was over a hundred miles from the abandoned San Patricio settlement, although in the same county, and to accumulate the herd and start the drive through this wilderness country would cut his chances for success almost in half. The springs could wait . . . they were a goal and a dream. More practical things must come first. Plenty of money, some legal papers perhaps, and more men to help him take over when he moved in there was his reasoning. Then he put dreams out of his mind completely, listened to Flaco, studied the men riding with him, forgot his youth and inexperience, and rode beside the silver-haired Bryson as an equal and a partner. A triumvirate indeed for conquering new country and accumulating power: Flaco, with his wisdom of the wild, his bellyaches, and a faculty for decision as firm as the viselike grip of his bony hand, was devoted solely to the trail and the adventure on it and felt no impulse to own or control the things he contacted; Silver Bryson, who surely had known and responded at some time to the normal desires of his kind to lead and possess, felt a compulsion he left unanalyzed to support Range Templeton's efforts; and Range

145

himself, ready to take full advantage of the qualities in these two men that would aid him in carrying out his plans. It was this willingness to use other men's talents as tools, in supplement to the impulses of his own positive nature, that would make it possible for him to accomplish things entirely out of proportion to his age and experience.

Along the trail that took them to the abandoned settlement, these three continued to lay out the work ahead. First, the wild horses would be hunted and captured, roped and sidelined, and left in Alfonso's hands for gentling enough to drive . . . only high-grade animals would be caught along with a few tough ponies to be broken and used as extras in the cattle work.

Indian signs were plentiful but not a redskin was sighted on the entire ride down the Nueces to San Patricio. Most of the time the crew rode near the river and camps were pleasant. Nights were clear with only the coyote's plaintive calls to break the starlit peace of their repose. The men were fed well and became rested and cheerful. Only Flaco complained and turned pessimistic over the good weather and good luck; he considered this necessary because he had observed that as sure as everything became right for everybody some disaster lay not far ahead.

When they arrived in the vicinity of the abandoned settlements, Flaco insisted on taking Tomás and scouting the area for inhabitants of any kind. He wanted a half day for the job. So camp was made one day at noon, and Flaco and Tomás went on ahead. When night came they had not returned. The fifteen men who waited, divided into groups of five, made a pretense of alternating between sleep and guarding, but there was little sleep and an all-night alertness to danger. When morning came, they rode out together and as they came in view of the lonely cabins and broken fences, suspecting some trap, they held their weapons ready and studied the scene from a protective distance. For a space there was no sound, then one that was completely unexpected — the tinkle of a bell, a small, sweet bell that a pet fawn or lamb might wear. The men all listened in a startled silence. The bell moved toward them through a nearby thicket.

Range, searching with a keen, shifting gaze, could locate no signs of life. The bell moved closer. The fifteen men continued to follow the point of sound, ears and eyes strained, feeling somehow spellbound.

The bearer of the bell finally emerged into full view. Some of the men cursed softly in amazement, others struggled to control laughter, realizing the harmless creature they saw might be the forerunner of trouble. For the amiable sight that filled their eyes was a huge ox, fat and shining, his burnished hide gleaming in the morning light, his horns polished, and only a speck of white in his forehead to break the coppery red of his coat. Here was a pet, recently fed, utterly content . . . the message was clearer than print. But where was the owner? Range and Bryson drew back and motioned the men to follow. They had hardly turned their horses about, before another sound, as startling as the bell, built their surprise still higher: it was a man singing, very loud and clear on the morning air . . .

> "Little Star, ah, Little Star,
> The morn it's clear
> But don't stray far
> Your home it's here
> Ah, Little Star!
> The grass you see
> Ah, pass it be,
> Me Little Star,
> For youse were born
> To eat the corn,
> Me Little Star.
> > The grass be high . . . and so be I . . .
> > The corn be strong . . . and life be long . . .
> > So hear me song . . . Ah, Little Star!"

By the time the song was finished, the singer too had emerged from the brush. He was a huge man, well matched in size with the animal. He whacked the ox affectionately on rump and side with the flat of his hand, scratched him between the ears, then looked up

147

in the direction of the riders as if expecting them. Range and Silver rode out to him while the other riders held back. The proportions and appearance of the man were astonishing all the way from his large bare feet spread flat like a short-fingered hand up a good seven feet to the top of a mat of sandy, tight-curling hair that hung at chin length. The part of his broad, red face not covered by a patchy beard was heavily pock-marked; he wore two very dirty garments reaching a ragged elbow and knee length. The long beefy arms were almost knee length too, and the abnormally broad shoulders were held startlingly erect. The voice, thick with the brogue of the Irish and the broth of the corn, boomed in speech as it did in song.

"Be the saints o' the mornin', if me poor foggy orbs are set in the sockets of a wakin' man's head, then it is Mr. Templeton and Mr. Bryson approachin' across the dewy carpet o' the new day!"

Range and Silver were in close now. They stopped their horses and stared at the Irishman and his ox. After the night of strain there was no humor and little patience left in them.

The Irishman and Little Star studied their visitors. Then the Irishman turned and addressed his ox, "Ah! and it is yourself that must speak to these strangers since the both of them, 's God's pity, are after bein' as wordless as the brute. Sure, now, and youse could be tellin' the dumb creatures — not the horses, me proud beastie, but the ones on their backs — me name is C. Cassidy, me nature is mild as a moth," the big, crude man spoke very softly, then exploded, "but me timper busts like a green rotten egg over him that's not answerin' a true Irish greeting with the spirit intended."

Silver smiled faintly. Range asked, "What about Flaco and Tomás?"

"Is it the skinny old one and the brown young one that yer brow is bleedin' with worry for?"

"The same," Silver answered shortly.

"Then simmer down, man, and don't be after wastin' your worry. It's close by they are, but dead to the world."

Range tensed.

"Asleep?" Silver inquired mildly, beginning to feel that the men were safe and the Irishman harmless.

"Tied to the earth with the silken cords of it."

"Eternal or alcoholic?"

"A deep, sweet slumber it is, safe in the arms of Morpheus! God rest the tired hearts of 'em."

"And who in the hell is Morpheus?" Range was edgy.

Silver almost smiled. "The god of dreams," he explained. "C. Cassidy, bendin' a little with the brew himself, is being poetic. Our scouts are sleeping off a drunk, no doubt."

"Flaco won't touch the bottle," Range said, "on account of his stomach trouble, and he won't let anybody with him hit it on the trail."

Although Range had addressed his remark to Silver, Cassidy threw back his head and bellowed with laughter.

"And did ye hear that now, Little Star? Then it is the whole story I should be tellin' you. . . . There they was, spyin' on me cornpatch, quiet as rabbits, thinkin' they was hid, not knowin' about the prickles as travel up and down me spine in pairs when there's aught but nature's dumb critters around. 'Is it the Mexican hawk, El Gavilán, you'd find?' says I, 'or, were youse after stirring up a Comanche from its nesting place?' 'And what is it I have stirred up?' says he, the skinny one. 'A God-fearing Irishman, and who else'd you think to find in old San Patricio?' says I. 'Nobody,' says he, 'so you make one too many.' 'Sure, now, and in that case,' says I, 'it'd make me the happy man to depart the place, takin' with me the hides o' two rabbits now prowlin' me premises.' More pleasantries there was, until parched throats and empty bellies gentled our natures, and it was meself as set out jerky and jug, first makin' all swear allegiance to the mighty Republic o' Texas, and askin' the brown one to swear also be all the saints of heaven and earth that he's no kin or favor of Antonio López de Santa Anna or any as followed after him. The sips they takes from me jug is an insult to me art and me name, and the old one all the while moanin' like a

149

banshee about the pain in his belly until me heart softens and I take down me ancient jug put aside for the sacred, the sick, and the dying, and pour from it a gourdful. 'Drink up,' says I, 'and turn y'r pains to pleasures, and y'r moans to music.' 'Drink y'r own poison,' says he, 'I'll have none of it.'"

Cassidy paused significantly. "That the poor little old man be ravin' out o' his mind was clear as the River Shannon, Little Star, and so it is for the good of his own self that I persuades — " he paused again for effect and repeated " — that I persuades him to drink deep as a man should. . . . Aye, and the young one, a-tremblin' there, it is also persuasion he must have. But sure now when they rise up they'll give thanks to us, feelin' as they will like new men on resurrection morn," he winked broadly at the ox, "and like children at play they'll go out to romp on the range of the wild horse."

"The ox, I'm sure, is charmed with your story," Silver spoke lightly, having made up his mind that the Irishman should not be antagonized. "And now may we view the remains of our comrades?"

The Irishman seemed to consider the matter soberly. "Though y'r countenances be bleak as a norther's breath, for myself, y'r welcome to follow into the settlement and abide there, but it's not alone that I am here." Range frowning and impatient shifted in the saddle as Cassidy paused to let his statement soak in. Then he turned to the ox again, thumped him on the side and asked, "Fellow citizen and wilderness companion, do we welcome these riders after wild horses and cows? Can we be sure now that the fine meat on your bones, and the brew in me cellar'll be safe in the presence of their campfires?" Little Star turned his head, appeared to pass judgment on the riders and nodded solemnly three times. Cassidy nudged the ox again and inquired, "No ripples of fear or doubt play along the hide of ye to say, 'Beware the serpent in the garden'?" The ox seemed to study the matter over, then shook his ponderous head from side to side. Silver laughed outright. Range smiled reluctantly. The Irishman, resting his hand lightly on the shoulder of his ox, turned without another word, and the man and animal moving leisurely side by side showed the riders into the abandoned settlement. There was no sign of life or recent habitation; neglected fences and hollow cabins, fields overgrown in short brush and weeds, everywhere mute evidence of disaster and failure and nature's effort to blanket it all over and obliterate the tragedy as soon as possible. On the far edge of the settlement, walled in with a natural growth of brush and fenced with tall pointed posts lashed tight together was C. Cassidy's living quarters, a cornpatch, a shed for the ox, a cabin with a cellar underneath. Sounds of groaning, babbling, and snores came from the cabin. It was not difficult to understand how C. Cassidy had learned so much about the riders and their purpose in coming to San Patricio. While the other riders sat their horses, Range and Silver dismounted and went into the cabin, preceded by Cassidy, who shook his head sadly over the two men lying on his cowhide pallet.

"They'll come out of it," Silver said, "eventually. That stuff must cast a spell as well as pack a punch. Was this what they drank?" He picked up a stone jug from a small table — a furnishing skillfully contrived from corncobs. The Irishman nodded and mumbled, "The very same." Silver removed the stopper, sniffed, tilted the jug for a taste. "I revise my statement. They may never come out of it. Mr. Cassidy, you must have the devil's own knack for producing liquid fire. I hope you know the antidote for your own poison for we hold you responsible for the lives and well-being of these two men."

"Why not carry them along with us and make camp away from here?" Range said, showing clearly in the look he gave the Irishman, he trusted no remedies that might come from this source.

"Go along with ya now and make y'r camp and get ready fer y'r drives. C. Cassidy is one as never yet killed a man without cause and cured many a one he has for less than the gratitude due. As for the trouble ye've had and the loss o' labor o' these lying here, the citizens of San Patricio'll make it up t' you. Y'r work you can do boldly with no thought f'r buildin' y'r campfire high. . . . No Indians comes nigh to the place . . . it is the plague that scares the feathers right out o' the bonnets of 'em and puts the wings to their

heels, and me it is they are sure has the evil spirit residin' within."
He grimaced to call attention to the pockmarks making great scars
across his face.

Then his voice became lonely and wistful, like a child who has
been too long without playmates. "It was only a scatterin' of us that
stayed when the last pulled out from here to Goliad. The redskins
from off the prairies and the brownskins from out o' the south kept
swoopin' down like hawks on a chickenyard 'til there was no heart
for stayin' on to die in the settlement. But it mattered little to those
of us with the sickness where we died, and when the devil brought
the Comanches again, hungry for scalps of the few left, it was myself they found last, fevered and ravin' on me pallet, and beholdin'
the sores eatin' me good face away they fled like the screamin' hyenas
they are, for 'tis the plague they fear like no other thing in the wilderness, may God strike the likes of 'em dead with it after an eternity
o' torture in the flesh!" Cassidy clenched his fists and raised his face
to heaven in a supplication that would have seemed melodramatic
had it not been for his ugly marred face and a tear or two that rolled
out of his eyes and lodged somewhere in the pits on his cheeks. He
turned to Range and Bryson with a movement that was apologetic
and added quietly, "Myself and one little bull calf hiding in the
brush was the whole that was left in old San Patricio. An Indian
has not been on these grounds since the day . . . the cow hunters
we have seen go by and the young Mexican demon El Gavilán has
camped here . . . we have seen them, but they have never seen us,
never laid eyes on Little Star and C. Cassidy. It is uneasy they all
are hereabouts and they leave the place quickly, for the spirits of
the dead do not rest easy in Old San Patricio, and unless the conscience of a man be clear as spring water, he cannot dwell long
among 'em."

There was a silence.

Range said, "Would you like to work for us on getting our drive
ready? We need another man."

"That I would."

"We will need a good lead ox for our herd," Silver said.

"That would be Little Star himself."

"Ever been to New Orleans?" Range asked.

"Never but from the land of Erin to the land of Texas."

"Come to the camp for supper."

"That I will do and gladly," he smiled broadly and gestured to the floor. "With a friend on either side of me."

It was clear now why his visitors had not been allowed to depart.

C. Cassidy's boisterous songs and the weird sound of his instrument, whittled from mesquite wood and strung with bobcat gut, had scarcely faded into the darkness that followed the late setting of the moon before Wong was waking the camp for a daybreak breakfast. This day the work would begin and there would be no letup until the drive was through and success or failure a settled fact. Cassidy advised that they all go out together, leaving no signs yet that the herd would be gathered at the settlement. He led them to abandoned dugouts where supplies could be safely hidden until their return. He knew something of the country to the south, and so astride Little Star, who struck a fast pace for an ox, and with Flaco squinting and surly on one side of him and Alfonso on the other, Cassidy led the search for a desirable location for building the pen that would be used as a trap to catch the wild horses. Alfonso, as the most experienced mustanger, was to have the say-so in these matters. Cassidy had not worked much at catching wild horses but was under the impression that they would find an abandoned pen within two day's ride from the settlement and this might be rebuilt much more quickly than a new trap. He had heard much talk of the place, had been there once, and would use all the powers he had in the world and out of it to find the old pen and thus make up for the trouble he had caused his new friends.

Silver rode with the Mexicans that day, speaking wholly in Spanish as if he knew no other language, asking endless questions on mustanging, listening carefully while Alfonso's nephew Romaldo told of his experience in walking down wild horses, for at this he was an expert.

It was a method the Mexicans had probably learned from the Indians and required some eight or ten days when all went well. Romaldo explained to Silver how careful, how cautious, how patient a man must be if he would be "accepted" by a herd of wild horses. It must be done by a lone man, following the band of mustangs until they became familiar with him and would allow him among them. The method had nothing to do with tiring the horses, but rather establishing a sort of companionship with them. But a man must be oh so careful not to change any part of his clothing or his equipment and to always ride the same horse. Even the smallest change would cause the horses to take fright and prolong the "walker's" job indefinitely. He must have a helper to keep him supplied with food and water and to advise the other drivers when he would be in the right position with the herd to rush them into the pen. Once a man was accepted by the herd with his own horse grazing, running, watering, or taking fright as the wild herd did, he would find himself able in a few days to move about in the direction of the pen and have the horses move with him until near enough to the other drivers his horse would apparently take fright and run, to be followed by the wild horses almost to the gate of the pen.

As soon as the location for the pen was determined, Romaldo would go out for his herd with his cousin Armando following and keeping him supplied with food. He would find the best herd in Texas, he assured Mr. Bryson enthusiastically, and be back to the pen within less than two weeks unless his cousin Armando was stupid enough to frighten the herd sometime with his noisy following-after. He looked to Armando for a rise to this remark, but Armando just grinned and said who could tell, maybe it would be Romaldo on whose shoulders a panther would choose to ride sometime as he passed under a low branch along the trail.

Range kept company with his one-way riders and learned rope-throwing tricks from a thin, weak-looking boy called Angus who was built like a jockey, had long thin fingers that seemed to ache for the cards, could make the rope snap with the deadly aim of a rattler, carried an unexpected strength in his wrists, and would, Range figured, be one of his best hands with the wild stock. Later, when he watched Angus day after day take chances with life and limb, handling wild horses and cattle as if he had steel rope for muscles and as many lives to spare as a newborn cat, he was secretly proud of his estimate of this pale, large-eyed young man whose skin wouldn't tan and whose features were as immobile as the skull that showed too plainly underneath.

The old pen Cassidy had hoped to find was located during the afternoon of the second day. It was constructed in an oval shape so that mustangs once inside would keep circulating and not trample themselves to death. Large mesquite posts, eight to ten feet tall, had been used. Placed as close together as possible, and set in a ditch about two feet deep, the posts had been lashed together with strong rawhide thongs. At the main opening in the pen, wing fences extended out about half a mile, making a wide V. These wings were made for the most part of brush and so disguised that the horses running into it would not realize they were trapped until they were well down into the V or even in the pen, since the gate too was well disguised. Although the fence now had many gaps and the wings were hardly more than an outline, many days of hard labor would be saved. Range, who had at an early age learned the tricks of wood-cutting under his ax-toting Uncle Jesse, took charge of the extra post cutting with Angus and three others to help; he kept Cassidy and Little Star well occupied dragging the posts to the right place. Silver, with Caesar and Cicero as right-hand men, saw that the old ditch was cleared and posts straightened and reset, while Alfonso and Andrés prepared the rawhide strips and others were assigned to constructing the wings. Wong busied himself solely with camp keeping and cooking, and Romaldo and Armando set out to find the manada that would be worth walking down.

One wing of the pen was near a watering hole and had evi-

155

dently been used in dry season for chasing the horses in when they came to drink. Alfonso examined the hole and thought it unlikely that horses would come there enough for any sizable catch since there was no drought on and tracks showed only an occasional watering. The hole was handy, however, for supplying the camp; but, on both Flaco's and Cassidy's advice, camp was made some distance away in one of those strange grassy clearings found in the brush country like an oasis in a desert. This was in a prickly pear thicket, and, except for a single trail, was almost as fortified as a structure of rock walls. Wong was to use as little fire as possible and Indians or other intruders would have to pass close by to know a camp was there.

In less than a week, the pen was ready. It was decided that the riders would spread out and try to scare up several bunches to work out before Romaldo got in with his herd. It had been a quiet afternoon with an early beddown. Wong had built only one fire in the early morning and had done the rest of his cooking over the coals and with the hot stone oven he had built into the ground. The stock were content and still. Tomás was perched high in a tree near the watering hole. A few horses and wild cattle had been watering there; he had volunteered to watch and see if there was anything worth the capture and report his find. There was enough moonlight for him to study the scene.

The men were not long asleep and Flaco and Angus were on guard when Tomás brought in the news that a small band of Indians (yes, he was sure not more than ten or twelve) were heading for the watering place. They were evidently traveling parallel to the river, avoiding San Patricio, and making for this particular water hole for a late evening camp.

Flaco gave the news out quietly and said they'd keep an eye on the redskins. If they watered and went on to camp further along, it'd be best to let 'em go. If they settled for the night, a buryin' party would be in order — not a single one must get away.

Range said, "Why don't we pen 'em?"

Flaco was startled. "Why don't we which?"

156

"They don't know about the pen. They're tired and so are the horses. The horses'll be heavy with water. There's enough wind in the right direction for us to make it up mighty close before they know we're around if we can keep the horses quiet. They may know about the old pen but they don't know about the new, and the old one had so many gaps it didn't mean anything. We'll rush 'em into the pen and — see if the posts hold. That way we ought to catch us some good horses and — some good Indians."

Flaco said, "That'll be different from any Comanche party I was ever on. I'm willing to play the game, but you're it!"

Range gave the instructions quickly. . . . The moon was bright enough for good fighting, but they must be extra careful not to let a single one get away. He gave specific directions as to which riders would ride the wing fences, who would close the gate, who would keep a special watch to see that no Indians escaped by climbing over the fence once they were in the enclosure. Except for the two who would be closing and guarding the gate, all would remain mounted, riding in close pursuit of the Indians right on into the pen and putting an end there to those not killed in the run from the water hole to the gate.

Angus said, "Can I rope me one, boss?"

It was the first time anyone had ever called Range "boss." It didn't sound strange or new to him.

"If it comes handy," he answered easily.

Flaco wanted to protest about the danger to the horses with shooting at such close quarters in the pen, and he wanted to observe that the Indians might not panic but instead turn on their attackers and try scattering into the brush. But there was such a positive quality in the instructions Range gave out, as if the whole incident had not only been well planned out ahead of time but also would most certainly happen exactly as he expected it to, that Flaco decided to keep quiet and along with the others do exactly as Range said.

CHAPTER VIII

LUVISA resolved to turn her mind from the dangers Range would be facing and remain quiet and composed until her child was born. She frequently sought diversion in Dr. Weideman's garden where she listened to his charming conversation on the latest items in his collection, or, most pleasant of all, helped Carlota care for Macduff, the strange, beautiful baby that Jeannie Dodson had borne. Luvisa was suddenly eager to learn all about babies, and "Duffy," as she affectionately nicknamed him, was the most convenient and pleasant to study. Carlota would place him in a basket in the garden where Luvisa could sit and watch him to her heart's content. He was an extremely quiet baby with eyes that seemed much too knowing. He did not kick and coo, but lay very still, studying objects with an intensity of concentration that Luvisa found disturbing.

One night, some weeks after Range had departed, Luvisa had a terrible dream. She was on horseback, with Duffy in her arms, fleeing from Indians down a passageway between great arms of brush. Racing toward an enclosure that seemed to mean safety, she discovered too late that she had entered a pen from which there was no escape. The Indians, yelling fiendishly, poured in and closed the gate. Then began the horrible chase around and around the pen. She could feel Duffy clutching her in terror, but neither of them could make a sound. When the horror had reached an agonizing peak, with an Indian racing beside her and snatching at Duffy, there were yells and shots outside the pen and the gate was thrown open. With Range in the lead, his riders dashed in to the rescue. The gates were closed again and there was an awful battle: arrows flying wildly, Indians shot at close range and toppling from their horses; some of the riders leaping from their own horses onto the Indians' horses, landing behind them, stabbing them to death . . . and one little fellow whose head in the weird night light looked like a bare skull, roping an

Indian, giving a jerk that broke the neck, dismounting to undo the loop and making another throw from the ground that was equally successful. Finally, it was over. And there in the awful arena of dead Indians, while his men went about the business of catching the Indians' horses, gathering up their equipage, and dragging the bodies out of the pen, Range rode up very close to Luvisa until his stirrup and leg touched hers, looked at her lovingly, put out a hand and touched her arm in question. Luvisa shuddered and drew back. He wanted to see the child she held — thought it was their child. She clutched Duffy closer to her, trying to hide him from Range. What would he do when he realized the baby in her arms was the one whose birth had been such a revolting experience for him? She tried to move away from him. He reached out and clutched her arm with a grip that brought a streak of pain. She looked wildly about seeking the aid that never comes in a nightmare. There at her feet the guide Flaco was scalping an Indian and beside him was a great giant of a man watching, intent on learning how it was done. Neither of them noticed her desperation. As terror mounted and pain increased, she was forced to loosen her hold on the child and let it fall from her arms. Range recognized Duffy and made no attempt to break his fall. Instead, his voice rang out bitterly, "Cradling the devil's seed in your arms!" His horse reared above the child, and Luvisa knew Duffy would be killed. The scream she had been choking on came out at last, and she awoke.

Luvisa felt gloomy and depressed for days afterward and Dr. Weideman had difficulty turning her mind back to the cheerful channels he had prescribed for her. She insisted that he try to explain or interpret the dream.

"You know that dreams often can mean something, Dr. Weideman — a message of some kind from the present or the future, a forecasting, a warning perhaps."

"Yes, my dear, I admit that. I also know that there are many more of perfectly meaningless character, and you'll do better to list yours in that category. Most of the experiences you had in the dream are

159

utterly fantastic, outside the realm of possibility, so discipline your mind and cease to dwell on the unpleasantness of it all."

"But, Dr. Weideman, you remember Mrs. Jeremy Williams, how she dreamed her brother had been scalped, stripped of his clothing, and left for dead. If she hadn't directed the searching party to the location as she dreamed it, he would never have been found. He would have perished but for her dream and the action she took upon it."

"Certainly. But there was nothing so clear-cut about your dream. Nothing you could act upon unless you choose to clutch Duffy to your bosom and go out scouting for Indians."

Luvisa allowed herself gradually to be reassured. She never told Range of the dream but was to ponder the significance of it time and again when certain events of her life would bring the distorted pattern of it before her like reflections in a faulty mirror.

On one of those clear nights in the fall when stars seem to multiply and come close to the earth, Luke and Laska were born. During the early hours of Luvisa's pain, Dr. Weideman allowed the window open, kept lights dim, and talked of the wonders of the universe. Then beauty was blotted out for a while by travail, but for Luvisa there was wondrous unexpected compensation in the thrust of exultation both physical and spiritual that she felt in the act of giving birth. Dr. Weideman knew of her rapture and was deeply thankful that it was so. When he told her that she had both a daughter and a son, as perfect and sound as any babies ever made, she murmured, "Now the beauty of the heavens has increased a hundredfold."

When Luvisa was able to go about again, she took the twins to Dr. Weideman regularly to have him reassure her that they were both in perfect health and at the same time renew her visits with Duffy. On one visit, she stayed longer than usual; the doctor's garden was glorious and Duffy's curiosity over the twins was additional enchantment. Ed Olson became uneasy and found them there. His anger was an ugly and hateful thing. Had Duffy been a rattlesnake coiled and ready to strike at the twins, he could not have exhibited more alarm at the proximity of danger.

"You dare let that Indian bastard touch 'em!"

Luvisa stood between him and the children. He raised his hand as if to strike her but her anger rose to match his.

"Grandfather! You're being wicked and cruel!"

Carlota came running for Duffy and took him quickly away. Ed Olson grabbed the twins and strode off, one under each arm and both screaming. Duffy was crying in the kitchen and Carlota murmuring to him. Luvisa stood very still and quiet letting the tears roll down her cheeks unchecked. Dr. Weideman had been in his study. He came out and stood by her awhile.

"Be careful, Lu," was all he said.

Luvisa could seek no comfort in wishing Range were near to console her — she knew he would be sympathetic with her grandfather. After that, she slipped off now and then to see Duffy but did not take the twins along.

Ed and Ella Olson, much impressed with their responsibility as great-grandparents to twins, considered Luvisa's role of caretaker so important that she was relieved of all household duties and charged with constant attendance upon Luke and Laska. This demand, she knew, was more of an indulgence toward the twins than herself, but she found it easy to comply, making the twins a full-time and fascinating study, prolonging the delights of caring for them, marveling and musing over their differences — for it was almost impossible to find any likeness between them. Laska's hair was a fluffy white down sprinkled ever so slightly with glints of gold and her eyes a gray that, except for the tannish flecks in them, would soon duplicate her father's. Luke's hair was dark and his eyes a deep, earnest blue; his fair skin was a contrast to Laska's creamy olive tint that made her such an odd and bewitching little creature to behold. As Luvisa sat hour after hour rocking the double cradle

161

that her grandfather had built, she talked to the babies of their father, weaving stories out of the things he might be doing — stories in which wild cattle and horses were easily rounded up, the fleet Toego made certain his escape from all enemies, and the events of the trail were all turned in their father's favor.

Silver Bryson watched with sharp interest the quick changes that were wrought in Range Templeton during the weeks of strenuous activity with wild horses and cattle. The changes came with the realization of having discarded youth and put on manhood. As Range considered approaching fatherhood his shoulders became straighter, his expression more grave, and his appetite keener. As a family man, he felt a stimulating responsibility to become important in the eyes of his wife and children. As a young adventurer, he felt a compelling zest for the risks and excitement of each unpredictable day. As a businessman, he knew exactly what he wanted to accomplish and what must be done to achieve the ends he had set. His inexperience made it impossible for him to plan all the methods to be employed in accumulating the money and land that were his goal, but every time someone called him "boss," or he issued an order to another man, his purposes were set a little firmer, his determination more fixed. He absorbed more than acquired the skills and cautions of the frontier: Angus's rope tricks, Alfonso's handling and gentling of wild horses, Flaco's reading of signs, the Mexicans' understanding of the cow critter, and even some of Silver Bryson's ways with words and weapons that proved useful in critical situations. And while he absorbed, he framed attitudes, clear-cut and unchangeable, about what he learned.

By the time Armando brought word from Romaldo that he was ready to drift his herd in close to the corral for the trapping, Bryson was well into his role as the silent partner, and Range was giving all the orders. Although it was through Alfonso's wisdom that he knew what must be done, and must have realized how his authority would suffer had he made a mistake, he stationed the men for the catch as if he had done it countless times before. He appointed advance riders to go out and assist Romaldo in getting the herd to the receivers, the men stationed farthest out on the two wings; other riders were stationed several hundred yards apart along the wings. Alfonso and Andrés were given two of the critical positions as encerrador and cortador (the one who shuts the gate and the cutter). If there were more mustangs rushing through the gap than the corral would hold without trampling and crippling, Alfonso would rush out from a blind made of green brush and through a gap to the entrance of the pen waving a blanket before the frightened animals; the cutter would dash in from the opposite wing to assist in cutting off the mustangs and putting up the bars at the entrance. Range and Bryson took positions as the receivers. It was Romaldo's plan to have the advance riders get in back of his herd; he and his horse would take fright with the herd as he had been doing in practice and he himself would run at the head of the herd right on into the pen and keep them circling after he was inside; this would be dangerous for Romaldo for if the cutter failed on his job and the pen became overcrowded or Romaldo's horse should stumble at any time, he would certainly be trampled to death. But if his plan went well, fewer of the horses penned would injure themselves.

The men took their stands and waited. For a while there seemed to be a complete stillness over the landscape. The riders became restless with the suspense as they waited for the advance men to reach their places. Sweat trickled down their necks and legs. They muttered soft curses as they swatted gnats away from their ears and eyes, and horses stomped and switched impatiently at flies. Then suddenly horses braced themselves, their ears pricked stiffly forward, riders tensed in their stirrups and their pulses began to throb with the pounding, thundering hoofbeats of the wild horses in sudden full flight. The excitement produced was almost suffocating as the thunder mounted from a dull roar to a deafening avalanche of sound. Then came the sight of them, heads high, necks arched, long tails and manes flying like flags of beauty and defiance.

163

Romaldo had kept his promise. He had picked a fine herd indeed, but in the run had accumulated more than the pen could possibly hold. It was plain that Alfonso and Andrés had their dangerous cutting job to do at the gate. They did it well, but some of the finest specimens were those cut back and the most exciting events of the catch those entirely unplanned. All riders had been mounted as lightly as possible, leaving off even hats and jackets, with girths tight and stirrups short, giving horses and riders every advantage possible in the race with the mustangs. Tomás, weighing less than a hundred pounds, rode on a saddle that was simply a sheepskin held by a sursingle to which were attached two brass stirrups. As the mustangs cut back at the gate turned and raced madly up the wings, Tomás spotted a sorrel with a golden mane, too fine a prize to lose. He raced out alongside the sorrel, crowding it against the others making their escape, and in a stunt that Range and Bryson witnessed close at hand and in complete astonishment, grabbed the sorrel's mane and seemed to slip with all ease and grace from his sheepskin saddle onto the back of the wild horse. He carried with him a hair rope about twelve feet long. The sorrel crashed into the brush of the wing and scurried through like a huge rabbit with Tomás glued to his back. Range and Bryson looked at each other with the same thought: that it was quite possible they'd never see the horse or Tomás again. At the same time Angus was putting on another unrehearsed spectacle. He too had spied a cutback too good to lose, a black filly of such gloss and spirit as to challenge any man's rope. And Angus, like Tomás, was prepared for his own brand of horse catching. He had ridden bareback in the chase with the end of his lariat tied in a horse knot about the neck of his mount so that any strain would not cut off its wind. It was no trick for Angus to get his loop over the mustang filly's head; the ordeal of muscle and rope would come after a race of perhaps several miles with Angus keeping his horse close to the side of his captive and with his own strength on the rope gradually choking off the wind of the horse. When the horse was down, he'd drop off and hobble him; then loosen the lasso until the horse got its breath, likely fixing the rope around the under jaw, Indian fashion, and after a while breaking down the desperate, plunging animal until it could actually be led or ridden into camp. Range and Bryson saw Angus disappear as a second punctuation to the disorder of fleeing mustangs, then turned their attention to the pen where Romaldo was still circling the mustangs within the enclosure and slowing them down somewhat. His horse was wet and winded and he finally gave the signal to Alfonso to open the bars and let him back through. With Alfonso lowering and raising the bars at exactly the right moment while Andrés used the blanket in the execution of a dance with the adroitness of a bull-fighter in order to keep the mustangs frightened away from the gap, Romaldo made his escape. His part of the job was finished and no one would deny his right to well-earned food and rest while the others got at the hard labor of roping and sidelining. Nor was any-one critical of the open vanity of his expression, showing clearly through the sweat on his face, as he rode by his companions gath-ered at the gate and on toward the coffee and dulce he would de-mand of Wong.

There were a few more than a hundred horses in the pen and around sixty-five or seventy of them were good horses that would be well worth driving to market, and perhaps twenty others were worth breaking and keeping in the camp's remuda. It was hard work, dangerous, muscle straining and back breaking, roping the mustangs, one by one, dragging them out through a side gap pre-pared for that purpose, and sidelining each one by tying a foreleg to a hind leg on the same side and allowing the animal about a twelve-inch step. Well-soaked rawhide in strips about two inches wide was use for the sidelining with the hair side placed next to the pastern. Not a single one penned failed to put up a fierce and exhausting fight. Several were so badly bruised and injured that Range ordered them shot.

It was Alfonso and his sons who would see that the horses were watered and grazed and gradually gentled enough to drive footloose and to bear a rider.

Everyone was much too tired for campside talk that night; everyone except Range, who was wakeful with a glow of energy that would not subside. There had been a small fire for coffee and he sat hunched over the coals with the red glow of them on his face, mapping his future with swift strong strokes of mental imagery. Silver Bryson, tired to the bone, watched him. Here were the beginnings of a surge of some kind of primitive genius and the older man felt pricked with a desire to observe close up the potent drama of life that would be generated by the pulsations of mind and thrust of will that belonged to Range Templeton. Events of the past that had warped Bryson's nature, wrapping it in cynicism and indifference, seemed to recede and loosen their hold on him, leaving his mind free to attach itself in a sort of selfish wonderment and curiosity to the analysis of his young partner. As he studied Range, he realized that the loyalty he could give to their friendship would be more of a gesture to fate than a response to sentiment; but he resolved to give it, permanently and without reservation, and to include in his dedication all family and properties of Range Templeton. Such a pledge, though known only to himself, would give purpose to living, something he had not possessed in a long time. And it had the stimulus of a gamble, with the rest of his life as the stake (not that his life was any great stack of blue chips he reminded himself cynically), and the winnings, whatever they were, most likely falling to Templeton. He felt excited about his decision and philosophically considered that his emotions might be akin to those ascribed by poets and playwrights to legendary figures who make bargains with the devil only to discover the anguish of losing their souls. Well, at least, his bargain was of his own making, unsolicited and unacknowledged. In the embers' reflections, he studied the face before him in an effort to determine if he'd made his pact with good or evil. Range sensed Bryson's attention.

"It's not the work, it's the waitin' that's hard," he said.

"Waiting on what?"

"Waitin' on my children to be born . . . waitin' on the time I can get my own land under me, all mine as far as I can see or walk or ride between sunup and sundown . . . waitin' for men to sleep . . . waitin' for daybreak . . ."

"Waiting for God-knows-what," Bryson added his own thought. "But I know what."

"I see. Then you won't have to bother about what God knows."

"God's got nothing to do with it. . . . A man knows where he's going, God or no God."

Bryson put down an impulse to chuckle as an older man does at youth and arrogance. "And man most generally makes a fool of himself as he goes . . . wherever he's going."

Range was silent again, Bryson's sarcasm having little effect on his line of thought. He knew himself as no longer young and certainly not a fool. And Bryson, continuing to watch Range, so immobile and yet so vibrant with thoughts of action, wondered if he himself might not be more especially the fool in underestimating the power of the man's will. How could this man who had not yet rounded out a score of years in the game of life be so sure he was not destined for an Indian's arrow or an outlaw's bullet? Why did he consider himself so exempt from disease and danger that he need not doubt his ability to accomplish what he set out to do? How could he be certain that betrayals and defeats would not overwhelm him? How much actual power resided in the maximum exertion of a man's independent will? Could it control the events of his life to such an extent that God, or at least something like a higher order or influence, could be ruled out? Could Range Templeton twenty years from now, or even ten, repeat with assurance, "A man knows where he's going, God or no God?" If it was in the cards, Bryson concluded wryly, for him to live long enough, he'd watch Range Templeton and find out. . . . Bold endeavors to shape life to one's own will were, in Bryson's opinion, no more than exercises in futility.

167

"Things happen in life that a man can't possibly be prepared for or know how to meet," Bryson said aloud.

"Like catching Indians in a horse corral?" Range asked with an aptness that took Bryson by surprise. Range had planned the penning of the Indians, an experience for which he was certainly unprepared, and it had been successful to the last dead Indian.

He could be laughing at me, Bryson thought, or he could have missed the depth of my meaning; anyway, he has an uncanny skill for crippling my philosophical thoughts with deadly practicality; we'll get along better if I never try to discuss the abstract with him.

"Tomás brought back a good horse," Range said finally.

"Yes," Bryson agreed, "and so did Angus."

"Angus choked his down. The way Tomás did it is better."

"Prettier anyway, and the horse was in much better shape when he brought it in. But Tomás is a rare specimen of mustanger. For that stunt there has to be a certain fleetness of limb as well as a body of light weight, and a nature sensitive to wild creatures, especially horses."

"I'll teach my boy to catch 'em that way while he's still young and lightweight."

"Would you teach a girl the same way?" Bryson inquired mildly.

"A girl?" Range looked up at Bryson in surprise. It was plain he hadn't given much thought to a girl. As he did so, the lines around his mouth relaxed, his eyes shuttered slightly, and for a moment there was an image before him of a small blond girl, duplicate of Luvisa, swinging lightly from the back of one horse onto another, and he mocked himself gently for the idea, "That would be something, wouldn't it?"

Horses and cattle were collected at last. The work had been hot and cruel. Men and mounts were fagged. There had been no casualties, only scratches and bruises and a painful sprain or two. Indian camps and trails, hardly cold, had been spotted time and again, but with unbroken luck the drivers went about their work unchallenged. On one of their far rides they came upon a small herd of amazingly gentle cattle, and in the herd was a milk cow with a small calf. No comments were made as to the docility of the animals. Flaco drove them into camp, took pains to run the milk cow by Wong, and accepted the hot milk Wong prepared for him at the end of the day as the others accepted coffee; no one observed aloud that he was not drinking coffee like the rest.

The horses were held on the far side of the river, a herd numbering a hundred and ten choice animals, well gentled and trained under Alfonso's direction. Alfonso would be in charge of driving the horses when the trek to market was begun and it was understood that he would keep well ahead of the cattle. The horses naturally moved faster than the cattle and it was Alfonso's plan to graze them well, keeping them broken in and conditioned to bring a good price. Although the average mustang would bring no more than five or ten dollars, Range and Silver planned to sell most of their string at around fifty dollars and none less than twenty-five for they had been carefully picked and handled with unusual care. They counted on selling many of the horses to planters in East Texas and Louisiana before they got to New Orleans. If they could pay all expenses of the drive with the horses and have the cattle money clear, the venture would be successful.

The cattle collected for the drive, numbering around six hundred, had not been taken across the Nueces but were being held on the south bank. There had been several weeks of very dry weather. Men had worked in clouds of dust until nerves and throats were raw. Back in Old San Patricio on the banks of the Nueces, Wong had broken out more supplies and after the first meal that hadn't been taken on the run in many weeks, all hands settled down to eat their fill and take a long night's rest. At least two full days of rest were in order before taking up the trail for the long drive to New Orleans.

Cattle were bedded down and all hands in the deepest sleep since leaving San Antonio. Range, with Wong as his assistant, had insisted on keeping the night watch while all others slept. There

169

were flashes of sheet lightning low in the north and west visible as soon as darkness set in, but the occasional blinks, far distant and lacking in brilliance, seemed to hold no threat. Clouds in that direction for several days and a slight rise in the river had indicated rains on the upper Nueces lately, and Range planned to get the herd across the next day to avoid any delay because of high water. Hard work and fatigue, and unusual good luck in gathering the horses and cattle, had dulled cautions. And Range was yet to learn the deceptions of Texas clouds and rivers.

The river rose that night quietly, before either Range or Wong became aware of the murmur and the rush. The night was much too dark for a hasty crossing, and this possibility was further ruled out when the clouds began to roll in on great accumulated crescendos of thunder and the sheets of lightning, now zigzagged with blue streaks of violence, took possession of the skies.

The riders, sleeping outside, hastily piled bedding and supplies in the cabins, and were ready to help Range and Wong hold the cattle before the storm reached its peak. Across the river, Alfonso with his two sons, his nephew, and Tomás, had sensed the coming storm in time to take every precaution for holding the horses properly.

As the storm roared, the river swelled, and it seemed the abundance of water in the clouds would never be exhausted. The cattle after stirring uneasily for a while became resigned and easy to hold. As the storm broke away, Range divided the men into two shifts, he and Wong returning with the ones who were to breakfast first. Then, just as the light began to spread slowly in the east, it happened: the long trail of luck came abruptly to an end, and, in a sudden explosion of events more surprising than the cloudburst, the attack came. El Gavilán, the Mexican hawk, was stampeding the herd.

On this dawn raid there were eight riders at El Gavilán's heels, and by his side an El-Gavilán-in-miniature, a smaller leader on a smaller horse that might have been taken for a shadow at a first quick glance. For El Gavilán's son rode with him. The raiders came in with shots and yells and strange harsh noises made with metal on metal — sounds best calculated to frighten the cattle out of all control.

Flaco's first thought was simply a verification of his convictions that for some time now good luck had been too long with them; it was his credo that too much good luck was a bad thing. Here was more proof. It didn't occur to him that El Gavilán might have been friendly to the owner of the gentle herd he had rounded up with the wild cattle and of the milk cow whose products had rested so gently in his stomach the last week or so.

Silver, who had stayed with the herd, reasoned: The war is still on. They're probably more interested in killing us than taking the cattle. What a damnably weird time for attack! Demons spewed out of a departing storm. Then like a demon himself, Bryson spurred his horse into the dimly lighted stampede and gun battle.

El Gavilán was in for a surprise too. He had expected all riders to be with the cattle. The other shift, just departed and led by Range, came back in on the side where Gavilán had attacked. The cattle, completely out of control, moved in a mad swirl and shove toward the river. There was no order to the battle. Each man conducted his own skirmish on the basis of keeping out of the way of the cattle, spotting an enemy rider and shooting before getting shot.

A favorite grazing ground for the cattle had been a wide strip of river-bottom grass that reached some distance back from the river to a high cliff worn out by an ancient flow of the river before it shifted to a softer bed. Only when the river was at flood stage, possibly once in ten years, did the water reach out to the rock cliff and up its walls. A few hundred yards upriver from the cliff there was easy access to the river-bottom pasture. It was not unnatural for the cattle to flee toward their grazing grounds, but their direction was marked more by terror than instinct and fully half the herd instead of following their regular course headed directly toward the edge of the cliff.

171

Riders were too busy trying to kill raiders to mark the course of the cattle's flight; that is, with one exception, "Barrel" West. "Barrel" had acquired his name because of his chubby torso and short legs. He was not a topnotch rider, but made up for his shortcomings in loyalty and hard work. He realized what might happen to the cattle and was more horrified at the possible loss in hard work and money than at the danger all around him. Then, too, Barrel was mightily homesick for Georgia; when he thought of additional weeks of work in thorns and dust and fear of Indians to gather another herd, he felt sick and mad all over and set his head to turn that herd back from the bluff. Barrel managed to get his horse in front of an outer fringe of the herd, but he had such trouble handling his mount that he was never able to fire his gun in an attempt to frighten the leaders into a turn. All of a sudden, it seemed to him, he was no longer on the edge but in the middle of the run and the crazed cattle were taking him with them over the edge of the cliff and into the rolling river.

The frantic medley of shots and shouts and maddened cattle finally subsided and the murky dawn revealed the muddy aftermath: There were the bodies of dead and dying horses and cattle scattered about . . . five Mexicans in the sprawling postures of the dead . . . Angus sitting in the mud cradling an injured knee and cursing in a monotonous stream of words that substituted for groaning . . . Logan, another of Range's riders, was walking about in a daze, wobbling as he walked, going from one dead Mexican to another, poking each with his foot as if to make sure he was dead. The central figures, however, were two Mexicans very much alive being searched and disarmed by a muttering Cassidy while Range and Flaco made sure there was no resistance. As Silver came up, Cassidy's muttering became coherent for his benefit.

"Sure, now, and it is El Gavilán himself we have here, and also the little bird of prey he has fathered, thanks be to the fine horse that stumbled and delivered them into our hands. It is a pity the rock that met him did not bust his head and do for us the unwhole-

172

some task still to be done . . . but, Mother of Jesus, what's to be done with the little one who has not seen ten summers since he left his mother's breast?"

"You mean he stayed behind when his father tumbled rather than turn back to the brush as the others did?" Silver inquired.

"That he did!"

"You're sure this is the bandit, El Gavilán?"

"As sure as I am of the river roaring out there. He has been to San Patricio before."

Silver addressed an inquiry to the bandit in Spanish but got no more response than if he had spoken English. El Gavilán and the boy, dressed almost exactly alike, maintained a rigid and fearless aloofness, their bravado as similar as their looks and dress. Their eyes seemed to look through their captors to focus on distant places.

El Gavilán's depredations were the most famous on the border. He preferred to prey on the pioneering white man, but was not averse to attacking his own kind if they possessed something he wanted or something he thought for some obscure reason such a person ought not to have. At times his services had been bought, and at other times he had given them freely and unexpectedly to some Mexican family in need. There had been nothing consistent about El Gavilán's career as an outlaw except his violence and boldness and a distorted but picturesque type of courage.

"Get this outlaw's horse," Range instructed Cassidy.

"His horse'll be no good, for a very lame one it is," Cassidy said, looking at the muddy, drooping animal that stood nearby favoring one leg already swollen.

"It won't have to go far, and it'll soon be out of its misery," Range said.

Cassidy got the horse.

Range took his knife from his belt and cut a strand from El Gavilán's riata. He tied the bandit's hands behind him.

"Tell him to get on his horse," Range instructed Silver.

Silver gave El Gavilán the command sharply in Spanish. The

173

Mexican stared at him for an instant, smiled a very small and insolent smile, indicated with his hands tied behind him he could not obey the command, and asked Silver if he'd be so kind as to help him.

Range said, "Wait a minute." He took the scarf from around El Gavilán's neck. "Tell him," he said to Silver, "that this is not to blindfold him — this is to blindfold the horse," and he proceeded to fix it through the bridle in such a fashion that it did blindfold the horse. The horse was too tired and lame to scare.

Silver explained the procedure to El Gavilán and assisted him in mounting.

"The horse thanks him," El Gavilán replied, and asked, "May the boy mount and ride away?"

Silver asked Range what he intended to do with the boy.

"A cub if it lives long enough grows into a full-sized bear," Range said. "But I'll let this one scramble home and tell the big bears on the border what has happened and maybe they'll stay holed up and out of the way for a while. Tell them the boy can go when I give the word, not before."

"It is arranged that the boy in a few moments now will be allowed to leave," Silver translated, "and unharmed," he added.

"Tell the boy to get on his horse, watch what happens, and then beat it," Range ordered.

Silver told El Gavilán, "Have your boy mount and give him any last instructions you would like him to have."

El Gavilán commanded his son, "Mount and draw near."

The boy's movements were swift and effortless as a brush swallow, but his eyes showed fierce and wild as he met the cool, unrevealing gaze of his father.

"I go to meet my father, Death," El Gavilán said, "and thus must leave you fatherless."

The boy tried to protest.

"I am not gone yet, and I am still your father to command you, and you the son who must obey. Is it not so?"

The boy nodded his assent.

"Then watch with two clear eyes until I have embraced the stormy waters there. Raise not a hand, make not a cry. Depart then, with bravado, but do not spread your wings to fly so far or high again until the corn ground on your mother's metate has made you as strong of body as you are of heart. Then you may take the name of El Gavilán, sharpen your claws, and pounce upon these, or any they may breed or bring upon the land. Is that understood?"

The boy nodded again, and swallowed with effort, the only sign he gave of emotions almost bursting the bounds prescribed by his father. The bandit understood and for a moment let his gaze lock with his son's in fond embrace.

Range said, "What's the double talk?"

"Just telling him to keep a stiff upper lip and go home to his mother," Silver translated loosely, feeling no need to speak the threat so implicit in the deed.

Range gazed for a moment down the river, reviewing the loss of the cattle and Barrel West. Then calmly and firmly, he grabbed the bridle of the horse up close to the bits, turned him around, his movements almost gentle and considerate for the lameness of the animal, and slowly, step by step, backed him carefully to the brink of the cliff where, with one quick jerk, he caused the horse to lose his balance and go sprawling over the edge. There was a heavy grunt from the horse as it twisted wildly in an effort to find ground, and then no other sound except the great splash.

El Gavilán had held the eyes of his son in a gaze of passionate concentration until the very moment he toppled out of sight.

The boy was the only one who rode to the brink and watched the finale of the execution. After it was over, he rode up close to Range. "Muchas gracias, señor, por su lección in brutalidad," he said deliberately, with all the violence and hatred he could put into his young voice. He glared at Range long enough to let it be known he was not going to break into tears, then spurred his horse fiercely and raced away.

"Thanks for what?" Range inquired mildly of Silver.

"Thanks for your lesson in brutality, mister." Silver translated literally this time.

CHAPTER IX

THE WORK of replacing the cattle lost through El Gavilán's raid was hard and slow. The herd was still about a hundred short when one of the cow boys, Finius Jones, sighted two Mexicans driving enough cattle to get Range Templeton started to New Orleans. Finius was riding alone, desperate with long months of homesickness, hating the wildness and freedom he had sought when he left his father's plantation in Alabama. His mood was mean and reckless. To get these cattle would mean starting toward the comforts of home. He was well hidden. They'd pass close. He readied his two guns and took careful aim. Damn greasers — probably stole 'em from somebody — he answered a belated prick of his conscience as he fired and the Mexican dropped from the saddle. The second Mexican, an instant before the shot marked for him was fired, sent his horse by a violent thrust of the spurs crashing through the brush to safety. Finius cursed at his miss and immediately got busy turning the cattle toward the Nueces. He was soon joined by Logan and another rider who had heard the shots. The three men hurried the cattle off to the San Patricio camp where the gloom that had hung over the place since El Gavilán's raid was soon dissipated in hurried preparations for departure.

The cattle were crossed and supplies and animals made ready for an early start the following day on the trail toward Goliad. Silver Bryson had carefully mapped the route of the entire drive. Flaco made plans to turn back to San Antonio from Goliad, and Range did not protest; even with the loss of Barrel West, he'd have enough drivers. Silver, with Cicero and Caesar, would go ahead and scout the trail, making decisions on grazing grounds, crossings, and camp sites, seeking out any threats to the safety of horses and cattle. The four Mexicans and Tomás would have charge of the horses, moving faster than the cattle and well ahead of them, stopping here and there along the trail where grazing was good. Range and Cassidy, with the other five drivers, would handle the cattle.

Silver and the two Negroes were out on the trail with the first faint light of dawn and Alfonso started the horses soon afterward. Wong and the supply mules were not far behind; he was to move between the two herds, taking occasional stops to rest and water the animals; he would make no meal stops during the day for the men carried noon rations of dried beef and hard bread in their saddlebags with the ever-present plug of chewing tobacco to quiet appetite and impatience until a better fare was available at the evening campfire.

As the first streaks of red-gold played across a thin cloud structure in the east to preface the sunrise, Little Star, his bell sending forth a jaunty clatter, stepped out proudly into the lead position on the herd, C. Cassidy walking at his side, one hand resting fondly on the mighty shoulder of the ox. Range selected Flaco to ride point with him as far as Goliad. The cattle moved easily, and the men's voices as they strung them out were gentle, as if saving their vocal energies for more strenuous times — and in the gentleness of their voices was a hopeful, singing quality, almost joyous, for it was a facing homeward to some of the men and a release from the long vigilance against Indian and Mexican for all of them.

There was no man and only one animal out of accord with the early and orderly movement out onto the trail: a lanky old bug-eyed steer that Flaco had named Highbones. Brought into the herd with the cattle rounded up by Finius Jones, Highbones had retained leadership over his part of the herd, and as he now moved a little apart and to the right of the main drive, he edged up into a position almost parallel with Little Star, showing his jealous contempt for

177

the sleek, fat lead ox. Flaco predicted Highbones would cause trouble and said they'd better shoot him and be done with it, and Cassidy commented that he'd seen that bony devil look at Little Star like nothing would give him more pleasure than to run a long horn through the chosen leader's heart and twist it out. But Flaco and Cassidy both knew that no one would harm Highbones except in extremity, for his ugliness and arrogance, his temper and strength, commanded a certain respect. His shaggy hide, dull brown in coloring with a scattering of black hair, showed the scars and lumps from many a battle for existence in the thorny realm where he had roamed. His unusually long, lean body, set high on polelike legs, was finished off at one end with a length of tail that just brushed the top of a sand-covered devil's-pincushion, and was crowned at the other end by a set of wrinkled, scaly horns extending straight out from his head about three feet and then turned at a right angle up two feet with a slight curve outward at the very tips. These right-angled horns and his bearing of aggressive self-importance gave him the appearance of continuous alertness and hunger for opposition.

"Watch that old Highbones edge up to point," Flaco called to Range. "Ain't he the most longacious brute you every laid yer eyes on? If it warn't for his horns and hoofs, I'd take him for a cross between some hombre's old chawed up rawhide lariat and a loose pole from a high picket fence. He ain't tactible. He'll git discombobbolated somewheres along the trail and mess things up good. As sure as hell's full of grassburrs, ye'll never git to New Orleans with that one."

When Flaco, on his return to San Antonio, came to visit with Firebush Olson one evening, bringing the first news of Range since his departure for the San Patricio camp, Luvisa stayed close by the men, determined to hear every word of the account. Wary and shy, the old guide departed from his favorite conversational trends of pessimistic forecast and general complaint to present as cheerfully

178

as he could those events he thought a woman should hear. In trying to lighten his account further, he constantly referred to the drivers as "cow boys" and failed to notice Luvisa's small frown of vexation every time he used the term; she did not like to have Range and his men campared even in jest to those reckless Texian raiders who roamed the Rio Grande and beyond rounding up cattle for their own profit without regard to ownership.

He was apologetic about turning back at Goliad. "I'm a thorn and thicket man myself. Them cypress swamps give me the creeps. I don't mind a river crossin' now and then, but I'm naturally turned against mud. Too much sand in my craw, I reckon." He got out his knife and started whittling on the calluses in his hands. "I figgered I'd best git back and give Dawson a hand with that freight to Chihuahua." Luvisa fidgeted. It always worried her to watch Flaco whittle on the rough ridges in his hands as another man would whittle on a stick. Someday, she thought, if his story gets too long or his concentration too intense, he'll be bound to bring the blood. She was relieved when her grandfather spread out an old map of Texas and Louisiana on the dining table and asked Flaco's help in marking the trail Range would likely follow from San Patricio to New Orleans.

"I left 'em here," Flaco's dark-stained fingernail underlined Goliad, "frisky and drippin' with the waters of the Santone River . . . by this time, I reckon the Guadalupe crossin' at Victoria is behind 'em, and they've follered this trail line here on yer map across the Labaca and on into Texana. Now which way they go from there depends on the weather. If it's dry, they'll go this way — if it's wet, this other way."

Their three heads came close together over the map and the candlelight wrought trick shadings into soft gold, fiery red, and shaggy sun-bleached locks. Firebush made careful markings as Flaco explained, "See this road that runs from Texana up north-easterly 'cross Jackson and Colorado counties to San Felipe de Austin on the Brazos? That one's the upper trail, the longest and the driest way to git to Houston. Here's another one that bends off the San Felipe road about twenty miles out of Texana and shoots nearly straight east, crossin' the Colorado and on to Columbia on the Brazos. If the rains hold back, and the swamps and rivers ain't roused up, they kin take this lower trail, cross the Brazos at Columbia, and from there make a beeline to Houston."

"I hope it's the shorter one," Luvisa murmured, and in her heart added fervently: Anything, anything to bring Range back to me sooner!

"Out of Houston, they foller the old trail to the Texas line," Flaco continued, "with crossin's of the Trinity at Liberty and the Neches at Beaumont . . . then they're on the Opelousas Road."

The Opelousas Road was a well-defined line on the map for it was already an established trail for driving cattle from the eastern part of Texas to the New Orleans market. It curved upward somewhat from Beaumont and across to Opelousas, Louisiana, avoiding the swamp and lake areas at the mouths of the Sabine, the Calcasieu, and the Mermentau rivers. From Opelousas, the trail took a sharp downward turn along the Bayou Teche through St. Martinville and New Iberia to Franklin; and there, in the treacherous bay area, it meandered on to Thibodauxville. Firebush Olson commented that he'd heard Thibodauxville was the first trading post established between New Orleans and the Bayou Teche country.

"Don't know much about it, 'cept it's mighty muddy country," Flaco muttered with depressing emphasis as his rough, stubby finger made a scratchy noise moving across the map from Thibodauxville to trail's end at New Orleans. Luvisa's thoughts took a frantic turn: So many rivers and bayous! Swamps, lakes, bays . . . where horses and cattle could flounder in turbulent currents — be swallowed up in bogs . . . Why had Range ever left her for things so fearful and far away? How long the trail and endless the time it would take to traverse it and return to her in San Antonio!

Almost in tears, she jumped up from the table, seized the candle in order to terminate the map study, and hastily invited Flaco to come and see the twins before she put them to sleep for the night. Flaco studied the twins for a long time. They returned his stare with a fixed interest.

"Too bad yer pa ain't standin' here in my tracks," he finally addressed them. "You," he pointed a knotty finger at Luke, "was expected; but you," he said to Laska, "I reckon you'll give him quite a start, and most likely he'll never — " Flaco broke off and looked at Luvisa self-consciously.

"She reminds me, ma'am, of a little kitten I saw once, a little baby wildcat it was, sunnin' itself and starin' at me, soft and cottonish with them flecked eyes that could look straight into the sun without blinkin' — " he paused in embarrassment, afraid he might offend, "beggin' yore pardon, ma'am, it was a dadburn cute kitten — an' different — different from any kitten I seen before or since — yep, it shore was."

Old Flaco's opinion amused rather than offended Luvisa for she had become accustomed to the surprised comment Laska drew from all who saw her for the first time. It was not only that she was so remarkably different from her brother, but also different in her own right. Far from being disturbed by Laska's strangeness, Luvisa was excessively proud.

When her grandfather and the old guide had left her with the babies, Luvisa talked to them to ease her loneliness and yearnings so intensified by listening to Flaco's talk of Range.

"To think old Flaco was so near Daddy just a few days ago — could talk to him — watch him — touch him. O mis queridos, someday Daddy himself will be here to see you — someday — if he has to swim all the rivers in the world! O Madre de Dios! Cuánto me hace falta! Cuánto me hace falta!" It was easier to lament love's anguish in Spanish.

Laska, always the hungrier and more impatient of the two, was fed first. "What are you, my golden one," Luvisa queried lovingly, "some restless little angel from the garden of the sun?" Laska paused in her feeding as if some celestial thought had rested for a moment in her infant mind. With her tiny hand resting on Luvisa's breast, they exchanged a long deep look as if in promise of sweet secrets soon to be shared. Never is one closer to God, Luvisa thought, than when gazing into a baby's eyes.

After her visit with the babies, Luvisa felt calm and ready to hear more details about her young husband's adventures, but she wanted the whole story, with nothing left out or glossed over. There was more to El Gavilán's raid, she felt sure, than simply the killing of the bandit and most of his followers, the loss of Barrel West, and the good work of Finius Jones in helping make up the loss. Flaco had made up his mind about what was right and proper for her to know and wouldn't have much more to say in her presence. But there must be some way . . .

Luvisa slipped into her grandfather's room and from a private cupboard brought out a jug of very old wine reserved for more auspicious occasions than this one. Firebush gave his granddaughter a glance of disapproval but could not very well ask her to take the wine away after she had set it before them. Knowing Flaco's reluctance about eating and drinking because of his ailments, she insisted that he take this rare old wine for his stomach's sake, that she understood it was a regular soothing syrup for such complaints as his. Firebush gave Luvisa a long quizzical look as she expounded the medicinal virtues of his most prized jug, but she avoided his eyes, excused herself, and said good night. By the time she had tucked the babies in for the night, the men were settled down with the wine and uninhibited male conversation was in full bloom. Luvisa settled herself too — on a footstool behind the door she had left slightly ajar — and listened with only the slightest prick of conscience for her eavesdropping plot.

She heard about the penning of the Indians, much as she had dreamed it: how every Indian was killed and all horses and equipment taken, with things happening exactly as Range expected — Indians tired and surprised, their horses waterlogged, and the erection of the pen something they did not know about. Firebush took utter delight in the gruesome event and had Flaco repeat certain parts of it time and again, roaring with laughter, assuring his visitor that such a yarn was worth several more jugs of his best wine. As Luvisa heard too the story of El Gavilán's execution, she knew with a stab of certainty that the "little hawk" would live to seek revenge for his father's execution.

As the men talked on, and she heard of Finius Jones's killing the Mexican, she kept wanting to know for sure if the cattle taken were wild stock or belonged to the Mexicans. Perhaps the Mexican killed was one of El Gavilán's raiders. Range could not know the circumstances, she reasoned, determined to believe her husband would not deal in stolen stock. Why was she splitting such hairs with her woman's worries anyway, she wondered peevishly, when by any measurement of the times a man had the right to take what he could find in that part of the country where the difference between taking and stealing was often no more than a point of view.

She left her place of listening when she was sure Flaco's news was spun out. It did not improve her humor to hear him toasting, as they drained the jug:

> Here's to cow boys
> An' ther keerless ways!

and Firebush adding:

> They'll ride herd on Texas
> One o' these days!

Good weather prevailed, and without losses or delays Range checked off Goliad, Victoria, and Texana on his drive. Out of Texana he turned off the San Felipe trail to attempt the lower crossings on the Colorado and Brazos; and when these were successfully completed, spirits soared high, for several days had been gained by the short cut through Columbia. Through the lush plantation area of Brazoria County, Range and Bryson chose to ride together ahead of the herds; the routine of the drive had been set and the two Negroes were sent back to ride with the cattle a few days. In

Columbia, Range and Bryson had heard that at the plantation of Victor Chenet they'd probably find beef cattle ready to market and Chenet glad to make a trade. They planned to make camp that evening in the vicinity of the Chenet plantation. They inquired of cotton pickers and learned when they were nearing the plantation headquarters. The field and the number of slaves were not large but the acreage was exceedingly well kept. There were several cornfields and some cane. When they rode in sight of the house, it presented a picturesque and alien look. It was neither pretentious nor of crude pioneer structure and it denied close kinship with Spanish or Southern architecture. Its lines were simple and inviting, its atmosphere distinctly French. A man stood at ease on the porch watching them approach. As they rode in closer, Silver observed that he was a Negro, rather light in coloring, an overseer of some kind, he surmised, noting the neat appearance and careful dress. They rode down the carriage drive and stopped close to the steps but did not dismount.

The Negro said "Good day" in a courteous tone.

"Is your master, Mr. Chenet, at home?" Silver inquired.

There was a pause. The Negro studied the two men in a manner they both resented. Just as Silver's lips tightened in impatience, the Negro spoke. "Gentlemen, I am Victor Chenet."

Range's eyes darkened and his body tightened as it always did in surprise and caution. Silver tried hard to hide his reaction to the introduction, his instinctive realizations: "The man is no Frenchman — he is a Negro — a free Negro — from New Orleans perhaps, maybe educated in France. Bryson's face took on a drawn look, his mouth outlined in white, his thought: A Negro owning slaves. What more of contrast and incredibility can be found in this land? . . . I'll accept him as a Frenchman if he can stand the test, if he's willing to compromise his identity. . . . Can I fool Range? I hope I can or this meeting will be bad business for us all.

"J'offre mes regrets, Monsieur Chenet," Silver Bryson's phrase of apology was soft-spoken and amiable.

"Ce n'est rien. Une faute naturelle," Chenet's French came as

184

easily and softly as Bryson's. "A natural mistake," he repeated for Range's benefit. "You gentlemen have been long on the trail, no doubt. Dismount and let me offer refreshment."

"We heard you had cattle ready for market," Range said, still sitting firm in the saddle.

"Hospitality before business is my way, Mr. . . ." Chenet smiled with charming courtesy and raised his eyebrows in inquiry.

"Templeton," Range answered shortly.

"And my name is Bryson," Silver added.

"Mr. Templeton, Mr. Bryson, I am delighted to meet you." Chenet almost bowed. Bryson noticed an expression of amusement in Chenet's eyes, shaded slightly with malice, he thought, but couldn't be sure. He'll play this carefully, and his way, Bryson figured to himself. He knows I'm a Southerner and he knows I know he is a Negro. But he cannot know the strange mixture of tolerance and prejudice in me, nor why this situation is so especially ironic for me. He cannot know that for me, too, it presents a bitter form of amusement, for I cannot predict from one moment to the next what compromises my emotions will allow me to make. Can I be his guest, do business with him, without betraying some part of myself? And yet, if I refuse, the old grief and passion will uncoil and sting and poison me again.

Silver Bryson dismounted even as he thought these things and Range followed his lead. They went up the steps onto the cool veranda. A Negro servant, much darker than Victor Chenet, opened the door and led the men to a parlor room on their left, a room rather small and formal, dominated by a beautiful marble mantle-piece; there were a few objects of art, obviously French imports, a crystal chandelier, and furnishings of fine polished wood in a simple French provincial style. The room had a pleasant and sooth-ing effect with large windows overlooking well-kept gardens and softening the formality of the interior arrangement. Chenet indicated chairs, certainly not designed for such men as Range Templeton un-less to put them at a disadvantage. Range sat awkwardly as if he

185

expected the chair to collapse under him. But Silver was at no disadvantage with the surroundings. He was chiefly concerned with the next inevitable gesture, for the servant had gone for drinks. Would he drink with Chenet? What could it matter? And yet there was a tight feeling like a hard ball in his chest and an unnatural heat rising in his face. As he exchanged a few remarks with Chenet on the herd he and Range were driving, he was telling himself that all men are fools and all men slaves to the tentacles of environment, to the emotional sets of childhood, but be damned if he'd drink with a Negro, especially a mixed one, which species he especially despised. He hoped Range was unaware of his agony, mounting every moment. He hoped the heat under his skin did not show in red splotches. Chenet was watching, Chenet was suspecting; but he could never know the full equation of the tension building up in Silver Bryson. Two servants came with the tray of drinks. There was French coffee in a tall, graceful china pot and brandy in a heavy crystal bottle. Chenet nodded and Bryson was served first. He took the delicate china cup with its mixture of coffee and brandy and was surprised at the steadiness of his hand. Range accepted the little cup and its contents with a certain disdain, having decided not to be intimidated by the formalities; then he supported the cup and saucer on his crossed knees, sensing some strain in the procedure, waiting. As the serving man turned to Chenet, he was dismissed with an unflung arm. Silver didn't miss the question in the servant's eyes as he turned abruptly and left the room without serving his master. Chenet smiled genially, held the suspense for a moment longer as if he savored it.

"Drink, gentlemen," he said, "and forgive me for abstaining — a slight indisposition of the heart." He made an apologetic gesture to the region of the offending organ. "I am limited to my morning cup and evening glass."

Silver felt weakness possess him. With a hand now obviously unsteady he took the cup to his lips and drank. He felt surrounded with a sort of haze and yet he could see the brightness of Chenet's

186

eyes. The man has bested me, he thought. He knows it. He found the solution, not I, and by finding it has made himself stronger than I.

Silver let his weakness draw him further downward. I wish I were dead, Châli, he allowed himself to wish as fervently as a distraught child. Oh, Châli, my dear, why am I alive? His emotions strained against the barriers that held back forbidden memories, and resistance collapsed. His beloved, vivid Châli Le Roi was before him — true love in her eyes — sweet fire on her lips. And this lovely creature was his betrothed — this peerless daughter of a French merchant — this beauty born of a beauty — the matchless Le Roi women, mother and daughter. "Raise your glasses high, gentlemen of Norfolk, in a toast to the incomparably lovely Le Roi ladies!" . . . The picture blurred for Bryson, and an evil mulatto face was there . . . the greedy mulatto uncle . . . the cursed mulatto uncle of the Le Roi women, his malignant shadow dissolving their life and beauty . . . not French ladies any more . . . quadroon and octoroon. . . . Dear God, what difference could it make! His heart cried out in renewed desolation: Châli was simply forever my blessed Châli . . . but not vivid any more — still and cold — bright eyes closed — red lips paled — warm breath still — dark tresses tangled in the deep water. O God, take my reason! O Châli, come back!

Bryson took his plunge into despair in a few seconds as one dreams a long sequence of events in a mere snatch of time, and the acute pain of it as he struck the jagged depths brought a shock that jerked him suddenly back to the present. He was amazed that after all these years he could be caught off guard enough to release the lock on that compartment of his mind so long sealed against conscious thought. He felt the mixture of strong coffee and stronger brandy supporting his effort to grasp firmly only the present moment. The haze cleared before his eyes. He looked directly at Chenet.

"To pass up good French coffee and brandy requires a measure of self-control that draws my admiration along with my sympathy for your denial," he complimented Chenet with careful formality.

"When he is very sure of certain things, a man takes those actions which may prolong his life, or at least make the portion allotted to him less painful," Chenet countered.

A long look passed between the two and Silver thought: Now I must do business with this man. He has cornered me and somehow squeezed the foolishness out of my senses.

Range watched the play between the two men and waited; he thought the man Chenet must surely be a Negro, but he'd never known a Frenchman and decided to let Bryson resolve the whole strange situation.

"These cattle you have ready for market . . ." Bryson began. "We have enough drivers to take on an additional herd. We're prepared to make partial payment if your prices are right, the remainder paid on our return trip."

"In these times of financial strain in our country a man is safer to stick to the barter form of trade," Chenet replied.

"We carry hard money," Range said, "enough for a sizable token."

"Then you're most unusual men," Chenet said, "and doubtless due to prosper. It's an easy matter to choke any kind of business to death these days with our confusing multiplicity of paper currencies and speculation land scrips. But I'm getting so accustomed to the barter system that I find in most instances I prefer it. Right now you could offer me barter more attractive by far than gold or silver. I need slaves, twenty or more. It is impossible for me to leave my plantation at this time to make such a purchase. . . ."

Impossible for you to leave it at any time on such a mission, Silver thought. You'd get put on the block yourself if you showed up in the New Orleans market place.

Chenet continued, "I'm just discovering the richness of my land. I want to grow more cotton and cane . . . cane is my big dream here . . . cane and a sugar industry . . . this is the land for it . . . and perhaps some rice too . . . but I must have labor."

"We're not in the slave business," Range said. "Cattle, just cattle,

188

that's our business with you. Can we see what you got and talk numbers and prices?"

"Surely, surely." Chenet was agreeable. "I have some three-year-olds and some five-year-olds. They'll top the market. You came at exactly the right time, gentlemen." He turned to the servant who had returned and stood, quiet and stiff, in the hallway. "My horse."

Chenet's steers were large and fat; he had 600 head ready for market, and 200 were three-year-olds; the others were fives and would doubtless bring thirty dollars on the New Orleans market. Chenet wanted ten dollars a head for the threes, and fifteen dollars a head for the fives. It was a good price; Range and Bryson could double their money if they could get the herd through to New Orleans without losses. They agreed they could handle the whole six hundred and the price suited them. Chenet explained it would take several days to round up the steers ready for the trail. Then they were back on the subject of payment.

"How much down?" Range asked.

"Nothing down. As I said, in the beginning, barter is the form of exchange I prefer. In this instance, it is the only way I will trade. I realize you are unfavorable to my proposition. But hear me through. I accept your refusal to take the cattle now and promise to bring back slaves. But do not close your mind to certain facts regarding the traffic in slaves. You know, I am sure, that likely blacks sell in these parts at prices ranging from five hundred to a thousand dollars, and this is not an unreasonable figure when in one good season with favorable weather a good working hand can pay for himself in the amount of cotton raised and picked. However, you probably have not had occasion to learn, as I have, that dealers in smuggled slaves along the Louisiana coast buy them for around $140, and Lafitte sells sound and likely blacks at a dollar a pound. All right, let us suppose that en route to New Orleans you come upon such traffic and are able to purchase some twenty or so. I will not inquire as to the prices you pay but will give you outright

189

five hundred dollars each for such as you can bring me in good condition — preferably males for the field, but a full-grown female or two would not be refused at the same price. I will then turn over to you my six hundred steers for seven thousand dollars and will pay you in cash the difference of three thousand or more . . . I could not handle more than twenty-five."

"And you could double that three thousand by selling about half a dozen good field hands to your neighbors at a thousand apiece," Silver added.

"That's one way of coming out," Chenet admitted. "But as I told you, I have dreams for my land, and only labor can make them come true. I want labor now much worse than I want money. As for making money, I am offering you the chance to make a small fortune in a few weeks time. Bring me the slaves; you'll make seven thousand dollars profit there. Then drive my cattle to New Orleans; there you'll get double the price you pay me for them — that's another seven thousand. Your herd, although they won't sell like my steers, should bring you around nine, maybe ten, thousand dollars. And you say you expect the sale of your horses to carry the expenses of the drive. With twenty or twenty-five thousand in cash, Mr. Templeton, you and your partner here will be able to set up a small kingdom in this southwestern Republic."

"It sounds good the way you tell it, Mr. Chenet. But like I said back there at the house, we're not in the slavery business. My folks back in Tennessee was always too poor to own any and I never learned their ways. I want to own land and stock but not my help — I'll hire them. If I don't like a man or his work, I want to fire him and get him out of my sight. When you fall out with a slave, you either got to sell him or beat him. That's not my way."

"Your philosophy is fitting for the frontiers of our republic, Mr. Templeton, but here in the eastern part of Texas the type of economy we are creating will be dependent on a stable and continuous labor supply. You can hire adventurers, even outlaws sometimes, to do your cattle work in season; but adventurers do not pick cotton and care for sugar cane. . . . We are straying from our argument. I am not asking you to buy slaves for yourself; own them only for the duration of a three-week journey, then exchange them for my cattle and cash. How do you view such a matter, Mr. Bryson?"

"I guess we're wasting your time, Mr. Chenet. Mr. Templeton's sentiments prevail in this partnership. It is possible that if we happened on a trade such as you describe, we would consider it; but since we will not be seeking it out, such an eventuality seems extremely unlikely. I am no abolitionist, but when I left the South, I fled to be free from being a master as the Negro flees to escape slavery. The black man came nearer owning me than I him. I do well enough to carry the burden of my own life. I do not care to sell myself into bondage again even for a few weeks."

Chenet looked hard at Bryson and then burst into laughter, genuine hearty laughter. "I have known slaves who escaped to freedom but you are the first escaped master I have ever laid eyes on." He laughed some more. "God save the Republic of Texas, sanctuary to misfits! Whatever we evolve in this land, we are most certainly destined to be different. . . . No offense intended by my offer, or my comments, gentlemen. A trade in which both sides stand to profit is not often quickly consummated. This one may yet be worked out. But I see you are impatient to be off. Good day, and good crossings. Watch the Neches. She's tricky. I hear you can hire extra hands there to help with the crossing for three dollars."

Bryson and Range thanked him and turned their horses to depart.

"Au revoir," Chenet called.

"Jusqu' au revoir," Bryson answered.

"So he's a Frenchman," Range said wryly as they rode away.

"Yes indeed, a different kind of Frenchman," Bryson said.

The Chenet house was the last scene of luxury and comfort Range and Bryson were to contact on the Texas side of the Sabine. The drive proceeded under clear skies with weather mild and unusually dry. The Houston gambling houses were passed without the loosening of a single money belt. This lusty, dirty boom town, sprawling in the noonday sun, momentarily quiet and harmless as a sleeping tramp dreaming of riches and fine robes, did not present an exciting appearance to the trail drivers with glamorous New Orleans as their goal. Then, too, it was understood that the supplies taken on there would include a reasonable amount of good liquor and that a few rounds of drink and card games in the evening would make up for the spree a man should allow himself before passing Houston by. As the dangers and hardships experienced on the Nueces River were left farther and farther behind and the crossing of the Sabine that would mark their entrance into Louisiana became an anticipation for the near future, the men became more relaxed and lighthearted. If Flaco had been along, he would have been uneasy because things were going so well.

When they actually approached this eastern border river of the Republic of Texas, there was no reason for trouble of any kind. The afternoon sun was bright and cheerful and shed enough warmth to make the calm river waters almost inviting, and certainly not formidable. It hardly seemed necessary to hire the extra hands that were available. The ones hired at the Neches crossing had been helpful but not actually needed; Range and Silver had been able to sell some of their horses around Houston, Liberty, and Beaumont, and had thus reduced the herd enough that Romaldo and Tomás could turn back after crossing the horses and help with the cattle. But as a precaution and a sort of forced courtesy, extra help was hired again at the Sabine. The seven men, two of them Negroes, who appeared at the crossing as if they'd been sent for, gave the appearance of really needing the three dollars that was their fee, and their eagerness to be hired was so pronounced it held something of a threat. They were a shaggy-looking crew, the two Negroes on skinny mules and the other riders on horses that were sad-looking mounts when compared with the good horses Range's men rode and drove. Silver and Range were convinced that if the didn't hire these men, they'd have more than twenty-one dollars' worth of trouble. So the services of the strangers were accepted, and they promptly showed the best places for taking the herd in.

Little Star slid off the riverbank and into the Sabine with the confidence of a rhinoceros entering his favorite pool and led out of the water in the tracks of the horses that had been crossed a few hours earlier. But his usual placidity was shaken when a water bird, crippled and unable to wing out of the way, flopped up out of the reeds and struck him in the face. He swung abruptly to the left and into a bog. Before a rider could cut in, Little Star and nineteen of his followers were bogged to their bellies. Range gave orders to leave them alone until all other cattle were safely crossed. Cassidy, however, was already beside his beloved pet, up to his waist in the mud, pleading alternately with the ox and the Lord to improve the situation, but his entreaties seemed not to get through to either one. So he pulled a bottle out of the inside pocket of his jacket — the contents reserved for "the sick, the sacred, and the dying" — grabbed the docile ox by the nose, elevated his head, thrust the bottle down his throat and emptied it before the surprised animal could resist. Then he untied a long whip from around his waist, raised it over his head and started a stream of invective and command that even an ox could not be insensible to. He punctuated his highly original and forceful language with sharp cracks and pops from his whip. Little Star began to struggle and roll and push — and slowly, by dragging inches, got nearer higher ground. But an unexpected development added to the difficulties. On the edge of the bog, his long legs planted like pillars, shaking his head as if his horns were itching to jab, swishing his long tail occasionally like a waiting cat, stood Highbones, his bug-eyes gleaming malevolently. The sweating Irishman paused to view the new danger.

"Ye dirty demon of the thorn patches! Ye long-livered old beast of the bad-lands — " He paused for breath. For the moment he was deserted in his dilemma, slightly screened from the main drive as the men pushed the herd on across. Then Tomás appeared through

193

the high reeds and Cassidy yelled at him to push the steer back into the herd. Highbones ignored the Indian boy and his efforts to draw attention away from Little Star. Tomás felt his dignity outraged. He had always imagined himself a bullfighter in a grand arena. Caramba! This was a chance to test the grand flourishes and movements he had practiced alone with nothing more challenging than a mission sheep or goat in front of him. He slid from his pony and slipped his poncho from over his head; on the wrong side it was a bright unfaded red; it would serve him well as a capote. He began to tease Highbones, but the stubborn steer continued to give his undivided attention to Little Star. Tomás became furious. He jerked his knife from his belt and threw it skillfully, planting it at a tender spot in the steer's shoulder . . . Highbones turned and lunged. Tomás tipped the steer's nose with his poncho and stepped aside. Madre de Dios! This was living! He screeched his exuberance. Highbones turned and with more carefulness attacked again. Tomás's escape was not so clean this time. He was thrown slightly off balance and stepped into the bog. Highbones followed. By this time several drivers had come over and were calling encouragement to Tomás while they guffawed at Highbones's ludicrous appearance, his long legs held to a harmless pace in the mud. Tomás struggled to the edge of the slough and then danced a mad dance before Highbones. The steer carefully pulled first one long leg and then the other up and out until he reached a firm position from which to attack his tormenter again. Tomás backed off, waving his poncho in invitation, placing one foot far behind the other in an effort to show special grace before his audience. His vanity proved his undoing for as he leaned back unnaturally far, his foot slipped and he fell sprawling. He saw Highbones nearly on top of him, rolled over in a flashlike movement and ran for his life, the men's laughter shrieking behind him. He leaped at a loose heavy grapevine, and swung out of the way of Highbones, at the same time climbing like a monkey. Highbones slid to a stop, turned and tangled a horn around the vine and shook it furiously. Tomás fell out, land-

194

ing squarely on Highbones's rail-like back. His mustanging experience, much more valid than his bullfighting, served him well. After several wild leaps and lunges, Highbones suddenly unfolded and stretched out, heading for the timber, Tomás still aboard. As he dived under the low limb of a big cypress, Tomás deftly lifted himself to safety, bringing his knife with him. This last was a gesture of triumph and the riders cheered him as he jumped to the ground and held the knife above his head to show them. Long streamers of Spanish moss from the cypress tree had caught in his heavy black hair and he wore them as a garland of victory, loving the cheers and laughter he had aroused, feeling more hero than clown. Distant crashes of brush announced the permanent departure of Highbones.

One of the Negro hired hands interrupted his whooping laughter to remark, "Ole bug-eyes sho' nuff done absquatulated."

One of the other strangers, wiping his face with a sleeve said, "Ain't shed so many fun tears since I saw a hog and alligator fight. Boy," he called to Tomás, "you're a little ole ring-tailed tooter even effen you ain't altogether a bullfighter."

"Shore, and why should he be?" another added, "since that old horny he was matched up with warn't altogether a bull!"

With fresh bellows of laughter and whoops of glee, the men turned their attention to Cassidy's renewal of whip popping, swearing, and shoving, and with further rough humor assisted him and Little Star to solid ground. Only thirteen head besides the lead ox could be ramroded out of the bog; six cows were too exhausted to make further efforts. Range considered shooting them.

"Don't fret yerself. Most times they git out after restin' awhile," one of the river hands informed him.

Most times you get 'em out and are that much to the good, Range surmised. He had no more concern for the lost cattle. The loss was his first and relatively small. He quickly paid off the seven men. He turned to his own riders who had joined in the rescue work. "We're in Louisiana now. Let's get on to Opelousas." Cassidy and Little Star, both covered with mud, had been standing still as a sculptor's model, heads down, relaxed, resting from their ordeal.

Cassidy roused, "Did ye hear what the man is saying, Little Star? 'On to Opelousas.' And here ye be kivered with slime and shame at the tail end o' the herd ye so proudly led across the Republic o' Texas. Now will you be leadin' or laggin' in Louisiana? Indeed, it's a sorry sight ye are, with even the clapper in y'r bell silent and clogged. But it's the lungs and not the looks that be needed for leadership, so begone with ye. . . ." He punched the ox with the handle of his whip and Little Star started off in a dog-trot to recapture his lead position.

CHAPTER X

THE CAMP on the Calcasieu River was the most pleasant Range had experienced since the Medina River camp on the freight trip with Eli Dawson a year and a half ago. It was the second night in Louisiana, and although they were still in unsettled country and a full two day's journey from Opelousas, the drive was more than two thirds done.

The beauty of the Calcasieu camp was not the same beauty experienced on the Medina. On the Louisiana river, the moonlight seemed to be filtered through a veil; there was a strangeness in the sounds of the night, and a sort of pulsation to the teeming abundance of life in river and woods, indicating that the laws of survival were less restrictive here. And the dry buoyant quality of air that put a certain stamina into all growth along the Texas river was exchanged here for a fragrant moisture-laden quality that brought lushness to growth and a lassitude to movement. Although the cypress tree with its characteristic Spanish moss was not a stranger to the San Antonio area, here in southern Louisiana it grew lustfully in the water as well as on the banks. For Range and his riders the long moss on the trees where they made camp on the Calcasieu was festive trimming for their musical concert. There were only two slightly orthodox instruments in the crowd: a jew's-harp that the rider Logan had kept self-consciously hidden until this occasion and a mouth organ that belonged to Angus and was of recent enough invention to be a curiosity to most of those in the camp. Cassidy's mesquite-wood and bobcat-gut combination which bore a distorted resemblance to a ukelele had been placed in Wong's keeping and carefully packed along with the camp supplies and was brought out for the first time since leaving the Nueces. It was Cassidy who began in the afternoon to organize the band that would perform in the moonlit evening. He helped Cicero and Caesar improvise a drum out of a proper length of hollow log and two pieces of rawhide. He instructed Tomás that he and his Mexican friends should accent the rhythm with gourds and castanets and hard sticks. He showed others how to make fifelike whistles from the hollow reeds on the river. And it was Cassidy who introduced a musical number in which all could participate. It was an hour perhaps after the music had started — Cassidy had done a highly sentimental Irish ballad, Angus and Finius Jones had led out in a long, loud, and lively session with "Bingo," taking the miller's dog through many heretofore unrecorded adventures, and the Mexicans had sung with mournful sweetness of unrequited love — when the word "Calcasieu" began to get musical in Cassidy's head and he started to improvise. Once the tune and pattern of words were established, it was anybody's song who could solo with an additional verse or even an additional line if he beat the other fellow to it. Cassidy's introductory lines were presented with true Irish sentiment.

> *Oh, the day 'tis done*
> *And we banish care,*
> *For the night 'tis soft*
> *As a maiden's hair.*

197

Sure, the moonbeams dance
And our troubles skiddoo
While we make music
On the Calcasieu!
  Sure, they do! Skiddoo! Skiddoo!
  While we make music on the Calcasieu!

And Cicero was inspired to follow.

Raccoon's a-peepin'
From topa dat tree.
Fox am a-watchin'
Still as can be.

Da alligator listens
And da bullfrog too
While we makes music
On da Calcasieu!
  'Deed dey do! Skiddoo! Skiddoo!
  While we makes music on da Calcasieu!

Caesar could not allow Cicero to get ahead of him.

Da willow tree bend
And da long moss sway,
While da cypress whisper —
You kin hear it say:

"My limbs hold da birds,
My roots hide da fishes,
If da owl hoot twice,
You get your wishes.
  'Deed you do! Whoo-oou! Whoo-oou!
  When makin' ya camp on da Calcasieu!"

Others got the feeling for the "Camp on the Calcasieu" and stanza
after stanza was born.

The breeze blows gentle,
There's a sign on the moon . . .

Gettin' mighty lonesome
For my pretty quadroon.

If I had this gal
So fair and true,
I'd camp forever
On the Calcasieu.
   That I'd do! 'Tis true! 'Tis true!
   I'd camp forever on the Calcasieu!

We been a long time
Behind this herd
And we'll get 'em to market —
Give you my word —

We're on the right trail
And we're goin' through
To Opelousas
From the Calcasieu!
   Right on through! Goin' right on through!
   To Opelousas from the Calcasieu!

We're on our way
To New Orleans,
Where women and money
Er thick as beans.

We're gittin' mighty restless
To git on through
And break up this camp
On the Calcasieu!
   Git on through! Skiddoo! Skiddoo!
   And break up this camp on the Calcasieu!

     *   *   *

The town of Opelousas in 1839 was very prosperous, very French, and very pleasing to the senses with its neat brick buildings, its flowering gardens and lawns, its cool streets shaded with heavy boughs of oak and magnolia, and its Latin character of happy living. Its residences, most of them two-story red-brick structures with white Doric columns supporting pediment and portico, gave the town an air of finish and security — qualities as foreign to the Texas riders as the language of the people who lived in these houses. Around the town square, the streets were lined with one- and two-story brick buildings which were the town offices of the French planters in that region, rich in stock and cotton and sugar. It was in several of these offices that Range and Bryson were paid off for the last of their horses.

Bryson's easy flow of French had been of immeasurable benefit in bringing about the sales in a community where English was rarely spoken. The horses had been driven through the town to show off their good points and excellent condition; the five Mexicans had dressed for the occasion as if for a parade, and Alfonso's careful gentling and training of the horses were evident in the way they handled; and though the unusual sights and sounds and scents of town life were highly exciting to the animals, their beauty and spirit were better exhibited because of this stimulation.

The general excitement created among spectators and the snorting and prancing of horses hitched to vehicles and tied to racks around the square made the occasion seem more like an entertainment than a commercial venture. The horses were held for further showing on the outskirts of the town although many of them had been picked and sold as they were driven through. Range and Bryson had been on the town square when the horses passed by, available for inquiries and price-quoting. Range hid his annoyance that the trading must all be carried on in French; he soon learned to read expressions that accompanied such phrases as "Mon Dieu oui," "Mon Dieu non," and "Bon!" and could suggest bargains or compromises on a trade without Bryson translating. A language barrier always awoke some sort of perverseness in Range Templeton; he considered the person who couldn't speak English much more handicapped than he might be in his own lack of comprehension of any other language. It never occurred to him to use, even as a form of courtesy, the few words of Spanish or French that he came to understand in spite of his indifference and resentment. Neither did it occur to him to wish he were like Silver Bryson or Dr. Weideman, accomplished in several languages; he was satisfied with simply being like Range Templeton.

After the sale of the horses in Opelousas, the Mexican mustangers were free to help with the cattle, and the drive through the Bayou Teche country for almost a hundred miles became a leisurely routine with each day's revelations in scenery and prosperous settlement a sort of wonder world of beauty and fertility. At St. Martinville, famous as the "little Paris" for refugee royalty of the French Revolution and now a fashionable resort for steamship travelers, the drivers from Texas frankly stared at the ladies and gentlemen of high fashion and were gazed upon with equal astonishment, the curiosity and amusement thus created being good-naturedly accepted on both sides.

Before arriving at New Iberia, they learned from travelers on the road that a yellow fever epidemic had hit the town; so the cattle were routed well to the west of the town. The news of the epidemic caused an uneasiness among the men, and, as they entered coastal country, actual discomfort added to their feeling of insecurity. There was a continual heavy dampness in the air, cloudiness, fog, and occasional light rain. Clothes and food became moldy, heat kept bodies moist with sweat, and they all yearned for sun and dry wind. Large sticky mosquitoes settled hungrily on bare skin, and there seemed no end to the string of lakes to circle and bayous and marshy lands to cross. They made no stop at the town of Franklin for Range was stepping up the pace of the drive in order to get across the Atchafalaya River as soon as possible; they were now in a treacherous area where they could be wiped out by the floodwaters of this greedy river at any time rainfall became sufficient to start feeding its far-spreading tentacles. They made camp on the banks of a bayou only a few hours drive from the point where they would cross the river and proceed to Thibodauxville, the last town before

New Orleans now only four, maybe five, days ahead. Shifts for guarding the cattle had been designated and those men not on duty were trying to sleep. Range and Bryson had built a fire at some distance from the others and were discussing plans for the completion of the drive. Range was the first to hear the boat out in the darkness of the bayou.

"Listen a minute. Something out on the water coming this way."

"It's more comforting to talk than to listen in surroundings like these," Bryson answered with an impatient gesture as if some inner tension were building up in him. "Especially so, if — "

"Listen!" Range commanded. "It's a boat headin' this way. Le's move a little out of the firelight."

They moved back away from the fire and into the shadows. The paddling ceased when the boat was a dim outline beyond the radiance their small fire cast on the water.

"Holà! . . . Hé! . . . Tiens!"

"Another damn Frenchman," Range said.

"Holà!" Bryson answered the call. "Qui est là? Que voulez-vous?"

Instead of identifying himself or his business, the voice questioned back, "De quel pays êtes-vous?"

"Texas," Bryson answered.

"Où allez-vous?"

"New Orleans," Bryson replied.

"Ah, boviers?"

"Oui."

"Dieu Merci!"

"He's overjoyed that we're cattlemen from Texas," Bryson told Range.

"Why?"

"I've no idea."

"Why don't you ask him a few back? Beginning with what does he want."

"That was my first question. He ignored it. He's not ready to declare himself."

"In that case, le's be quiet until he's ready."

They were silent. There was some slight movement in the boat, an uneasy shuffling as the silence lengthened, then an appealing, "Parole d'honneur, je suis un aime."

"He insists he's a friend."

"We aren't huntin' for friends. Tell him to state his business or start paddlin'."

"Mais, que faites-vous ici?" Bryson put the question sharply. There was another long silence. Then one word was pitched back at them with a mixture of defiance and invitation.

"Esclaves!"

Range needed no translation of the word. So here it was . . . a bargainer out of the bayou . . . a dealer in slaves . . . the type of smuggler Chenet had anticipated . . . a trader in illegal human cargo. He felt a strong rush of aversion to such a business. He expected Bryson to hurl a denunciation at the voice in the darkness; then he realized that Bryson, as usual, was waiting for him to state his wishes in the matter. . . . What were his wishes? To send the man on his way with a threat? To learn how these smugglers did business? That was it . . . a man ought to know what was going on even if he wanted no part in it. "Ask him what's the tie-in between us and his slave business," he said to Bryson.

Bryson did not immediately renew his conversation with the stranger. He took a deep breath and sighed heavily, and then in a voice that had a cold precise quality Range had never heard before, he attacked the man in the boat with questions that had in them an undertone of violence. Range would not have been surprised if the trader had disappeared without a word. There was a hush after Bryson's demands were uttered, and then a torrent of excited explanation came from the man. The distress in his voice told Range more clearly than words that this man's slave business was giving him trouble of some kind. In that case (Range began to reflect as if he understood the volant conversation in French being hurled from bank to boat and back again) the trader probably had some special bargain to offer — a bargain that might tie in with Chenet's trade so that he could actually make that fourteen thousand dollars . . . fourteen thousand if he got the slaves to Chenet and Chenet's fat steers back to the New Orleans market . . . that would double what he had expected to make on his drive of horses and cattle . . . more than double it. . . . What would it mean to be able to return to San Antonio with thirty thousand dollars? . . . "A small kingdom," Chenet had said. . . . No tellin' how much land he could buy with that kind of money . . . and the big house at the springs — that would take thousands to build . . . there'd have to be more drives such as this one to New Orleans, but not so many if he dealt with Chenet . . . and a chance like this might not come again in his whole life. What were the risks? How distasteful would the transaction be? When you came right down to it, why be squeamish? He wouldn't buy a nigger to keep at any price, but trading — that might be different — might be worth the trouble. This creepy soiled feeling that seemed to surround the whole idea was a sort of weakness on his part, he reasoned; he was no longer a kid, he was a man. He'd get his land sooner — he'd be with Luvisa longer — and these slaves would meet the same end whoever handled them. He started to ask himself what Luvisa would think of such business but cut off this line of thought sharply by reminding himself that women shouldn't ever have to think of such things.

There had come a pause in Bryson's sharp questions and the stream of emotional answers.

"What's his trouble?" Range inquired. "And why did he pick us to tell it to?"

"He's stuck with twenty-seven smuggled slaves," Bryson relayed coldly. "Twenty-six males, one female. He's a native in these parts — a sort of middleman — gets the slaves directly off the boat, pays cash, hides them out for his customers and demands a reasonable profit of about fifty dollars each. He pays around a hundred and fifty and sells at about two hundred. He doesn't have to move them about and keeps them only a few days; usually his expenses are small and his risks negligible. His present difficulty is that his customer failed to show up for this cargo as arranged; he's had the twenty-seven on his hands for a week; they're eating too much and they're still hungry and restless; he has three guards who are demanding their wages and threatening to take out on him. His expected customer, he thinks, has either fallen on evil ways or plans to inform on him."

"What does that mean?"

"Informing the authorities is almost as profitable as handling slaves and sometimes less trouble. An informant gets fifty dollars apiece for every smuggled slave seized and half the sale price when the slaves are auctioned off in the regular market. In fact, traders such as this fellow have been known to inform on themselves under false names and realize a fine profit. Suppose the slaves sell in the market at seven hundred each — he'd get three-fifty each plus the fifty-dollar-a-head bounty — that would be a total of four hundred for each black; and since he paid only one-fifty apiece for them, he'd stand to profit two hundred and fifty dollars on each slave. On a bunch the size of this man's here, twenty-seven slaves, that's a profit of almost seven thousand dollars."

"Then why hasn't he informed on himself?"

"He doesn't get out of the woods. He's a swamp man. He's smart enough to know what goes on but too ignorant to go about doing it himself. He's been satisfied with his modest profits of a thousand or so to a cargo, and lets bigger men take bigger risks for bigger profits. A buyer that pays this man two hundred per black can get from five hundred to a thousand when he sells direct to a plantation owner."

"What's the risks for such a buyer?"

"Being informed upon and losing his whole investment, or being killed for the loot and losing his life. The more lucrative and illegal a trade, the more vicious are depredations made upon it."

"Once we were out of these swamps and well on the way to Texas, there wouldn't be much danger," Range said meditatively.

"My God!" Bryson exclaimed. "The eternal short cut. Don't you ever think around or over anything? You've hit the kernel of our

205

friend's argument for selling to us. We'll have a good market and few dangers, he says."

"How did you get so much out of him?" Range asked. "There may be a trick to his story. You'd think from all he told you he expected us to cry as well as buy."

"He's scared."

"Wonder if he's thought about yellow fever mixing up with his slaves. Did he mention any of his help being sick? They could all die off mighty quick, slaves and all."

For a moment Bryson thought Range wanted this information about the health of the guards for his own protection; then with a sharp awareness of the truth, he knew Range simply wanted to throw a further scare into the man as preliminary to a better bargaining basis. Why he should have expected scrupulous thought in any direction once Range had decided to consider the trade, he didn't know. And, he wryly reminded himself, he was committed to follow Range all the way, not to influence, only to observe. So he told the man who waited about yellow fever at New Iberia and mentioned it might spread around considerably, and inquired suspiciously of his health, the health of the men he hired, and the condition of the slaves. The man groaned that this threat should be added, and then cursed his fate in one long stream of profane complaint until he was breathless. Finally, he subsided and added a quiet comment.

"After his preface of colloquial profanity which could not with accuracy be translated into any other language, he assures us by all the saints and his own sweet mother's soul in paradise that they are all hale and hearty, and only a little hungry."

"What does he want for 'em?" Range asked.

"Two hundred dollars each."

"Tell him we won't deal in cash, but I'll swap him cattle."

When Bryson relayed this message, the Frenchman again gave himself over to unrestrained lament.

"Why don't he go away if the swap idea gives him convulsions?" Range asked.

As if he understood, the trader became calm again, and inquired tremulously, "Combien de bétail?"

"Seven," Range said. "Tell him seven cows to one slave."

"He'll plunge into the bayou in despair," Bryson commented achieving a viewpoint of grim humor in the unexpected turns the trade was taking. "Sept!" he called out.

There was no outburst. No word spoken. The paddles began to make soft sound and thin ripples caressed the reflections near the shore. But the sound of the strokes stopped not far away; then slowly they were set in reverse motion and the boat was again on the edge of the shadows. The man explained in flat tones that in the best cattle market seven cows per slave wouldn't bring the price he had already paid for the blacks; if they, kind fellows, would reconsider, he'd rather sell them for cash at a hundred and fifty dollars each and just get his money back.

No response from the bank.

Then he'd sell them at a hundred and forty dollars.

No response.

Then — finally — if God would forgive him for dealing with demons right out of the devil's den, he'd be there at dawn to get the cattle, and, if they weren't good cattle, there were certain Texas cattlemen who might find their eternal resting place, not on their native soil, but hung up on a cypress root in a Louisiana swamp.

Range laughed at Bryson's translation of the threat. "Tell him he's scared us so bad we'll throw in a bull for good measure so he can start a herd and make up his losses."

The trader replied that he was in no jesting mood; he'd take the bull and it better be a good one; moreover, he'd refuse to trade in the morning if he didn't like the looks of the cattle.

Range sent the reply that the slaves wouldn't be accepted either if they turned out to be a puny lot.

The boat slid into the dark and the quick, angry strokes that propelled it soon were no longer audible.

Range chuckled. "Maybe we've cured him of slave trading and made an honest cattleman out of him."

"An *honest* cattleman! Mon Dieu, comment est-il?" Bryson exclaimed.

"Who are you talking to?"

"Anybody who can tell me what an honest cattleman is like."

"The man came looking for a trade. We gave him one. What's dishonest about that?"

"Honesty is a point of view worn by the mind like a long garment swung graciously from the shoulders is worn by the body; it can conceal a beauty and perfection of conscience — or, it can hide some very unattractive motives."

"Save your riddles, and tell me more about that informing business. You said a man that turns in a smuggler gets fifty dollars on each slave seized and half the money the slave brings on the market. So when a slave sells for seven hundred, the informer gets three-fifty of it. Who gets the rest?"

"Theoretically, it goes into the public coffers — actually, it fattens the pockets of those in authority."

"What kind of law is a slave trader violating anyway? If it's all right to own slaves, what's wrong with handlin' 'em for profit? When did we get such a crazy law anyhow?"

"It's been more than thirty years since the United States legislated against further importation of slaves from Africa and by constitutional action abolished traffic in slaves. The law was meant not to regulate the buying and selling of those Negroes already in bondage here but to abolish the *capturing* and selling of free Negroes, either in Africa or in our own country."

"A law that people don't pay attention to for thirty years ain't much of a law in the first place."

"Especially if there's no money set aside for its enforcement while the institution of slavery continues to dominate an economy where more and more slaves are necessary to development and prosperity, thus guaranteeing big profits for the slave smuggler. Attempts to win moral victories by legislating against traffic in slaves are like efforts to cure smallpox by medication of the sores — if the ravages of the disease on the body are to be checked, the cause must be made plain and eradicated."

"You told Chenet you were no abolitionist. That sounds like abolitionist talk to me."

"There's a difference between conviction and analysis. Now that you are about to become a dealer in slaves, are you aware of any new-found convictions?"

"I don't know about that, but I got a lot of plans in my head. Listen. How do you think this would work out? . . . You and Cassidy and the five white drivers will take the cattle on to market. You can handle the sale and pay off the men so they can go on to their homes in the States. I'll take the rest of the crew back with me to Chenet's. Cicero and Caesar can help me handle the slaves. Wong will feed 'em. The Mexicans can help guard and scout ahead so we won't have to meet up with travelers on the road. I'll go into Franklin and stock up on supplies. Since we made no stop there on the way through, there won't be any questions about our turnin' back before we've had time to make New Orleans."

"That reminds me," Bryson put in, "our visitor said a lawyer could be found in Franklin to fix up proper sale papers on smuggled cargo for a reasonable fee."

"Don't want any papers. If he'd fix up papers like that, he'd just as soon send someone out to inform on us. More risk in havin' him know than traveling without papers. Might help Chenet for me to have papers but he can fix up his own."

"If they're stolen from you or escape, or if you're asked to prove ownership, you'll be without recourse."

"I won't lose 'em."

"The men we've hired may not like the change in plans."

"Maybe not, but they'll like the extra pay that goes with it."

*　　　　　*　　　　　*

Range sent Cicero and Caesar with Bryson and Cassidy to watch the cattle through the early morning hours and called the other men to a predawn breakfast. He'd asked Bryson to tell the two Negroes of the deal that would take them back to Chenet's plantation with him.

"Offer them a hundred dollars apiece if they'll stay with the slaves night and day and help me handle them until we deliver to Chenet, and after that ride with me on the drive back to New Orleans with the steers."

"In other words, you're going to make them the overseers, and you want me to make them like it?"

"It'll help me out if you will. I notice they always step pretty lively for you. Cassidy'll fall in line with you too. Make your own deal with him — if he wants to go back to San Antonio with us when we're through down here, that's all right with me. He'd come in handy on some other drives we'll be makin'. That lead ox is a big help too. Reckon he'll sell him in New Orleans?"

"He'd sell his own soul into eternal hellfire first."

"I guess so."

As the time drew closer for Range to speak to the men, an unexpected reluctance settled upon him and he knew words wouldn't come easy. The drivers realized he had called them together earlier than usual for some special reason. They ate in silence; then as they drank coffee and smoked, squatting or standing around Wong and his breakfast fire, they eyed Range with curiosity and waited. The Mexicans, standing to one side in a cluster, more wary and withdrawn than usual, and Wong with his masklike expression and soft movements were somehow irritating to Range. No one of these men he had hired was a close friend, and likely he'd never see the white riders again; but they had given him respect and obedience to orders and they were his first crew; and he dreaded whatever loss in respect must come to him with the announcement that he was a dealer in slaves. Not that it would change their regard enough to matter much — such business was too commonplace — but there would be a shading of difference in their attitude, and he postponed as long as possible this inner loss he must experience. For some unaccountable reason Luvisa's dearness and sweetness, the purity of her person and her spirit, seemed to surround him with a sort of protest. The silence was growing too long. He must shake off this weakness and get down to business.

"Made a little business deal last night," he began. "Changes our plans some." Eyes focused on him more attentively. Expectation increased.

"The fellow that called on us in that boat was having trouble." He hesitated, then stated flatly, "He's a slave dealer with twenty-seven blacks on his hands — his customers didn't show up." The men continued staring at him, waiting for the rest. Was he imagining it, or had some change come over them already? Why was it so infernally hot so early in the morning? He felt small trickles of perspiration crawling down the back of his legs. He swatted angrily at a mosquito buzzing around his ear. Say the rest and get it over with!

"That plantation owner over on the other side of Houston — the one with the good steers — said if we'd bring him back slaves, he'd deal with us on the steers. We told him we weren't in the slave business, just cattle, but he told us to keep our eyes open."

Tellin' 'em too hell-blistered much! Cut it off!

"The upshot is we got twenty-seven slaves on our hands if this trader shows up this mornin'. I'm takin' 'em back to Chenet and then drivin' his steers to New Orleans. Bryson will go on through with this herd. He'll take Cassidy and you five fellows who come along for the ride. With the crew cut in half, you'll have more ridin' and less sleepin', and chuck won't be so handy for Wong will go back with me; but we're less'n a week from market and I'll make it worth your while — ten dollars apiece extra pay for your work from here on in. Will you take it on for that?"

Range thought each of the five nodded. He couldn't be sure. No word was spoken. He looked at Wong. The cook's expression had not changed, but for an instant Range wondered fiercely what train of thought his news had provoked in this impassive Chinese man for there was some small gesture of disapproval or distaste expressed through his hands as he poked at the fire and reached for the coffeepot.

He turned to the Mexicans. "You mustangers will go with me." He looked directly at Alfonso since the older man was jefe to the other four. "I'll need your crew to help handle the steers." He purposely failed to mention that he wanted them to act as scouts and guards on the trip with the slaves; he'd let Bryson explain that in Spanish and settle their wages with him — they'd take it better that way.

"Cicero and Caesar will go along with me too," he added. "Anybody have anything to say?"

There was a prolonged silence. Then Alfonso spoke softly. "Por Dios, señor, we are so worthless to you — " With his shoulders and hands he gestured how worthless. "Cierto, we saben the wild black horse, saben the wild black cow tambien, pero no saben the wild black man."

It was the first time Range had thought of the origins of the slaves or considered how primitive their state might be. How wild were they? Had they had any training as — as — slaves, or, were they straight from Africa? It was a disturbing thought.

"You don't have to know anything about 'em," he answered Alfonso. "I want you simply to scout the trail ahead of me so we won't meet up with anybody and can — " he fumbled for the right explanation — "can make better time." He wished for Bryson to take over this conversation for there was an expression of mild stubbornness on Alfonso's face.

"We hire to catch horses, maybe drive cattle, pero no can drive — "

Range interrupted sharply. "You don't drive anything except the steers back to New Orleans, and if you don't want that job you can pull out for San Antonio when we get to Chenet's and I'll hire some more drivers to take your place. Right now I just want scout

duty out of you in the daytime and guard duty at night — nothin'
to drive — understand?"

"Sí, señor." Alfonso made his assent sound unpleasantly negative.

"Mr. Bryson will talk to you about the pay."

"Sí, señor."

The dawn had begun to sketch in outline the camp and its surroundings when the sound of boats coming along the way of last
night's visitor was heard. The men all turned and peered into the
dimness of the early light, and their backs were to Range. Although their movement was natural and unrelated to their feelings
for him, the position in which he was placed made him feel terribly
alone and he wished with a fearful intensity that he had not involved
himself in this trade. He could still back out, refuse to swap. But that
would show him a man of uncertainty, unwilling to stand by his
commitments, a weakling who talked up a good bargain and then re-
neged when faced with the risks and dangers attached. What was he
thinking about? He could handle this business all right! After all,
hadn't he killed bears and Indians! Let them bring on these wild
black men! Let the Mexicans sulk if they wanted to! Let that stinking
noisy French trader try to double-cross him! He'd show 'em all!

He strode out from behind the men and down close to the water,
placing himself squarely with his back to them, and stood there, his
legs planted wide apart, his hands on his hips, his head thrown back.
The morning light spread and the boats drew in closer.

A slight breeze drifted across the bayou in Range's face and
brought the sickening odor of the slaves — the beastlike stench of
long confinement — the body's protest against being deprived of many
of its normal functions, severed from the stimulations of exercise, sunshine, and water. The sweet fragrance of flowering bayou growth was
also carried on the breeze and held close to the ground by the heavy
damp air; this sweetness mixed with the foulness of the human
cargo on the boats in a way to make a man's stomach rebel. Range
swallowed and held his breath to keep from retching. Morning birdcalls engaged in a chorus of beauty with an intensity that further

213

accented the loathsome quality of the scene. The three boats came in to the bank and the trader jumped out, agile as a squirrel. He was small and stooped and his features were disguised in a heavy growth of beard that gave him a look of callous fierceness. He strode over to Range in a gait as aggressive as his short legs could express. He came close, and, without greeting, glared up at Range, showing no intimidation at his own disadvantage in height. There was enough light for the two to size each other up. The masklike expression on Range's face would have done credit to Wong. The smuggler's heavy eyebrows were drawn together in banked-up indignation; finally, he spat disdainfully, and tried to provide an opening.

"C'est votre tour."

Range understood generally that the man expected him to take the lead now. He attempted no word of response — simply gestured with his head that the smuggler was to come with him and moved toward the spot where Toego and another saddled horse were waiting. The Frenchman hurled abrupt orders toward the boats, each crowded with one guard and nine slaves, and then turned to follow Range. Already mounted on Toego, Range indicated to the trader that he was to ride the other horse.

The swamp man was ill at ease as a horseman, but he was stubbornly determined to show this big man from the faraway land of Texas that he was his equal; he mounted awkwardly but without fear or hesitation. The stirrups were too long and his legs dangled. Range gave him a cool glance but ignored his discomfort and rode off toward the grazing ground where the cattle were being held; the smuggler trailed along handling his horse and his discomfort as best he could.

Bryson and Cassidy came to meet them. Cicero and Caesar were already busy cutting out the cows for the trader. Range thought: Bryson knew I would go through with this. Bryson greeted the man and the French phrases immediately identified him with the transaction of the night before and brought forth a stream of protestation and woe.

"Has he backed out?" Range inquired.

Bryson smiled. "No. He's just unhappy. You've crowded him. He's simply voicing a lament that he should come to this — that we should deal with him so harshly. He knows now, he says, that men from Texas are a cruel, heartless breed."

"He'd do worse by us if he had the chance," Range commented. "And what kind of a heart he's got, I don't know, but to my notion he's got no stomach a'tall — any man that could ride in a boat with all that stink he just come up the bayou with — "

"Perhaps he's able to ignore that by concentrating on profits . . . or dangers."

Range's only answer was a snort of disgust.

The cattle were soon cut out. The trader admitted reluctantly that they were as good as any in the herd. They returned to the breakfast camp where Range ordered Wong to cook up the greatest part of the remaining food supplies to feed the slaves.

"Fill up their bellies and they'll handle easier, won't they?" he inquired of Bryson.

"A truth that has wide application for both man and beast," Bryson replied.

The drivers herding toward New Orleans could restock on food supplies at Thibodauxville, Range explained to Bryson, and he would take care of his own crew and the slaves by taking on new supplies at Franklin.

Since the slaves were chained together for transport in groups of nine, they were staked out at three trees well apart when taken from the boats. Range observed quickly that they seemed in fairly good condition, although emaciated and hungry-looking, and that on the whole they were more weary than wild. He asked Bryson to inquire of the smuggler where they had come from and learned that they were captured in Africa and trained for field work on an island off the coast of Honduras. Several of the slaves wore irons around the ankles and one had an iron about his neck; these had been hard to handle at some time, Range surmised, but the only chains now used

215

were attached to iron cuffs on the wrists. Each slave wore these wristbands, Range noticed, and they were held together by a short length of chain that would permit only limited use of the hands; forged to the band on the right wrist was the long chain that attached them one to the other. There were no locks; they could be separated only by cutting the chain and joined again only by forging it. The long end of the chain that held them together was carried by the lead slave in each group and used for staking them out; this was accomplished by looping the chain around a tree, drawing it up close, and then taking the end some distance away to tie securely around another tree. This system of chaining made it easy and safe for one man to guard nine slaves.

The black who wore the iron about his neck was almost as large as Cassidy; he had been placed next to the end of a group and behind him was the woman, his daughter, an ugly soft-eyed girl about fifteen years old. Her hair, about five inches long, was a bushy mass standing straight out from her head. Her teeth were large and slightly protruding. Firm-breasted, small-hipped, and straight-legged, she walked with a light tread, her shoulders back, her expression alert. A ragged, greasy, one-piece garment hardly reached her knees and was belted with a strand of old rope. Her only ornamentation was huge ivory earrings. Cicero was the only man in the camp that gave her more than a passing glance of curiosity, and Cicero was the only one on whom she allowed her shifting glance to pause. The appeal in her eyes gave his heart a strange twist — and he read the appeal aright: she had smelled the food Wong was preparing — she was dreadfully hungry. Cicero conversed with himself. So he was an overseer, was he? In charge of these black folks, was he? Well, as sure as Moses had whiskers, he was going to fatten that ugly little gal — get some meat on her bones. He looked at her again. She gave him a big toothy smile. He felt his heart twist again.

Range was impatient to break camp and get started back to Texas with the slaves. He wanted to get to Franklin as soon as possible and get properly supplied for the trip. He wanted to get the slaves cleaned up; their filthy condition was an offense to the basic cleanness of his nature. He wanted to get them outfitted so they wouldn't look like they had just come in on a slave-runner; then, if he were seen on the trail with them, he'd be less subject to suspicion. He reasoned too that the slaves would be easier to handle if they were comfortable in every respect. He did not admit to the surface of his mind that he was trying to offset some deep disquietude within himself for having become involved in an illegal slave transaction.

The departure of the two crews was managed with dispatch. Bryson talked quietly with the Mexicans and made agreements about their pay for turning back and their duties with Range — scouting the trail so that he might be advised of travelers and avoid meetings that might lead to inquiries about the slaves. They would also be expected to share guard duty at night. After the slaves were delivered to Chenet, they would have a choice of returning to San Antonio alone or hiring to Range for the drive back to New Orleans.

"The Mexicans want nothing to do with the slaves," Bryson warned Range. "They are frightened of them and at the same time repulsed by their being in chains. They don't like guard duty at night but have agreed to it as long as two of them can be on duty together with you or one of the Negroes keeping them company. Don't worry about them trying to release the slaves — they fear them too much for that — but the Mexicans themselves might do a disappearing act if you keep them too much in the company of the slaves."

Range took the instructions without comment or question.

"Cassidy and I have made plans to stable Little Star in New Orleans, and, after we've looked around a bit, take a pleasure cruise upriver to Opelousas and be there waiting to join you for the return drive through Teche country."

"Thanks." Range looked at Bryson, frankly grateful. He would not have asked for the help Bryson could give him trailing through the French-settled country with his knowledge of the language and sharing of responsibility in the treacherous bayou area, but he was glad it had been offered. They shook hands silently and parted.

Range took Cicero and Wong into Franklin to help him in the selection of supplies. Franklin, settled chiefly by English families, had been founded about forty years before by a Pennsylvanian and named for Benjamin Franklin. It had remained predominantly English in character and had become an important shipping and trading point. Range found unexpected pleasure and excitement in this buying expedition carried on in his own language. He missed Bryson but felt a satisfaction in being completely on his own in an atmosphere that relegated Frenchman, Spaniard, and Negro to the background. He was generous in his purchase of food supplies, laying in an ample stock of tobacco and coffee, and cautioned Wong to make his estimates in terms of feeding the whole crew, slaves included, so that they would rest easy and tire slow. He bought cheap straw hats, trousers, shirts, blankets, and a covering of heavy waterproof canvas to go with each blanket. The nights were always damp, often rainy, and sometimes now quite chilly; so he considered the bedding more important than shoes for the slaves; Cicero agreed with him. These blacks had always gone barefoot, he said, and if they tried to fit them in shoes or sandals they'd all be unable to walk in a few days' time. If any of them got footsore on the long walk, there were extra horses they could ride now and then. For the woman, Range let Cicero select a piece of calico with bright blue figures on a red background. Since neither of them had any ideas on yardage, the merchant sold them ten yards. They each made a further selection that was a curiosity to the other. Range bought a wooden pail of homemade soap and Cicero added a small padlock with a length of lightweight chain to their stack of purchases.

"What you got in mind to do with that?" Range asked Cicero.

"Gonna loose that woman's chains and let her help me and Caesar feed slaves and work around camp. Better for her to work and be chained by herself."

Range looked hard at Cicero. He didn't mention that he had seen Cicero buy a long string of carved wooden beads, green and yellow, and slip them into his pocket. He noticed Cicero had used his own gold to pay for the gift. The Negro met Range's eyes in a straight unwavering look.

"Go ahead," Range said shortly, perfectly aware that Cicero's interest in the slave girl was more than his job called for. But Cicero was steady — Bryson trusted him — he'd just let such matters take their natural course. It even occurred to him that when he got back to New Orleans he must buy something very special for Luvisa — some jewelry, some silk or satin, and something for their child. He stood in a brief dream trying to figure out what on earth a man bought for a baby, until Cicero roused him.

"If's nothin' mo' on yo' mind, boss, I better load them pack mules so's we kin git outta here."

Back in camp, Range instructed Cicero and Caesar to take chisels and hammers from the tool kits they carried for shoeing horses and other blacksmith duties along the trail, and cut the chains of the slaves so they could be released for washing in a pool and exchange their filthy tatters for the new clothes. Everybody in camp was excited over the procedure. The slaves themselves had already lost much of their restless fright and discontent because of the good food furnished them and the thoughtful supervision of Cicero and Caesar. The Sudanic dialect they spoke, sprinkled here and there with muddled French and English phrases, became such a frenzied babble and jumble when they realized what was about to happen to them that the Mexicans were frightened by it. The many intonations for words of identical sound gave a weird and baffling quality to their excited speech. But Cicero only laughed heartily.

"Boss, ain' they funnier'n Satan in a ditch? They's great repeaters, ain' they? Sound like they's got nothin' to say, mighty few words to say it with, and they just keeps on a-sayin' it over and over. But don' you worry, I'll teach 'um meanin'ful words 'fore long to take place o' dem heathen sounds."

Cicero began his word tutelage by giving special names to the girl and her father. Caesar listened dubiously while he explained.

"That gal need a purty name. What her papa call her sound like a bark ruffled with a grunt. A little gal that ugly need to have a sweet honeyed name to call her by. I'se gonna name her Adelia — that right-soundin', don' ya think? And her papa, he so big and importan' lookin', we calls him King George. Whadda ya think?"

"I think King George gonna wop a chain aroun' yo' neck sometime for moonin' around his Adelia-daughter."

"Ain' moonin' — jus' overseein' like we s'pose to do."

"Doncha think layin' good gold out on yaller beads is overdoin' ya overseein' a mite."

"Le's git to chiselin' them chains, and whiles we's about it, we takes that collar from around King George's neck and them other irons offa ankles."

"Did boss say to?"

"He didn' say not to. He don' want 'em to look boat-fresh, and he wan' 'em to walk easy and long. So I reckons — "

"Git to ya tools, man. We can't cut dem chains with dis chatter."

The bathing was a gay affair for the slaves even though they were closely guarded; they must stay bunched up, and Caesar had made it plain that any who attempted to stray would immediately be placed back in chains. Cicero had given a demonstration in the proper use of the soap Range had bought at Franklin and they went into the water carrying handfuls of grass and fern with which to scrub themselves. Cicero had been stubborn in his insistence that Adelia should be allowed to bathe alone, out of sight and unguarded. He attached her new chain to one cuff and then by use of the padlock fixed the other end around a tree on the bank, thus leaving one arm free and allowing enough slack in the chain for easy movement in bathing and dressing. He left her alone with the ten yards of calico and the beads, well concealed in a clump of willows and as much bewildered by the modesty thrust upon her as the gifts he had made.

The results of the bath and the clothes and the big evening meal that followed were highly satisfying to Range and almost stilled the qualms that had been with him since swapping for the slaves.

Adelia's response to the red calico and the beads had been in the feminine tradition of all races and times. Inspired and exalted by the means of adornment, and without needle, thread, or pin, she had achieved highly original grooming. One strip of the cloth had been wound around and around her head in a tight turban that allowed a few straight tufts of her hair to peep out of the top. She had made a slit in the material to admit her head and had torn off a length that reached slightly below the knees in both front and back. The remainder of the cloth had become a sash that she wound tightly around her body beginning just under the breasts and continuing to a line just below the hips — here she looped it and let it hang nearly to her ankles. The beads were around her neck, the loops of ivory in her ears freshly polished, and a large purple water lily was tucked in at the top of the sash just below one breast. Her skin was like black satin and her eyes big with delight. When Cicero came for her, she gave him the shy, questioning smile with which a woman seeks approval.

It was inevitable that the slaves should sing that evening and that Adelia should dance. Range knew instinctively that this was good for him, too — so he let them sing. If they should have visitors, he reasoned, these unchained, happy Negroes would not be suspect as smuggled cargo. It began with humming and chanting and moved on into specific sound and rhythm patterns. Then Cicero and Caesar began to put the physical elation of the slaves into their words, and the slaves began to pick them up, led by King George, and twist them with the Sudanic tongue; and with it all Adelia's swaying and singing became more active and interpreted their mood in primitive dance. . . .

> I feel so good
> So boo-ga boo-ga good!
> I feel so-o-o good,
> So so-ga boo-ga good!
>
> How zat you feel?

221

Why, I feel like a bear in a honey dance:
Wanna jiggle and wiggle
And shuffle and prance!
I feel so good,
So ji-ga wiga good.

How zat you feel?

I feel like a squirrel in a pecan tree:
Wanna whisk and frisk
And fiddle de dee!
I feel so good,
So fiddle faddle good!

How zat you feel?

Why, I feel like a rabbit in a clover bed:
Wanna stomp and romp
'Till I'm outta my head!
I feel so good,
So stompa rompa good!

How zat you feel?

I feel like a bluejay on a spree,
A strutter in a flutter
For a jamboree!
I feel so good,
So jamba bamba good!

How zat you feel?

I feel like a catfish on the run:
Wanna leap from the deep
And play in the sun!
I feel so good,
So lee-pa dee-pa good!

The three-week trip back to Chenet's plantation was for Range a time of supertension and strain. He knew no deep slumber, catching his rest only in short naps, and in the daytime was constantly in fear of meeting some wayfarer or intruder who would cause him trouble. In the more settled areas he could not avoid being seen by field workers and an occasional traveler, and at such times with studied caution he set an unhurried pace and himself presented a calm bold front. The slaves gave him little cause for worry. He had chained them back together in three groups but had not restored the short length of chain between their wrists and the freedom of arm position made it possible for them to walk with greater ease and tire less; they were too weary at nighttime to cause the guards any uneasiness. Range made the trip with as much speed as possible but was careful not to crowd the endurance of the slaves; they made early morning starts, took noon rests, and walked on until late in the evening. From day to day Cicero taught King George more and more "Christian" words. At any time the big black lapsed into his Sudanic dialect, Cicero would yell at him.

"Stop yo' heathen mouthin', big man, and learn some Christian words!"

King George would take the word or phrase that was his lesson and make it into a chant; sometimes the other slaves would accompany him, two or three at a time, and they would walk for miles to the monotonous rhythms and sounds. These rituals wore Range's nerves raw, but he could find no good reason for stopping them and realized the slaves were less likely to be troublesome when preoccupied by Cicero's word games and King George's chants. The weariness of the long walk lay heavy upon them during the last few days before arrival at Chenet's and the lamenting quality of their chants was harder to ignore. King George, tired and glum, allowed the long staking chain to drag instead of carrying it as usual looped around his neck.

"Pick up 'at chain, elephant man," Cicero finally ordered. "Can'cha feel it a-draggin' — how it keep draggin' ya down?"

King George ignored the command for a while, but finally pulled up the chain and threw it over his shoulders, and started his chant:

Chain
It keep draggin' ya
Draggin' ya
Draggin' ya down
Down
Down
Chain
Chain
Draggin' ya . . .

Cicero was as relieved as Range when afternoon storm clouds gave excuse for setting up early camp and putting an end to the chain chant. The Trinity River had been crossed and they were in a section vulnerable to coastal hurricanes. Range had no idea how the slaves would act in a storm. He checked Cicero closely as he looped and tied the staking chains. With unexpected swiftness the dark clouds seemed to take possession of the sky; an eerie gray-green light gave warning of nature's violent intentions; the unnatural silence of bird and insect and animal life, even the waiting stillness of trees and grasses, created a fearsome preface to what must come. Occasional flashes of lightning seemed to signal, "Get ready!" Then a dull continuous roar began to build, climbing up one side of the sky and rolling down the other, meeting an ascending roar that overlapped and climbed as the other faded. Cicero, shaking with fright he tried hard to control, locked Adelia close to King George, murmuring to her in an attempt to comfort.

"Don' fret, 'Delia, nothin' happenin', nothin' a'tall — jest 'at ole tater wagon rollin' across a sky."

When the wind and rain hit with full fury, the lightning snapped, the thunder banged to earth with a violence that made the very ground tremble, and great limbs of trees that did not have their full green strength snapped and broke all around. The slaves were completely terrorized and leaped against their chains. Range and Wong

224

and the Mexicans were wholly occupied with keeping horses from breaking away and supplies intact.

The smatterings of Protestant instruction and fervor that had come to Cicero in his youth returned to him now and served like a raft in a churning sea. Caesar huddling on his knees with his face covered, letting out an occasional shout for mercy and rescue, suggested an example that Cicero decided all should follow.

Shouting, "Pray God!" and "Pray Lord!" he stumbled around among the slaves, kicking, shoving and tripping until every one was on his knees or on his face. They seemed to comprehend the purpose was for supernatural intervention and their wails and cries began to compete with the storm sounds, blending, rising, swelling to fit the pattern of nature's turmoil. But for once Cicero, instead of leading and instructing, was caught up and led by the slaves and taken back into a primitive somewhere that was an emotional harbor for his ancestors. As the storm began to subside, the frantic but highly unified shoutings and writhings increased in passion and tempo, as if, in competition with the clamor of the storm, they felt that now they were getting the best of it. Range yelled at them and threatened them to no avail. Then he stopped and studied them for a while. Finally, making up his mind that this orgy of sound and motion would continue until no strength was left in them and would require a day or so for recuperation, he pulled out his pistol and shot directly over their heads; then moved in closer and shot again with his other pistol, planting the bullet in the tree closest to Cicero and Caesar. He had penetrated. The sound was cut off. As he deliberately reloaded his pistols, he stared at Cicero until the Negro self-consciously got to his feet and brushed at the mud and leaves and twigs that clung to him.

"Do you have enough mind left in ya to help Wong get fires goin' for supper?"

"Reckon I do, boss." His voice was husky, his movements stiff and awkward, and on his face the look of a sleepwalker awakened in strange surroundings.

*   *   *

225

The day after the storm Cicero rode close to Range whenever possible and tried hard to start a conversation, mumbling about inconsequentials and then withdrawing when he had made an opening. Finally he made a hurried and shaky statement of his case in one long breathless string of words, gripping the horn of the saddle with both hands as if to fortify himself.

"Speakin' straight out, boss — I wants to buy 'Delia — wants to buy her 'fore we gets to where we're stoppin' — her papa like it if I takes her — 'cause I'se free — I wants 'er — wants 'er bad, boss — how much you sell her for? I pay much as anybody — much as anybody pay."

Range was silent for a while. The request did not surprise him and he could see some advantages in the sale. After all, Chenet hadn't promised to buy more than twenty-five.

"I been promised seven hundred apiece, but you been good help. I wouldn't charge you that much."

Cicero's body sagged into a position of relief and repose in the saddle. "Say five hunnerd, boss?" he proposed with the undisguised eagerness of a poor bargainer.

"Sounds all right. You got that much?"

Cicero shifted around in uncertainty before he answered. "Got what's comin' on this trip and got a little bag buried in my blacksmith shop — three hunnerd all way round, might be. But we work for ya, boss — that 'Delia-girl work out her price some for your missus and I work for you — time and place don' matter."

"Ready to tie yourself up to untie that girl, are you? Well, I'll tell you what. I'll put your wages for this trip on Adelia — you keep the gold in your shop to live on. The rest of it you and Adelia can work out one way or another."

It was Cicero's turn to be silent. Range studied him with curiosity. Could it be that the big black fellow was about to cry?

"Boss, I been thinkin' ya heart got hard spots in it — but — now I — thinks different — and I — 'at funny little big-toothed gal mean more to me than gold — 'er anything, boss — and I'uz scairt you might not — but you did, boss — so frum here on out, count on me, boss."

226

"That's all right." Range was made awkward and a little ashamed by Cicero's gratitude. And it crossed his mind that he was thankful Bryson wasn't riding with him to pass an opinion on what had just been said.

In the heart of New Orleans Silver Bryson and C. Cassidy were strolling aimlessly, letting city sights and sounds soak in gradually. Business duties on Range Templeton's cattle were done. Bryson had received almost nine thousand dollars in gold, had paid off the riders, held back a proper amount for his and Cassidy's return trip to Opelousas, and placed the remainder on deposit until Range should arrive with Chenet's steers and complete his sales.

It was early evening. The street gas lamps were lighted and sounds of entertainment began to push out the daytime noises of business and trade. Coffeehouses and saloons, gambling houses and theaters, beckoned with gaudy displays, music and laughter, tantalizing odors of food and drink and the heady perfumes of women and flowers.

The huge, shaggy Irishman, dazed with this bombardment of his senses, and the casual Southerner who seemed so unaffected by it all were a strange-looking pair indeed; but in New Orleans such incongruity went unnoticed for here was a metropolis giddy with the wealth of frontier resources, and in the flow of people along its streets was all the diversity and oddity to be found among those who adventure in wilderness country and those who profit from the exploits of the adventurer.

In returning to New Orleans, Silver Bryson realized that he was imposing upon himself a sort of test: Had Time and Texas toughened the scars of heartbreak and regret, healed the open sores of hate and revenge, enough so that he would feel no pain under the pressure of memories? He was ready to ignore what New Orleans held of his past, enjoy briefly its comforts and pleasures, and depart in a few days on a leisurely river trip to Opelousas.

He hadn't been paying much attention to Cassidy's amazed mutterings until the Irishman questioned appealingly, "And would you

227

be tellin' me what is a quadroon or be showin' me such a one? A lovely sort of woman creature she must be indeed with all the singin' and yearnin' men do after her."

Well, here it is, Bryson told himself — the pressure on the scar and a dull pain.

"She is often as lovely as the songs say," he answered with a deliberate casualness. "There was a time here in New Orleans when quadroons must observe an ordinance that they not go out in public dressed in silk, jewels, and plumes. This ruling was made because of the disturbing competition they gave women of purer strains and firmer social status. The quadroon is one-fourth Negro, the offspring of mulatto and white."

"Are they slave girls then?"

"Very seldom. It is the custom in this city for white fathers to free their quadroon and octoroon children — the octoroon being the offspring of white and quadroon."

"Would they be noted as careless women?"

"As in all classes, there are women of easy virtue. But it is an old custom for quadroon and octoroon women to be reared in strictest chastity until they acquire a protector at the quadroon balls — a function to which only white men are admitted."

"Aye, and what might a protector be — not a true husband surely?"

"Not in any sense a true husband — more often a husband of some less attractive but more socially acceptable woman. But the exchange is understood — the quadroon to be set up in economic security and to serve her protector faithfully in love."

"Such a thing saddens me heart. It's a God's pity to bargain beauty and love for gold, and the poor creatures with never a chance to know the blessed state of man and wife."

"There have been exceptions. I know a French merchant who married a quadroon and returned to his native land with her as his acknowledged wife."

"Did you so? Now what — " The discussion was interrupted as Cassidy, engrossed in what Bryson was telling him, stumbled over

228

a blind beggar sitting crouched almost in the path of the passers-by. The beggar was a wretched creature, nearly naked, full of sores, his legs withered and useless. He sat hunched far over, his bare brown back showing the deep scars of brutal lashings, and he turned his head with a deformed twist of the neck so that his mutilated sockets were exposed while he mumbled unintelligible pleas for attention of some kind.

"God's Mercy!" Cassidy exclaimed. "Ye poor old carcass! A heap of misery indeed that gold would not be healing." But he dropped two gold pieces which the blind man grabbed, one in each hand, as they struck the ground beside him. His precision astonished Cassidy, and the blind man grinned at him as if he perceived the astonishment and was pleased with his performance.

"Saints surround us!" Cassidy murmured in horror. "Have you ever seen a worse sight, Mr. Bryson, in the land of the Comanche and the plague?" He turned to Bryson and was startled at his appearance — the tall thin frame drawn up in unnatural rigidity and his face almost as white as his hair.

Through lips stiff with shock of some kind, Bryson said, "An escaped slave. A mulatto."

The beggar heard him and cringed.

"Show me your hands," Bryson commanded the beggar. "Show me the back of your hands, before I kill you!"

The blind man groaned. He tried to say something but his mouth only sagged and trembled. He finally held out his hands, shaking so violently that the gold pieces, so deftly garnered, dropped from between his fingers. The hands were covered with scars and sores. Bryson leaned over to scrutinize them. When he raised up, the violence was gone from him and he looked tired and sick.

"Not the one," he muttered. "For a moment there I was sure. Thought he was the one."

The beggar began a frantic crawl away from Cassidy and Bryson, falling against people, against walls and steps — whatever sense he had achieved in blindness for the moment lost in fear.

229

Cassidy tugged at Bryson's arm. "It is dying of thirst that I am," he pleaded. "No man-sized drink have I had since the crossing of the Sabine. It was me last bottle of sacred fire that was poured down the thankless gullet of Little Star." As he talked, he urged Bryson to and through the door of a saloon. "And it is right certain I am that you could do with a nip yerself."

Bryson in absent-minded detachment took his seat with Cassidy at a table and made no objection when the Irishman ordered "A bottle of the strongest and best for two honest men not right easily deceived by the contents of a bottle."

The saloon was not crowded so early in the evening. At the far end of the room there was a small stage set with piano and sofa and an ornate backdrop, but no entertainment would be offered until the audience was of a size and mood to receive it.

When the bottle came, Cassidy poured the drinks, offered Bryson a glass, and with a supreme effort at putting aside their unpleasant experience, proposed heartily, "To the mighty Republic of Texas!" Bryson murmured, "To the Republic," and merely touched his lips to the glass while Cassidy drank with thirsty gusto. He poured himself a second drink and wondered uneasily what to do or say when it was plain Bryson wasn't the type to drink his troubles away. What was it they had been talking about before stumbling on the beggar? Quadroons.

"That French merchant, Mr. Bryson — the one married to the quadroon. What was the fate of him and her? Did ye know?"

Bryson at first appeared not to hear. He turned the glass in his fingers several times and finally took a small drink. Why not talk about it? It would entertain this lonely giant across the table. It might relieve the pressure of despair and futility that was threatening his sanity. That the wretch of a beggar had so resembled another mulatto was a ghastly coincidence. Or perhaps he had simply been betrayed by the force of aroused memories. Anyway, the old wounds were broken open. Might as well let them bleed.

He began to speak quietly. "Yes, I know the fate of them very

230

well. They lived happily in France for a while and they had a daughter. Then they moved to Norfolk, Virginia, and the merchant became quite rich. He moved onto a country estate in an aristocratic section. His wife and daughter became renowned for their beauty — the two Frenchwomen were the pride of the countryside and the toast of all Norfolk, and happiness trailed them like a bright-liveried attendant!"

The Irishman's eyes glowed with sentimental appreciation, and Silver Bryson saw a grand banquet hall, men and women in all the color and shimmer of finery, the sparkle and musical clink of crystal, laughter, and a gay masculine voice: "Raise your glasses high, gentlemen of Norfolk, in a toast to the incomparably lovely Le Roi ladies: To the beauty of Christine and Châli Le Roi!"

Silver Bryson tasted the drink before him and resumed, "There was a certain vain young man of much property and some prestige who discovered that love can be the most important thing in life, and he tasted real happiness for the first time when he became affianced to the daughter of the French merchant."

"Ah! The sweet wonders of young love," Cassidy exclaimed, his Irish heart warmed by the story, his mood mellowed by the contents of the bottle-of-the-best.

"But the story, alas, has a sad ending, as do most stories of quadroon love," Bryson warned Cassidy. "The French merchant was killed in a mysterious shooting affray, his beautiful quadroon wife went into strictest seclusion, and, according to public belief and sentiment, died of a broken heart soon after."

Cassidy was dismayed. "God pity the pretty quadroon. But perhaps 'twas a mercy since her good husband was gone." He waited for Bryson to continue, then as the silence lengthened, prodded him. "The young man and the maid? Did ye learn how they fared, Mr. Bryson? Did ye not say it was a true love?"

Bryson could not answer at once for it was as if the fatal letter were in his hands again, the small ornate script clear before his eyes, and the final line clearest of all: "I do this that our true love may always remain the same, and thus I am forever, Your Châli."

In a trancelike voice, he finally answered Cassidy, "A very true love indeed. So true that the maid, rather than deceive or injure the vain young man who loved her so, took her own life and thus was forever unattainable. She drowned in a deep blue pool in her father's garden . . . a deep blue pool where exotic fish played in the tangled loveliness of her dark tresses."

"Holy Mother of Jesus!" This was too much for Cassidy. He studied Bryson. Was the man crazy? Could the mere tasting of strong drink affect a man so? He quickly refilled his own glass and drank it dry before exclaiming, "Ah! it could never be!"

But Bryson continued matter-of-factly. "She had found out, you see, that her mother was a quadroon. And she an octoroon. The taboos of the times labeled her a Negro, not a Frenchwoman. And she had been about to wed a white man from the first families — a man of much property — slave property."

Cassidy wanted to hear no more. It would take another bottle, maybe two, to make him forget what he had already heard. Somehow he knew the scene with the beggar out there had some connection with the story and that the white-haired man across from him had been the young man of property. The saloon was becoming crowded, the general noise of revelry building up. Cassidy was relieved when the waiter brought the second bottle.

"Drink up, Mr. Bryson, and wash away yer dismal thoughts." Cassidy quickly followed his own advice and was relieved to note that Silver was at last taking a sizable drink.

But Cassidy found he was held prisoner to Bryson's attention. Bryson looked at him with a new directness — as if Cassidy's desire to hear no more was a stimulation to go on.

"Let's do away with pretense, Mr. Cassidy, and let me finish. I am no Catholic and you are no priest." Bryson actually chuckled at the Irishman's startled expression. "But it will do us both good if I finish this melancholy tale in more order. The villain of the piece was a mulatto — the quadroon's uncle and an extortionist of some talent.

232

When he threatened the merchant with revealing himself as a true kinsman of the family, there was an altercation in which the merchant was killed. Then the mulatto extracted payment from his niece in exchange for his silence, and she soon died in sorrow and fear. He applied to the daughter then, and her answer was . . . in the deep blue pool. I — " Bryson emphasized the *I*, paused, and went on, "I later traced the villain to this city where he resided as a free mulatto. I tricked him into thinking I was executor for the estate of the French family he had despoiled and that he was to gain thereby. I led him through an orgy of indulgence that ended in the room of an Oriental tattoo artist. There I had the pattern of a scorpion, sign of the scourge, punctured on the back of his left hand and given a vicious pose and coloring. For the right hand I had the artist design an open human eye, baleful and accusing. By further manipulation I sold the mulatto into the harsh existence of heavy labor on a remote plantation. It was my intention that he be confronted by the fearful symbols on his hands as he labored in the fields, and when he hid them in fear or idleness, he would feel the sting of the lash. Out there tonight I was beset with an illusion — a few mad moments when I thought the beggar was this same mulatto — that he had somehow escaped the full measure of my revenge. But it was just a trick of memory — a resemblance distorted by the fog of hate. I'm satisfied that the dog of murder I branded so well has either expired in his misery or continues to suffer according to my plan. I find that revenge is almost sweet enough to compensate for lost love, Mr. Cassidy — almost sweet enough."

Cassidy took a big drink, Bryson a small one. "And remember, Mr. Cassidy," the cool amber eyes looked deep into the clouded blue of the Irishman's, "remember the confidence of confession is inviolate."

The giant shivered a little. "I would sooner kiss a rattlesnake, Mr. Bryson, than trifle with your confidence."

Bryson smiled. "Your entertainment from now on will be more pleasant, I think." He nodded toward the stage.

A tall blond singer in a gaudy revealing costume of plumes and satin had moved to the center of the platform. A small, comic-faced man took his place on the piano stool and brought the room to attention with a series of chords and gay runs. The blonde leaned toward her attentive audience and in a throaty contralto began recounting a departing lover's request to:

> *Light me three candles, darling,*
> *Every day that I'm away.*
> *Light me three candles, darling,*
> *While these words you softly say,*
> *"One for I, one for Love, one for You.*
> *I love you . . . I certainly do!"*

The ballad continued through several verses while the singer swayed and crooned seductively. Suddenly, there was a commotion near the stage, a deep bass voice began to blend in duet with the blonde.

"As I live and draw breath, it's our Angus," Cassidy exclaimed to Silver. And soon the pale face of the mustanger and rope artist was visible above the crowd as he took his place boldly by the singer and tilted his head far back to look up at her as he joined in the song. The performance was so completely ludicrous — the big blonde in all her glitter and the nubbin of a man in rough frontier garb, big weapons stuck in his belt and a horsehair rope wound around and around his waist — and the harmony so delightful that the customers yelled and stomped in gusty applause. Silver and Cassidy, feeling that they were sponsoring home talent, stood to shout their encouragement and approval.

The singer too was enjoying the novel turn her act had taken by the addition of this jockeylike man with the profundo voice. She patted him approvingly on the head.

"What's your name, dearie?"

"Anything you want to call me, duchess."

"What do you say we call him 'Poison'?" she asked the audience. "See how his skull of a face would go with crossbones?" She stood back of him and crossed her arms under his chin so that his face

234

peered out between her wrists, making the pantomime weirdly effective, for indeed his tight skin and thin lips with eyes so hollow and hair so light and close to his head, made the symbol an apt description. There was a roar of laughter as Angus grimaced in acceptance of the ridicule.

He broke the pose by grasping the blonde's elbow and steering her with mock courtesy to the sofa.

"Rest your beautiful bones, baby," he said, and turned back to the front of the stage. "Give me some good chordin' in the key of G," he commanded the piano player. "And let me give you feather-bed boys a robust ballad from outta the brush of the mighty Republic of Texas. So I'm 'Poison,' am I? Why, that's the truth, and you should know it!

> *I'm a mighty mustanger from outta the brush!*
> *I live on bull-meat stew and corn-meal mush!*
> *I catch wild horses by the herd!*
> *I leap on their backs as light as a bird.*
> *I walk 'em and stalk 'em —*
> *I break 'em and stake em.*
> *I ride 'em sideways and ride 'em astraddle —*
> *Ride 'em bareback or with a saddle.*
> *When a panther follows along my trail,*
> *I double back and twist his tail!*
> *If a rattlesnake stops to give me a battle,*
> *I skin 'im alive before he can rattle!*
> *When a redskin bothers me, I rope 'im, by heck!*
> *It saves my bullets and breaks his neck!"*

Angus interpreted every line with hilarious movement. Soon the whole saloon was resounding with the song of the mustanger as all the revelers joined in. There was a violence and a release in the exhibition that restored Silver Bryson to an emotional equilibrium he had not known for years. To hell with the past and the codes of gentlemen! Hurrah for the Republic of Texas with its wild men and its wild ways!

CHAPTER XI

WHEN Miguel Sándivar returned from his journey to the springs with La Brema, he awoke his father from a sixteen-year lethargy. Gazing upon his son, confident and secure, astride a glorious golden horse, accompanied by La Brema with twin heifer calfs — one the sacred all-white — made Emilio feel that his life was transformed, his luck completely changed. He no longer surveyed with cynicism the fact that Iturbide's bones had recently been honored in Mexico City and the once-disgraced emperor made a hero; perhaps this meant that a living Sándivar whose family had been faithful to Iturbide would find himself in favor with the present government.

After hearing the whole story of the wonderful springs — the Regalo de la Vaca — Emilio opened the pouch of family documents he had so carefully preserved and, with Miguel, feverishly reviewed all the old papers and records kept there. The grant between the Nueces and Rio Grande was an enormous one and he thought it might include the springs. Such a prospect put Miguel into an ecstasy of delight, and the enormous pride with which he viewed his parent who possessed this great contract with the King of Spain was a heady stimulant to Emilio. He resolved that he would restore the House of Sándivar; he would see his son a gentleman of honor and wide possessions. He immediately started negotiations with a neighboring ranchero and sold the extensive acreage on which he had lived so indifferently since his flight from Mexico City. The amount of money he collected from the transaction was adequate for the venture he had in mind, and since the buyer was interested only in the grazing land, Emilio managed to retain ownership of the shabby buildings and a few surrounding acres. Here he left a bewildered and grief-stricken Francisca with the younger boys and a promise to send for them when the family fortunes were recovered. Having observed his lack of resourcefulness for so many years, Francisca expected never again to see him or her beloved eldest son.

Emilio and Miguel set out for Tampico where they were appropriately outfitted for their important trip to Mexico City. Once in the national capital, they had little difficulty in presenting the old Spanish grant and having it properly recognized and entered into the government records for legal and tax purposes. Although government officials warned Emilio of the dangers in settling between the Nueces and Rio Grande and pointed out that many Mexican landowners had abandoned their holdings in this region because the Mexican government could offer them no consistent military protection, still such settlement was encouraged because it would be helpful when the time came for Mexico to show her strength north of the Rio Grande.

Emilio had no fear of the obstacles outlined; he was possessed by the dream he shared with his son. He hired a party for surveying, and back in Tampico picked ten men to take to Texas as fighters and vaqueros; he and Miguel together passed on each of the ten, all mestizos without family ties, all eager to travel and fight and some seeking a necessary obscurity. There was a quality of fierceness in them all and a similarity of temperament that would make it possible for them to fight or work together without turning on each other. It was as if Miguel and Emilio recognized the necessity to supplement their more gentle natures with the rugged and ruthless qualities exhibited in the men they selected to take across the Rio Grande with them. Thus fortified, they felt bold and happy in their new venture, and the luck of the white calf was consistently with them.

When the survey was completed on the old Spanish grant to the Sándivars, the beautiful springs did lie within its boundaries, and Emilio set up temporary living quarters and corrals there. Soon he and Miguel would have better buildings erected, hire more men, bring Francisca and the boys to the new home, and begin to realize income from vast herds of cattle and horses. There was only one

237

thing that worried Emilio. What if the Texians should eventually prove their boundary at the Rio Grande and hold it? What of the title to his property? Would his Spanish grant be valid with the Republic of Texas? He could not believe that now was the time for testing such validity with the two countries in a state of enmity. He preferred to think that his new ranch lay in Mexico and always would. But as a precaution and a compromise, he wanted to get a Texas title for Miguel on a small acreage that would include the springs; then he'd take his chances on getting Texas recognition of his Spanish grant in case it should ever be established that his property lay in the Republic of Texas. But he wanted no chances taken on Miguel's beautiful springs, the heart of the Regalo de la Vaca acreage. He had heard in Laredo that there were traveling boards of land commissioners who saw to such things and that one of these boards was now in San Antonio.

Emilio had an isolated memory of the time when a family relation, native to Spain, had been sent as an official to San Antonio de Bexar. If he could find this relation or some member of the family who would vouch for him, he would dare to go to San Antonio, appear before this board, and seek title to the springs. Why not? The luck of the Sándivars had turned, and the good fortune that had followed on all his endeavors since Miguel's return made him bold and confident.

So it was that with a fateful sort of timing (Range Templeton was concluding his first big business venture in New Orleans and getting ready to head homeward) Emilio and Miguel Sándivar, accompanied by several of their fighting vaqueros as protection against the hazards of such a journey, took the Laredo road to San Antonio.

Ed and Ella Olson had always given Luvisa such love and attention that she was scarcely conscious of her orphaned state. Most of her thoughts and memories of her parents were relegated to a dream world, seldom visited or explored. The unbroken rule in the Olson

238

household not to speak of the sad events of the past had closed the door also on discussions of relatives and ancestral background.

Since Range too had been early orphaned, he and Luvisa since their marriage had made only the vaguest references to their parents; without reminders of relatives through letters or visits, they found no occasion for discussion of family history. Their time together was always much too short for the realities of the present, and perils of day-to-day existence focused more concern on survival than origins. For both of them, it was as if life had begun with their love and events prior to that were hazy and unimportant.

There was perhaps something too of instinctive caution and injured pride in Luvisa's silence about her Spanish lineage. She had no memory of her Spanish grandfather who had left San Antonio after her mother's death. She was convinced without anyone ever having discussed the matter with her that she had never been accepted by her mother's father — had even been resented and ignored by him.

The established order of Luvisa's memories and attitudes was not disturbed until two strangers called at the Olson House one afternoon to be received by Ed Olson with a reluctant courtesy. They were distant kinsmen of his daughter-in-law and had come to beg a favor. Out of respect to the girl his son had married, he felt he must receive and hear them. And since he could not in good conscience deceive Luvisa about their identity and purpose, he called her into their presence.

"Señores, my granddaughter, Mrs. Templeton. My dear, these two gentlemen, Señor Emilio Sándivar and his son Miguel, are distantly related to you, I believe."

"Sí, sí," Emilio hastened to explain. "Your esteemed mother and I were third cousins. We never met. But I have the small clear memory of the time when a family relation, native to Spain, your distinguished grandfather, was sent as an official to San Antonio de Bexar."

The Sándivars, excited by Luvisa's delight in their meeting, her

239

personal charm and easy flow of Spanish, plunged into happy explanations of family relationships and their own fortunes and affairs. Since they spoke no English, Firebush, whose Spanish was not polished or fluent in the manner of Emilio and Miguel, withdrew from the discussion and kept an unhappy silence.

Witnessing Luvisa's eager, almost affectionate attention to the Sándivars, Ed Olson felt a sting of remorse that he and Ella had told her so little about her mother. But actually there wasn't much to tell, he reflected: A beautiful, sweet-natured girl, lovable as Luvisa herself — only child of a widowed Spanish official who didn't think Ed Olson's son was good enough for his daughter, who disappeared without ever acknowledging his only grandchild and heir.

Meanwhile Emilio was explaining with a familiarity that Ed Olson resented, "In exile on my property in Tamaulipas, I never knew the fate of your noted grandfather. But I supposed I might find some descendant of the family still residing here who would be able to vouch for me in a business matter very close to my heart. My inquiries among the eminent first families of Spanish colonization led me directly to you, Gracias á Dios!"

The business matter referred to by Emilio did not emerge until after the guests had dined and the family was seated in the patio, Ella Olson silent and busy with her needlework, Firebush thoughtful and apart, puffing on his pipe and making no effort to keep up with the highly animated conversation. As the full purpose of their visit was revealed, Luvisa's happiness in the meeting began to fade and her uneasiness to mount. For Miguel in telling the story of his cow La Brema, the discovery of the beautiful springs, and the coming of the horse Lustre, was no longer simply the charming distant cousin for whom she was beginning to feel a real affection — he was the Mexican at the springs for whom her husband felt such contempt and hostility.

"Perhaps your paternal grandfather with whom you reside would be so kind as to appear with me and my son before these commissioners of land," Emilio was saying, "so that we may get an attentive ear, be received as trustworthy. I carry the gold to pay for the land, but I know political conditions here are such that I may not be well received as a Mexican unless I am properly presented. And I hope I may die a beggar and be rejected in paradise if the señora or her grandfather ever has cause to regret such sponsorship of the Sándivars as men of integrity."

Entirely persuasive and carried away with his enthusiasms, Emilio continued to outline his plans while waiting for an answer to his request.

Luvisa was engulfed in anguish and uncertainty, burdened with a decision that must be entirely her own. Her grandparents, so protective and so near, must themselves be protected from the painful complexities of the problem. The aloneness of her position was a new frightening experience. To help Miguel fortify his hold on the springs would be a form of betrayal to Range, for to possess the springs was the very core of her husband's dream. And yet what possible excuse could she offer to so simple a request? Emilio was asking only that her grandfather introduce him to the proper authorities and vouch for the sincerity of Miguel's intentions to make the property at the springs his permanent home. She began to reason that the uncertainties of the times and the wilderness condition of the country would likely prevent Range from ever making a home in that difficult land between the Nueces and Rio Grande. There was no certainty, either, that Emilio and Miguel would permanently settle on the property; their eagerness and zeal for the plan seemed to discount far too much the obstacles that lay ahead. They had lived in quiet isolation and then been visited by unusual good fortune. They had been far removed from the harshness, the actual terrors, of the times. They were bound to meet disappointment and suffering soon and probably actual violence and death . . . so her thoughts ran. Why should she hurt them with an unexplained refusal to do them a small kindness? She'd probably never see either of them again. They were deserving of her favor. And, after all, Miguel had been first at the springs. She was affected too by the

241

tie of kinship; although it was a distant connection, yet it was a blood tie, and for the moment she felt it close and compelling, linking her like a silken thread of the spirit to her mother who might have been, through some chance heritage, like these gracious cousins before her.

So she told Ed Olson what they wanted.

Although it was plain he had no eagerness for the business, he nodded his agreement.

The next morning, after a haunted, sleepless night, Luvisa realized her ordeal had only begun, for her grandfather insisted that she come along with him to the land commissioners and do the talking. It was a real chore, he said, to keep up with the lingo of those two Spaniards. He was careful not to call them Mexicans.

There was a certain prejudice against Mexicans as landowners; but in the case of Emilio and Miguel, there was no difficulty — Ed Olson's presence and the fact that they were distant relatives of his granddaughter gave them a decided advantage with the land commissioners. Then, too, the acreage and amount involved was so very small — only 160 acres at 25 cents an acre in an area wholly undesirable for settlement promotions. Emilio's doubloons were accepted with an easy joke about President Lamar now being able to pay off the regular army. It was a small piece of business, of no particular significance to the board, accustomed as they were to dealing in immense tracts for contracted settlements . . . no significance to the land commissioners at all, but to Luvisa, with cold fear at her heart, the most significant and sinister event in her whole life.

Thus Miguel's modest piece of land became a homestead, inviolate, protected by a very special law hardly a year old in the Republic of Texas: the Homestead Law.

Luvisa Templeton and Ed Olson were asked to sign their names as witnesses to the transaction. Luvisa was so hesitant and so obviously pained about the request to place her signature on the document that her grandfather grew impatient, explaining over and over that it meant nothing at all. Miguel looked frightened as Luvisa struggled to think of a pretext for not writing her name. She became aware of his anxiety, quickly dipped the pen and wrote, feeling as she did so that she was signing some fatal documentation in a book of doom.

When Miguel and Emilio bade Luvisa farewell, there were actual tears of happiness in Miguel's eyes and his voice broke time and again as he tried to express his gratitude.

"Beloved cousin," he said, "will you and thine consider my home your home forever? I shall try to make it a lovely, gracious home worthy of your presence should you ever appear there. And if you'll forgive me the familiarity, it is a part of my cherished dream to find someone as charming and full of kindness as you to live by my side and bear me such beautiful children as yours are. Our blood tie may be weak with the dilutions of the generations since our respective ancestors were brother and sister, but my fondness for you is a strength to my heart and an inspiration to my spirit." He pressed her hands tenderly and was gone quickly to hide the weakness of his tears.

Once more alone, Luvisa was struck with the full realization of what Range would have felt about her visitors. He would not have liked Miguel or Emilio, even if he had never had the unpleasant meeting at the springs; this she knew for certain. He might have endured their presence with strained politeness for her sake — he could not have endured her expression of affection for them. He would consider her help to Miguel a betrayal and affront. It would be impossible for him to understand how she could do such a thing if she really loved him. Lonely as she was for him and passionately as she loved him, she was appalled at the idea that he might actually turn against her, despise her. Suddenly she was dreadfully ill, then hysterical, and ran to her room to fall on the bed sobbing and moaning.

Ella Olson, thinking her granddaughter was weeping for memory of her mother and loneliness for her husband, came to comfort her,

243

but, unable to penetrate her hysteria, became concerned and sent Firebush to bring Dr. Weideman. When the doctor came, he asked to be alone with Luvisa.

"Tell me about it," he said, as serenely as if she were sitting before him in all calmness bidding for his attention. He waited. Soon, the whole burden of her thoughts and fears were laid before him, first in broken whispers, then in a leaden voice of despair.

"You have betrayed no one, Lu," he said with conviction when her recital was done. "You have simply been betrayed by your tender woman's heart. Tell no one what your experience has been. Erase from your mind these evil forebodings for they tear down strength and encourage weakness. And I know two very sweet babies who do not deserve to be denied the fine nourishment and attention they have become accustomed to, who will cry with fright and pain if you offer them the despair and fear now contaminating the milk that is their life substance."

Luvisa had forgotten the twins and was shocked that she had neglected them. The idea that her condition might cause illness or discomfort acted immediately to dissolve hysteria and restore composure. Following Dr. Weideman's instructions, she took a cool bath, drank the rich turkey soup her grandmother offered, and went to care for Luke and Laska.

Dr. Weideman made a point of advising Ed and Ella Olson never to mention the visit of the Sándivars. They had for so long practiced silence on this subject that they agreed readily with his instruction and attributed Luvisa's hysteria to an awakened memory of her parents. Thus Dr. Weideman reduced the chances that Range would ever learn of Luvisa's connection with Emilio and Miguel Sándivar.

CHAPTER XII

From Luvisa Templeton's Account —

. . . How WOEFULLY I underestimated my husband in those early days of our marriage, accepting many of his dreams as boyish fancies, even joining in the dreaming myself, failing to comprehend that special power in him — the power that carries a man quickly from dreaming to planning and doing.

At the same time I underestimated Miguel. There was one likeness between Range Templeton and Miguel Sándivar: the uncanny ability to translate fancy into fact. Otherwise, their differences were so great, no thought or preachment could merge them into compatibility. Theirs were the kind of differences, if I may be forgiven for speaking so bluntly, that must be bred out. And when circumstances accentuated the contrarieties of their natures, rooting their dreams to the same spot, conflict was not a choice but a compulsion. Caught in the struggle between these two dreamers of determination, I could give one only a burdened understanding while the other possessed my heart.

After the visit of Miguel and Emilio, I began to take on what might be called, I suppose, a false maturity, a sort of protective covering against what I had done. I began to plan what I would have Range do and think, how we'd make our home in San Antonio and send the children to the States for an education, away from the harshness of the frontier . . . and, if we could make enough money, possibly go with them. It was the only time I ever took the lead in our life together, even though it was only in my thoughts, for he would return to me from New Orleans a man of means, able to finance a small kingdom, manifesting such strength and forcefulness in thought and action that it would never occur to me to do otherwise than follow him with confidence anywhere he wanted to go, eager to bear his children and share his fate. And the love we had known before I bore Luke and Laska was to grow into something as magnificent and awesome as the spectacle of a giant waterfall that suddenly appears after the quiet meandering of a deep river. . . .

The Christmas of 1839 was the most wonderful Christmas of my life. We knew Range was trying to get home by Christmas because he'd managed to get word to us from Houston before turning back toward New Orleans with the fat steers he'd bought from a Mr. Chenet. I had been saddened by this turn of his affairs that kept us longer apart than either of us had expected, but I began planning for Christmas and tried to feel cheerful that he was being successful in his money-making ventures — at a time, too, when money was so hard to come by in the Republic. I couldn't be sure, however, that we'd be together on Christmas and was beside myself with joy on that afternoon of December 23 when they rode into San Antonio, tired and haggard from extra-long hours on the trail but in good health and spirits. There were twelve of them in all, including the Negro woman Adelia. The party quickly broke up on the plaza, the five Mexicans and the Negroes off to their homes, and the four others — Range, Mr. Bryson, the giant of an Irishman Mr. Cassidy, and Wong — made haste to the Olson House. It was well that I had prepared Christmas gifts and helped my grandmother to have everything ready for company and made festive with holiday decorations, for after Range's arrival I was so deliriously happy that all practical things left my mind. And you cannot imagine the astonishment, the fun and laughter, the utter delight caused by the twins! It was the first question Range asked me while he still held me almost too tight for breathing, and Grandfather welcomed Mr. Bryson and Mr. Cassidy, and Grandmother tried to tell Wong all at once everything that had happened in the house and yard while he had been gone.

"Luvisa — the baby — is he — ?"

"Oh, he's wonderful, darling."

Range glanced over my shoulder and gave Mr. Bryson a triumphant look.

"Well, Bryson, you'll have to put that locket away for a while. It's a boy." Then he explained to me. "He bought a locket for a present to a *girl*."

"Oh, how sweet!" I exclaimed. "She'll adore a locket, Mr. Bryson. I know she will!"

"Luvisa!" There was reproach and disappointment in Range's voice. "You said a boy."

"*And* a girl — Luke and Laska!" It was my triumphant moment, and I shocked them so, there was no immediate word from anyone.

Then Mr. Bryson yelled, "Twins!"

Range looked completely blank. "A boy and girl *both?*"

I nodded. He came to life, swung me off my feet around and around, hugged me so hard I thought my ribs would crack, gave an ear-splitting shout, kept saying, "Luvisa, twins!" over and over, and half-carried me as he rushed into the house to see them.

As Range stood looking at his son and daughter for the first time, they stared back seriously for a moment and then began to laugh and kick in glee. They were not yet four months old and exceedingly friendly in disposition — but it seemed to Range that they were welcoming him in particular. He reached out his hand and touched Luke, then Laska, as if he were afraid his slightest touch would be too harsh. And then I saw his eyes fill with tears that he would not acknowledge, letting them slide on down his cheeks and onto the front of his jacket. It was the only time I ever saw Range shed tears. Finally, he laughed shakily, still unable to say anything.

I laughed too. "They won't break," I said. I picked Luke up and placed him in the crook of Range's arm. Then I took Laska and arranged her on his other arm. He looked bewildered and frightened. Laska wiggled and squealed in playful mood, and Luke lay quietly, his hands folded in judgelike manner gazing fixedly at his father as if to inquire what manner of man was this. The others

247

had come in by this time and all burst into laughter for Range looked so desperately awkward and funny holding both the babies. I took Laska for she was about to squirm out of his grasp.

Grandfather said, "Let me have that young sprout before you fall down with him," and took Luke. Then we all started talking at once and Grandmother had a hard time getting us stopped long enough to eat supper.

When I left the company to give the babies their bedtime nursing, Range came with me, carefully transferring Luke from Grandfather's arms to his own, and walking with slow and cautious step as he followed me. He sat and watched us in absolute stillness and so solemn you'd think he was afraid something might break a spell and we'd disappear. He adored us all three with his eyes and held Luke stiffly as if he dared not move. After Laska was through feeding, I placed her in her father's arms and took Luke. Range was not quite so unsure of himself now and his arms enfolded her possessively. I hadn't wanted him to love the boy more than the girl, and now, watching him with her, I was content. I was so happy I could have cried but I contained myself, not daring to speak, just feasting on his presence, smiling at him, loving him with all of my being. So many joys I had then to balance against the time when I would have them no more: that glorious, light and heady, almost spiritually intense feeling that comes over a woman with the return of the man she loves after a long and anxious absence; that wondrous pride with which she holds a son or daughter in her arms to show him the very life of their blended love, thinking here may be the very best of them both, here the whole wonder and beauty of their love; and that shining faith and hope through which she envisions the future of her home and family as a charmed circle encompassing all the love and goodness this world can afford. I was later to learn that life can be as bitter as it can be beautiful, but to this moment, even as I recall and set down these things in the pain of my affliction and the desolation of my heart, I am convinced that such glorious feelings as I had then are no betrayal of life but rather assurance of a

248

divine quality through which man and woman can someday realize the intended fullness of joy to be found in this world through the blessedness of harmonious living. Of course, such a state of existence cannot be until greed and hate and violence are replaced by brotherly love, reverence for God, and appreciation of the world's natural bounty. Shall I, a weak and dying woman, predict when such things shall come to pass, or what forces of evil and destruction may go before? No, I think not. I have a simple mind and a simple faith. I say that love will triumph in this world, no matter what darkness of the ages or corruptness of man may lie between now and then; I can say this because I have been enfolded by the wings of love. I say moreover that goodness will eventually encompass the earth; this assurance I have because I have encountered the power of goodness.

(Ah, Mr. Bryson, I am being too profound. I see pain and pity in your eyes. Your affectionate concern is a great comfort to me, dear friend, but I will be happier through these final days if you do not consider me an object of pity, but rather pity those women who have neither sighted the grandeurs of this life nor dwelt for any span in their glory. Hand me a glass of cool cistern water, and after I have revived a little, let us turn the account back to that wonderful homecoming Christmas. Do you recall the gay dance we did together, Mr. Bryson, and the beautiful rose gown and bonnet Range gave me and the other lovely gifts you all brought from New Orleans? I will need no help from you in enumerating them every one.)

I had never before possessed cloth so fine as that in the garments and bolts of material Range brought to me from New Orleans. The lovely colors and the feel of the fine fabrics to my fingers and against my skin were a tonic to the senses. The rich rose velvet Parisian gown and bonnet were the most gorgeous of all — the bonnet, pleated and quilted, with its ribbons and rosebud trim, made me feel the grand lady indeed. The gown was of low-cut-neckline styling such as I had never worn, but since my husband had bought it for me, I reasoned away the slight embarrassment that my modesty imposed; the neck was outlined with flat pink roses of lighter shade than the gown and spreading green velvet leaves, and here and there these same roses and leaves had been worked onto the material of the full boned skirt. The waist fitted ever so tightly and my arms were almost bare; there were long mittens of creamy imported French lace and a matching shawl (even lace stockings!) and all the necessary undergarments soft and fancy with trimmings such as a woman dreams of but seldom has the time and goods for making or the money and place for buying. How on earth Range ever came to buy all these things, who helped him make the selections, by what miracle they fitted me so well, I never looked into; it was sufficient that he had taken the time and trouble to express his love and call my attention to his success in this way. Of course, most of the things were not practical for a woman living in a frontier settlement and I would actually wear them very little, but my joy was as complete as it would have been had I been attending parties, balls, and theaters every day. His generous purchases also included several pairs of fine kid shoes in different sizes so that out of them Grandmother and I might be fitted and the extras could be given to some of our good friends who would never have opportunities to shop for such things. Besides all these, there were three special pieces of cloth in generous yardage of such fine quality as I had never touched before. When Range showed these to me, we were alone and the romantic declarations he made to me were more precious than the gifts. The pink cashmere, its woolen as soft as a new downy chick, he said he was giving to me to match the color in my cheeks; the golden yellow satin for the glow of my hair; and the fairylike filmy mass of blue-gray Japanese silk because it reminded him of the lovelight in my eyes. He said more — words too dear and too personal to expose in speech or written form. . . . Those who have truly loved will read between these stilted lines anyway;

250

those who have not would only profane such lover's language with their curiosity or ridicule. Ah, a woman does not care whether she is actually beautiful by the world's standards or not as long as she is mirrored thus in the heart of the man she loves!

There were clothes for the babies too — long, long dresses elaborate with ribbons and laces, and beautiful silk wrappers in pink and blue lined and delicately embroidered. They actually looked as if they'd been made for royalty. We dressed the twins in these clothes on Christmas Day, and what a picture they made! They were charmed with the bows and laces and gurgled with delight as they amused themselves plucking at the trimmings and apparently engaging in conversation about the wonders of their new clothes. Mr. Cassidy gave them an adorable music box that was an endless pleasure and kept them entranced as long as anybody would keep winding it up. Range had had a silver cup engraved in New Orleans for his baby. It carried the words: "To My First-born from Range Templeton." So that was Luke's present from his father that Christmas. It was quite appropriate since Luke was actually the first-born, but I think Range was a little envious that Mr. Bryson had brought the only gift especially for a baby girl. Wong had remembered the family too; but he brought a single present and placed it on the mantle. It was an exquisite carving in ivory showing two children in a pose of adoration for a butterfly poised delicately on a flower.

"Why," Grandmother kept asking me in a puzzled manner, over and over, "did he select a piece with *two* children in it? You'd think he might have divined you were going to have twins. I certainly missed the old wizard while he was gone, not only for the work he does, but the things he seems to know. It gives me the creeps sometimes how much he knows without ever prying or saying anything. . . . I'll always puzzle how he knew to bring an ivory piece with *two* children in it."

Range's gifts to Grandmother and Grandfather were a small pitcher and a mustache cup colorfully decorated with New Orleans scenes. Mr. Bryson brought Grandfather a bottle of very old French wine and Grandmother a lovely brooch — and for me a most unusual set of combs for my hair done with seed pearls in an elongated pattern of two doves in flight. Then there were several boxes of sweetmeats and confections, strange and exotic in flavors; just which of the men brought these, I cannot say — I simply recall what a novel delight they were to all of us and our visitors.

There were eight of us for Christmas dinner: Grandmother and Grandfather, Mr. Bryson and Mr. Cassidy, Dr. Weideman and Eli Dawson, Range and myself. Wong had Cicero and his new wife Adelia to help him in the kitchen. I had yet to get a good look at Adelia or learn where Cicero had found her; she scooted about behind things like a frightened gopher and it was some time before I became aware of her as a family fixture and inquired into the matter.

All afternoon Christmas Day and far into the evening, friends and neighbors dropped in to hear all the news brought back from along the Opelousas Trail and New Orleans. Wong kept the large crystal bowl filled with eggnog and surrounded with trays of Christmas cookies and at suppertime platters of cold meat cuts, pickles, and the small biscuits that were his specialty. I was very gay in my new rose gown and loved the whole wide world! I received many compliments and attentions and I'm sure now my bearing was a little on the side of vanity that day, so proud was I of my tall and handsome and very prosperous young husband, my beautiful children, and yes, I must admit, not at all displeased with myself — my appearance and my good fortune.

We were fortunate to have two musicians who could play for our dancing Christmas night. In those times we were often dependent on the Negro fiddler for dance music and Cicero was one of the best. So we danced to his fiddle and Mr. Cassidy's melodious stringed instrument until they were both played out. Range was not the type to let himself go and have fun dancing; he was stiff and clumsy in the execution of any step. He tried a few times for my sake but I knew he was relieved to deliver me to another partner and appreciated that I did not insist he exhibit his inability further. This streak of restraint and withdrawal in his nature disturbed me from time to time. I felt that through it, he was denied some of the lighter, sweeter joys of life. But dancing and singing both were forms of expression alien to his disposition. He could show dignity and a pleasant countenance before company, but only now and then would he participate in a lively conversation. As he grew older, he dwelt more and more in silence. In his quietness lay a great strength and reserve that gave him a kind of power, but there was too much restraint about him for as complete enjoyment of life and love as I myself knew. He was always too solidly sure of my devotion and loyalty to be jealous of my gaiety with other men, provided he admired those men and trusted them. It was Mr. Bryson and I who put on the top performance of the evening for he could move with grace and skill through the most intricate steps, and although I had never been to many balls, dancing was as natural to me as breath and laughter. Range cheered us as roundly as the rest, and it did me much good to express my exuberance in this way. Mr. Cassidy entertained us highly with an Irish jig, and Dr. Weideman led me through some beautiful Russian dance movements to which I added a few steps of the Spanish fandango, suggesting by twirling, stamping my feet, and snapping my fingers that we combine the two. But some small warning in his eyes stopped me. I know now it must have been that in abandoning myself to the typically Spanish movements I showed my heritage too clearly and he did not want me to lose myself in the exaltation of the dance and become conspicuous in this way. Cicero was an artist at the Spanish fandango tunes as well as the stomps, swings, and waltzes so popular then. And he had been playing one of these adapted by his peculiar genius to the steps Dr. Weideman was exhibiting. It was odd the way I responded to Dr. Weideman's wordless warning; it frayed the edges of my high spirits somewhat and cast a small nameless fear into the pool of my joy.

*   *   *

If Range and I had taken the money he made on the New Orleans drive, moved to a settled part of the United States and made a modest home there, we would not have had to suffer the long separations imposed on us by conditions in the Republic of Texas. We could have escaped the constant dangers attendant on Mexican invasions and Indian attacks, for San Antonio was the favorite striking place for the invader and savage alike. We would not have had to live in the midst of the turmoil and uncertainties of Texas affairs: a government destitute of finances and so without the necessary military defenses for its citizens, annexation problems, boundary disputes, border banditry that made the thorny brush country between the Nueces and Rio Grande rivers even more inhospitable and threatening than nature had intended — and finally, the Mexican War.

It was not until ten years had passed after Range's first drive to New Orleans that we were able to establish ourselves on our ranch in southwest Texas. Of course, in all those years Range never for a moment turned his face wistfully to the east as I did, thinking that out of this wild land lay a place of security and safety for the children and a closer companionship for ourselves. Since I knew this so well, I never said one word that expressed any displeasure with his plans for acquiring large landholdings in an unsettled area and building for himself and family a self-sufficiency independent of community life; instead, I encouraged him in his determination to overcome all obstacles in attaining these things. I realized that he was as wedded to Texas in mind and spirit as he was to me in heart and body. I even understood — or thought I did — the passion that drove him toward possession of the vast acreage south of the Nueces that had challenged him so, a passion that was as much a part of him as the love he bore me and the children. For me to have opposed this force in him would have been, in his eyes, a form of unfaithfulness as disloyal as offering myself to another man. I say I knew these things early in our married life, yet it was years before I came to acknowledge that the land and I were rivals. Was it some weakness in me that I should have overcome — devoting my every word and action toward making him stronger within himself and

254

more confident in all his undertakings? Should I have raged or pouted or withdrawn from him, or pleaded and used my woman's wiles to turn him into quieter ways and a more peaceful existence? Was it wrong, unfair to myself and my children, that I never opposed the hasty departures to follow Captain Hays after marauding Indians or to strike out on long trails for surveying his land or rounding up more cattle to sell — that I met all these advances of loneliness and fear with the quick hug, the fierce kiss, the too bright smile? There were times when I did not approve of the means he used to achieve his ends and I worked carefully at bending him in the direction of a dormant nobility that he chose to ignore or deny. I tell myself over and over that had I been with him more (fighting, expeditions and business trips kept us much apart), and had I been granted some further wisdom to season the bounty of my love, I might have been able to sustain him in some manner that would have caused the nobler elements in his nature to triumph. But it is unwise to dwell long on what might have been. As I follow the circle of my thoughts around and around, I always get back to the simple fact of loving Range Templeton beyond the point of reason or explanation.

Although much of sadness and loss must go into any account of the turbulent events between 1840 and 1850, I wish to make it clear that as we feared and fought, and death and disaster crossed our paths time and again, all was not dreariness and pain. Once you have given yourself wholly to life on a frontier, there is an excitement and stimulation running through all endeavor. It was intoxicating to Range, so temperate in most respects, and was not without a certain savor for me. The dearness of family and friends is deeply accented when survival is constantly under threat. Strong and weak points of character are swiftly delineated under the pressure of circumstances that repeatedly demand the utmost in courage, boldness, and judgment. Small unexpected pleasures are treasured more in time of peril; and out of tribulation there can come spiritual elations otherwise never encountered. . . .

*   *   *

255

Range had not been back in San Antonio a month before Indian troubles were stirring. Early in January of 1840 three Comanche chiefs rode boldly into San Antonio for a conference with Colonel Henry Karnes, bringing the message that the tribe wanted peace with the Texians. After the colonel had heard their story, he told them that no treaty could be made until they had brought in all prisoners. The Indians appeared willing to meet this condition, agreed they would bring in the prisoners and sign the treaty, but Karnes was convinced they would try to pull some kind of trickery and went about preparing for trouble.

San Antonio's plaza was soon enlivened with three companies of infantry under the command of Colonel William Fisher. Then there was a period of anxious waiting, for some of the white prisoners held were relatives of San Antonio residents. The Indians took their time about putting in a second appearance.

It was not until March 19 that runners appeared to announce the coming of the Comanches. There were about sixty in the party, many of them chiefs rigged out in all their finery and exhibiting their wealth in horses and buffalo robes, some young warriors, and a few women and children. The menfolk of the Olson household went along with many other men of the town to watch the proceedings and to be near at hand in case of trouble — and Firebush Olson was convinced there would be trouble. He instructed his wife and granddaughter to bolt the doors securely and left guns carefully loaded.

The Comanches brought only one captive with them, a girl named Mathilde Lockhart. She told the Texians that the Indians were holding back the other prisoners and intended to bring them in for ransom later on. The Indians were questioned and their replies considered most impudent and unsatisfactory. They were then informed that the council house was surrounded and they themselves would be held as hostages until the other captives were brought in as promised. The Comanches considered such proceedings a preposterous indignity and immediately resisted, some dashing for the nearest

256

outlets, others starting a general conflict in the council house.

Soon the fight was raging in the streets and spilling over into yards. Arrows whizzed, knives flashed in the sun, gunshots resounded across the plaza and down the streets, and an inferno of screeches and yells sounded a fearsome alarm. Women and children quickly sought cover. Behind thick walls, barred windows, and bolted doors, Ella Olson and Luvisa were in little personal danger. While her grandmother kept the babies well back from the window, Luvisa watched the fighting in the street, held a rifle ready, and was on the alert to unbar the door for anyone who might need to enter the house for refuge. Some of the Indians had managed to mount and were fighting with lances; others were dodging in and out among the houses on foot, letting fly their arrows and using knives in close combat. Dr. Weideman was on Nightmare and zestfully making the most of the fray. He drew up not far from Luvisa's window and paused to reload his pistols, apparently in no immediate danger. An Indian careened around the corner, his horse in a high run, his lance raised for the doctor, who was directly in his path. Dr. Weideman saw him but was for the moment defenseless. There was little thought and less skill in the action Luvisa took, raising the rifle, pointing at the spot where the Indian and his horse should cross the path of the ball if she pulled the trigger at that instant — and she did. The horse toppled. Dr. Weideman had his pistol ready by that time and with one shot stilled the floundering Indian. The doctor recognized Luvisa at the window, smiled and bowed.

"I thank you, Mrs. Templeton, for delaying the inevitable and more especially for assisting me in obtaining this fine specimen." He waved his pistol at the dead Indian, then dismounted to examine him.

Luvisa spotted two other Indians hugging the walls, slipping from house to house on the side of the street nearest the doctor, and called to him, "Dr. Weideman! Look to your fighting!" In a swift movement he was back on Nightmare and running the two down.

Later Luvisa heard how Mrs. Maverick and Mrs. Higginbotham,

watching together, had observed some of Dr. Weideman's curious and startling conduct immediately after the fight. He had placed a severed Indian head upon the sill of Mrs. Higginbotham's grated front window, addressing her, "With your permission, madam." He had repeated the performance with a second bloody head. It developed that he had selected them for a special study of the skulls, male and female. He explained his action to the shocked witnessses: "I have been long exceedingly anxious to secure such specimens — and now, ladies, I must hurry and get a cart to take them to my house."

To the horror of many residents the doctor boiled up his grisly trophies, including two entire bodies, and assembled the skeletal specimens in his garden. There was a great hue and cry raised about his polluting the city's drinking water by emptying the contents of his boiler into the public ditch that ran by his house. He had to appear before city authorities and defend his action. He explained that the water was quickly purified because it was a running stream. Although there was much loud and excited talk among his accusers, and it was reported many women were sickened and vomited, the doctor was unmoved by the procedure, cheerfully paid his fine, and left the courtroom laughing. Thereafter, many of the Mexicans referred to him as "El Diablo" and would go far out of their way to keep from meeting him.

There were thirty-five Indians killed, twenty-seven captured, and more than a hundred horses — along with many buffalo robes and peltries — taken in the Indian Council House fight. The Texians had seven men killed and seven or eight wounded. They sent a squaw, well mounted, back to the plains country to tell of the disaster that had befallen the Comanche chieftains. She was supposed to return in a few days but was never heard of again. The exchange of prisoners that the Texians hoped to bring about with the captured Indians never took place. Instead, the Comanches, in retaliation for the slaughter of their leaders, tortured to death the white captives they held, executed a frightful raid on the port settle-

258

ment of Linnville before the summer had passed, and began to harass the settlers anew with robberies and abductions.

The Olsons shared specifically in the dreadful aftermath of the Council House fight for Firebush Olson was among those wounded, and the arrow that lodged in his back was fatal. He lived for nearly three years but lost the use of his legs and became more and more the invalid. His mind weakened and failed and a near madness descended upon him — a madness which engaged him in endless horrible conflicts with the Comanches.

Because of Ed Olson's suffering, Range felt more vindictive than ever toward Indians, and Luvisa suffered more sharply than ever before over the tragedy that had taken her father and mother — a scene of horror that Firebush enacted over and over in his delirium. But it was Ella Olson who shared the agony of the old Indian fighter to the fullest and deepest. Range was away from home much of the time, and Luvisa was diverted through the many demands made on her by the twins; so it was from his faithful wife that Firebush got the fullest measure of time and strength, love and grief, and a tender, constant care. One consolation came to Ed Olson in his affliction. He lived to hear and understand all about the big Plum Creek fight in which aroused Texians made the Indians pay dearly for plundering the town of Linnville. Almost a hundred Comanches were killed and not a single Texian lost. Range was with the men who had gone out from San Antonio to join in the fight. When they returned, the fighting party stopped first at the Olson House to give Firebush the whole story, putting him in the best spirits he had known since receiving his wound six months before. He called Range and John Coffee Hays close to his bed and scrutinized them as if seeing them for the first time. "Like it fightin' together?" he quizzed.

Range and Hays exchanged a glance of mutual understanding and assent that pleased the old Indian fighter.

"When it comes to fightin', let him lead," Firebush told Range. "Best leader in these parts."

Range nodded agreeably. He liked fighting with Hays.

Not long after the Plum Creek victory, Hays was made a Ranger captain and Range thereafter joined in the Hays expeditions whenever he was in San Antonio and available for volunteer duty.

The Plum Creek victory cured the Comanches of attempts to penetrate into settled areas and conduct raids on a grand scale. But they continued to rove in small bands, stealing horses, capturing and killing women and children. Yet, the watchfulness imposed by these robberies and abductions was only one facet of trouble for the settlers around San Antonio. Constant rumors of invasion from Mexico fostered a state of uneasiness, and the robber bands that headquartered in Laredo preyed ever more rapaciously on the traders whose goods were so essential to the frontier economy.

Agatón Quiñones continued to operate as chief of the freebooters, and in April 1841, Eli Dawson was robbed of a large cargo on the Laredo road, losing several men and barely escaping with his own life. Captain Hays quickly gathered up a company of twenty-five volunteers and struck out for Laredo. Range, Silver Bryson, and C. Cassidy went along. It was Range's intention to visit the springs before his return, and, in a general way, determine the boundaries of his ranch land.

Captain Hays was soon back in San Antonio with prisoners and a job well done. This border town did not yet consider itself a part of Texas, but on this occasion it surrendered to the young Ranger captain and promised protection for the traders. Range came in several weeks after Hays, and his state of mind was not a happy one for he had found the Sándivars well settled at the springs.

"I guess they've lived around there a long time. It's the same family that boy and cow belong to — the one I saw at the springs first time I was there," he told Luvisa.

She listened to his account silently, not trusting herself to comment, burdened with her deeper and much more accurate knowledge of the conditions and motives of the Sándivars.

"They own a big stretch of land toward the Rio Grande," he explained. "The land that will be ours lies to the north and east of the springs. I want the Nueces River on my northern boundary and I want the springs to the south. I've decided we'll build our first house on the Nueces where things will be safer for you and the children — then from time to time I'll put up some pens to the south spotted here and there where the riders workin' for me can pitch camp when they're out after cattle and horses. When the children are older and the Indians and Mexicans are cleared out — boundaries settled and all that — we'll build the big house at the springs."

Luvisa's outward calm and attention belied her inner turmoil: I'm glad I'm sitting not too close to him and I'm glad the light here in the patio is dim, she thought, and glad he's too absorbed to expect me to say anything.

"I asked those Mexicans if they'd sell some of that land now, thinkin' they might want to get out with something to the good, but they wouldn't hear to it. That little Mexican I met up with when I was lost, recognized me. He acted mighty haughty up on Luis Martiniano's fine horse."

When he used the word "Mexican" with such contempt, Luvisa felt a stab of personal injury and held back the impulse to set him right. If he knew I was half Spanish, if he knew I was distantly related to Miguel and had extended him hospitality and some affection, what would he say? . . . how would he treat me? . . . would he still love me? The likely answers to her self-torturing questions chilled her heart.

Luvisa could not understand such pure racial antagonism as Range had built up against Miguel — antagonism that had spread quickly and without reservation to include all Mexicans. It was all right, she reasoned, to hate the Mexican bandits who attacked traders and killed innocent men for profit (hate them for their acts of violence, not for being Mexicans), and certainly Texas must be free from such despots as Santa Anna, but couldn't Range see in such men as Eli Dawson and John Hays the importance of judging men by character rather than race?

"They treated us like that part of the country was Mexico and we were foreign trash of some sort," the contempt was still strong in his voice. "They'll learn the hard way after while that they belong on the other side of the Rio Grande, and they'll be lucky if we don't push the boundary back further than that."

She wanted to say: Remember, Range, when you went with John Hays to Laredo in that company of twenty-five men, thirteen were Mexicans under command of the courageous Captain Antonio Perez. The gallant Hays would be hard put to defend us with Americans alone.

"They'll see the time when they'll be glad to get out alive," he continued. "I'll keep my eye on 'em. The Indians or border bandits may clean 'em out any time and save me the trouble of dickerin' with 'em. I'm not going to be in too much of a hurry about some things. I know what I want — and I know what it'll take to get it. I expect to be around in that part of the country for a long time, and my children after me."

Your children are one-quarter Spanish, Luvisa told him in her mind, or part Mexican, I guess you'd call it. And in the intensity of imagined reactions she saw shock and shame and a sort of cold violence rise up in him. Then she experienced a very real shame for herself that she was dealing in deceit and concealment — that her love for this man outweighed her courage, outweighed the pride she had in her mother and her mother's origins.

Range moved his chair closer to Luvisa and reached for her hand. He held it tightly, stroking her wrist with his thumb in a way he had when confiding in her about things he felt deeply.

"Your hands are cold, Luvisa. Do you want a shawl?"

"No, dear, I'm all right. Just excited with all the news you bring." His strong touch, his affectionate concern, dispelled some of her fears, and she dared to hope that time and events would so work things out that he and Miguel would never meet again, never come into conflict, and that Range himself as he grew older would temper his intolerance with reason, would allow their love to be the most important thing in their lives — more important than origins, more important than land.

"I thought about calling our land the Rawhide Range, Luvisa. Do you like that? Is it all right to use my name like that?"

That he sought her approval of this expression of his vanity amused Luvisa. She gave it wholeheartedly. "I think it's a perfect name, dear. That country is certainly tough as rawhide and a wonderful natural range for cattle and horses and the wilder animals too. And you yourself, Range Templeton, are tough as rawhide," she teased, "so it couldn't be better . . . the Rawhide Range."

"We'll make our fortune out of the stuff that rawhide comes from — cattle — by the thousands. And we'll be helpin' Texas to grow strong and tough as rawhide too. There's got to be more money in this Republic — not money borrowed from other countries, but money made here and spent here, like I made on that New Orleans drive. I believe if enough Texians could get into the cattle business, we could hold this Republic together with rawhide! I'm gonna slap my brand on every wild cow I can get a rope on — a brand like this — " He illustrated by using his finger to draw imaginary lines in the palm of Luvisa's hand. "A big T for Templeton with two R's ridin' on the T for Rawhide Range." His fingernail was sharp and his excitement strong. Luvisa could actually feel the design of the brand

burning in her hand. "I'll get a head start and be the biggest cattleman of them all!"

Range seldom spoke with such excitement, but now he went on. "I'm against this talk of annexation. We can take care of ourselves, build Texas up and stay independent. We don't need the United States to fight the Indians and Mexicans for us. All we need is to get John Hays, Ben McCulloch, Old Paint Caldwell, Ed Burleson, and a few others like 'em outfitted with enough men, horses, and weapons and the Republic will be made safe for settlers from border to border. For my part, I'm gonna show 'em what a man can make out of that wild land between the Nueces and the Rio Grande — it's a mean part of the country that most settlers don't even like to cross and a land speculator wouldn't offer to a coyote. Most of it I can get for a survey and a song, and never have to sing the song."

"You'll pay for it with a rarer coin that gold," Luvisa said, thinking of the risks he must take, the dangers he must face . . . the labor, the endurance, even the pain and bloodshed that this land was likely to demand of him.

"I reckon my biggest expense will be ammunition," he answered wryly.

For the next several years little notice was taken of the Rawhide Range, the herds gathered and marketed and the work carried on there. Texians were deeply concerned with Mexican refusal to accept the boundaries stipulated by the Texas Congress in 1836. President Lamar brought trouble upon the Republic much sooner than was necessary, many were inclined to think, by sending an expedition to occupy Santa Fe, for the place was entirely Mexican even though it lay within the far-flung northwestern boundary of Texas. The hungry, trail-weary members of the expedition were received by the people of Santa Fe as enemies, thrown into prison, and later marched under cruel conditions to Mexico City and confined in the infamous Perote prison; moreover, the ill-fated trip brought retaliation that struck at San Antonio in March of 1842 when General Vasquez captured the city and withdrew after two days of occupation. Many residents became panic-stricken and fled, but the Olsons stayed on with those to whom San Antonio was home — deep-rooted — to live or die in, whatever the fortunes of war.

Six months later General Adrian Woll entered the city at the head of a Mexican army numbering about thirteen hundred. Captain Hays and his little band of Rangers stood all alone against the Mexicans, all other forces having been disbanded because of the poverty of the Republic. Hays put out his spies to watch the movements of the enemy and spread the word afar that San Antonio had fallen.

Woll had occupied San Antonio a week before Texas volunteers were of sufficient strength to meet him in battle. This week of occupation was one of almost unbearable suspense for Luvisa. Range was somewhere in the vicinity of Victoria delivering cattle to a drover there, and she had no way of knowing if he would hear of the disaster and be among the volunteers to oppose Woll. Although abandoned homes were looted and many demands made on the Mexican families, those at the Olson House were not molested. At one time Mexican soldiers came to requisition food and blankets, but Firebush, under the delusion that Indians were in possession of the town, was aroused to one of his wildest exhibitions, and the soldiers, terrified of the madman, made a quick departure. Dr. Weideman made one hasty backdoor visit late at night to see how they fared and to assure them the Mexicans would be routed before long, and then went on his mysterious way.

On Sunday, September 17, Matthew (Old Paint) Caldwell with only two hundred men in his command engaged General Woll's force of six hundred infantrymen and two hundred cavalrymen at Salado Creek several miles out of San Antonio. It was a battle of savage intensity, lasting all day, and spread carnage and confusion over the whole settlement. Although he had a four-to-one advantage in numbers, General Woll finally fell back before the fierce attacks of Old Paint's volunteers; but, as he withdrew from San Antonio, he took with him the personages of the district court and prominent citizens as prisoners. Caldwell's force and the Rangers under Hays followed Woll, making his retreat to the Rio Grande as difficult as possible.

San Antonio's becoming a free city again did not put an end to Luvisa's anxiety, however, for Range, having managed to join Captain Hays, stopped at home only long enough to tie extra supplies on his saddle and give her and the children each a hasty embrace. The heart of a woman can break as she so briefly sights her husband dashing from one danger to another, tired, hungry, feverish with the fight that has been or may be just ahead — yes indeed, Luvisa mused, as she stood very still while the dust from Indian Toego's galloping departure settled around her, the heart breaks time and again, but is somehow mended . . . I suppose it has always been like this for the women whose men must go out to fight in the big and little wars — hard to reject self-pity — hard to support faith. But I shall indulge myself in the fancy — nay, the belief — that man's eventual destiny is to outgrow the compulsions of war and learn to fashion the weapons of peace.

When Range came back from chasing Woll, he stayed around San Antonio to await developments on a planned invasion of Mexico. President Sam Houston was trying to avoid an open declaration of war. He hoped the stronger countries who had recognized the Republic of Texas as a sister nation (the United States, Great Britain, and France) would exert pressure on Mexico to recognize Texas independence, but in response to Texas anger, he officially sanctioned the move on Mexico being organized at San Antonio and placed General Alexander Somervell in command.

For a period of two months the volunteers assembled on the plains of Bexar. Their number reached over seven hundred. Orders were delayed. They were without discipline or financial support, and bad weather made camp life miserable. They were poorly clad and poorly fed, full of restlessness and dissension. Their condition brought much hardship to bear on the residents of San Antonio. When General Somervell finally issued the orders to move toward the Rio Grande, civilians in and around San Antonio felt like discarded remnants. The events of the year had drained them of both substance and morale — the main settlement and all the surrounding countryside had a desolate and dilapidated appearance. The population was pitifully thinned out and the sentiments of those who remained were sorrowful and uncertain. Nature chose to accent the hardships with an extremely severe winter, striking early with freezing north winds.

Range tried to improve the personal safety and condition of his family by building an addition to the back of the house to be used

266

as permanent quarters for Cicero and Adelia; he figured this would give Luvisa and her grandmother both help and protection. He never wavered once in his conviction that Mexican troubles would be over before long, and his dream for the Rawhide Range was as secure as ever. He had already picked the site and started the structure of the house on the Nueces River before being called back because of Woll's invasion. He had left Silver Bryson and C. Cassidy in charge with some hired help that continued the building and the cattle work while he himself was involved in the fighting and waiting around San Antonio.

Somervell's departure order came on November 25. It was a bleak and bitter season for journeying or fighting. "I won't be back for Christmas," Range told Luvisa. "Might as well face it. If old slowpoke Somervell takes as long getting across the Rio Grande as he has getting out of here, we'll be all winter on this jaunt. And soon as my duty's done, I might as well get back to work on the Rawhide Range so's to get the house ready for you to move in by spring."

"Then you won't be back for four, maybe five months?" Luvisa tried to make the question casual.

"That's the way it has to be now, but later on — "

"I understand. But Luke and Laska won't. You've been home for two months now and they've had their first uninterrupted companionship with you."

"They don't need to know I'm leaving."

"They already know. They've watched preparations. They sense how we feel. They've looked like a duet of sorrow ever since you came in this morning with news of the orders. You could ride off from babies in a cradle and not be missed, but a couple of three-year-olds you've been romping with are already tuning up to give plenty of trouble at parting time."

When Range was ready to go, the twins were as difficult as Luvisa predicted. They clung to him and cried, they tried their wiles and tricks, and finally, he had to force their arms from around his neck while Adelia helped Luvisa hold them from him, Laska screaming wildly and without restraint, Luke accompanying her with choking sobs and pleading, "Daddy, don' go 'way! Don' go 'way!"

Range leaped on Toego and left at a run. Luvisa finally got the twins to subside in her arms and gave up completely and cried with them. Adelia hovered around lamenting over her charges and finally got the three of them off to bed utterly exhausted with their grief.

By Christmas Luvisa was still without news of Range and must somehow make the children happy in spite of his absence — in spite of her grandfather's suffering and her grandmother's pinched, tired face. Dr. Weideman came to her assistance by inviting the twins to his house to share a tree with Duffy and the two children of José and Carlota — a very special tree just for these five on Christmas night.

"We will create a children's oasis in this our wilderness, Lu," he told her. "It can do no harm. And I think to witness the utter happiness of children for a few hours may be a tonic both your spirit and mine can use at this time." The doctor was sad and a little wistful, a mood most unusual for him.

Luvisa had recently been taking the children occasionally to play with Duffy in the doctor's gardens. They were very happy together and Laska was entranced with the animal collection. She seemed to have a natural understanding of bird and beast, a great sympathy with and power over dumb animals, a sensitivity for all living things. Luvisa could see no harm in an association so wholesome and happy — she and the twins would be leaving San Antonio before long — their lives were so restricted because of Range's absence, Ed Olson's affliction, and the severity of the times — and it seemed unfair to penalize children for adult prejudices.

That Christmas night was the oasis the doctor had promised. No five children were ever any happier over the beauty and promise of a Christmas tree and small gifts for childish pleasure never more gleefully accepted and appreciated. José played Santa Claus and

268

Carlota plied the guests with good things to eat. Dr. Weideman and Luvisa joined the children in their laughter and it was indeed a grand tonic for the spirit. During the evening the doctor told Luvisa some of his plans for Duffy. He would take the boy abroad at twelve; he would travel with him, teach him many languages, and place him in a school where he could be happy and have every opportunity to learn and become an individual independent of his bleak origins. He realized what an uncertain life he himself led in this wilderness, he told her, so he had made provision for Duffy in a will which also included conditions that would bring responsibility and some profit to José and Carlota.

"I don't know why I'm telling you this, Luvisa, unless it's that I feel a call, a strange call from far away, as if my wife and child beckoned to me and I might have to go. My papers are with a man of integrity, but a woman's touch might be needed — somehow — somewhere. You may not be around, but in case you are — or perhaps it's just that I wanted to share this — feeling with you."

He appeared quiet and happy so his peculiar reference to a call did not disturb Luvisa.

When San Antonians learned the full story of the Somervell march to the Rio Grande, it was a disheartening one which lengthened the list of Texas men held prisoners in Mexico.

Early in January a man named Hervey Adams who had served in Captain Bogart's company brought Luvisa news direct from Range. The Bogart volunteers had acted with Captain Hays as advance spies for Somervell's army and thus Range had become personally acquainted with this man and had charged him with messages to deliver at the Olson House on his way back to his East Texas home. Range had returned to his headquarters on the Nueces and wanted Luvisa to know of his safety and in general how the expedition had fared. Adams and part of his company had been lost in the brush on their return journey and had suffered terrible privations. He was convinced, he told Luvisa, half jesting, that she had married a very crazy man — that anyone wanting to live in that wild country was not quite right in the head.

"My husband is a man of great strength and will, Mr. Adams," Luvisa said proudly. "He will accomplish what he intends. He will profit from the very wildness of the country."

Her guest, a discerning man of cultured demeanor, smiled at her intensity and loyalty. "I was aware of this quality in your husband, Mrs. Templeton. And I see he has in you the purpose and encouragement needed for succeeding at such hazardous ventures."

"Thank you, Mr. Adams. Now tell me just how it was with the men who accompanied General Somervell."

"Well, all the delays at the Rio Grande set the men perfectly wild. They called the general an old grannie and many more uncomplimentary names. They accused him of being too scared to advance on into Mexico and settle scores for Woll's invasion. They accused him too of having secret orders from Sam Houston to drag them around until they were tired enough to go home."

"Do you think President Houston actually did that?"

"No one knows for sure, but it is a likely possibility since he is now reported trying to negotiate with the United States for annexation, and war with Mexico might jeopardize an early agreement."

"What did *you* think of General Somervell, Mr. Adams?"

"I thought him a fine, kind gentleman, Mrs. Templeton, but no more able to handle the self-willed, angered Texians than a ten-year-old boy. A large body of the men, about three hundred in all, expressed their complete contempt for his retreat orders by electing Colonel William Fisher to lead them into more aggressive combat with the Mexicans and an attempt to free the Texas prisoners being held in Mexico. My company took a vote on the matter, and, I must admit, contrary to my own feelings, the decision was to return home. Your husband wanted to follow Fisher too, but under the influence of John Hays and Ben McCulloch, who felt honor-bound to obey the orders of their commanding officer, he turned back."

"Madre de Dios, I am thankful!" Luvisa muttered. "And what

do you suppose has happened to Colonel Fisher and the men who followed him into Mexico, Mr. Adams?"

"We can only hope and pray, Mrs. Templeton, that they have succeeded in freeing the prisoners taken at San Antonio and Santa Fe."

When later messengers filled out the story to its dreadful conclusion, Texas history felt the impact of another episode as critical as the Alamo: the Mier Expedition.

After the men under Fisher left the main body of Somervell's army, they proceeded on down the Rio Grande to cross over at Mier. Their fate was soon sealed in this little desert town of Mexico where they were forced to surrender to General Ampudia. Later, after they were sent to the interior, they made a break for liberty but were recaptured and a tenth of their number shot in penalty. Santa Anna really intended to shoot them all, but the British and United States ministers protested so that he selected only a tenth of the number for execution and determined which they should be by a drawing of black beans.

The black beans were placed in a pitcher with white ones so that all must draw. By this piece of sensational cruelty Santa Anna did fatal injury to his country's cause. It was the kind of story that spread the world over. It hastened Texas annexation and the war with Mexico. It aroused the people of the United States to elect a President who favored annexation of Texas even if it meant war with Mexico. It made the people of Texas forget their ardor for independence as a separate republic and seek instead a condition of statehood in the Union that would place them forever beyond the reach of Mexico; and, should the present threat to their security continue, the strength of a mighty nation could be raised in their defense. An unnatural whim of cruelty . . . a pitcher of beans . . . and the course of history was changed. . . .

A hundred and fifty-nine white beans . . . seventeen black ones . . . A man reaches his hand in and draws out life or death. . . . A man is too deeply stirred by the horror of un-

*certainty, the terror of chance, to think of any way to feel out
a black bean. Does black have a different feel to it than white?
Does a man pray for a white bean? Does a man will that his
fingers see a white bean? Does a gambling man say, "This
beats all," and hold a handful of beans, letting them dribble
down to one? Does any man say in his heart, "What I draw
is all right, but please, Lord, let my friend over there get a
white one." Can a man be made of such calm stuff that he
watches the whole procedure with a steady pulse and clear
mind? Big Foot Wallace notices that the black beans are poured
in on top of the white ones and his big hand rummaging at the
bottom of the pitcher brings up a white bean. . . .*

There were countless versions of the bean-drawing, but none
altered the grim and awful fact that the men did draw the black
beans and were shot. People all over the United States and in na-
tions across the sea who knew little or nothing about the Texas
situation were aroused to denounce Mexico and clamor for the
defense of Texas. Although it was two more years before annexation was assured, and three before war with Mexico removed the
threat to the south, in the year 1843 Texas citizens began to feel a
little safer. Political matters were still far from resolved, and the
Texians burned with resentment that Mexico would not release their
prisoners, but further Mexican aggression was held up by the new
tide of feeling in the United States expressing strong sentiment for
annexation. That was the last thing Mexico desired — to drive Texas
into the Union and either lose the territory for good or have to fight
the United States for it. Britain and France also were anxious that
Texas remain outside the United States and began to work on Mexico
to recognize the Republic of Texas and cease molesting its people. So
President Houston was in a position to drive a good bargain, and
proclaimed a temporary truce with Mexico.

Such was the political status of the Republic in the spring of 1843
when Range decided to move his family to their Nueces River home.
It was Luvisa's first trip away from San Antonio and she had no

regrets at departing. All the disturbances and losses since the Indian Council House fight, the long separations from Range, the sadness of her grandfather's affliction and death, and the haste and pitiful eagerness with which her grandmother followed him through death's door made her almost frantic to leave the place. So she said farewell to the graves under the queen's-crown vine, now four of them, packed those belongings most necessary and useful for her new home, and left the house with most of its furnishings in the care of Adelia and Cicero. She and Range had decided to keep the Olson place as a refuge for her and the children in time of war. Cicero was to open it to Eli Dawson and other friends who would be in and out of San Antonio. So Luvisa left behind many things that she planned, in more settled times, to bring to her permanent home. Her most prized possession was a beautiful hand-carved chest that had belonged to her mother. She had not discovered its contents until after her grandmother's death. She had always loved the chest, placed inconspicuously in her grandmother's room and covered with a large, elaborate, rainbow blanket. When she had inquired of its contents as a child, Ella Olson always said the same thing.

"Family things, not to be prowled amongst. I promise you the chest shall be yours someday, if you do not worry me overly much about it."

Luvisa had decided that it contained things personal to her grandmother and grandfather and curiosity had gradually subsided. But when they were gone and a place must be found to store their personal belongings, Luvisa searched for the key to the chest. She found it in a little wooden box that was a carved miniature of the chest and had been carefully placed in the very bottom of her grandmother's trunk.

As she unlocked the chest, she felt a hesitancy, a trembling sort of uneasiness; her breath came short and she held her hands tight on the lid a moment before slowly raising it. And she knew before it was fully tilted back, she knew as she caught the first scent of the sweet fragrance that rose from its depths, that no article here had

273

ever belonged to her grandmother. It was filled instead with the clothes and jewelry, the countless little things of personal use or fancy, that had belonged to her mother. The perfume still lingering in the folds of the garments raised the images of childhood clearly before Luvisa — those early days when she had clung to these garments, felt their softness in her baby fingers, been enfolded by this fragrance still so alive. Luvisa was transported into a state of mind that was like a dream — only much more vivid, for the sweet-scented fabrics she touched and gazed upon were reality and stimulated the depth of her memory until she recalled her mother with a wonderful clarity: the fragile beauty, the tiny figure, the fond smile. And with the vision she heard gentle Spanish phrases of endearment addressed to her: "Ah, querida mía . . . mi alma y mi vida . . . niñeta carísima!"

When Luvisa departed, it was hard to leave this precious possession behind, but she resolved to bring it on some later trip when there would be no necessity to explain or show its contents.

Range had made excellent preparations for the trip to the Nueces. His good fortune in money matters made it possible for him to provide more comforts than was the lot of many settlers. There were two sturdy wagons, a coach, and a number of good pack animals. Range had ordered the coach many months in advance and had it brought overland from Galveston during the dry season — it offered much better protection than a regular carriage. He had several spans of fine mules for the wagons and a string of good horses for the coach — and some gentler horses for Luvisa and the children to ride when they grew tired of the coach. C. Cassidy, Silver Bryson, and Wong, as well as six regular riders for the Rawhide Range, were in the party of travelers. In addition, Range had picked up four more men in San Antonio to take back with him and assure full protection for his family.

For the first several days of their journey they followed the Laredo Road. Range was reminded of his introductory trip along this road five years before. It was the same lush flowering springtime with perfect weather as a delightful framework for nature's marvels. For Luvisa, it was the adventure of her life, and the twins shared her wonderment to the fullest, their high spirits never subsiding except into sound slumber. The three of them rode horseback several hours daily, growing healthier and happier with every mile, and Wong, like a magician, made every campsite a luxury.

Eli Dawson had given the twins a white dog named Ned, and he too shared in the delights of travel. Ned was no purebred — his face was that of a diluted bulldog — but he loved all his traveling companions, especially the children, and his happy capers seemed to be constantly telling them it was a wonderful world filled with wonderful people and events.

The men hunted and brought in fresh game daily, and the company of the children seemed to keep them in a fun-loving mood day after day. It was the perfect journey, or so it seemed to Luvisa so drugged with the happiness of accompanying her husband to their first home. If there were discomforts of any kind, she failed to notice them.

It was the beginning of three years of unbroken happiness for the Templetons. There were occasional alarms or anxieties, and Range had to be gone now and then for weeks at a time — but no wars, no serious threats from Indians or other marauders, no calamitous illness.

The Rawhide headquarters, enclosed with a high fence of sharp-pointed poles, was as much a fortification as a home. The double gate at the entrance was made of heavy logs and could be securely barred. Besides the main house, there was a long one-room bunkhouse and a chuckhouse nearly as large where Wong cooked and served the men their meals. There were also corrals and shelters for the best animals, and in each corner of the enclosure a small raised structure made of heavy logs and used as a lookout or for defense in case of attack. There were holes in these little guardhouses for sighting and firing, and since they sat on stilts, entrance was by ladder through an opening in the floor. They were the delight of the twins because the peepholes allowed them glimpses of the world outside the fence

275

where they could not go unless accompanied by several of the men. The main house was long and low and cool-looking, built facing the south with a porch extending all the way across the front. There was a large open-at-the-front hallway in the center and two rooms opened off each side; at the end of the hallway was the entrance into the dining room and back of that the kitchen — a porch extended across the west side of both of these rooms. And there was the comfort of good fireplaces, one in every room. There were two storehouses — dugouts well roofed and securely built — one to hold arms and ammunition and the rigging that the men on horseback used in their work, and the other for household supplies and foodstuffs.

Luke and Laska flourished as naturally in this life as the mesquite trees and the prairie grass, but the older they grew the more their differences stood out: Luke's quiet steadiness, his thoughtful manner and instinctive cautions, his fairness and generosity; Laska's uncurbed enthusiasms, her recklessness, the fierceness of her childish loves and hates. They were alike only in their affection and loyalty to each other. From the time they played together consciously, they compromised their differences. Luke would allow Laska's caprices to rule him without restraint for a certain length of time; then he would exclude her from his own little circle of play, ignore her with a certain thoughtful deliberateness, until she coaxed him and worked to win him back into partnership. Although they were not allowed beyond the main fence, they took many risks in spite of Luvisa's watchfulness. Luke was usually with Laska, engaging in the same pranks, but somehow it was she who always stuck her head into wasp nests, ventured too far out on a limb, or learned firsthand just how sociable a polecat will be. On occasion Luke would refuse to follow her and simply view sympathetically the havoc she created. One such instance concerned the big black rooster that ruled the poultry yard. The rooster was much prized by Wong because of his victory over the large Mexican hawks that swooped down and tried to pick up a chick now and then. Luke knew that the rooster's spurs were sharp as a knife and his temper black as his feathers. Laska

276

knew this too but wanted the excitement of crossing the chicken yard because it was forbidden territory. She was sure she could outrun the rooster but she forgot he could fly as well as run. She was badly flogged for her daring. When Luvisa saw the gashes on her shoulders and arms, she wanted Wong to kill the rooster, but he just shook his head and smiled while he helped her wash the wounds with soap and water and apply salve. Laska screamed so that Luvisa was completely unnerved. Wong sensed her distress.

"No worry, Missy Lu, she so plenty much mad at that old rooster, she got no pain!"

Luvisa laughed shakily and Laska screamed all the louder.

Luke never exulted over his sister's distresses and disasters; he gave her his sympathy and consolation and whatever aid he could devise.

No tendency of Laska disturbed and embarrassed Luvisa so much, however, as her heathenish worship of the sun. From the time she could crawl, she preferred a sunny spot on the bed or the floor and would crawl into the bright light and coo with pleasure. Then to her mother's consternation, when she learned to dress and undress herself, she displayed the strangest notions of playing and sleeping in the sun stripped of all but the very last bit of a garment she had on. It was not, Luvisa realized, that she lacked modesty, she just wanted the sun's rays on her body. Sometimes Luvisa would find her, after Luke had gone to take a nap in a comfortable shady spot, sleeping blissfully in some concealed sunny nook about the house, every stitch of her clothing cast aside. Alarmed, she tried to talk with Laska about it but didn't feel that she accomplished much. When Laska was four, Luvisa partially solved the problem, although her tiny daughter continued to behave like a sun sprite and best her in every discussion.

"If you'd sleep in the sun without your clothes, Mama," she informed Luvisa, "you'd know how good it feels. I bet Indians know, Mama."

"But you're not an Indian," Luvisa protested.

"Are you sure I'm not, Mama? When you found me, wasn't I a little baby Indian lying in the sun without any clothes on?"

277

"Indeed you were not!"

"Then what was I when you found me?"

"A sweet little baby girl with white-gold hair that I adored."

"Did I have clothes on, Mama?"

"You had some of the most beautiful clothes a baby ever had," Luvisa evaded. She couldn't bring herself to punish the child. They were in their own little world. Sunshine was a wholesome thing. If Luke and Laska could work out so many compromises on their differences, Luvisa reasoned, maybe she should try their system. So she helped Laska make her own little sun garden by the house and went with her there for a while every sunny day — and most of their days were sunny ones. She kept a wooden tub in the garden and each of them carried a bucket of water when they went there. Luvisa usually took along some sewing or a mending task and sat on a bench in the shade to watch. Laska would have her bath and then pour the bathwater on the grass that soon grew soft and green. Afterward she lay in the sun and basked like a kitten, her body taking on a soft lustrous tan coloring like chinaberries in the fall. The comments old Flaco had made when he saw her for the first time, an infant in her cradle, would come back to Luvisa: ". . . a little baby wildcat . . . sunnin' itself and starin' at me, soft and cottonish with them flecked eyes that could look straight into the sun without blinkin' . . ." They carried out this sun-garden ritual with the agreement that Laska was at all other times to stay properly clothed. Luke showed no jealousy of this extra time and attention Luvisa gave Laska. He took pride in the fact that he was left alone in the house to take his bath and his nap without supervision. He began to develop manly independence and self-sufficiency at a very early age. Luvisa's role of motherhood with Luke was tranquil and satisfying, a continuous quiet joy; with Laska it was an adventure in extremes: laughter and tears, amazement and vexation, shock and relief. She did not understand her daughter, she simply loved her with all her heart and tried not to be afraid.

Range seldom spoke of the springs during that time and Luvisa began to think he might be satisfied with their home on the Nueces, although she knew he was gathering his cattle further and further to the south and more and more absorbed in extending his land-holdings. She had during those three years only one bit of news concerning Miguel. Silver Bryson returning from a trip to Laredo found her working alone in the kitchen, took the refreshment she offered, and as he gave her an account of his journey, mentioned that he had heard the Sándivar family, living at the springs, was having a hard time.

"What troubles them?" Luvisa asked, trying to mask her interest by moving busily around the kitchen.

"They were almost cleaned out once by raiders but they hung on. Then they tied up with the Laredos who have been ranching in those parts a long time and working together the two families have managed to keep their families unmolested and some of their stock out of the hands of marauders."

"I'm glad to hear that," Luvisa murmured.

"But the whole story of their trials, as related on the streets of Laredo, has the usual Spanish flavor of romance and tragedy."

Luvisa dropped the lid of a kettle with a clatter. It rolled across the floor. Bryson recovered it for her and continued.

"Miguel Sándivar married Rita Laredo, a very delicate and very fair señorita, so they say. Then there was a daughter born, one Rita Marina Sándivar, but the frail young wife did not live to see her child. Beautiful mothers who die thus pass along an even greater beauty to their daughters, according to the old Mexican who told me all about it."

Luvisa was very quiet. Then she said, "How sad for a young lover to be bereft so soon of the substance of his dreams."

"Your comment, sad and poetic, puts the true Spanish flourish on the end of my little story," Bryson said.

Luvisa became aware of Bryson's scrutiny, realized he must know she had more than a passing interest in the Sándivars. It annoyed her somehow that he should be so discerning, even though she knew

279

if he had any curiosity about her past, it was only because of his desire to be helpful. She wondered if he had heard somewhere of Miguel's visit with her.

"Why have you brought this story to me?" she asked him.

"Aren't you interested in these people at the springs where your husband hopes to build you another and grander home someday?"

"Yes, Mr. Bryson, I am. I am a curious, prying woman." She was close to tears. "Therefore, I am also interested in your past. There must have been a woman — "

The expression on his face silenced her. She regretted her asperity. She did not want to hurt him whatever his reason for bringing her news about the Sándivars.

"I bow out, Mrs. Templeton," he said gravely, leaving her to dwell on Miguel's sad circumstances and to wonder too what burden of sorrow had placed such a permanent shadow on Bryson's life.

When Range took cattle out or brought in supplies, there was news to be talked about and read about for weeks afterwards. Annexation and relations with Mexico continued to be the major political problems, and the trends of public affairs were felt very personally at Rawhide Range headquarters for the Templeton acreage lay like a small buffer state between Texas and Mexico.

Back from a trip to Galveston in March of 1845, Range brought the biggest news to date, relating it in snatches as he dismounted and was welcomed by his family.

"The American Congress approved annexation just a few weeks back. We can become a state if we agree to the terms by January."

"Are the terms what we want?" Luvisa inquired.

"Mostly. The United States agrees to settle the boundary ruckus once and for all. It's understood that the Rio Grande will be the line even if it means war, and, to my notion, that's good — that's the best part of the whole business. Also we get to keep our public lands — that's good too. . . . I think it'll pass our congress. . . . I think we're as good as in the Union right now and war with Mexico's just around the corner."

Range Templeton's thinking was in tune with the times for the Texas Congress accepted annexation unanimously, turning down a last-minute proposal of Mexico to guarantee independence if Texas would agree never to become a part of the United States. And before the year was out, General Zachary Taylor had moved into the controversial territory between the Nueces and Rio Grande to let Mexico know the United States intended to fix the boundary at the Rio Grande. President Polk signed the act that made Texas a state in December, and the ceremonies of transition from Republic to State were held in February of 1846. At Rawhide Range headquarters a few weeks later, Silver Bryson was reading aloud from a newspaper the speech of President Anson Jones, while the family and most of those employed on the ranch gave him grave attention:

> . . . The Lone Star of Texas, which ten years since arose amid clouds of obscurity and shone for a while, has culminated — and has passed on and become fixed forever in the glorious constellation — the American Union. Blending its rays with its sister stars, long may it continue to shine, and may gracious Heaven smile upon the consummation of the wishes of the two Republics, now joined together in one. The final act in this great drama is now performed. The Republic of Texas is no more.

A complete silence greeted this pronouncement. It was as if they had listened to an epitaph. After a moment, Silver Bryson added, "And the *Texian* as a nationality is no more . . . but may he be speedily resurrected, more virile and aggressive than ever . . . pattern for the proud brood to come."

No such reverent silence greeted the next piece of sensational news that one of Range's far riders picked up and brought to the big house on the Nueces as fast as his horse could carry him there: General Taylor had clashed with the Mexicans and hostilities had commenced. The tumult and excitement that followed in the Templeton

281

household was simply a small reflection of the passion and the storm that gathered throughout the state. Range Templeton was only one of many Texans forced by Mexican aggressions to forsake the Texas dream of a free and independent republic — a husky, brand-new frontier nation — and vote for annexation in order to gain the support needed to meet these aggressions. Now there were old scores to settle, and 5000 Texans, wildly exultant, stampeded into the military service of the United States. Range decided that Luvisa should return to San Antonio until the war was over; Silver Bryson agreed to escort her and the children there and then return to operate the Rawhide Range. So Range got out his favorite old buckskins and battered felt hat, polished his weapons to a mirror brightness, and prepared to join the Hays regiment gathering on the Rio Grande, for the Texas Rangers were to be placed in the vanguard of the invading armies.

Luvisa's response to the arrangements was not in the pattern Range had learned to expect at parting time. She went about the duties of packing with a haste and detachment unlike her calm and careful self and showed none of her usual cheerful acceptance of events and the plans he made.

"You'll enjoy a visit in Santone," he told her, seeking to lighten her mood. "See some women again . . . buy some things for yourself and the kids and the house . . . pack up your furniture there and we'll haul it down when I get back. . . . We'll have Cicero and Adelia come along next time, and Caesar if he wants to. We'll want to do some more building and I need a good blacksmith shop. This job down in Mexico won't take too long — be back before the year's out."

She was on her knees packing a trunk with linens as he talked. She threw the last things in without noticing where they landed and then slammed the lid down as if to stop his talking, but she didn't answer him. As he stood waiting, the silence lengthened, and finally she looked up at him — a look such as he had never had from Luvisa — a look of deep smoldering fire that could burst into conflagration. He was startled. He did not know whether to accept it as anger or

282

passion or a mixture of the two. It made him feel very strange and uncertain. He took a step toward her, his heart pounding. The look deepened, but before he could reach her, could find a word to say, she got quickly to her feet and fled from him.

Luvisa was not fleeing to give way to tears but for a much more subtle reason. She did not want Range to know yet that this parting for her had become an ordeal of the flesh as well as of the spirit. The three years of uninterrupted happiness and closeness they had known were even more treasured in retrospect, and she found rebellion against the long separation ahead rising in her with a violence that was shocking, for never before had she felt the highly emotional Spanish temperament which she had bequeathed to Laska arousing in her own nature. She had given Range up to battle and business ventures on many occasions but this war seemed more threatening, and Range more eager to be off than ever before. She could understand why the war must be, what was to be accomplished by it, and the many reasons a man like Range would have for feeling he must participate; but no matter what the whys and wherefores of war, resentment against circumstances could burn reason out of a woman's mind when a husband so dear, a very component of her flesh and blood, was being taken from her and might never return. And Range — her resentment mounted at the thought — was actually looking forward to his reunion with John Hays and the fighting adventures that lay ahead of the Rangers. Luvisa had never known the torture of jealousy before — had never known her passionate nature could betray her into this fiercely jealous mood against war in general, John Hays in particular, and for good measure all the beautiful women reputed to be in Mexico. She resolved for once to make the parting as hard for him as it was for her. She would forsake the pose of I'll-stand-smiling-until-you-return. She would do something more memorable, more haunting than tears. A love as great as hers must have powers still untried. His power over her she knew. Her power over him she would put to a test. If she succeeded, he'd weep when he left her and long for her while he was gone. There was something devastating about seeing a strong man cry, but after all, a woman had to know, had to be sure; and a woman fighting the competition of war could not afford too much tenderness — too much softness.

On the day before Range's departure, Luvisa became a sort of imperious queen over her household. She kept Wong busy preparing the things that Range liked most to eat, cautioning and scolding him about the smallest details. She kept Luke and Laska hurrying about at numerous small tasks and awed into quietness by her unaccustomed sternness. Her personal grooming was in every respect the garments, the colors, the little details she knew Range loved. Her beauty was for this day a provocative, a daring, a dangerous beauty that she had never before felt the challenge to achieve; and on every occasion that day in Range's presence she managed to accent it with words and gestures that tied in with the loving intimacies that had developed with their years of marriage, remaining at the same time slightly aloof.

In the late afternoon as she stood in the yard clipping yellow roses that she had selected for the dinner table, Silver Bryson came in from a long day's work with the cattle; as he spoke to her, she motioned him to come nearer, and then asked with an effort at lightness, "Tell me, Mr. Bryson, are the women of Mexico really as irresistible as they are made out to be?"

Bryson smiled knowingly and looked at her with an awareness of the deliberate effort she was making. "For your information and consolation, Mrs. Templeton, none more irresistible than the mistress of Rawhide Range," and then added with a sort of tender admonition, "War is a lamentable condition, especially for women and children. Be careful that in sharpening your weapon to such a keen edge you do not wound yourself."

Luvisa's eyes, bright with a feverish intensity, filled with tears and she bent hastily over the rosebush again.

When the final anguish of parting was upon Range and Luvisa in the early morning of the next day, she realized that in exacting an actual measurement of the physical power of her love she had merely

284

achieved new depths of despair for them both. The victory through passion that she had sought was hers but the reward was only poignant regret, for the true nature of her love was to give bountifully — to meet demands, not make them — to fortify, not weaken, the courage and pride of the one she loved. But now it was too late to reverse the tide of passion and pain. The man in strained and wakeful silence by her side would soon be gone — soon be translated from lover and husband to Ranger and fighting man — for the time had come when he must put aside his love, take up his weapons, and ride away.

The children still slept — Range had told them the night before that he'd be off on a journey before day and they hadn't been unduly upset, thinking this farewell no different than the ones they had become accustomed to. He'd also told the men good-by. His gear had been made ready the night before. His horse was saddled — whoever had done this last service had slipped back into his bunk. . . . Now this parting he had planned with careful detail and some eagerness had become an almost unbearable pain for him. And love had given Luvisa both a triumph and a defeat, for how could she not share his pain? Now that he was suffering, she'd rather have had him ride away a little bit gay, a little bit eager, feeling bold and brave. As it was, she knew he was searching for a reason, hoping she would help him find one, for delaying his departure, putting aside his duty. But they both knew none could be found.

She turned to him and stroked his face — it was drawn into rocky ridges. She kissed his lips to find them parched and cold, almost as if in death. Then his arms were around her like bands of steel . . . no tender words, no warm tears, only the agony of his dry, hoarse sobbing . . . and her own wonderment that the body and mind could reach such peaks of anguish and ever return to breath and thought. . . . But there was no oblivion. . . . She remembered that one time she had fainted in a thrill of surprise and pure delight, feeling his arms around her at the end of their first separation. Now, when she would have welcomed a release from pain, there was no

285

such escape. . . . Finally, that bleak bridge of time between presence and absence was crossed, and her husband was gone. She sat on the edge of the porch, leaning against a post, weak and trembling, eyes dry. A mockingbird took possession of a hackberry tree nearby and with joyous abandon welcomed the radiance of the new day, made more elaborate the design of her despair.

wwwwwwwwwwwwwwwwwwwwwwwwwwwwwwwwwwwwwwwwwwwwwwwwwwwwwwwwwwwwwwwwwwwwwwwwwwwwwwwwwwwwwwwwww

CHAPTER XIII

wwwwwwwwwwwwwwwwwwwwwwwwwwwwwwwwwwwwwwwwwwwwwwwwwwwwwwwwwwwwwwwwwwwwwwwwwwwwwwwwwwwwwwwwww

LUVISA was in such a hurry to get away from the Rawhide Range, to find new interests and surroundings that would dull the sharp edges of her desolation, that she finished packing and got the family started on the long coach ride to San Antonio in a mood bordering on panic. Luke asked her once, "Mama, are the Comanches coming?" And she only added to his bewilderment by replying, "No, dear, I don't think so. But if they do, that will be exciting, won't it?"

Silver Bryson and Wong teamed together to contribute the only calmness and efficiency evident on the long, tiresome journey. C. Cassidy sulked because he had wanted to accompany Range but instead had been assigned specific duties at the ranch; so he kept too close company with the jug and sang for the travelers many more doleful tunes than they cared to hear.

When they finally arrived in San Antonio, they found the city much changed and filled with a contagious excitement. The Mexican War had transformed it into an important military base — brought it vigor, hope and trade. There were troops marching through — strangers on the streets — ox-carts everywhere piled high with freight or farm products — sturdy new homes being erected to accommodate newly-arrived German immigrants.

And at the Olson House, Cicero and Adelia were waiting to welcome the arrivals from Rawhide Range as though they had been

286

miraculously delivered from the wilderness. Luvisa found it delightful to move into the unexpected ease and comfort provided by these
two faithful caretakers. Silver Bryson and the other riders who had
been escort for the coach were soon refreshed and off on the return
trip, for C. Cassidy and Little Star were scheduled to start leading
herds off the Rawhide Range as soon as possible to supply bases for
the U. S. Army.

When they were gone, Luvisa thought of Dr. Weideman and
wondered why he hadn't called. "I must take the twins and go see
our good neighbor, the doctor," she told Cicero eagerly. "I wonder
why he hasn't called."

"Dat doctor, he no longer hereabouts."

"Dr. Weideman? You mean he's gone, Cicero? But the house and
garden look the same." She realized with a sense of shock how much
she had been counting on the doctor, his counsel as a physician and
friend, the stimulation of his personality and philosophy, to carry
her through the loneliness of wartime waiting. He was, she felt,
both protector and confidant, the only person who had ever known
her heart and mind, understood her motives and desires.

"Where did he go, Cicero? Did he take Duffy?"

"Duffy he still here. De doctor — he — he drown."

"Drowned? Oh, Cicero! No! When? Where?"

"Not so long after yo'll folks lef' here. He over aroun' Gonzales
and try to cross Peach Creek on a rise. Him and dat mean ol' black
mare wash away downstream and bof drown."

Luvisa felt destitute. "Wasn't anyone with him? Didn't anyone
try to rescue him?"

"Nobody seem to know much about it. 'Nother man drown too.
Maybe he try to help de doctor or doctor try to help him. I couldn'
say. Some mo' along nearly drown too, I heard, but da's all."

Luvisa remembered the Christmas party and the only confidence
about himself the doctor had ever shared with her: "I feel a call,
a strange call from far away, as if my wife and child beckoned to
me and I might have to go." Had the doctor, in some mad moment

287

of fancy, in the roar of the rushing stream heard again the call from his wife and child and deliberately pursued the sound? Had the crossing been made in some urgency of rescue, or a jovial spirit of risk and dare? Luvisa could only wonder. She was certain, however, that Dr. Weideman had made no ordinary exit from this world. She was certain too what the doctor would want her to do. She would go to see Duffy at once.

The door of Dr. Weideman's house was opened to Luvisa and the twins by Carlota who registered her joy and astonishment in a great gush of words and tears and repeated embrazos. Then she sent the twins into the garden to find Duffy and lamented to Luvisa with sighs and more tears.

"The good doctor left the instructions that my José and I would make his house our house until this child we love as our own has twelve years. Then he must be taken from us and go to a strange faraway land — for learning. Just what he will learn that we cannot teach him I do not know. But I do know there will be no one to love him as we do in this land across the seas. And my poor heart is in constant pain, as is José's, to think of that time of parting."

"Oh, Carlota. How you borrow grief!" Luvisa chided. "That is four years from now. Then Duffy will be much more the man. And he will not stay away forever. He will become wise, as the doctor was wise, and return to comfort your old age perhaps. Dry your tears now, and tell me, does Duffy have lessons of any kind? I'm sure Dr. Weideman wanted him instructed."

"Only such lessons, Señora, as José and I can give him in honest work and true worship."

"I'm sure you instruct him well in the virtues. Does he read and write?"

"Oh, yes, Señora. He spent much time with the doctor on such things."

"Then I'll continue his instruction for I am already giving Luke and Laska regular lessons in reading and writing and simple sums. I think the three of them would study well together."

"Oh, Señora, how kind you are! I know such a thing would please the good doctor, and the child will not be so lonely — will not be spending so much time with the caged things in the garden as he does now — and while you brighten his mind you will lighten his heart."

Somewhat pleased with her discernment, Carlota led the way into the garden where they found Duffy entertaining the twins with the antics of a pet crow.

"That Daño," Carlota fussed, "a bird of ill omen that should never have been brought to the garden. A demon in black feathers . . . but the boy has taught him many pranks and will not be persuaded to part with him."

Luvisa did not on this occasion share Carlota's aversion to Daño. She saw nothing but the happy excitement of the three children provoked by the wonder of being together once more and the enchantment that always accompanies the performance of a pet. And she found herself laughing aloud at Daño's open vanity as he responded to Duffy's calls and commands in the mood of proving how very shrewd a crow could be — carrying pebbles, nuts, and bright objects here and there, or flying up and dropping them at Duffy's command so that Luke or Laska could catch them or letting them fall in the hair of the frightened Carlota and cawing noisily as the children laughed. Soon Laska was feeding him nutmeats and he was attaching himself to her as a kind of favorite.

Duffy in a burst of generosity, wanting to express his joy in Luke and Laska's return, said, "Daño prefers you to the rest of us. He is yours."

Laska's eyes grew big with pleasure, but before she could accept, Luvisa interrupted, "No. No. That is generous of you, Duffy. But Daño's home is here in the garden. Laska has no such suitable place for him. You can all play with him here."

This first meeting with Duffy and Daño was the beginning of many things for Luvisa, both pleasures and problems. The classes

289

she held for the three children were always experiences in the un-predictable. She taught the children as best she could, but some-times she felt the instruction was too unorganized to do much good. Duffy being a year older and having had so much attention from Dr. Weideman was more advanced than Luke and Laska and he enjoyed much more teaching them the lessons Luvisa assigned than learning his own — and the twins preferred him as their teacher. And the matter of language got completely out of hand. Although Range never allowed the children to speak Spanish in the home, and Luvisa had tried to subdue Laska's preference for it, here in San Antonio where it was spoken so much, Laska dropped back into it and seemed to forget about English. Duffy spoke a very precise English and tried to please Luvisa by using it when talking to her; he also had a collection of Russian, French, and German phrases left over from the doctor's conversations that he threw in for good measure, but since he had been reared in Carlota's care, it was her language that served him best. When Luke led in con-versation or recitation, he started out in English but often would switch to Spanish to keep up with Laska and Duffy. Under pres-sure of excitement, when the three tried to talk at once, the use of two languages, with Duffy adding expletives in three others, created some highly amusing sounds and meanings and no little confusion to Luvisa in assembling actual facts of argument or incident.

Meanwhile Daño became a privileged character and his nuisance value increased daily. He was properly caged in the garden at night, but during daylight hours he was usually in Laska's possession and the two of them were often in mischief together. On their outings, the crow usually rode on Laska's shoulder, but was sometimes perched insolently on the top of her fair head or on her forearm held out in falconer position. She used a long string on his leg to teach him to come and go at her command and would occasionally give him his freedom.

Daño was by nature a thief as well as a great prankster. He learned sounds that were almost human — laughing, crying, and screaming — and Laska taught him how to make the most of his talents, startling people and animals alike with his imitations. Luvisa began to despise the bird — it was as if he complemented the more unruly side of Laska's disposition. Many of the townspeople longed to make an end of him too, but Laska's affection for Daño was well known and he was spared — even when he stole bright trinkets on public display in the market place, or snatched a candy or flower from a vendor and brought it to Laska with great cawing and preening, pleased with his mischief, enjoying the commotion he caused. There were some among the Mexican population who were terribly frightened of Daño, holding Carlota's opinion that he was most certainly a bird of ill omen.

It was the summer of 1847. San Antonians were making ready to celebrate a wartime July Fourth — the second time for the Texans to honor this national holiday of the United States for they had been in the Union now for well over a year. Range had been to San Antonio once since the war started, after the Mexican capitulation at Monterrey, and as discontented as other fighters with the eight weeks' truce granted the Mexicans by General Taylor. He had returned to Rawhide Range alone for several weeks of cattle work and then had gone with Ben McCulloch to rejoin Taylor when hostilities were resumed. The men with McCulloch were enlisted for only six months; so Range would have an opportunity to visit his family again sometime during this month of July. This prospect made the holiday especially cheerful for Luvisa, made it easy for her to share Luke's and Laska's excitement over the day's program. There would be foot races, horse races, fireworks and games, a parade with soldiers and a military band, and many stunts that included catching a greased pig, climbing a greased pole and other funmaking. The twins had two paint ponies named Duke and Dolly that they were going to ride in the parade; Duffy was to ride a black filly foaled by Dr. Weideman's Nightmare, the mare that had drowned with him.

291

The morning of the parade when everything was about in readiness for the children to take Duke and Dolly from the stall, an accident erased all happiness from the scene. They were already on their ponies, the lot gate was open, and Cicero was checking the saddle girths. He decided Luke's should be tighter and was drawing it up when Ned started a furious barking at the watering trough and routed out a large rattlesnake from its seclusion in a cool spot under the trough.

Cicero was not in a position to see what was happening. The snake darted across the lot in front of the horses, Ned dashing about and yelping in frantic warning. Dolly reared, but Laska had full control of her. Luke was sitting carelessly in the saddle, reins loose, watching Cicero, and Duke's sudden side-jump and rearing almost unseated him. He clung on, but the horse in its fright knocked Cicero out of the way before the girth was securely buckled. The saddle turned, and the pony dashed from the lot and up the street.

Luke's foot had been thrust too far into the stirrup by the pony's lurch and he could not get free from the saddle. He was swinging under the horse's belly in a position to be dragged to death within a few moments. Duffy, waiting in front of his house, instantly realized the gravity of Luke's predicament. He dashed in pursuit of Duke, caught up with him, leaned out of his saddle and with true Indian mustanger skill leaped from his own horse and clung desperately to the bridle of the runaway.

The pony dragged the weight on his bridle for a short distance and came to a stop; Luke was still conscious enough to get his foot untangled from the stirrup, but, while he was doing so, his pony continued to twist and pull and prance, the saddle under his belly still making him wild. Duffy held on until he saw Luke drop free, then strength seemed to leave his arms and he let go the bridle, falling to the ground in a heap.

With the release of the tug on the bit, the pony reared again, lost his balance trying to avoid the boy under his feet, and came down full force, his forefeet striking Duffy solidly in the chest. Duke snorted and shied at what he had done, gave up to mad fright again and dashed on up the street until he lost the saddle and came to a bewildered standstill.

Luke was badly bruised and scratched and had several ribs broken. Duffy was more seriously injured. They were carried into the Weideman house and Luvisa sent for a German doctor who was a new resident and highly reputed for his skill as a physician.

The doctor soon reassured Luvisa about Luke, and gave his undivided attention to Duffy, who was dazed and quiet, lying with his eyes closed, breathing in a shallow way, but apparently in no pain. Luvisa noticed that Laska stared at the doctor as if to read his mind, then took up a quiet watch standing by Duffy's bed, gazing steadfastly at him. When he opened his eyes, José and Carlota and Luvisa were there too, but it was Laska he recognized and smiled for. She smiled back.

"Daño," he whispered, and frowned a little. "Bring Daño."

Laska was out of the room like a flash. But when she came in from the garden with Daño, Carlota met her at the back door and barred the way.

"Alto ahí! You shall not enter this house with that feathered demon! Por Dios! Bobita, don't you know a bird in the house means death in the house also?"

"Zoquete! Let me by. Duffy wants Daño. Get out of my way, you old toad, before I stomp your toes!"

Carlota began to cry but stood her ground. "Ay Dios mío! Quita de ahí!"

"Qué animal! Cochino! I'll have Daño peck your eyes out!"

Carlota, tears streaming — for she knew her precious Duffy would die if this hideous bird were allowed to enter — pleaded, "Chica, querida, the bird must stay out. He carries death. You do not want to bring in death to the boy, do you, chica? Ave María Purísima!"

This approach infuriated Laska all the more. Her love for Duffy

293

was of a fiercer quality than Carlota's. "Al demonio con tú! Bruja del infierno!"

Luvisa heard the quarrel and went to arbitrate, but she was so· stunned by the things Laska was saying to Carlota — by the fierceness in her eyes — that she was speechless. When under heaven's dome had the child learned such phrases of wrath and violence?

Carlota was shocked too. She backed away from the blaze in the wildcat eyes, cringing under the lash of vituperation, delivered so fluently in her own tongue. She was usually mild in manner and sensitive. She had never before been described as such a loathsome creature and at the same time condemned with such utter finality to all the horrors of hell. Daño was the only one enjoying the scene, and with his head cocked to one side, added his derisive screeches to Laska's abusive ones. Then, as if to aid in routing Carlota more completely, he hopped onto her shoulder and tried to pluck the sparkling earring from her pierced ear. Carlota jumped away from the door and screamed. Laska sharply commanded Daño back on her shoulder and marched without further hindrance to Duffy's bedside.

In spite of Carlota's horror at Daño's presence in the house, he stayed until Duffy drew his last breath about twelve hours later. Most of the time, the shrewd-looking black bird sat on the foot of the bed watching Duffy, but he took occasional flights into other rooms to bring back bright objects from mantel or dresser tops, piling them as a sort of tribute by Duffy's pillow. Laska sat watching Duffy, wide awake, not making a sound, listening for each breath Duffy drew, her face taking on a drawn and tortured look.

Luvisa recognized that the intensity of Laska's nature would make this heartbreak in childhood more devastating than any adult loss. And her heart cried out with a mother's natural protest: My darling little golden kitten who loved to purr in the sun — if only she might have dwelt in the sunny glades of irresponsible childhood a little longer!

When Laska asked, "Will Duffy die, Mama?" Luvisa couldn't answer.

"I think he will," Laska answered herself and went back to her vigil.

Duffy seemed at no time to be in pain, but when the hemorrhages started, the doctor shook his head and told them the boy would not recover. Duffy would rest awhile, open his eyes, smile at Laska, look at Daño on the foot of his bed, seem content and close his eyes again. He seemed hardly to recognize Luvisa or José and only once turned to Carlota.

"Don't weep, Carlota mía," he said softly. "You will not have to send me away to school now."

Finally, shortly before he died, he called to Laska in a frightened voice. She was instantly at his side and took his hand.

"What is it, Duffy? What do you want to know?"

"Luke?"

"Luke is fine, Duffy. He'll be all right." She said it distinctly and with such conviction that he couldn't doubt her. He smiled a small, satisfied smile, then asked her another question:

"You will take care of our Daño?"

"Always, Duffy, always."

"Bueno." He smiled his pleasure at her reply again and ceased to breathe.

Laska held on to his hand tightly for a moment, then commanded Daño to her shoulder harshly and went directly to Luke, who had been placed in a room across the hall from Duffy. He had been sleeping lightly but woke when she entered.

"Duffy is dead," she told him bluntly and stood staring at him until tears started rolling down his cheeks, then she threw herself on the bed beside him and burst into convulsive sobbing and wailing. Daño sat on the bedpost just above them, immensely disturbed and making hideous sounds that resembled a human cry of distress.

The children did not talk with Luvisa about Duffy — they chose rather to keep their grief some sort of secret pain between them.

295

Not only had they lost Duffy, but the beloved garden was gone. The place had been sold, the proceeds given to Carlota and José, according to the doctor's provisions, and the collection disposed of in some wise by the new owner. Luvisa would occasionally overhear some bit of conversation between the twins concerning the accident. One time they were sitting quiet and thoughtful with Daño, all three perched on the low limb of an oak tree just outside her window.

Finally Laska said in her abrupt manner, "Duffy saved your life."

Luke nodded.

"If he hadn't stopped Duke, you'd have been dragged to death, wouldn't you?"

Luke nodded again.

"If Duffy hadn't jumped for your bridle, he'd still be alive and you'd be dead," she pursued relentlessly. How heartless she can be! Luvisa thought in pain; it's as if she were trying to estimate which one she'd rather have alive.

Luke still had no word, but his head was bowed and the tears came and dropped unheeded.

Then Laska seemed to realize what she'd done, pleaded, "Don't cry, Luke, don't cry," and added her tears to his.

She treats him like she does me, Luvisa observed with clarity and sorrow; first the sharp wound — then the healing application of remorse.

Luvisa spent many hours with them in games and small tasks — many hours thinking up diversions that would take their minds away from the tragic episode that affected them so deeply. She grieved too and longed for their return to the house on the Nueces where it would be more difficult for memories of Duffy to intrude. She resolved to do her utmost to persuade Range on his next visit that they should return to the Rawhide Range and wait the end of the war there.

Range Templeton was a tired, bearded man back for a little while from a war not yet finished. He would rest a few days in

San Antonio with his family before the final fray, before the big fight in the heart of Mexico: the win-lose-or-draw, the do-or-die finish with Santa Anna.

He was telling his wife it wouldn't be safe to return to their ranch home until the fighting was all done.

He was holding his two animated children, one on each knee, while they adored him, asked endless questions, curious about his weapons, unaware of his weariness, ignoring his dirty apparel that hadn't been off his body in two weeks — slept in, ridden in, fought in — ignoring the odor of sweat and fatigue.

Their eyes said to him: Here is our hero! Our big, brave, wonderful Papa, who isn't afraid of anything in the whole wide world!

He knew he must ask them a few questions too . . . mustn't send them to bed too soon, no matter how tired he was . . . that sparkle in their eyes made a man glad to be alive no matter what. His pride in them could rise above a fagged body and mind. What a boy! What a girl! My son and daughter!

"How's Ned?" he said to Laska. "How's Duke and Dolly?" he asked Luke.

The sparkle dimmed out. Their eyes clouded with bleakness. Laska's body slumped against him. He heard Luvisa catch her breath.

"What's wrong?" he asked them all. "Something happen to the ponies?"

Then Range Templeton heard how Duffy (Macduff, the atrocity child wrested from the reluctant womb of Jeannie Dodson by Dr. Wiedeman nine years ago) had saved the life of his son. Laska did most of the talking in short painful sentences that began at the end of the story and worked back.

". . . Duke didn't mean to kill him. . . . Daño belongs to me now. . . . What makes you look so queer, Papa? You're not going to cry, are you? . . . We miss Duffy something terrible. . . . He taught us about animals, Papa, and how to creep up on things quiet like an Indian. One time — Papa! What's the matter? What makes you look at Mama like that?"

297

"Hush, both of you, and go to bed!"

Alone with Luvisa, he stood very still, his eyes accusing her but unable to speak his thoughts: You allowed the children to play with that despised half-breed, that unwanted bastard, bred in the debauchery of an Indian camp, forced on a captive mutilated white woman who never intended it should be born! You allowed them to become fond of him — to be affected like this when he died! You were fond of him yourself — it shows in your eyes! Now you expect me to be grateful? Grateful to that Dr. Weideman for ripping it out of Jeannie Dodson against her will? Grateful to IT for a freakish stunt that seemed to save my son's life? I'd rather kill somebody or hate somebody than feel like this! Now I've got to let the thought eat into me that if that bastard had never lived, my son might have been lying in his grave tonight instead of sitting on my knee. . . . Must I believe that? Why must I? How do I know someone else wouldn't have saved him, or his foot come loose from the stirrup before — before it was too late? But that's not the way it was. My son's alive, and that baby Dr. Weideman fought me and Firebush to keep alive is dead because of my son. The doctor told me I might live to see it straight someday. He'd like the way things are now for me. If he could be around I know how he'd be looking at me. I know what he'd be saying. ("See, Range Templeton, that's the way life is. What if I hadn't saved that baby? What if I had allowed you or Firebush Olson to destroy it? I'd have been taking your son's life at the same time, wouldn't I? And you — *you* would have struck down your own child, wouldn't you? Remember no matter what the derivation of life, we cannot afford to reject the hope and triumph inherent with the act of being born, the plan still far removed from our understanding for achieving the divine average somewhere down the eons of time.") Tommyrot! Why should I let that crazy doctor get at me now, putting things back in my mind that he said nearly ten years ago. He's dead and so is the Indian bastard. Luke's alive and safe and sound in his bed. Let it go at that.

298

All he said to Luvisa was, "I've got to have some rest," and left her to seek her bed alone, stricken and without comfort, comprehending his mood as completely as if he had spoken every bitter thought, every harsh word that lashed through his mind.

July Fourth continued to be a day of both personal and historical significance in the Templeton family. On this national holiday in 1849, two years after the accident that took Duffy's life in San Antonio, a special celebration was being held on the Rawhide Range. It was, first of all, a housewarming, for the big headquarters family home now wore a face representing prosperity more than pioneering. It was an imposing two-story structure painted white with green trim, and the original long front porch was now complemented by an open banistered upstairs porch of the same dimensions. Lumber had been freighted in to furnish weatherboarding for the front two-story section of the house. Huge chimneys on the east and west dominated each end. The dining room had been enlarged and a kitchen shedroom added; two of the front rooms off the open hall had been made into a large parlor and music room graced by one of the rarest pieces of furniture to be found in this wild land: a large square piano imported from France, Range's gift to Luvisa on their tenth wedding anniversary. Upstairs rooms included Silver Bryson's quarters, a library and study room for the twins' instruction, and Luke's bedroom.

The Rawhide Range had been welcoming its guests since the first day in July. The men camped out of doors, storing their gear in the long bunkhouse. The house was occupied entirely by the women and children. There were visitors who had come from points as far away as Houston and Galveston, joining others at Corpus Christi before the journey up the Nueces — men and women Luvisa had heard of only through her husband and Mr. Bryson, and a few who were friends of friends and had never met either the host or hostess. There were also old friends and acquaintances from Gonzales and San Antonio, U. S. soldiers from posts along the

Rio Grande, Rangers who had ridden and fought with Range Templeton, cattle raisers, drovers, mustangers, cow boys, and several freighters, including Eli Dawson and Flaco.

Out of Wong's and Luvisa's kitchen came the vast supply of pastries, breads, beans, and supplementary dishes for the meats prepared in barbecue pits out of doors — a great variety of game, and beef cuts in profusion. Large kettles of coffee were constantly steaming over the live coal beds, and the storehouse yielded jugs and bottles of livelier content to decorate for a short while the shelves of the bunkhouse before quenching the deep thirst that accrued with horse racing, roping exhibitions, and hunting on the Rawhide Range in the daytime and the dancing and campfire conflab that filled the evenings.

The conversation among the menfolk on this Fourth of July in 1849 was not easy casual talk but a hearty outspoken mixture of jubilation and protest, for this day had a patriotic significance to Texans above and beyond the traditional one of American independence. It was the first anniversary of the Treaty of Guadalupe Hidalgo which had marked the termination of war with Mexico. Mexican claims to territory north and east of the Rio Grande were at an end and the lower Rio Grande was the established international boundary. This was an achievement to celebrate. But a year had passed and all was not well. Many little private wars continued unabated in the tradition of survival-of-the-fittest: between Texas and Mexican landowners, between freebooters and those they preyed upon, between Indian raiders and their chosen victims on either side of the border. It was one thing to settle the boundary line by treaty, it was another to tame the wild border country. The United States Army, not the Texas Rangers, was now charged with keeping the peace, and federal agents tried to handle the Indians as wards of the government. Around the holiday campfire at Rawhide Range, the protests were vociferous, even though there were U. S. soldiers among the visitors.

"Damned pore gov'ment policy," a leather-faced drover expressed it, his mustache bristling with indignation, "sendin' greenhorn soldiers in here to do our fightin' when the Rangers are cut out for the job. Why ain't somebody up there got sense enough to arm the Rangers, put 'em on federal pay, and let 'em clean things up proper: chase all the Mexicans across the Rio Grande and all the Indians right on into their happy huntin' grounds!"

"You're mighty right!" a trader who had suffered a big loss in the Linnville raid agreed. "The way they dicker aroun' with the Indians is a putrefyin' business."

"Yeah. Washington sends some peaked-lookin' agent out to pat them on the head and say, 'Nice Injuns. Great White Father say you love Texans now — no lift their hair. You love Mexicans across Big River too — no steal their ponies.'" This sarcasm from a freighter who was finding business more hazardous than in Republic days.

"Ah, grassburrs!" Flaco joined in. "Them Comanches and Apaches think the Great White Father in Washington is plumb loco. Us Texans 're their pet enemies and they're gonna itch fer our scalps as long as they breathe. And they been raidin' Mexico fer ponies fer two hundred years. They're as liable to quit stealin' horses as they are to quit ridin' 'em."

Range listened to all these things but did not add to them. He was vastly relieved that the land between the Nueces and the Rio Grande was no longer disputed territory and all the acreage he had acquired or intended to acquire now lay within the State of Texas. Even though Indian raids and outlaw depredations of both Mexican and American origin were a constant menace to life and the peaceful pursuit of the cattle business, he preferred to fight his own wars. The Rangers could be called on in special emergencies and he saw nothing but advantage in the inadequate protection the United States offered Mexican landowners such as the Sándivars. The confused loyalties of these Texas Mexicans whose lands had been under the dominion of four national governments within one generation and their vulnerability to savage pillaging of both Indian and Texan were matters that he felt were being rather fortunately fumbled through the inexperience and restrictions of the soldiers and agents. Silver Bryson also refrained from pointed comment or criticism on the way the United States was handling border difficulties, but he enjoyed throwing a bit of ironic humor on the fires of protest. "It is a contradiction worthy of a toast that we celebrate peace and pursue war at one and the same time," he observed, and then offered, "So here's to the little wars that are left out of the big treaties. May we survive them all!"

After this, the men were drawn away from their campfires and into the house by the novelty of piano music.

The piano was the central indoors attraction. Luvisa and the twins had learned with instruction books some simple melodies which they performed, but there was no really accomplished musician to bring the fine instrument to life. One of the lady guests played charming accompaniments to the popular ballads of the day and a soldier who had one time been a student at Brown University in Rhode Island had a lively repertoire of college songs and general harmony at his fingertips that added to the gaiety of the evening gatherings. It was Cicero, the Negro fiddler who couldn't read or write, one generation removed from the African jungle, a black man uneasily free in a land where his race was enslaved, who finally awakened this grand pianoforte to make it talk and cry and laugh and dance in a manner never dreamed of by the classical forebears of piano music in the lands where the instrument was developed. And when Adelia danced for his music, the applause broke the bounds of all restraint in clapping, stomping, and yelling — jarred the rafters — momentarily leaped the barriers of race and culture in a great surge of pure enjoyment.

Adelia's dancing and Cicero's playing were not the only sensational exhibitions in the big parlor at the Rawhide Range. Laska plotted with Cicero to play for a dance she and Luke would do; she produced a costume that Cicero said gave him the bug-eyes, and they combined their inventiveness in working out the dance steps which went far in the direction of the Spanish fandango and the rest of the way in the natural fire of Laska's disposition fed with instinctive genius by the fuel of Cicero's playing. Laska assured Cicero that she had her mother's permission to do the dance but wanted to practice in secret to surprise her. Luke was an able but not overly willing partner in Laska's act. The costume she wore was one assembled from the gorgeous things she had found in the old chest — the one with the key kept hidden; she had peeped one time when her mother opened the chest and knew where the key could be found. The beautiful comb for her hair, the big silky lace shawl, the fan and the jewelry, the tiny slippers that were just a fit, offered no problems in costuming; but the full skirt that was like cloth of gold had to be made a bit shorter, a bit tighter at the waistband; and the bodice must be made to fit more snugly. Since Mama had said so often it was disgraceful for a girl of ten not to know how to sew, Laska reasoned that in making such good use of this maidenly skill which she despised, certainly in the long run Mama would be so pleased with the job perhaps she would forgive the matter of the hidden key and plundering of the chest. Anyway, the plot and the practice proceeded without mishap to the appointed time as agreed upon between her and Cicero. The parlor crowd was in the proper mood and spirit, conditioned by Cicero's performance, when Laska heard the chords that were a signal for her entrance. Then she was terribly afraid for what she had done, trembled and felt her body chill with the moisture of fear. She was ready to flee and let Cicero simply go on with the music. She tried to push Luke out of her way. He shoved her ahead.

"Don't be a coward. Finish what you start."

Cicero spotted them, subdued his music and announced: "Laadees an' gen'men, us got a surprise piece fo' yo'all by little master an' mistress o' Rawhide Range — ready yo'selves to see some right fancy fandago footwork!"

No one present was more surprised by the piece of fandango footwork than the parents of the performers. Luke, whose only concession in costume was a red satin sash worn with his best white blouse and dark breeches, played a minor but graceful role in the dance with his twin sister. Laska did all the steps she and Cicero had planned, and then as she felt the spellbound attention of the crowd — saw the utter astonishment on her mother's face — became aware of a reflective sort of anger stirring in her father that always aroused her to a sense of power over him, an urge to make him a little more angry (like answering him in Spanish or annoying him with Daño) — she proceeded to create a dance of wild excitement that was an expression of her own self and the rebellious spirit that had flowered in her with the loss of Duffy, her father's strangeness and hatred of Daño, her mother's irksome mantle of concern. . . . She was a streak of golden flame, a whirl of golden fire, an angered golden sprite in a tantrum of delight, a frenzied little goddess of the sun, stomping feet and snapping fingers, golden hair flung all about; then with a shout in Spanish fashion, she was done.

Luvisa and Range Templeton accepted the avalanche of praise, the outbursts of curiosity, the stares and astonishment. Their color was high, their words few. Luvisa did not go to Laska that night; she simply sought her own pillow when she could decently leave her guests and wept in a silence of scalding tears. Much later when Range lay beside her very still and quiet, she let him know she was awake.

"Why did you let it happen?" he asked.

"She did it, somehow, without my knowledge."

"I ought to kill that piano-crazy nigger. He taught her."

"No, Range. Laska did it all herself. I'm sure of that."

"Where did she get those clothes, all that Mexican stuff?"

"She's been in — the chest."

"What chest?"

"The one that belonged to my mother. I don't know how she found the key. I — I — must punish her for — prowling among my things — and making such an exhibition of herself."

"You mean you haven't talked to her yet?"

"I — was too upset."

304

"How come all that fancy Mexican stuff in that chest?"

"Those were — Spanish times, you know — " Luvisa choked on a trembling sort of sigh, and her breath caught in short gasps such as a child makes after sobbing long and hard.

Range patted her shoulder with awkward tenderness. "Never mind now. Get some rest. We'll get her straightened out somehow. What stumps me is, I can't figure where she gets it to act and talk like a cussed Mexican all the time."

Since the celebration at the Rawhide Range was in the nature of a public function, there was no such thing as an uninvited guest, but the appearance of a well-known wanderer, known simply as the Neighbor, for the last few days of festivity was something of a surprise. The Neighbor had become a familiar figure in the Southwest during the past ten years. Bearded, weaponless, wearing nondescript garments, always riding a mule, he paused in his wanderings wherever he could help someone in distress or need.

This was his first visit to Rawhide Range, and after Range and Luvisa had made him welcome, other guests were eager to recite for them his peculiarities and good deeds.

"He spent nearly three months with the Barnes family over near our place," a woman from Victoria eagerly related. "Mr. Barnes had his leg broke. The Neighbor farmed his crops, helped the family like a hired hand, but wouldn't take any pay, just moved on."

"He's good at nursing the sick," another praised, "and can read the Good Book in proper style or say a prayer over the dead."

"He was buryin' some dead Indians one time to keep the buzzards from 'em," Flaco related to Range with skepticism and reluctant admiration, "when he found one was still breathin'. He took keer of the varmint and finally turned it loose to git back to the tribe. . . . To my notion, that's carryin' good deeds too fur . . . thousand wonders his scalp wasn't lifted."

"He'd take care of anything in trouble from a sick dog to a horse

305

thief," Eli Dawson added quietly. "And besides that he's taught many a boy and girl in the lonesome river valleys of Texas to read and write and say the tables."

"Somehow or other he put a quietus on that feud between the Burks and the Lawrences," a cattleman from Gonzales recalled. "He's got a special brand of religion, but don't give it no name. Never gives himself a name either. By way of introduction, he just says, 'I'm your Neighbor' and looks at you in a way that makes you right glad he's around."

Range listened to these things and kept watching the Neighbor as he moved from group to group, unobtrusive in manner, eating sparingly, polite in his refusal of strong drink, appearing more hungry for companionship than food. Something about the man bothered Range — somewhere in the past was a place, an incident, that Range wanted to associate with the Neighbor. It pricked at his memory until he was miserable. Finally he approached the man when an opportunity to speak to him alone was presented, stared frankly at him, and remarked "Somewhere or other I've met up with you before."

"Yes, Mr. Templeton, you have. Ten years ago I worked for you."

Range studied him intently, tried to imagine him without the beard, in a rider's proper riggin', and suddenly he knew. "Why, you're Finius Jones, the best cow boy I ever had!"

The Neighbor seemed more pained than pleased by the praise.

"Why, I remember plain as anything. You brought in more than a hundred cattle after El Gavilán's raid and got us started on that first drive to New Orleans in good time. You were good at the cattle huntin' business — had a real knack for gettin' 'em outta the brush. Why didn't you stick to it? I thought you were on your way back to Alabama. You could've had cow-boy work with me anytime. What happened to you anyway?"

"I felt the hand of God."

"Yeah?"

"I had to return to the Republic of Texas and serve out my days."

"What for?"

The feverish intensity of the Neighbor's eyes worried Range, made him feel ill at ease.

"For murder!"

"Murder?" Range was shocked.

"Yes, murder, Mr. Templeton. I committed murder to get those cattle for you. I shot a Mexican in cold blood. I wanted to get home to comforts and a life of ease. So I killed a man deliberately to get that drive started — and would have killed another but he got away. I never got home — I turned back from New Orleans. The tortures of conscience, I found, are worse than hardship, worse than home-sickness, worse than anything that can beset a man."

Range did not openly smile at Finius Jones, but there was a blend of both amusement and sympathy in his expression. "You mean you let yourself suffer all this time over that? Why, to my notion that was a good deed. Don't you know you probably cleared the brush of one more thievin' Mexican." And as an afterthought he added, "Too bad you missed the other one."

The eyes of Finius Jones flashed with a wild anger, but he answered quietly. "I knew no such thing. The Mexican just as likely owned the cattle and I was the thief . . . and murderer."

"Killin' and murder are two different things," Range answered thoughtfully. "After all the fightin' and tight spots I been through, if I let every killin' rest on my conscience as murder, I'd be crazy as a loon." He looked at Finius as if he considered him a little bit crazy and concluded, "Give your conscience a rest, Mr. Jones, and if you decide to settle down, let me know. I'm short on help and I'm going to take another herd or so to California. I'd pay well for a good man like you."

Finius Jones glared at Range as if he'd like to strike him, and then gradually let an expression of serenity wipe out his anger. "Thank you, neighbor," he said, "but I think I shall continue to work at fulfilling the law."

"What law's that?"

" 'Bear ye one another's burdens, and so fulfil the law of Christ.' "

That night before he pulled out, Finius Jones talked some to the guests at Rawhide Range. It began when someone asked, "What religion do you follow, Neighbor?" He was sitting on the top step of the front porch leaning against a pillar. The men sitting around on the edge of the porch and settled on their heels in a sort of semicircle in the yard were quiet and tired, weary of talk and dance, surfeited with food and drink, smoking, ready to be off, each to his own endeavor, each on his own path. The women sat at windows that opened on the porch or in the rockers and on the benches placed on the porch. Some stood at the banisters upstairs and dreamed in the moonlight. The moon, round and full, stared down with a pure, clear July intensity. Cicero came around the house, silent as a shadow, and squatted in the corner the steps made with the porch, his head about on a level with the feet of the Neighbor. The wanderer, his head slightly bowed, made no immediate answer to the question directed to him. When he raised his head, the light of the moon picked up bright glints in his uncut light-brown hair and on his bearded face and he spoke with a gentle measured quality.

"The religion that I follow is an experiment with goodness as exemplified in the life of Christ. If I were worthy to exhort you, I would say know the power of goodness and the sin of greed. I would say minister unto the weak, the sick, the aged, and the infirm — for who of us shall escape these calamities and not in turn need ministering unto?

"It is well to refresh the spirit often at the fountain of giving — to drink deep of the joy of sharing.

"Perceive how hate corrodes the spirit, how indulgence in gossip and condemnation weaves a snare for the destruction of human happiness, and how prejudices among men passed along from generation to generation poison the mind and canker the thought.

"Cultivate prayer. The heartfelt prayer of no man goes unattended at the ear of the Infinite.

" 'Bear ye one another's burdens, and so fulfil the law of Christ.' . . . 'For all the law is fulfilled in one word, even in this: Thou shalt love thy neighbor as thyself.'

"Such are the tools of the spirit for clearing the path where the soul of man may walk unfettered."

The speaker was silent. No one of his listeners stirred. The cadence of crickets and cicadas continued as a burry background for the sounds of the summer night. An owl hooted with soft, sad tolerance. A whippoorwill called and was answered with a faint far cry that reached back like a drowsy echo.

He rose, said "Good night, neighbors," went in ease and quietness down the steps and across the yard, and on to the tree where his mule was tied, packed for departure. He mounted and rode off down a moonlit trail to the south.

When the guests were gone and the men of the Rawhide Range back at their work — when the houses and yards and kitchens were straight again — a great blissful calm settled over the Templeton household and the summer heat encouraged long, lazy siestas for days afterward. Only Cicero failed to sink into the pleasant lethargy that followed. His spare time was spent at the piano in the cool darkened parlor kept tightly closed against heat, dust, and strong light. His touch gentle, his foot on the soft pedal, he disturbed no one with his struggle to find proper words and music for the song within him, a song born in his heart the evening he sat and listened to the Neighbor, "da man on a mule."

> *Isya all bog down*
> *On dat muddy road?*
> *Isya back a-breakin'*
> *Wid all dat load?*
> *Lemme turn yer wheel,*
> *Lemme tote yer sack,*

Gotta heart-song in me
An' a good strong back.

Ah learn my song
'Bout da golden rule
By a-listenin' hard
To da man on a mule.
He cum a-visitin',
An' den one night
Did a little talkin'
'Bout livin' right.

Isya faggin' an' a-hunger?
Isya weary to da bone?
Lemme make ya down a pallet,
Feed ya good corn pone.
Isya porely and a-pinin'?
Den we hum a little tune,
Make de burden lighter
An' ya fellin' better soon.

Isya ol' an' gray
An' lef' all alone?
Does ya reach fo' da bread
An' git ya a stone?
Lemme set by yer side
An' hol' to yer han',
It all cum right
In da promise' lan'.

Dis song Ah sing
'Bout da golden rule
Ah made f'um da words
Of da man on a mule.

CHAPTER XIV

LUKE AND LASKA were never sent to school, but the matter of their education was not ignored. Luvisa had taught them the rudiments of reading and writing and simple sums. When the subject of their proper schooling came up after Range returned from the Mexican War, there was mutual agreement between Range, Silver Bryson, and Luvisa that it would bring unnecessary loneliness to the whole family to send them to a Southern or Eastern school for a formal education. Mr. Bryson suggested stocking a library with appropriate schoolbooks and reading matter and allowing him to act as their instructor in a routine of study; when this was agreed upon and begun, he seemed more content than at any time during his partnership with Range and settled down to teaching the children and spending long hours pursuing his own reading and meditation.

"My fees for instruction will be simply to buy all the books I want for myself as well as the children," he told Range. Thus it was that the freight hauled in to the Rawhide Range frequently included large heavy boxes of books along with the barrels of sugar and flour, ammunition, bolts of cloth, and leather goods. And the children's minds, filled with the nature lore of the cactus country and the stories of hunting and fighting on a bloody frontier, began to take on new dimensions under Mr. Bryson's guidance and expanded to a consciousness of states beyond Texas, countries beyond the United States and Mexico, and peoples of many times and places. Listening to his cultured voice, reading his assignments in history and literature, they happily explored the joys of learning. There was a deep affection between Silver Bryson and the twins but little demonstration on either side; they were challenged by his manner of dignity and reserve and absorbed his instruction like sponges, but their application of what they learned was a different matter. Laska seemed to go to her lessons with the zest of an adventure, but when it was done, she threw it off like a mantle that might prove cumbersome or uncomfortable and continued living more by feeling than by reason or judgment. Luke, on the other hand, carried his learning experiences with him and made them a part of his deeper thoughts and used them in shaping his actions at home or out on the range. Their studies occupied only a few hours of the day, but continued throughout the year with only occasional interruptions for holiday festivities or special work with the cattle when Bryson felt he was needed.

Luke, after he was ten years old, rode with Range and Bryson when cattle were gathered for market and on many of the mustang ventures. There was complete compatability between Luke and his father; and Range and Bryson both got much secret pleasure from the hero worship Luke tendered them. Luke was Range's nobler self, and in adoring his son he could adore his own better qualities as well. The obvious congeniality and satisfying companionship that existed between them did not make for a better understanding between Laska and her father. She longed for the same attention, and, when she failed to get it, substituted the kind of attention she could get, using Daño as her favorite device for starting trouble.

On one occasion — the first time Luke was allowed to ride out with the men on a roundup that would take them away from headquarters for several days — Laska felt the sting of neglect so strong that she plotted a more daring reprisal than usual. It was very early on the morning and little attention was being paid to her as the mounts and supplies were made ready. Luke was wholly occupied with the frisky mustang he was to ride and extra proud of the fact that for the rough brush work ahead he and his father were both riding fresh-broke horses. Laska slipped away from the group and ran to her room. There she selected from her collection of brightly-painted gourds a big red one very light in weight. The seeds in it made a fine sound, like a rattlesnake, and a piece of cloth string was tied securely to the neck of it. She called Daño and he made no objection when she looped the string around his neck so that the big gourd would dangle there when he flew.

As good-bys were being said, both Luke and Range looked around for Laska. Range was in extra-high spirits at the prospect of having Luke constantly by his side in the workdays ahead, but he was reluctant to leave without a reassuring glimpse of Laska.

"Where's my golden girl?" he asked Luvisa. "Thought I saw her around a few minutes ago."

About that time, there was an almost human scream over their heads and Daño darted down, not very sure of his flying balance, the big gourd swinging wildly, rattling hideously, hitting Luke's horse across the ears and Range's between the eyes. The mustangs went wild in an explosion of pitching and plunging, and Daño stayed with them, flapping and cawing in raucous delight, until Laska — vastly pleased with the act that she alone could call off — rushed downstairs and whistled him in.

After it had seemed certain that Luke and Range wouldn't be thrown, everyone watching the spectacle had given in to hilarious laughter and yells.

Range hated practical jokes and hated Daño. Except for Luvisa's intervention, he would have killed the bird before they left San Antonio. It was hard for him to control himself now — hard not to shoot the crow on the spot — not to get off his horse and give Laska a good shaking. But he knew better than to violate the laughter and good fun that had broken out over the incident. Laska always bested him in such things. It was humiliating; both as a father and a man his pride was vastly injured. And the stunt was dangerous besides. Luke might have been hurt. He was surprised the boy had stuck on and allowed himself to be pleased with his son's performance; because of it, he softened a little towards Laska. He conceded her a small tight smile, but his eyes were cold, and he said nothing. He saw that Luvisa was worried about what he might say and do. So he did what he often did as a substitute for acting or speaking violently . . . let his anger solidify into a stillness that always brought a feeling of uncertainty and sometimes actual fear to those in his presence. Now those around him grew quiet, the tension built up, and Laska's

313

features sharpened with a sort of pain that Range observed but could not interpret. He shared the pain for a moment and at the same time felt some satisfaction in the assurance that at least she was responsive to his displeasure.

Laska sought desperately for words that would break through to her father. "Good horses, Papa!" she said loudly and tossed her head in defiance of the ready tears. "And you and Luke can really ride 'em."

"It's a good thing," Range said. That was all. Then he turned to his riders. "Let's get goin', men. We've lost too much time." A wave of his hat was good-by to them all and purposely ignored the little golden girl, clutching the black crow in her arms, a big red gourd tied freakishly around its neck.

Laska did not know why her father despised Daño so, but she was aware that it was in some way connected with Duffy. She was also quite conscious of his lack of sympathy and gratitude where Duffy was concerned. Duffy's death had left a lasting scar on Laska, and, when she came to know that Range did not share her grief, understand it, or even approve of it, she expressed her hurt and loss in defiance and deliberate trouble-making. She knew he loved her, and since he wouldn't act as she wanted him to, she used that knowledge to hurt him. Unable to change either of them, Luvisa must simply watch the conflicts, large and small, share in the pain they meted out to each other and mediate their differences when she could. She disliked the pet crow almost as much as Range did but endured him for Laska's and Duffy's sake, knowing how sacred the promise and strong the tie that he represented.

Daño appeared from his actions to know something of the quarrels raised in his behalf, to enjoy being the object of them, and often took pains to initiate trouble on his own. One morning, several weeks after the gourd incident, he was presented an opportunity for mischief that required no direction from Laska. Keys were always a special temptation to Daño because by snatching them he could be sure that a lot of delightful noise and commotion would follow. So when his sharp eyes spotted the storehouse keys on a bench where

Range had laid them while he gave his attention to mending a bridle, Daño darted down like a hawk after a chicken, snatched the keys and flew out over the fence and into the brush. Range had been about to use the keys and there was no other way to get into the supply room without breaking down the door. He was pale and speechless with anger. He picked up his rifle and stood waiting for Daño's return, for he knew the crow would be back in a moment cawing and gloating over his mischief, the keys hidden where no one could possibly get at them. Luvisa saw what happened. She knew she couldn't keep Range from shooting the crow but perhaps Laska could. Laska was upstairs in the study with Luke and Mr. Bryson. Luvisa called her and told her of Daño's offense. She dreaded the fight between Range and Laska but not nearly as much as she dreaded Laska's grief over a dead Daño and the consequent feeling she would have toward her father.

Laska ran out to Range like a streak of fury, leaped at his rifle and clung to it, screaming at him, "You can't shoot Daño! If you do, I'll hate you forever and ever just like you hate Daño! You can't shoot Daño!" Then as usual in peaks of excitement, she broke off into Spanish. Luvisa shuddered at what she heard. Range sensed something of the meaning for he put down his gun, took her by the shoulders and gave her a good shake. Laska began crying, and Luvisa knew which had won.

"I'll get your old keys," she said, when his hands dropped from her shoulders. "I'll get your dirty-old-coyote keys." She turned from him and ran to one of the watchtowers, climbed inside, and began whistling for Daño. He was soon answering her. The calls and answers went on for some time as if in argument. Range sat down on the bench, his shoulders drooped, his hands resting on his knees. It was not long until Laska came running to him, threw the keys in the dust at his feet, then turned and ran on into the house and back upstairs. Laska called Daño to her from the upstairs porch before returning to the study. Luvisa knew she would sit reading with Daño perched on the back of her chair and Mr. Bryson would not object.

If there had been any validity in Carlota's superstition that a bird in the house meant death in the family, Luvisa thought wryly, the members of our household would have by this time all been in their graves.

Laska's obstinacy began to extend beyond her outbursts with Range and occasionally touched Bryson or Luvisa. She had no fear of horses, tamed or untamed, and observed none of the cautions urged upon her. She openly defied Bryson one afternoon when she appropriated a tough little Spanish pony brought into the home corral with a bunch of mustangs Range had rounded up to use on a drive to California. The pony, light dun in color, wiry and full of fire, attracted her attention. Range was not around. She told Bryson she wanted the horse for her own. He told her it was no horse for a child — too mean and full of sting.

"I'll call him Stinger," she said. He's my horse. And I'm no child." Before Bryson could recover from this pronouncement, she was over the fence and in the pen with the mustangs, walking toward the dun that she had just named Stinger. Bryson commanded her to get out of the pen. She ignored him, moving on toward the dun, murmuring a soft strange jargon, mostly in Spanish, the tones both caressing and compelling. The other mustangs reared and snorted and crowded together in the far corner of the corral. Bryson dared not get in the pen and disturb them further. The dun stood as if rooted to the spot, watching the little creature that approached him so steadily and fearlessly, spellbound with the sound she made directed to him alone. He pulled back on his hind legs, almost sitting down, trying to resist the power she had over him; his eyes protruded as if in great fright, his nostrils distended, and his ears lay back close to his head, but he didn't move out of his tracks. At last, she stood directly in front of him, still murmuring but not touching him. Eventually, she reached out her hand in a slow sure movement, touched him gently between the eyes, stroked his head, but did not reach up to his ears. Stinger trembled violently. She removed her hand, talked to him some more, then turned and walked back to the fence. As she climbed over, Bryson reached up and lifted her to the ground. He met her triumphant look and said not a word.

"You see, he is my horse," she said and left.

The dun, strangely gentled, walked over to the fence and watched her go. Bryson, pale, his face beaded with sweat, came in the house and sought Luvisa. She was frightened at his appearance. He reassured her, and then seated himself as if his knees would no longer support him. She brought him a spot of brandy although it was not his custom to take spirits at midafternoon, and he took it gratefully. When he had finished the story, she shared his amazement to the fullest, and but for subjecting him to further shock would have shared his brandy too.

"The little witch!"

"The wonderful little witch!" he echoed.

Stinger became as much of a fixture in Laska's life as Daño. She rode him as often bareback with halter as she did properly saddled. She taught him more tricks than a circus horse — her commands by whistle and call were his law. Frightening as it was, her family began to accept her stunt riding without protest and finally began to find it rather entertaining. Bryson once remarked to Range in the presence of Luvisa and the twins that here was the one he could teach to ride as Tomás the mustanger rode, catching the wild horse by leaping on it from the back of a trained mount. Range looked so startled that Bryson laughed and told how Range out on his first mustanging expedition just before the twins were born had been much impressed by the work of the young mustanger Tomás who could leap so nimbly from his own horse onto a fleeing mustang, taking a halter rope with him and returning with a tamed animal. Surmising that he was soon to have a son, Range had remarked to Bryson, "I'm goin' to teach my son to catch 'em like that."

"I asked him what if he had a girl," Bryson continued his account of the campfire conversation, "and he looked as startled at the idea as he did just now at my mention of the limber-limbed Laska as a likely pupil in the art of mustanging, Tomás-style."

By recalling that incident, Bryson unintentionally started a kind of family feud. Luke and Laska both were now determined to learn to catch wild horses as Tomás had caught them, and Range had no intention of teaching either of them such a dangerous business. Nevertheless, when preparations got under way not long after for a wild-horse hunt, Luke boasted to Laska that he intended to try out the Tomás stunt for bringing in some extra-good horses.

"You're too big and fat," Laska said. "You'd fall between the horses and get stomped. Tomás was small, like me. I could do it, but you couldn't."

This blunt appraisal, made in an outburst of jealousy, was exaggerated, but nevertheless she was lighter in weight and much quicker in action than Luke. They were around twelve years old at the time and Luke was large for his age, though certainly not fat. Laska was tiny and thin-looking, many pounds lighter than Luke, but surprisingly strong.

Luke seldom contradicted Laska, even when she berated him. He kept his silence now. He'd been going with the men on such expeditions for two years and was always sorry that Laska was left behind.

"I'll go this time," she told him. "I'm old enough and I can shoot as good as you can and ride better. I'll tell them I'm going and they can't keep me from it unless they lock me up!"

"But you're a girl!" Luke couldn't help protesting.

"I don't care! I know more about horses than anybody on this range and I can catch horses just like Tomás caught them! You'll see!"

Laska's announcement to the family of her intentions was dismissed all around as ridiculous, and she retired into a mood of sullen quietness, brooding on some form of retaliation for the injustice done her.

Bryson, feeling that he had brought on the difficulty by reviving the memory of Tomás and his mustanging, offered a solution. The children and Luvisa were good travelers, he said, as illustrated by their trips to and from San Antonio — why not take them along?

Wong could pack up an extra mule or two, take along a tent for Laska and Luvisa, and make a pleasant outing for them all. Range protested at first that it was too dangerous, but Bryson insisted.

"It's the country you chose in which to rear your family and make your fortune," he reminded Range. "They might as well get acquainted with it. We're well supplied with six-shooters now — we ought to be able to hold our own against most challengers between here and the Rio Grande; after all, we've been doing it for quite a while now."

Luvisa eagerly backed up Bryson's arguments. She had never seen the Rawhide Range beyond the few miles she had ridden out from the house on rare occasions. She and the children rode well, and they could in emergency shoot well enough. Range finally agreed that it might be a pleasant excursion and not too dangerous. Laska was in a perfect frenzy of joy. As she helped her mother plan and pack for the several weeks of camping out on the range, they indulged in a lot of private banter about being the first lady mustangers in Texas; and when the menfolk weren't around, Laska's high spirits poured out in noisy exhibitions — happy foolishness of song and dance that was both distraction and delight to Luvisa.

"I'm a mustangin' woman ridin' fast and free," Laska would shout as she skipped and whirled up and down the long hall, bringing something to Luvisa to include in saddlebag or bundle.

"When I get goin', watch out for me! Yippee!!

"In a buckskin suit, with a gun I can shoot — Bang! Bang!

"Ya-hoo! Vamanos!! To the land of the roving mustang!

"Yippee! The land of the roving mustang!"

Laska chided Luvisa about her sidesaddle and bulky riding habit. She insisted it would be more appropriate if her mother wore buckskin trousers and jacket as she did.

"You'll leave clear sign behind us," Laska said, "bright blue scraps of your skirt waving from every bush."

"My heavy poplin habit does not snag so easily," Luvisa defended. "And although I don't indulge in the kind of antics you do, I'm not

319

so old or awkward for riding that I must brush against every tree or bush on the trail. You know I don't like trousers for women. I've simply learned to endure them for your safety, that's all. And that reminds me — I do wish you'd humor me on this trip by wearing a sturdy boot and a head covering." Luvisa's brow furrowed with the old worry that Laska preferred moccasins to any kind of shoe or boot and had worn no head covering since baby-cap days.

Laska laughed. "Banish your snakebite and sunstroke worries, Mama. The snake that bites me will die a horrible death, and if I had to cover my head from the sun I would be crazier than I am."

They were a happy family, setting out together like a company of nomads. Daño was left behind, properly caged and very fussy, with Cicero appointed by Laska as overseer and burdened with endless instructions.

Range Templeton was surprised at the pleasure he experienced in having his family with him, camping out in the wilderness that was his own land. It was as if the trip were a sort of ceremonial union between his land and his family. He had a chance to study Luke, so strong and quiet — the boy would make a good partner a few years from now. He watched Laska closely, trying to find the key for understanding and controlling her, searching for some characteristic that would let him hope she might outgrow her boldness and temper and become like Luvisa. He took pride in her courage and her fine hand with horses, but the faculty she had for making him feel elated one moment and like a weak fool the next brought him as close to fear as he ever came. Was it his imagination that she looked so much like a Mexican? If she could only be cured of talking and acting like one —

It was good to have Luvisa along too. She seemed happier, closer to him somehow. These long drives to California the last few years had taken him too much away from home, drained him of all thought and energy for anything but getting the herd there and getting back with the money and pushing the lines of his land further south. But one more drive would be enough — he'd be done with dangerous trips and long absences. He wasn't an old man, but fifteen years of ridin' freight and drivin' cattle, fightin' swamps and deserts and Indians and Mexicans aged a man some. Luvisa still looked young and pretty. They'd settle at the springs in a few years now, turn the Nueces quarters over to Luke. Maybe they'd have more children, a sort of second family, no reason to think they couldn't — if he was able to be at home more. He looked at Luvisa, found her watching him intently; he smiled at her possessively and felt a warm satisfaction in the loving response of her expression.

He also found himself in the mood for looking back over what he had accomplished since coming into the brush a greenhorn with big ideas for money-making and land-getting. He hadn't done so bad. In that five years before the Mexican War, no cattle driver in Texas had made more money than he had on New Orleans drives; and even while he was away in the war, the cattle and horses had been increasing, waiting for him to come back and make a cleanin' when the gold rush started in California. Funny thing, the gold fever had never hit him, at least not the kind you dig for; he'd gone over the deserts and the mountains and through that deep dangerous Indian country for gold already mined and minted . . . and he got it, too . . . well over a hundred thousand dollars clear if he came out all right on this next drive — it stacked up pretty fast when you got a hundred dollars apiece for your four-legged hunks of meat. Other drivers hadn't had his luck — lost out to the Indians . . . those East Texas cattle raisers didn't have as much sense about fighting Indians as a sucking calf had about a panther. Well, their losses were his gains — kept pushing the price up. Too bad for them, but after all he broke the way . . . showed 'em how . . . made the first drive of any size without wagon-train protection. He could remember how some of the would-be drivers had hung around him at the house-warmin' in '49, gettin' his ideas, waitin' for him to lead out. One of 'em had said, "Pretty risky business, Mr. Templeton; no slave traffic to make up losses." He had pretended not to hear. Wonder where that old story got picked up? Wonder if Luvisa had ever heard it? He'd admit the deal gave him some early gray hairs, but he'd do it again. Chenet turned him a lot of business after that . . . Luvisa had good help out of Cicero and Adelia . . . sure, he'd do it again and not be near so squeamish about it.

He sat late over the campfire embers with Silver Bryson one night, wakeful and driven along in his thoughts by the old impatience to be done with what he had set out to do. He still didn't own the springs, the crown of beauty his land must have, the very core of his dream.

"A touch of land fever?" Bryson inquired with mild cynicism.

"Whatever you want to call it. When I get this drive off, I'm gonna get to the bottom of that business on exactly who owns those springs and why that particular hundred acres or so can't be bought up."

"Maybe the people on it like it as well as you do."

"The Mexicans livin' there may not even own it. I'm gonna have the titles looked into."

"I'm surprised you've waited this long. Have you been expecting divine intervention on your behalf through an Indian raid or similar types of eviction?"

Bryson's cynicisms had long ago ceased to prick Range.

"Could happen yet, but I'm not dependin' on it."

"What if you should find out that these Sándivars have a good title, say a Texas homestead?"

"These border Mexicans never heard of a homestead law. I don't mind payin' reasonable for any old title they can dig up — then they got to get out."

"Well, I have heard it rumored that along the border there are services to be bought guaranteeing riddance of title-owner when title is proved inconveniently valid."

"Stop trying to twist my thinking."

"I'm trying to untwist it."

"I think we'll have another look at that place on this trip."

322

"Why?"

"I want Luvisa and the kids to see it . . . they've never been there."

"And yearning yourself for a sight of that which you covet."

"You want to come along or stay with the catch when we get 'em penned up?"

"I'll come along. I'm thirsty for a drink of good spring water."

When Luke had proved his ineptness at catching mustangs the Tomás way and had taken several hard falls in the process, he graciously joined the whole camp in awesome admiration for Laska's feats. Three different herds of wild horses were penned on the expedition and out of each Laska had picked a favorite before they reached the pen, crowded swiftly to its side on Stinger, and carrying a short horsehair rope slipped easily from her horse onto the mustang. Far out on the horse's shoulders as he stretched out in a dead run she looped the halter properly, placed it over head and nose, and later returned to camp with the horse subdued and in good condition. Laska was subdued too; these races took the restlessness from her, gave her appetite and sound slumber.

Luvisa stilled her anxiety for Laska's safety with Silver Bryson's philosophy. "The risk is much better than the sullen mood, the brooding, and the devising of trouble for us all. Better a broken bone or two than a broken spirit."

When the horses had been penned, caught, and sidelined, Range suggested that the party move on to the south for another day's ride and see the springs before returning home. He'd leave hands to care for the horses, holding them for two or three days until the main party returned. The children were eager to go further and see more, and Luvisa hid her fears at the possible meeting with Miguel.

"I want to take you the rest of the way so you can see what I'll have when I finish takin' over," Range told Luvisa. "You've heard me tell about the springs — now I want you to see for yourself that it's just the place to build that biggest house in Texas like I always promised you."

"I like the house we have, dear," Luvisa's voice was a gentle protest. "And — what about those people now living at the springs? I guess — they like it too. I don't much like to go there — and look around — with the place occupied — and all. It might start trouble of some kind — mightn't it?"

"Just a Mexican family, and they're about cleaned out. Won't give us any trouble. We'll just be travelin' and lookin'."

"But — the owner may be around and recognize you as — as the one who has tried to buy him out."

"What if he does? I won't have anything to say this time. I'm holdin' off for a while yet. He don't know it but I've got an option to buy all the land he's grazin' now except for a hundred or so around the springs that's tied up some way or another. Most of his holdin's are based on an old Spanish land grant that the court down this way is gonna throw out. When I get back from California, I'm gonna get it all ironed out. I wouldn't be surprised if the Mexicans haven't pulled out from the springs by then. If they haven't — "

"If they haven't, what will you do?"

"Don't know yet. I'll have to see. Don't you worry, I'll get it, and in another five years — "

"But, Range," Luvisa's protest was stronger now, "I love the home we have! Why must we plan another?"

"We've got a son, you know. Could be in not much more'n five years he'll be thinking of settlin' down with a partner of his own. I could run my land right, with him on one side of it and me on the other. And I've figured on buildin' at these springs from the start — you know that. You'll like the place when you see it."

"Are you going to build a home for Laska somewhere too?"

"Laska? . . . Do you think anybody'll ever be able to put up with her besides us? If she gets much wilder, I'll be buildin' a cage for her, not a house."

"Range!"

"Don't get riled. She does give us some hard times, but maybe she'll grow out of it. Funny little scamp. She's done all right on this trip. Her recklessness sort of makes my hair stand on end, but she seems to have put away that mean way of hers for a while. . . . I always figure about a girl that the man she gets will want to take her his way. Luke'll never want to leave the land — if Laska does, I'll give her money for her part."

Luvisa thought: He talks about leaving the land, not leaving home or family.

As they neared the springs, Luvisa prayed: Mother of God, let me not have to face Miguel. And Range's animation increased. They met a lone vaquero. Bryson talked with him, found that he was of the Sándivar range, asked how far to the springs, and if they could camp there. The vaquero studied the woman and children, the Chinese man in charge of the pack mules, let the suspicion begin to fade in his eyes and then die altogether when Laska rode to Bryson's side and made several excited inquiries in her singing Spanish. Bryson quieted her with a stern look in order that the vaquero might not think her undisciplined and out of a woman's place. The vaquero insisted on conducting them personally to a comfortable camping site on the stream just below the springs and in sight of the Sándivar headquarters. He assured them they were welcome and that the master would surely come out to greet them if he were home but both the young master and the old one were in Laredo and not expected back for perhaps two days. Luvisa sighed and murmured thanks to the saint that had taken Emilio and Miguel on a journey.

The following morning when they came to the springs and stood together where Range had drunk so thankfully after being lost in the brush, Luvisa understood the attachment he had for the place and could have shared his feeling but for knowing he was coveting that which belonged to another and could come by it in no way that would be lawful and right.

As Range and Luvisa became lost in their own thoughts, Range reviewing for himself and for her his first visit to the springs almost fifteen years before, Laska and Luke rode off unnoticed through the willows and on up to the Sándivar house. It had been several years now since they had seen any house other than their own, or visited with children near their own age. Wouldn't it be exciting to find some children here?

Francisca kept her cherished only granddaughter out of sight when she saw the children coming, although Marina trembled with eagerness and begged to be allowed a closer view of them. But Laska's glib tongue proved as effective on Francisca as it had once been on Carlota, and soon the three children were together: Luke, staring, completely tongue-tied before the fair little black-haired stranger; Laska, chattering gaily under the stimulation of curiosity and the delight of having before her a girl companion younger and much shier than she; Marina, her heart pounding, her cheeks flushed, making soft polite phrases to fill the small gaps Laska allowed her.

Bryson came after them much sooner than they liked and watched in astonishment the leave-taking. Luke, with Old World gallantry, kissed Marina's hand. What in heaven's name has the boy been reading? Bryson asked himself.

Laska, not to be outdone, gave the startled Marina a regular Mexican embrazo and kissed her on both cheeks, giving Bryson more food for humorous thought on this spontaneous overlapping of cultures. Marina, quite unable to cope with her feelings, ran away to hide tears of disappointment that her new-found friends must be snatched from her so quickly.

The Templeton family returned from their mustanging expedition without mishap and with an unusually good string of ponies to make up the remuda for the California drive. But every member of the party was glad to sight the big white house that stood like a sanctuary of rest and comfort and protection at journey's end. Among Luvisa's happy thoughts, however, there was a discord of anxiety.

"How wonderful to be back!" she exclaimed aloud, and then

326

thought: Why must we ever leave this place? Why can't we live our lives out right here — comfortable, happy? Why must we have more land than we need — more money than we can spend? Land and money — suffocating our love. How can I uproot a dream that has grown into a passion and a greed? How can I show my husband that here in this home with his family around him is a reality that outstrips the dreams of most men? Perhaps I can turn him into happier and more unselfish ways — if he never learns about Miguel's homestead and our kinship — if he can forget the springs . . . what a foolish thought! . . . he could easier forget me.

Range rode up close to her. "What are you thinking?"

"Thinking how rich I am!" she said gaily, putting aside the shadows of the future. "My good husband, my children, my comfortable home. Oh, Range, I love it here. I wish for nothing more!" It was all she dared say just now. Range smiled at her, said nothing, but somehow she divined that he was thinking: This is only a small part of what I intend to do.

There was a closer and more tangible threat to Luvisa Templeton's happiness than those invading her thoughts as she viewed with such fondness the staunch and friendly lines of her home on the Nueces. Undetected, unsuspected, a lone Mexican rider had followed the campers soon after they left the springs. He was mounted on a sorrel stallion with flashing mane and tail of bright copper color. The rider himself was clothed in inconspicuous colors of brown and green so that on foot he blended with the landscape like a lizard or a snake. In his body was the careless grace of the untamed, and when he walked it was with the light springy step of a predatory animal. His dark eyes, when not animated by thought or emotion, had the cool blackness of a cave's end where light has never touched. They could light up, however, with venomous fierceness or dangerous charm. His trailing of the Templetons was leisurely during the day, and he made a cold camp in the evening at a safe distance. At night he crept close on foot, and in utter stillness watched the family, his black eyes taking in detail after detail until he knew the relationship

327

of each one: the son, the daughter, the wife, the white-haired friend. His piercing glance dwelt longest on the daughter, puzzled, intent . . . this one looked more like the daughter of a grandee than a gringo . . . yet she addressed the big one as father . . . maybe the father was a fool in such matters and the mother had — (he watched Luvisa awhile) no — one man only. He studied Laska further and found faint tracings of her father's features, enough to reassure him they were indeed true father and child. He was satisfied, and in no hurry. He had learned patience in twelve years of waiting and growing up. Here was heavy ransom and revenge in so many forms it was a deep pleasure to contemplate. The Mexican did not study Range Templeton. This member of the family he knew already although Range would not have recognized him, for the sinister watcher had been a boy of ten when his father had been sent over a bluff into the flooded Nueces River in payment for the life of Barrel West and the loss of a herd. This was the son of The Hawk, the second El Gavilán, dedicated to vengeance, living by rapine.

CHAPTER XV

AFTER HIS VISIT to the springs with his family in 1851, it took Range Templeton five more years to make his cattle drives over the California Trail pay off to his satisfaction. During that time his wife achieved a sadder, deeper patience and his children passed into an early adulthood.

Luke became the respected young master of Rawhide Range, ever at Silver Bryson's side, ready always for the long ride and the hard work with cattle and horses. His arm was quick and steady for roping or shooting. He was purposeful and determined in action with a force that reflected his father's temperament, yet he showed more warmth of disposition than his father — more regard for the feelings of the men he worked with and the animals he handled. He seemed deeply satisfied with the land and his place on it — satisfied with being who he was and where he was.

There was no such stability and satisfaction in Laska's actions. Deprived of Luke's company, utterly unable to be contained in the household duties that occupied her mother, she became more and more the solitary rambler. She took long rides alone out from the ranch headquarters, and on these rides spent countless hours training Stinger and practicing the stunts that were too daring to perform before her mother's anxious and frightened eyes. Her only quietness was achieved in her preoccupation with creatures of the wild; the delight of watching a mother polecat on a training tour with her young or a fawn hiding itself in pure stillness . . . the fascination of a spider constructing its web and then pouncing on its prey to weave a quick death encasement, or a rabbit in a pose of utter placidity — green grass at the corners of its mouth — staring into her eyes for long moments of purposeless communion. . . . But, for the most part, she continued, as in childhood, to live in emotional extremities.

Luvisa took what comfort she could in the fact that Stinger's speed and Laska's skill with a gun were reasonable protection against the dangers she might encounter. Then, too, there was always Daño — old and cross and despised by the household, he still served a purpose for which Luvisa was thankful: a great alarmist, he accompanied Laska on every ride and could be depended on to give warning of the approach of danger in almost any form. He rode much of the time perched on her shoulder, but never failed to take scouting flights ahead and around, and to Laska his noises and flutters were a form of communication as clear as an instrument reading.

There was one phase of the rides that would have alarmed Luvisa more than any other. Laska had outgrown the sun-garden ritual with her mother, but her delight in being exposed to the sun had never diminished. So, in secret, she had fashioned two skimpy garments that she considered the ultimate in comfort for practicing her tricks on Stinger in the sunny private arenas of grass and sand that were her own discoveries. She had pretended to discard a pair of buckskin trousers as too worn for further use, but actually she had slashed them off high above the knees and used the surplus to make a covering for her breasts — a strapless binding tightly laced in front. She had a special hiding place for these garments and before going on her long rides would slip them on under her regular riding trousers and long jacket. When she arrived at a spot that pleased her for sunning and performing, she would remove bridle and saddle from Stinger, take off her outer garments along with the tight belt that held gun and knife, and clad only in the buckskin briefs with worn moccasins on her feet and a quirt on her wrist, begin the game of signals and stunts with only Daño as audience. By now she required no halter for guiding Stinger; a whistle, a call, a flick of the quirt, a slap of the hand or prod of the heel, and his response was exact and instantaneous.

But there came a day when she had an audience other than Daño, and whether it was wind direction or the lassitude of old age, the bird failed to discover any cause for alarm. Laska had ridden out further than usual that day and found a spot that was especially pleasing to her — an almost circular grassy clearing near the river — and also near, dangerously near, the daytime camp of another lone rider. For in the seclusion and comfort of thick low shade on the edge of the clearing El Gavilán slept, more soundly than usual, well satisfied with his spying on Rawhide Range headquarters and under no threat of pursuit since Range Templeton was in California and his men working far to the south. It was a time for gathering information, for resting and planning the full campaign of his vengeance. He awoke to the sounds of a horse running, gay commands in a feminine voice, and the hoarse cawings of an old crow. He looked into the clearing and what he saw led him to believe that he was not awake, that a strange dream was upon him. He achieved different positions and views of the performance before him, rubbed his eyes, felt his knife and gun, reassured himself that he was alive and awake,

330

and then settled back to observe the strangest and most entertaining sight he had ever witnessed. While Stinger ran full speed, or rared up, or seemed to stand on his head, Laska rode him standing, tumbling, and sometimes apparently flying as she clung to his mane and flung herself with feather lightness from one side to the other. As his incredulity subsided a little, he realized that here was the daughter of Range Templeton, here was the little golden tan one he had observed at the Templeton campfire. Since that time she had changed — still a little one — but no longer a child — a little bird woman. He liked the idea. His eyes brightened with pleasure and excitement. As her stunts increased in tempo and daring, El Gavilán found himself swept away on a wave of sheer admiration that for the moment ruled out caution and thoughts of revenge.

"Hola!" he shouted, "Bravo! Bravo!" as Laska swung from Stinger's high-flying tail, tipped her toes to the solid earth, and with an easy spring was landed back on the horse.

He was unprepared for the magiclike disappearance. She slid out of sight on the other side of the horse and the horse himself seemed to leave the ground and literally fly into the brush across the clearing. But the brush was silent too soon. She had not run away. He could not see that she held a gun for a moment before she abandoned herself to the haste of dressing and getting saddle and bridle on Stinger.

Moved more by impulse than intrigue, he called to her, "Come back, bird woman, come back, if you are a true thing and not a phantom."

After a while Laska called, "Who are you?"

"A lonely rambling mortal of no importance, bird woman — no importance whatsoever. Have no fear."

There was a long silence punctuated by Daño's warning angry cries.

Convinced that Laska wasn't going to appear again, El Gavilán, still acting under compulsions strange to his nature, invited. "Ride this way again, little phantom. Let us meet again. I leave here a token of my reality and intention to return. Can you do the same?"

There was no reply, and soon the signs of the brush told him she was gone. When he searched the spot to which she had retreated, he found a small quirt of exquisite design with silver trim in the handle and plaited from multicolored thongs. He knew she did not lose a quirt so fine and with so secure a wrist loop. He smiled in happy satisfaction. He tried to slip the quirt onto his own wrist but found his hand too big for the loop. He laughed aloud at the wonder of his good fortune, and twirling the quirt around his finger went to call up his horse, for as a precaution he must finish his day's rest in another spot.

Laska waited three days before she returned to the spot. She was fully clad in her long riding trousers and jacket, and in addition to her usual light weapons a holstered rifle was strapped to her saddle. But her cautious approach was not intercepted and no bold voice called a greeting when she reached the place. She saw that her quirt was gone and went in search of the token he had promised. It was Daño who found it at the foot of the tree where El Gavilán had rested; and with a screech of pleasure he brought the object to her. It was a thumb-size piece of carving in rich rose onyx, a hideously fascinating little figure representing an ancient carnival spirit, its wide-open laughter depicting not so much triumph of evil as delight in wickedness. Laska studied it for a long time, puzzled, pleased, and deeply curious. As the coolness of the polished stone faded to warmth in her hand, a flaming excitement replaced the caution she had been building up for three days. She wanted to hear the bold young voice again. Why had she been so foolish as to wait so long to return?

She thrust the onyx piece deep into her pocket, clutching it tightly, and seemed to hear his voice in startling clarity repeating, "Ride this way again, little phantom. Let us meet again."

She answered with a resolve to ride this way again and again until they did meet.

*   *   *

It was almost a year before Luvisa noticed that the old casualness was gone from Laska's horseback excursions. They were not so frequent but had taken on more purpose. An element of timing and preparation had replaced the former impulsive departures.

With Range at home for a while between drives to California, her fears were redoubled. She wanted so much to avoid clashes between him and Laska that she dared not tell him about the long rides without escort, much less voice the suspicions that had been tormenting her.

In deep distress, she approached Silver Bryson one morning. Range and Luke had taken Wong and several of the riders out on an early morning hunting jaunt, and Laska had slipped away soon after.

"Mr. Bryson, I must make a painful request of you today." As many years as she had known Silver Bryson — as well aware as she was of the understanding and affection he gave her children — her pride suffered at having to submit such a problem to him. It was hard to look at him directly and say, "I need your help with Laska." She should be making such an appeal to her husband, not her friend. And the attention and concern with which he would hear her was even more of a reproach. But she said it.

He recognized her tension and smiled warmly. "Has she brought home a pet bear?"

"No. I wish it were so simple a thing. She is out again on Stinger — one of those long rides. I — I fear for her welfare on this — this kind of ride. There is something different happening to her — something dangerous. I can't tell Range — can't send him after her. You know how her willfulness angers him — and if he should find out — To be wholly honest with you, Mr. Bryson, I think Laska occasionally meets someone on these rides. And yet — yet who could it possibly be in this wild unsettled region? Oh, my fancy carries me into the most frightful places!"

"You're letting your anxiety carry you too far. I'll admit Laska draws unusual adventure to her as a loadstone draws iron, and whether she's engaged in taming a wildcat or an outlaw" (why in God's name had he made that comparison, he wondered, but went smoothly on), "the victim is probably as obedient as Stinger." Then he added more seriously, "There are some settlers newly moved in down the Nueces a way with properties to the north. She may have discovered interesting neighbors."

"But no one within a half day's ride," Luvisa countered his reasoning.

"Well, when two people each ride half a day toward each other, they can bridge quite a gap. But our surmises won't put your mind at ease, I know. So I'll be off at once and see what I can find out. I have never matched wits with Laska on trailing and spying. I find the prospect appeals to me." His voice took on a teasing quality to reassure Luvisa. "Don't you realize, madam, that in sending me on such an assignment you're placing me in more danger than I'm likely to find her in. If she returns with a white scalp at her belt, you'll know I failed to accomplish my mission."

Luvisa relaxed a little and rewarded him with a small smile, but as he turned to leave, she called, "Mr. Bryson?"

"Yes?"

"Take care for yourself. It is rumored, you know, that El Gavilán rides much further north than he used to. It is well — to be careful — when you ride alone — " Her voice trailed off as if some despairing thought had deadened it.

"I presume if Miss Laska can ride unharmed in the land, so can I," he answered with a forced cheerfulness that fell flat between them as they shared a single awful thought that neither would have dared put voice to.

He was even more disturbed when he heard Daño's strident complaints coming from the large cage on the upstairs porch where Laska occasionally confined him. Why had she left the bird behind? So she would be harder to trail? So that Daño's fussing in the company of a stranger would not betray a meeting place?

*   *   *

Silver Bryson trailed Laska with all the accumulated skill of his fighting and hunting years on the frontier but finally had to admit he was beaten. Only an Indian or a hound, he told himself in disgust, could figure it out. He had been out several hours and to go any further would be merely guesswork. He decided to wait where he was and try to sight her as she returned to the ranch. He had reached an elevation where he could see some distance to the north and east. He took from his saddlebag a binocular instrument of French make that he had secured in New Orleans. Because of its awkward and complicated adjustments, he hadn't found it practical, but he tinkered with it now, thinking it might be of some aid in his search. At last he was rewarded — he glimpsed, far away to the east, a lone rider. It was a Mexican — he had enough detail in his glasses to be sure of that. The man was riding rapidly away and soon passed from view. Frantically, Bryson tried to change the focus, hoping to bring the rider back in view again, but with no success.

"Looking for someone?" a pert voice inquired just back of him.

Startled, Bryson dropped his instrument with a clatter and turned an angry countenance to Laska, annoyed that he had been too engrossed to hear her approach.

She laughed and whistled to Stinger to join her for she had left him some distance away while she slipped up on Bryson.

"Are you ready to go back?" she asked him sweetly, as if the meeting had been agreed upon. "I am."

Bryson didn't answer her. They both mounted and rode off toward the ranch in silence.

Finally, Laska baited him. "At spying I'd say you'd grown a little rusty, Mr. Bryson."

"At intrigue I'd say you'd taken on quite a gloss, Miss Laska."

She looked away from him. After a while she said, "Mama sent you, I suppose."

Bryson didn't bother to reply.

"I've done no harm, but she wouldn't understand. You wouldn't

335

either. Nobody would! I don't intend to tell her or you or anybody! You'll just have to let me alone!"

Bryson gave her a cool, hard look. "Stop screaming. You've told me more than I want to know already. . . . Someone's approaching up ahead. Your father most likely." He said nothing more.

When Range and five of his men met Laska and Bryson, there was little said but the undercurrent of feeling had an explosive quality. Range gave a gruff greeting with, "Pretty risky you two riding out this far alone."

"It was my fault, Papa," Laska spoke softly. "I kept leading Mr. Bryson on. He had those glasses he brought from New Orleans to see a long ways with, but they didn't work very well. It was a sort of lesson, you might say."

"Dangerous kind of lessons. Most likely you took out on your own and he came after you."

Laska deliberately switched to an argument that would sidetrack Range. "You always take Luke on hunts, but you never take me. Where is he now?"

"He's at home where you ought to be, helping Wong take care of the game."

"I thought you were still hunting."

"We are. Bird huntin' now. Out for a hawk. Got wind of El Gavilán workin' up close and felt like scoutin' around some. Seen any tracks or signs where you've been?"

"Hawks don't leave tracks. They fly," Laska said, knowing such flippant answers always set Range on edge. Several of the men smiled. Range looked grim. "Maybe so. Maybe they do fly. But they don't swim. Pitch one into the Nueces when it's on a good rise and he'll go out like a rat in a rainbarrel, won't he, Bryson?" He didn't expect Bryson to answer. He was trying to even the score with Laska — excluding her from the meaning of his statement while astonishing her with it. "And if this one keeps circlin' around in these parts, it would be right fitting and some pleasure to float him out like a dead rat. It sure would!"

It was as if the idea pleased him so much, his humor changed. He looked at Laska. Her averted face — her rigid posture — touched him with sympathy. She wasn't listening to him, he thought; she was pouting — boiling mad — because he'd taken Luke out on the hunt and left her behind. She'd run off by herself. Luvisa hadn't told him, but he had it figured out now. Luvisa worried and sent Bryson out after her. His imagined explanation satisfied him.

"Simmer down, chick, and run along home. Your Mama's worried. So long, Bryson."

But Silver Bryson didn't turn away. He had made up his mind about something. "Ride east a ways," he said to Range. "I saw a rider in my glasses — not one of ours — you might strike a trail."

"Rat tracks, maybe? Well, rats don't fly." Range looked at Laska and chuckled, pleased with his attempt at humor, and then turned quickly to ride away, disconcerted by the hostility in her eyes.

"What did he mean about a hawk can't swim?" Laska demanded of Bryson. "You know what he was talking about, I know you do!"

Bryson, unmoved by her urgency, replied with finality. "You have already stated with some spirit that you intend to tell me nothing. Such an attitude is now entirely mutual."

They rode the rest of the way in without speaking another word.

Other than her relief at Laska's immediate safety, Luvisa found no comfort or reassurance in either Laska's vague explanations or Silver Bryson's evasive answers to all her questions. Their efforts to protect her from deeper anxiety only nurtured her suspicions into convictions and forced her to build still another barrier of deception between herself and Range.

Range Templeton found that he did not have the men or the time to conduct a running war with El Gavilán and at the same time get ready for another drive to California. So he decided to work out one more drive and then settle down to cleaning out thieves and establishing his boundaries to include the springs.

Luvisa pleaded with him not to make the trip again. He had

gambled with many risks and dangers the last fifteen years — driving to New Orleans, on Ranger expeditions against Indians, in the Mexican War — and had won on every count, she pointed out. But the California drive over a fifteen-hundred-mile trail with cruel scarcity of water and grass and constant threat of fierce Apaches involved the greatest risks he had ever taken. He had made it safely three times, but on the drive he had just completed Dame Fortune had shown him clearly that he was no longer in such high favor. And he had intended that drive to be his last. Why tempt further chastisement, Luvisa argued.

Range would not be dissuaded, however. Too stubborn to take his losses — more than a hundred head of his cattle had died at a water hole from some kind of poison weed, and Apaches in a night attack had made off with that many more — he was determined to make another drive that would be large enough to make up for his bad luck . . . determined to match his stamina and ingenuity against Apache savagery and desert barriers until his gold outweighed his losses — such losses as he knew about or could compute in figures.

During preparations for this last drive, Range kept Luke working with him more closely than ever before and felt a deep satisfaction in the companionship of a son who was at fifteen so much of a man — almost as tall, almost as strong as his father, and always striving in behavior and dress to look as much like Range as possible. It was pleasant to plan on the father-son partnership that lay only a few years ahead. He found himself wanting to confide some of his ambitions to his son or at least direct him toward his own goals. As they rode into headquarters late one evening, side by side, relaxed in the coolness and golden haze of sundown, he spoke of the springs.

"You remember the springs, son, the place I showed you when we were out on that camping trip three years ago?"

"Oh, yes, sir. . . . And I remember — " Luke was thinking of a little black-haired girl of enchanting shyness who had allowed him to kiss her hand.

"Remember what, son?"

"That — that it was a very beautiful place."

"That's right. It is. And, mark my words, you'll be living there someday. Would you like that?"

"Yes, sir . . . yes, sir." Luke was eager, his eyes shining, as Range liked to see him: "That would be nice to — to — " He wanted to say it would be nice to have neighbors — nice to see the little girl again — her hand had trembled so when he held it. But he finished — "to live in such a place."

Luke's excitement over the idea pleased Range so much that on impulse he asked, "Would you care to see the place again, son? Mr. Bryson is making a supply trip to Laredo for me next week. I can't get off just now. But I might let you go along. You're old enough to be gettin' around some, I reckon. And he'll be comin' back by way of the springs to check up on some things for me. Like to go along?"

"Oh, yes, Dad!" The privilege of traveling as a grown man with other men, away from the family, away from home, almost on his own — it was a thrilling prospect. But his father's reserve, and his own, kept him from expressing his enthusiasm further. Range understood that he had given his son happiness, and himself felt a deep paternal joy that things were always so right between them.

The home of the Sándivars, although not constructed in the grand hacienda manner, had an air of permanence, of Spanish grace and privacy, and the whole headquarters of the Regalo de la Vaca gave the appearance of a family in native soil with roots going down fast.

Silver Bryson was aware of this as he observed the improvements that had been made since he had last seen the place. But he was given little opportunity for close inspection. Miguel and his brothers came out on horseback to meet the men from the Rawhide Range and there was no warmth in the polite exchange of greetings.

Bryson, knowing well that he had been purposely intercepted before he could arrive at gate or door, ignored this evasion of hospitality, and explained, "We journey from Laredo back to Rawhide

339

Range headquarters. How is it here with you? Is the ranching business going well?"

"As well for me as for any Mexican ranchero in these uncertain times," Miguel said. "No matter how peaceful the heart or legal the holdings, there are troubles. But I do well enough. It is not in my nature to sell or desert the land that has belonged to my family since the time of Spanish kings."

Any questions that Bryson might have asked about the Sándivars selling out were answered. He knew all that he had come to learn and was ready to go on, but Luke, sitting on his horse close by Bryson's side, caught Miguel's attention; and Miguel observing the close resemblance to Range inquired, "This is the son of Señor Templeton, is it not?"

Luke eagerly supplied the answer. "Yes, señor, I'm Luke Templeton. My twin sister and I were here once before, when we camped at the springs nearby, and we talked to your daughter Marina."

Miguel frowned. "Ah, yes, I was not here, I recall." And he recalled several things more: the name of Luvisa Templeton on his homestead papers, the distant cousin, so charming and helpful, and the twin babies she adored. He had on several previous occasions forced the thought to the back of his mind that there could be any relationship between the name on his papers and the name of the owner of Rawhide Range. Now the thought would be forced back no longer and he accepted it with a stabbing sadness, remembering with painful clarity how Luvisa had shown such frightening reluctance to write her name. What a burden he, Miguel, had placed upon her! And in her fairness and goodness she had done what he asked, knowing, of course, her husband's desire for the springs. What tragedy that one of her tender nature should be matched with the arrogant and greedy Range Templeton! He looked at Luke with softness in his glance but kept his manner cool for he did not like to contemplate any meeting between his daughter and Range Templeton's son, no matter how innocent the acquaintance. So he did not meet the eager comment, the inquiry in Luke's eyes, with any remark about Marina.

Bryson said, "If we may have your permission to water at the springs, we'll continue our journey, for it is our intention to camp on our own range tonight."

There was relief in Miguel's quick and gracious response to Bryson's request, but Luke hid a rebellious disappointment at this turn of events. He had thought they would be camping at the springs and during the whole trip had enacted over and over in his mind the chances he might have to renew his acquaintance with Marina — the things she might say and he might say. Now he was so near and must pass on. He felt a hot flash of anger at both Bryson and Miguel who seemed to have deliberately thwarted him, acting as if they knew his intentions and were trying to keep him and Marina apart. He dropped back behind Bryson and the other riders on a pretext of checking the loads on the supply mules that carried the purchases made in Laredo. Miguel and his brothers had ridden on in the opposite direction. Near the gate of the wall enclosing the main house, Luke dismounted and tightened the straps on the pack animal at the very end of the string. At the same time, he searched for some sign by which he might locate Marina. But the heavy wooden gate was very forbidding; the walls stood thick and high, dense foliage of trees and shrubs reaching over here and there and on the outside a protective border of formidable cactus plants; and what he could see of the spreading adobe structure within looked cool and sealed and discouragingly far away. Still he killed time. Surely, he thought, she must be watching from somewhere . . . travelers this way were so few, and he knew about a girl's curiosity from Laska . . . but Marina was not the same kind of girl . . . she would be quiet — afraid to be seen — too shy to speak. He searched the wall for he knew there must be places for lookout, or defense in time of raids. He noticed that at regular intervals at about the height of a mounted man's head there were small rectangular barred apertures, most of them camouflaged with foliage of vine or shrub, all view to the inside carefully shut out. He got back on his horse, aware that his separation from the other riders had become conspicuous; but reluctant to give up his search, he rode up close to the wall and slowly past every opening to the east of the gate. He stopped at the last one near the corner; it was crowded with the brilliant blossoms of an exuberant vine and he thought he detected some unnatural movement there. Then he heard the approach of running footsteps toward the opening — the labored running of a heavy person — and a breathless angered instruction: "Marina! Marina! Come down at once! You bold disobedient girl to take advantage of my fat and aching feet! Your grandmother and your grandfather and your father shall hear of this. Peeking at strangers like a wanton one!"

"Why don't you follow me and look too?" Marina teased her guardian in a sweet soft voice.

"You know I am no squirrel to clamber up pegs on a wall!"

"Then be a quiet guinea while I — " Marina saw Luke so close to the window, his face on a level with hers, and was speechless.

The sound of her voice had set Luke to trembling. He must see her! "Marina!" he dared to call softly. The vines parted and there was her face framed in the blossoms, her hair blacker than he remembered, her skin fairer, and her smile sweeter. He removed his hat quickly. She recognized him and with her lips framed the word "Lucas," but in shyness or caution her voice was so low he heard nothing. They stared at each other in thrilling wonder, Marina's lips slightly parted, her cheeks pinking. Luke was brought out of his trance of delight by a call up ahead. He must go on — he must not cause trouble — but it was hard to pull away. Wasn't there anything he could say or do? The bag of hard candy in his pocket for Laska! He pulled it out quickly and pitched it on the ledge in front of Marina. Her hand reached for it. "Gracias," she murmured, her big eyes lowered then raised to his as adoringly as if he had set a casket of jewels before her. It was a look that affected Luke with a depth of emotion he had never before experienced. For a moment he couldn't bring air into his lungs — couldn't find voice. Then he said, the soft Spanish words tumbling out in a tone that was part caress, part desperation: "I'll be back, Marina, I'll be

342

back! Wait for me, little one, always wait for me!" And surprised and alarmed at the power of youthful passion in him, gave his startled horse a sharp kick and raced ahead. He did not stop when he reached Bryson's side, but galloped on to reach the springs ahead of them all. He leaped off, threw down his hat, and doused his head and face in the water. When Bryson rode up, Luke was sitting quietly, balanced on his heels, gazing at the reflections in the water. He did not look up at Bryson or speak a word about his experience; he had sealed over his emotions with his father's granitelike reserve.

Luke waited until Range was off on his drive to California before learning to play the guitar; it was the only accomplishment he had ever desired that he felt his father would not look upon with approval. He had no guitar of his own but several were at his disposal in the bunkhouse, and the riders who played them with varying degrees of ability were all eager to instruct him. His heart was so filled with dreams of Marina that melody came easily to his fingers and his singing carried a haunting quality that soon brought him a regular audience on the evenings when he took up his strumming at the bunkhouse, on the front porch, or in the parlor where he and Cicero soon began to team up with guitar and piano. He and Laska found a closeness they had lost when Luke began to work regularly with the men. Laska sang with him and not infrequently added to the musical performance with lively dance and satirical pantomime of the animals and people who were a part of life on the Rawhide Range. The entire household and all the men who worked for Range were brought into this new circle of enjoyment and relaxation, and there was more laughing and singing than had ever been heard before within the high wall of pointed poles that enclosed Rawhide Range headquarters. In it, Luvisa tried to submerge some of her uneasiness, and partially succeeded; Laska artfully hid her driving restlessness and found some relief of spirit in these entertainment sessions with her family. Silver Bryson felt at times as near

343

contentment as he ever expected to be and at other times heavily depressed with the irony of contradictions in Range Templeton's family and the burden of knowledge he carried about each one. But he, too, put aside the forbidding future for a while in favor of the enjoyable present. He realized, however, when he made his next trip to Laredo almost a year after the one on which Luke had glimpsed Marina, that Luke was about to add to the emotional entanglements of the Templetons an element of crisis that could easily rival Laska's when the final reckoning before Range should come. Luke insisted on going to Laredo with Bryson, bought a guitar while he was there, and further insisted that they make the return trip by way of the springs. Bryson indicated he would rather take the shorter route.

"Mr. Bryson, sir" — Luke in determination or opposition was always extremely polite — "I must go by there. I came along for that purpose."

"Your father's fever for the springs?"

Luke looked at Bryson as if he didn't know what he was talking about.

"Why, no, sir. I want to see Marina Sándivar. I'm old enough to pay my respects to a young lady if I like."

"Do you think you will be an acceptable suitor in the eyes of her father? Do you think they will even open the door to you?"

"Possibly not. But now I can sing to her at least — not too badly, I hope — and in the Spanish tradition."

"If you do such a thing, you'll be courting trouble more ardently than you'll ever court a woman. Your father has a deep and terrible violence with which you are unacquainted. I know of nothing that would arouse it more than to know you were singing love songs to Miguel Sándivar's daughter."

Luke gave Bryson a cool look so much like his father's that Bryson felt a chill creep along his spine.

"This is my own affair, Mr. Bryson. If you do not care to accompany me, I'll go alone."

344

They made evening camp at some distance from Regalo de la Vaca headquarters, and Luke rode out into the moonlight alone. He sang first at the gate, hoping to be admitted into the yard, but there was not even the smallest notice given that he had been heard. He moved to the little vine-covered opening in the wall where Marina had received his gift of candy, and sang there, his themes ranging from love's joys and wonders to its losses and laments. Still there was no sign — the place was more silent than when he approached it — more unresponsive to his music. At last, he turned sadly away and, deeply despondent, let his horse move slowly back toward camp. Before he had gone far, he realized that he was being pursued by someone on foot, running to catch up with him, and a small frightened voice called, "Señor Lucas, stop for me." He waited, his heart pounding, and in a moment a Mexican boy was at his stirrup, breathlessly announcing, "The Señorita Marina says your music touched her heart and she will wait to hear it again."

The world was suddenly a most wonderful place and love man's most glorious estate. "Bless you, hombrito, for your message, for your swift feet and your brave heart! I know the risk you run for love's sake. Now listen to me closely. Say to the señorita for me that the music was my heart speaking to hers, and to know she waits for me is a music that will sing in my heart until I come again. Now hurry back. God protect and reward you."

Luke bedded down away from the others to lie wide awake in blissful stillness as the moonlight intensified and then waned.

On the homeward journey, he seemed to enjoy the discomfort he caused Silver Bryson by playing his guitar as they rode along and singing with joyous abandon a song of his own invention:

> I'll marry Marina . . . I'll marry Marina . . .
> You can be sure that I will!
> And I'll love my Marina . . . I'll love my Marina
> Till the beat of my heart is still!

345

CHAPTER XVI

From Luvisa Templeton's Account —

. . . It is June 25, 1858, a little over two months since I began my account of events shaping the destiny of my family and perhaps in some inscrutable way forming a fragment of the larger destiny of all mankind. The urgency that I felt in the beginning to record all these things has abated as the strength of my body has diminished. It is only my aversion to an unfinished task and Mr. Bryson's presence with the poised pencil that keep me at it. When we started this documentation, I was the aggressor, you might say, with Mr. Bryson humoring me in my whimsy by setting it all down. Now it is he who persists, and I have divined the reason why: it is not that he attaches so much importance to things I am recounting as that he knows when I am finished with the task, I will indeed be finished with all things in this life — so he intends to keep me at it as long as possible. The disease will complete its devastation upon me before long, however, regardless of either my own or Mr. Bryson's will in the matter; but it is likely I would have succumbed sooner without the stimulation of these morning and evening visits devoted to our writing. I feel best in the early morning before sunrise and in the evening as twilight sets in, but a terrible weakness is on me now at all times for I have had three weeks of chills and fever with heavy night sweats, and last week I had a hemorrhage of the lungs that was very different from the others, being of a dark clotted nature. I presume that in looks I am about as poor an object as might be seen in human form . . . but I care not . . . and had much rather be off than to stay. These hard shakes, coming as they do in the heat of summertime are such a shock to the system that I am placed in a regular frenzy of irritation. The doctor has done all he thought best, giving me a sirup of quinine for the

346

chills and hoarhound sirup for the cough. But the disease is stronger than his medicine and makes rapid progress. I tried an experiment of my own yesterday: just as the chill came on, I had Adelia dash cold water over me. I continued to shake for about an hour, but when the time for the next one came, it seemed to be frightened away . . . but not for long. Mr. Bryson has tried to prevail upon me to go to one of the establishments outside of Texas where they say some wonderful cures of consumption have been performed. I have not considered it. I am sure that my case is one of the many incurables . . . and I find it a comfortable thought, somehow, to take my leave of life here on the very bed where I was conceived and brought into the world. It will not be long now until I complete that cycle, so I must hurry on over the years with Mr. Bryson before this weakness completely engulfs me. Things come clearest in these early morning hours between three and five o'clock. . . .

After we visited the springs in 1851, Range made two more drives to California instead of the one he had planned as his last. I tried hard to dissuade him from that last trip. It would mean another absence of almost a year, or longer, and I protested on that account. He promised me that, good luck or bad, it would definitely be his last. After all, we were still young, he said, and had many more years in which to settle down — long years ahead when there would be no more separations — when we'd live in that grand house at the springs — and he was taking the risks, facing the dangers, enduring the separations, only that he might provide better for his family than most men. A man tells himself and his wife things like that, I realized, to hide the vanity of doing a thing simply to prove his invulnerability and exhibit his power.

It was almost two years before Range returned from that last drive, a very sick and weary man, not so invulnerable after all, and yet in no mood of defeat, for he showed no inclination to admit he should not have gone, or to allow me a triumphant moment for pointing out that I was right. . . . His saddlebags were heavy with gold, and so he was willing to take a rest and recover his health. I'm sure

347

we would never have known the cause of his trouble if some of the men who returned to the Rawhide Range with him had not let it be known. They were very careful to get it circulated in such a manner that Range would never know who betrayed him. For the wound that had made him so ill, that had imposed medical attention and a long rest in California before he could make the return trip, had been received in a most unheroic fashion when he was chased on foot by a thirst-maddened steer, tossed into the air, and painfully bruised and gored before one of the riders shot the crazed animal.

It was late fall of 1856 before Range was completely restored and could return to hard riding. Luke at seventeen had been taking a man's responsibility for three years, and was as full grown as his father had been at that age. Under Luke and Mr. Bryson the work with cattle and wild horses had continued on the range but on a smaller scale and not without difficulties. Range had not been able to keep as many men as he needed to work the Rawhide Range or even know what took place over all of it; cattle drives and the gold rush took men from him that were hard to replace, and since he didn't hire Mexicans, the rank of his riders grew awfully thin at times. Cattle and horse thieves flourished and much of our land to the south was profitably worked by them. So Range had his job cut out for him when he was able to go again: He'd clear those thieves out — and he'd take care of getting his southern boundary defined, including the springs. So the old uneasiness came close again and I felt that circumstances would not too much longer defer to me.

My children were children no longer and I began to fear that the isolated life we led was depriving them of the normal exercises of sociability with young people their own age. Luke had made trips with Mr. Bryson to the coast, to San Antonio, and Laredo for supplies. He had taken on a dreamy detached manner that made me wonder if he might not yearn to go off on adventures of his own rather than take root on his father's land. Laska, although somewhat more agreeable in disposition as she got older, would accept no curbs on her reckless behavior, and I learned to tolerate most of it

348

without protest. . . . I even succeeded in shutting out the fears I could not quite justify regarding the long rides she insisted on taking alone. For a while I considered sending her to the Ursuline Academy in San Antonio; I had heard some very fine things about the teaching of the sisters which included a certain amount of time each day devoted to the study of politeness. Since neither Mr. Bryson nor I had done so well with this subject in Laska's education, the idea had a special appeal for me. With girls her own age and the sisters to guide her, perhaps — but my plan got no further than Laska's ears. She said promptly that she didn't care to go, and that if I insisted, she would run away. Some children make such a threat idly, but I knew Laska would run away. She was so adequate unto herself that I sometimes felt she could have lived self-sufficient on the Rawhide Range without any of us around.

I had promised the twins that for their eighteenth birthday we'd have a celebration as grand as the one we had on the Fourth of July in '49, but the things that came to pass in our home sent them defiant and heartbroken from the Rawhide Range before that birthday arrived.

(Now I come to the hard part, Mr. Bryson. . . . Why did I set myself this tormenting task?)

El Gavilán, the Mexican marauder, was the evil force that opened the door on disaster. The depredations on the Rawhide Range began to take a more vicious turn than common thievery. An important water hole was poisoned. Prairie fires were set. And our riders were preyed upon, several losing their lives. El Gavilán had been robbing for several years in the tradition of his father from Matamoros to Laredo and beyond, but he began to give concentrated and particular attention to our property after Range returned from California. It was some time before Range realized that El Gavilán was almost wholly responsible for his losses and he declared a personal war of vengeance on him. When he had recovered his health, he was still in no position to go after El Gavilán. He did not have enough men. He decided to go to San Antonio and pick up some

riders who were willing to be fighters. When he let it be known the trouble he was having, a plan developed to form a sort of minute company that would use his riders and a small Ranger force as a fighting band to go directly to Laredo and on down the Rio Grande valley to hunt out El Gavilán and rid the border once and for all of this plundering. Although the state maintained no highly organized Ranger force at this time, the trouble we were having was the kind of civil disturbance for which Governor Pease was willing to authorize an emergency company. This was good news to Range. So, rather than wait around in San Antonio until the matter was approved at the state capital, he decided to go on to Austin with the Ranger captain in charge and if necessary give special testimony on the extent of depredations. While in Austin, he found time to go to the land office and examine records on his own property and the land surrounding it. There, at last, he learned that the springs had been purchased and was held as a homestead by Miguel Sándivar — that the transaction had been made while he was on his first drive to New Orleans and building his highest air castles — and that, unbelievably, there were the signatures of the wife he loved and the grandfather-in-law he had idealized, as witnesses to the sales transaction. How stunned he must have been! How he must have questioned first his eyesight, and then his sanity! Then tried perhaps for a short moment to believe the signatures were of two other people named the same as his loved ones, but two entirely different people. But he knew the handwriting of each one too well to deny the evidence before him. First bewildered, then bitter, I know how he probed into his memory, reviewed our life together in the smallest detail searching for the reason why he had been so betrayed. Possibly, he tried to believe that I did not know the piece of property was the one he desired. But, whether or not I knew, why had I kept the matter a secret from him? Suspicion ate deep into him, I know. He must have recalled how I had discouraged his interest in the springs and expressed my preference for the home we had over any he might build there. I think he thought of kinship between Miguel

350

and me and even opened his mind to the painful possibility that my origins were not clear of Mexican strains. The fury that built up in him, the self-torture that his thoughts inflicted, were devastating. When he returned home six weeks later, he looked older by twenty years, completely ravaged by the forces that battled within him. He sent no word home of his plans to pursue El Gavilán. I think he must have considered never coming back — then the long ride and the hard fight gave him the composure needed to face us.

No scene of my whole life is so clearly etched in my mind, burned into memory with the needle of agony, as that evening of Range's return. We were sitting on the porch — Laska, Luke, Mr. Bryson, and I — and Wong was weeding and watering my cherished yellow rosebush. I had been fretting because we'd had no word from him, and they had all reassured me, pointing out how he often got sidetracked on business deals of one kind or another. Then we heard his horse whinny, and knew he was approaching. Old Ned, fat with age and pampering, woke up and went to the edge of the porch to send forth his lazy welcoming bark. I arose and hurried to the yard gate. Wong straightened up from his weeding and waited still as a statue. The children arose, more languidly than I, and followed me. Mr. Bryson stood leaning against a porch column. Then we saw him, and I think our hearts must have stopped in unison for those first few seconds as we tried to comprehend what might be wrong. I thought at first he must be seriously injured. His position in the saddle was that of a man almost unconscious from strong drink or a mortal wound. Luke and Laska came up close on each side of me. Mr. Bryson remained where he was. Then Range was there looking down at us, as if he were trying to place in his mind where he had seen us before. It was most frightening. I'm sure Luke and Laska thought some madness was upon him; I felt them move closer to me as if in protection as Range without a word dismounted slowly and stiffly like a weary old man. Not a one of us could speak a word. My throat felt completely closed and I could hardly breathe. I was the only one who knew what must have happened to him —

351

what must have wrought this change in him — yet I moved toward him for the welcoming kiss and embrace that was always our greeting on his return. I don't know why I did, knowing already how he felt; I had the fleeting thought perhaps that he'd want to pretend things were all right until we were alone. But the fierce and accusing look he gave me caused me to step back as if he'd struck me.

Luke was the first to find his tongue.

"Dad, what's wrong?"

Range had stood holding the reins after he dismounted. He let them fall to the ground, acted as if he hadn't heard Luke, and walked to the porch. He gave Mr. Bryson a hard look as if to measure how much he knew. Mr. Bryson returned his stare impassively and said nothing. It was a horrible moment, all of us standing there, waiting for something terrible to overtake us that would change our whole world. Wong remained in statue stillness. Range, about to mount the steps, turned and looked at Laska, Luke, and me again. His eyes had a cold, curtained quality now; a small muscle in his throat twitched, a certain sign of deep, almost uncontrollable anger. Laska's expression spoke an anguish of concern for her father, and she did the worst possible thing, gave voice to her sympathy in Spanish (not intentionally for provocation, as she had often done, but unconsciously, speaking out of her heart in response to his suffering).

"Pobre papá!" with all love and compassion.

Range was so affected that he actually bared his teeth for a moment like an enraged animal, and his eyes showed such hostility that she cowered before him.

There is no rage as fearful as silent rage.

Finally, our eyes met and held, and I felt trapped, smothered, experiencing the actual physical pain of unnatural travail.

"Been to Austin." His voice was tight and rasping, the words painful as deep thorns plucked from tender flesh. "Saw the papers on the Sándivar homestead. Saw the signatures. You knew what piece of land it was?"

352

I nodded.

"That Mexican some relative of yours?"

"A distant cousin."

"Not so distant, I take it, that you didn't feel more beholden to him than to your husband?"

My throat closed again. My breath was cut off. But I must speak. I don't know how it came out. A jumble, a struggle for words. I remember my waistline felt so tight and my bodice bound me so, I thought I must faint. I mentioned the Sándivars had come to us simply for information and an introduction, that Grandfather had taken me along to help him out with the Spanish, that he knew nothing about what piece of land it was.

"You knew though?" Range asked me again.

"Miguel described it to me."

"Miguel!" My use of the given name indicated an intimacy repugnant to him. There was jealousy and hate and insult in the way he threw the name back at me.

"I never saw him but the one time in my life. I felt some — sentiment about the meeting — the only meeting I ever had with relations of my mother."

"Your mother was a Mexican?"

"She was — Spanish. I — I — knew so little about her — until Grandmother died — and I opened the chest."

I stopped. He said nothing, just kept staring at me, as if I had been transformed into something odious.

I stumbled on. "I was afraid — to tell you these things. You feel so strongly — I didn't want to — wreck our happiness — I was afraid — afraid — "

"Not afraid enough to keep the Templeton name off of that paper — not afraid enough to do something to save what you knew I wanted and was workin' and fightin' and ridin' my guts out to get."

"I hoped they'd give up and go back to Mexico — prayed things would work out — "

"I guess your Holy Virgin must have been takin' her siesta while

353

you was prayin' . . . unless you wanta call the cleanin' out we just gave the Sándivars an answer to your prayers."

Oh Dear God, what had he done!

I was conscious of some change in Luke — a more startled attention. "Cleaned 'em out?" His question to his father had an urgency outside the crisis between Range and me.

Range shifted his gaze to Luke. "We started out from San Antonio with a special force to get El Gavilán."

Laska cut through sharply. "Did you get him?"

There was something intensely personal and demanding in the question. And a suspicion that my heart had long denied became a dreadful certainty in my mind.

Range was surprised at this interruption, but wasn't sidetracked from his consuming anger with me and his frightful account.

"Is he some other relative I don't know about? . . . Couldn't be sure we got him. But he left a good trail of blood. We can hope and pray — like your mother does about these things. I hope he drags his thieving carcass to the other side of the Rio Grande — I don't want him foulin' up the soil of Texas. I shoulda sent him over the bluff with his father when I had the chance — woulda saved considerable trouble, not to mention some lives and some herds."

Laska gasped and put her hand over her mouth as if to hold back a scream.

"What did you do to the Sándivars?" This time there was harsh bluntness and (could it be?) a threat in Luke's question.

"Cleaned 'em out, like I said. Found El Gavilán hidin' out on the place with some of his stolen stock in Sándivar pens. The whole bunch a pack of robbers — regular thieves' den. Had a runnin' fight with El Gavilán and his gang and killed off enough to quieten 'em down considerably. Told the Sándivars to pack up and we'd give 'em an escort across the Rio Grande. They argued about it."

"The Sándivars are not thieves!" Luke cried in passionate denial.

"They aren't now, son. At least, the four dead ones aren't. When

354

the dust had cleared, we let the two that were left pack up and get out with the old woman and the girl."

There was no need to ask if Emilio and Miguel were two of the four dead. My despair sought greater depths. Of course the Sándivars were not thieves. They had been tricked, falsely accused somehow, and Range and the men with him overly eager to make an example of them.

"While you mourn your thievin' Mexican relations, I think I'll go in an' rustle something to eat." He went on up the steps and into the house.

"Wong," I called and wondered if the old man were too petrified from what he'd heard to ever move again. "Will you please go in and attend to Mr. Templeton?"

He looked at me with a kind of composure that heartened me. "Yes, Missy Lu."

"Make him comfortable. He's worn out — not himself."

"Yes, Missy Lu."

"Come, sit down, Luvisa." Mr. Bryson was at my side.

"Mother, do you want me to take you away?" Luke's voice was trembling with an anger I'd never known in him.

"No, Luke."

"Then I'm going away, Mother, right now."

"Not just yet, Luke."

"I've got to, Mother. I'm going after Marina."

"Why? What good can that do?"

"I've got to find her! I've been seeing her — on these trips to Laredo. I was going to wait — until we were older. She's — no telling where she is! I've got to go to her! I've got to find her!" He whirled away and was off toward the corral.

I could not move or speak.

"Laska," Mr. Bryson said, "see that Luke has something besides his heart tied on that saddle when he leaves here. And — don't go with him. Understand?" She nodded and moved after him, in trance-like obedience, stumbling as if her feet were weighted down.

I found that I was sitting in the porch rocker, my hands clinching the armrests, rocking gently, wondering if this was the way one felt when reason was about to depart. Suddenly I was racked by a hard chill, although the heat of the summer day was hardly passed. Mr. Bryson got a blanket from somewhere and put it around my shoulders, then pulled up a chair close to my side. He unclinched my hands and held them tightly in his own.

"You know I want to kill him," he said.

"Yes."

"Why don't I?"

"Because I love him. Because he is suffering in his way equally as much as I."

"He is a ruthless blunderer, and he has treated you with contempt."

"I have blundered too."

"You were trapped into a small deceit — trapped by your own kindness and gentle nature, and held there by love and fear."

"He too has been trapped — by a storm of passion and prejudice."

"My God, Luvisa!"

I began to shake again, and he held my hands more tightly, muttering words to me I could not distinguish . . . I felt afar off. Then I came back, and was in possession of my senses and the chill departed.

"You're not going in to him tonight?"

"Yes."

"No, Luvisa."

"Yes, Mr. Bryson. . . . Good night. . . ."

"Good night, Luvisa. . . ."

He left me, but did not go into the house. I do not know where he went that night. I went in to Range.

This was the night my third child, the stillborn mentioned in the beginning of this account, was conceived. This was the night I made my second attempt to use the full power of physical love to rout the more complex diversities between us. I disregarded the bitter lesson I had learned on his departure for the Mexican War: that a

woman who loves a man truly and beyond self reaps only regret when she transforms that love into a weapon for reducing him to abjection. I had vowed in that crucible of pain never again to violate my love in such a fashion; but now in more desperate circumstances I broke that vow, only to enter upon a longer and sadder season of regret. My defeat was more abysmal than before, the ordeal of spirit, the abuse of body almost beyond human endurance. But the resilience of the human frame we live in, the fortitude of the spirit with which we are divinely endowed are capable of most unexpected extensions when put to the test.

Range took his men out the next morning with supplies for several weeks of hard work in the brush. That was our last night together. When he returned to the house after that, he occupied Luke's room, had his breakfast alone, very early, and took the rest of his meals with the men.

I was very ill and unable to wait on myself for a time — I cannot recall how long. Adelia gave me loving care, Laska was the sweetest and most attentive to me she had been since childhood, and Mr. Bryson sat and read to me — the sound was soothing, but I know not what it was he read from. Cicero thought once to cheer me with piano music, but I had to ask him to leave off; I could not bear the sound of music. I was beset by chills and fever and began the cough that has continued with me. But I finally accumulated enough strength to stir around again. And the breakfasts Mr. Bryson and Laska and I took together from a small table placed in a cool nook on the back porch became almost a pleasure.

We heard nothing from Luke. Mr. Bryson told me about Marina and I took comfort in the love between Miguel's daughter and my son, surmising that here perhaps was some part of the answer to the riddle of my life had I the spiritual insight to decipher it. My whole thought for them was an intense desire that they might be absolved from the misfortunes that had beset the two families and their love become a full fruition of all our dreams.

There was a final ordeal to be passed through and when its course

was run, I knew there was no reason for me to remain longer on the Rawhide Range.

As soon as I was able to pry my thoughts away from my own woeful condition, I observed that Laska was living in a state of deep and detached melancholy. She gave every possible consideration to my feelings and comfort, even to putting on a false cheerfulness in my presence, but I knew that she was enduring a hidden anguish, that she had no intention of confiding in me, and that if I intruded with question or accusation, I might lose her altogether.

Late one afternoon, after being out on Stinger all day, she came in tired and dusty, looking more forlorn and haggard than usual. She and Range met just off the back porch, she coming in and he going out. She deliberately got in his way so that he would have to stop and look at her, although he had been acting as if he were the only one alive about the place and the rest of us invisible beings who could be neither seen nor heard.

"I want to know if *you* killed him?" she questioned with fierce demand.

"Killed who?"

"El Gavilán!"

"Couldn't be sure, but I b'lieve so. There was plenty shootin' both ways at the time. Could be I wasn't the one. Like to think I was though. It looked that way."

"You can't be sure he's dead though, can you?"

"No, I can't be sure. That's too bad. But I'll tell you one thing, if he's alive, and I ever get another chance at him, I'll be sure. That goes double if he means anything to you. This is the second time you've jumped me about gettin' him. Now get this through your head: Even if you are more like a Mexican than a lot of 'em I saw across the border, you're my daughter, and I'll kill that thievin' devil Gavilán or any other Mexican that even acts like he wants to make up to you. Got that straight?"

They glared at each other, the tempest between them mounting, he towering above her in paternal rage and she so tiny, tightened like

a whip about to strike, each equally strong in the power to wound the other to the heart.

"I got it straight," she told him evenly, "but about two years late. It's too bad you feel that way about the only man I've ever — "

Range slapped her, hard.

She put her hand to her cheek, unbelieving for a moment, for in all her life her father had never struck her.

"Sangre de Cristo! You slapped me! And you're my father! I can't even hope you might not be, knowing Mama for the faithful creature she is."

In slapping Laska, Range gave her the victory, for he could not recover as quickly from what he'd done as she could. I felt an echo in my own heart of the agony that surged in his, for in spite of all her misbehavior and stubbornness he had clung to his idealization of her as his "golden girl," a pet phrase he had used since she was a baby.

Laska pursued the course of cruel condemnation he had set off by slapping her.

"You wanted me to be like Mama, didn't you? Meek and quiet and adoring, forever seeking something noble in you. Let me tell you a thorny truth: I am *not* like her. I am like *you*, and if there's anything noble in you, try to find it in me — you'll have a harder time than she's ever had searching for it in you. And I'm going to slap you back! Do you hear? And I'll hit harder, and it'll hurt more, because I'll strike you with shame — with shame!"

Range had all he could stand. "Get out of my way," he ordered.

She gave him a final thrust, "Vete al diablo!" and moved from his path.

When she came on the porch and realized I had heard it all, she gave me a stricken look, then ran to my arms sobbing, "I didn't want to hurt you — I didn't want to hurt you any more!"

"I don't think — I can be hurt any more — now. Tell me all about — El Gavilán."

359

So this was part of his finer revenge on Range, I thought. To steal his cattle, lay waste his land, then take his daughter — one way or another. But why had he waited so long? Why hadn't he kidnaped her, held her for ransom, or — harmed her in some way that would strike at Range more grievously?

"Laska, has he ever molested you in any way?"

"Oh, no, Mama!"

"You know — surely you know — he is a very wicked man. He and his father before him have lived by violence, ravishing the land, preying on the people."

"Of course I know, Mama. Everybody on both sides of the border knows about El Gavilán, and he himself has told me how wicked he is."

"Then how could you — weren't you afraid of him?"

"Afraid of him? Why, no . . . I have never been afraid of him." She drew back from me, and I saw a pleasurable sense of power rise in her eyes. "There are times though when he has been afraid of me. It is a new kind of experience in his life to have someone not afraid of him, especially a woman. He cannot understand . . . it frightens him . . . and attracts him. And I am drawn to him too, Mama — not for his wickedness, but in spite of it. He is not all wickedness. If his father had not been a bandit before him — "

"Laska! Don't make excuses like that to fool yourself. The man is all bad! He murders, he robs, he pillages! I hope you never see him again. I hope he *is* dead!" The words were no sooner out than I regretted I had spoken, knew I had struck fire, stopped the flow of confidence.

"Don't say that, Mama, unless you wish me dead too. You have spent a lifetime of making excuses for the man you love. Range Templeton may not have murdered, but he has killed; he may not be a robber, but he has taken by force what should have belonged to others and sometimes did! He may not have pillaged and plundered for the love of it, but he has wrecked the lives of those who love him and destroyed innocent people like the Sándivars. I prefer El Gavi-

360

lán's kind of wickedness, Mama, and I'll take it if I ever get another chance. I haven't gone away with him because I didn't want to disgrace the family. There isn't a family any more."

"You know Range killed El Gavilán's father, don't you?"

"El Gavilán never told me but I figured it out that evening Papa came back and said he should have sent them both over the bluff, and another time I heard him say something boastful about hawks not swimming. Tell me about it, Mama. I should know."

"It was before you were born. Your father was rounding up his first herd for the New Orleans market, had them about ready to go, and El Gavilán — the first one — raided the camp. It was after a big storm — several hundred cattle were lost — went over a bluff into the flooded river, and one of Range's men went with them. In the fight the bandit and his small son were captured, some of the others killed."

"Captured? I thought you said Daddy killed him."

"He did." I had fumbled the story. I intended to say simply that Range had killed the bandit and released his son. I didn't want to tell how it was done. But of course that was the next question.

"How?"

Reluctantly, I told her the rest of the story, and concluded, "So you see the son has brooded for a lifetime over doing us some injury in retaliation, some fiendish revenge. Oh, my darling, you are that revenge — what he does to you — if he lives — "

"Couldn't be much worse than what my father did to his."

"But his father was a bandit caught in bold robbery!"

"And my father was a brute. I'm glad you told me. I see it all more clearly now and I'm ready to go with him if he comes back. I think his plans for revenge went astray, Mama. He first saw me doing tricks on Stinger, and he thought it was fun. Later we put on riding exhibitions for each other — showing off — playing. I don't think he had ever played before in his life. He liked Daño and Stinger. Sometimes we killed game and ate together at a campfire." She sat dreamy and thoughtful, calm after the storm, relieved that

she was confiding in me. "I know he loves me truly or he would have done me harm."

"I cannot be so generous in interpreting his motives. He knows in whatever manner he takes you, it would be a full revenge on your father."

"He would never take me unless I was willing to go."

"That is just a finer point in his plan — if you go willingly — if he can keep you — the revenge will be sweeter and last longer."

"There's no use, Mama. If he lives and comes for me, I'll go, and whether it's revenge or not, it will be as sweet for me as for him."

In my way, I had done no better with her than Range. I began to try from that moment, and will continue to try as long as I have a conscious thought, to believe that no man is so wicked or so debased there is not some kindness, some spark of goodness, some capacity for true love in him, for my tawny Laska, my little sun sprite, must not be abused and handled cruelly. I will admit too that I take some comfort in the fact that to abuse her might be an uncomfortable and dangerous business even for one of such reputedly callous nature as El Gavilán.

My attacks of chills become more frequent and my coughing more continuous. I closed my room tight at night and tried hard to keep others in the house from being disturbed. I knew by now that I was to have another child and the realization was almost more than my mind was willing to take on. I had wanted other children so much through the years, and now that I could not live to care for one (I had already accepted the consumptive's fate) and there were no other arms to welcome it and hold it with loving tenderness, why, oh, why had the great creative force of life victimized me in a time of such physical and spiritual devastation? I was brought to dwell again, after all the years, on the tragic lot of Jeannie Dodson, and was comforted, not by the thought that my sorrow and shame were less than hers but by thinking of Duffy, the child that I had adored — the child that had brought joy and a beautiful companionship to

362

my children. And I decided that this little soul so painfully derived should be housed in my body without resentment, and I put out of my mind the temptation to consider this or that kind of action or accident that might prove fatal to us both. I could not, however, erase the dread that engulfed me as I thought of that time not far off when I must face my whole household in full knowledge of my condition . . . Laska's pity and shocked concern . . . the puzzled wonderment of all those who worked for us . . . Mr. Bryson, incredulous and full of compassion . . . and Range — would he despise me more, ignore me still, debase me further with some added contempt or repulsion?

I might have spared myself the torment of such thoughts for arrangements were soon under way to take me to San Antonio to be near a doctor, the cough and chills having become so bad that Adelia and Laska, attending me night after night, aroused the household with their concern and insistence that I must have medical treatment of some kind. I don't know who took the initiative. Laska simply started packing our belongings and said her father was making arrangements to send us in the coach and getting together supplies for the trip. Mr. Bryson would be in charge of the riders sent along for our protection.

"I hate him for sending Mr. Bryson to do the duty that is his own!" Laska said, "not that Mr. Bryson won't be more pleasant company!"

I kept silent. I had no energy to spend on protestations. And in the business of packing, I had only one specific request: that my mother's chest be taken with us. I knew I would never return to the Rawhide Range. I was glad my grandfather's house had never been sold.

When we departed, Range stood on the upstairs porch watching, but made no gesture of farewell. Before I stepped into the coach, Indian Toego, who had been retired for years and privileged to roam about the place at will, came up to me and in gentle curiosity nudged first my elbow, they my cheek. Toego had always been a one-man, no-women horse, holding back his finest gaits and best conduct for

Range alone, but in his old age he had enjoyed the attentions I gave him and repaid me with occasional expressions of affection such as he was exhibiting now. I paused to stroke his head and lean against him for a moment, but lest sentiment overwhelm me, did not dare look up at Range, and turned away in haste to take my place in the coach and have the door closed behind me.

There was one aspect to the trip that had pleased me from the start. It would take Laska away and help her to forget El Gavilán. I knew Range had watched her much more closely after their quarrel, and if El Gavilán lived and came for her there would be little likelihood of their going undetected and escaping his wrath. And if he did not come back, her resentment against Range would mount, her bitterness increase, until the antagonism between them would become intolerable.

At the first camp on our trip out, a tent was set up for Laska and me, and I was made very comfortable; we camped early in order that I might get extra rest. It seemed to invigorate me to be out of doors but the motion of the coach was extremely tiring. Laska had ridden with me in the coach all day and was very restless. And so while camp was being set up, she got on Stinger and went for a ride, remarking that she'd keep an eye out for game. She shrugged off offers of company, said she wouldn't go far, just wanted exercise, and was out of sight before there could be protest or objection.

The game she brought back was indeed a most surprising specimen — a variety that had been sought in vain by many hunters more intent on their task and better armed than Laska. She brought her prize directly to me, while those in camp sat or stood rooted to the spot in amazement that such a thing could be. For she had found the hawk, El Gavilán, and dared to bring him into the company of honest men and into my presence that we all might know what she was about to do; and in the hope, I'm sure, that my grief and anguish might be somehow diminished.

She spoke in the highly excited manner of her childhood days. "He has been waiting around for days, hoping to find me, Mama,

364

and when he saw the coach and Stinger, he knew I was along. I must have known somehow, Mama, it seemed so awfully urgent to take that ride." El Gavilán and I looked at each other, searchingly, as Laska's words whirled around us. I cannot say that I liked what I saw, but I was in some small measure reassured: simply that he had allowed her to bring him to me. When Laska paused, he spoke to me.

"Laska tells me you are sick. She regrets to leave you, and I am sorry she must go while you are like this. I must be back in Mexico soon — very soon — and it is her desire to go with me. I will protect her with my life."

My face must have shown what I thought of his life and the protection it would be to a woman. He sought to offer me further consolation. "We will find a priest soon, if that is your will."

"Indeed it is!"

"I wish you a good journey and a quick recovery, señora."

The things I wished for him and Laska seemed more impossible even than the simple statement he had made to me. I could not find a word to say.

Laska embraced me with all her wiry strength, crushing me, hurting me. "Adiós Mamá querida" . . . "Adiós, señora." They were quickly gone.

I held back the coughing that had been provoked until they were on their horses and away. I did not want her to be haunted by my cough, shadowed by my pain.

Five months later the sacred burial rites were said for my stillborn child, a girl that I named Anita. I was amazed at my grief for the child, not having realized before that the full passion of mother love can be so overpowering from the moment of giving birth. I had long flights of fancy in which I seemed to know exactly what kind of girl she would have been; then I would simply whisper her name and the tears would flow . . . "Anita," the name of one who would have kindness in her soft gray eyes, and gentleness in her hands.

Now I am beginning to indulge in a selfish consolation that she has gone on before me. I will never be lonely there, for among the cherubim I will find my Anita and hold her in my arms.

wwwwwwwwwwwwwwwwwwwwwwwwwwwwwwwwwwwwwwwwwwwwwwwwwwwwwwwwwwwwwwwwwwwwwwwwwwww

CHAPTER XVII

wwwwwwwwwwwwwwwwwwwwwwwwwwwwwwwwwwwwwwwwwwwwwwwwwwwwwwwwwwwwwwwwwwwwwwwwwwww

Silver Bryson's Supplement
to Luvisa Templeton's Account

LUVISA TEMPLETON is dead. I must write it out bluntly like that in order to believe it myself. The earth has claimed her and a marker reads: "Luvisa, wife of Range Templeton . . . Kindness was her stronghold, and love her fortification. . . ."

The pen that inscribes this appendage is moved in the execution of a promise.

"Mr Bryson, to these things you have so patiently recorded at my request, you will add in your own words some appropriate conclusion to the account, will you not? You are a part of my life — of my family's life. . . ." So I promised her.

I never told Luvisa Templeton the story of Châli Le Roi, although at times I came near it. In her last days when we were closest, it would have been easy to tell her, but I chose not to burden her with more sadness, and she understood this. The last time I took notes for her, I commented on the lovely gentle name of Anita, and she asked me, "What was *her* name, Mr. Bryson?"

"Whose name, my dear?"

"The love of your youth."

"Châli."

"How beautiful!"

Then she said it over to herself softly several times, "Châli . . . Châli," and we mentioned it no more.

366

Luvisa with her Spanish heritage and Châli, daughter of a quad-roon, were so different, and yet alike in their capacity for boundless devotion, and both were born to follow the path of the dark star and encounter the doom shaped by racial antagonisms.

Had I told Luvisa the full story of Châli she would have learned something else she never discovered about me — that revenge is a weakness of my nature. When I am deeply injured, I cannot rest, cannot assuage the pangs of grief or the stings of insult until I have carried out my own ideas of balancing offense and punishment. This I did in the case of the mulatto who destroyed the Le Roi family and with them all the values of life that I knew then. And now I must confess that I am engaged in plotting another revenge, balancing injury and retribution, this time on Range Templeton. . . . I have Luvisa's cough. I shall return to the Rawhide Range and spend the rest of my life there. It may not be a long life, but the disease will not find me as easy prey as the delicate body and crushed spirit of Luvisa. I shall cough at night, and Range will lie awake and think of her suffering. I shall have my meals with him, and my coughing will drive away all appetite. I will ride with him and her ghost will ride with us, ever-present in my racking cough. And as we ride, the heavy fragrance of the agrito bush will sicken him with its sweetness and burden him with yearnings, and the golden beauty of the huisache will be a torture to his senses. I will know all the ways to recall her wherever he goes, whatever he does.

In a bleak sort of way, I expect to enjoy myself.

But these morbid musings do Luvisa an injustice — she who was able to sustain through all adversity an unfaltering faith in the divine origin and goal of man and a holy conviction that the time must come when man's inhumanity to man will altogether cease. My cynicism falters in the presence of her philosophy and my weakness turns on me, for in the visions of her that I conjure up for Range Templeton who shall say which one of us will suffer more? Though I find pleasure in his pain, how can I put aside my own?

As I look back through the notebooks I have filled with her ac-count, I read on one of the opening pages: "If I am to die in peace,

although despised and put aside by the one I love, I must believe, in spite of all mistakes and suffering, in the divine purpose of the life span . . . the gradual accumulation of goodness in the consciousness of the human race until pain and ignorance and greed are all crowded out, and somewhere down the passages of time the way cleared for more joyous living on earth."

". . . down the passages of time" . . . are they so hopelessly long that to make our own contribution seems merely another exercise in futility? And later she had me set down the words of Dr. Weideman: "Attainment of the divine average, I have decided, must be measured in thousands or tens of thousands of years."

Assuming that this doctor spoke with prophetic wisdom, is responsibility for a condition of existence so far removed from our own short and puny span of days to be wholly denied by those of us who now tread the earth with such uncertain step?

I can only surmise from the wreckage of experience that if it were possible to fan the spark of idealism that glows in youth, to nurture the nobility that is planted in the human heart by shielding it from the destructive forces of greed and prejudice, the process of disillusionment and development of self-interest under which we now mature might be reversed. Hope for such a reversal rises strongest in us when we behold in each new generation the spark of idealism still unquenched, the seed of nobility still fertile with promise.

I saw this hope surge high in Luvisa Templeton before she died and my barren heart could not help but reflect some portion of the light. And it was made possible because Luke and Laska came to her. I had sent a courier to Laredo and to the springs on a chance that the message might get through to them that their mother lay dying. I instructed the messenger to pass the word among the Mexicans that roved across the border, specifically those that might know the whereabouts of El Gavilán.

Luke arrived first. His presence was such a surprise, such an unexpected happiness and stimulation that I think her life was actually prolonged several days by his appearance. We all knew a brief respite

from the valley of shadows while Luke told us of Marina and how he had found her living with her grandmother and two uncles on the few acres that held the ramshackle buildings of the old Sándivar place in Tamaulipas. He had stayed with them awhile and persuaded them all to return to the Sándivar home at the springs. He had explained to them how it was Marina's property now and he would stay by her and protect her. He had built a small house for himself and Marina, hardly more than a cabin, close by the springs. They were married and their love was a happiness so great that — He looked at his mother, unable to express himself, and she smiled understandingly. I'm sure Marina couldn't be as beautiful as he described her to us — love is a force that fashions beauty to its own exaggerated proportions. He climaxed his story by telling us they were soon to have a child. Color flowed into Luvisa's pale cheeks. "Why, I'm a grandmother! Luke, darling, how wonderful!" We drank a toast to Luke's unborn child and savored with an intensity out of all proportion to the occasion this bit of festivity at her bedside, a few seconds snatched eagerly from the grudging Timekeeper who hovered so near.

Laska almost failed to make it in time. She arrived on the very day of her mother's death. She had ridden alone and like a madwoman for over two hundred miles — from some point across the border in Mexico. She was wild-looking, dirty, grieved. She embraced Luke and me in her manner of sweet impetuous violence and frantically inquired about her mother. Luvisa was now in a state of semi-consciousness, sometimes aware of things about her, sometimes not. Luke and I were horrified that she might in some last moment of lucidity see Laska like this. Laska had no thought but to rush to her mother. Luke took her to a long mirror and had her look at herself.

"You don't want Mama to see me, do you?" she asked after staring a moment.

"Not like that. If you'd wash up and put on something different, maybe — "

Laska flashed a grim look at him, and the old fire of challenge leaped up.

She left us and we were totally unprepared for the appearance she made after a while. We stared in utter fascination. She enjoyed her triumph for a moment and then said to us, "Will you take me to Mama now?"

Laska had invaded her Spanish grandmother's chest for a second time. The clothes fitted as if made for her alone. She had on the full-skirted, tight-bodiced golden gown that she had danced in, but this time it needed no alteration. She wore two ornaments, a pair of thin gold earrings and a plain gold cross on a chain around her neck. She explained about the cross.

"I wear it for my mother and her mother."

Her hair was curly from fresh washing and her skin the sun's own dust of gold.

When she entered the room where Luvisa lay, she stood quiet for a moment gazing on her mother's still pale face, the eyes closed, the breath so uncertain.

"Mama!"

Luvisa opened her eyes wide in astonishment. Her mind did not accept the scene just as it was.

"Range!" she called clearly with a bright, unnatural excitement. "Range, my dear, come quickly! Here is your golden girl!"

Laska stood trembling.

Luvisa continued, "You are such a lovely thing — my little golden witch — my little sun sprite."

Laska rushed to the bedside, fell to her knees, flung out her arms over her mother's body and buried her face in the covers, completely overcome with her feelings. Luvisa's frail fingers found Laska's hair and caressed it, and the phrases of endearment that she used were from the wayward memories of her own childhood — the ones spoken by her Spanish mother to her: "Ah, querida mía . . . mi alma y mi vida . . . niñeta carísima!"

As Luvisa Templeton beheld for the last time that contour of the river of life that had contained her love for Range Templeton, she gazed with wonder and reassurance into the quiet pool of calm depth

370

that was her son's life, and in Laska glimpsed the beauty of a tumul-
tuous craggy little cascade sparkling in the sun. But when I go,
the only view at hand will be a dry and rocky gulch through which
the life-giving waters have rushed by some misdirection and disappeared altogether.

I had thought to go no further with this account, but it would be
unfair to those who may read the Luvisa Templeton story not to
record one other event concerning Range Templeton and myself.

When I returned to the Rawhide Range and brought word of
Luvisa's death, some new and deeper mantle of darkness was flung
over Range Templeton's mind. After a while, as one will experi-
mentally toss a stone into a deep well to find if there is still water
in its murky depths, I told him that Luke was living at the springs
married to Marina Sándivar and they were to have a child.

I knew that hate surged strong in him still, but I was unprepared
for the storm of passion that broke over him and took possession of all
his faculties. He was never articulate in anger, and now the violence
of his feelings brought on an inner devastation appalling to behold.
The blood drained from his countenance, his eyes bulged, and the
heavy cords in his neck were drawn tight and hard with strain. Then
he was thrown into a paroxysm of chills as if some giant grip were
laid upon him and shaking the very vitals out of him. I thought he
was about to fall in a death convulsion and reached out to lend his
body support. When I touched him, he became still and solid. His
color flooded back. He licked his lips as if some flavor of venom were
there, and his fingers twitched in a gesture of cruelty.

In twenty years of association with Range Templeton I had experienced time and again, in moments of extremity, the opening of
some channel of the senses that would reveal to me his sensations and
intentions as clearly as if he had conveyed them to me in words. This
was such a time. He was submerging his senses in the blackest Mexican hate he had ever known, feeding his fury with the fact that by
his only son he was to have a grandchild in whom the Mexican
strain would be stronger than his own and yet it would bear the

371

name of Templeton and possess the springs. The birth of this child would represent a triumph for Miguel Sándivar, his family and his race, and would be an outrage against the single element of life that Range Templeton held sacred: perpetuation of self through offspring.

He seemed completely unaware that I was near him — his eyes never once sought mine in question or recognition. His first controlled movements were to check his guns and the ammunition in his belt. Then he turned and strode with heavy purpose toward the stables and picked out a good horse that could carry him for a long ride. He mounted and rode off headed for the springs.

Without any attempt to be furtive in my movements, I followed. I felt him to be completely insensible to my actions, wrapped as he was in the evil mood that makes killing easy, driven by the searing desire to destroy that which was inflicting his agony.

That night in the brush country, following Range Templeton across his thorny acres, from the headquarters of the Rawhide Range on the Nueces River to the springs of the Regalo de la Vaca, was a ride through hell's own provinces. The moon was on the wane, its light eerie and deceiving, and the coyote calls were like the lost and lonely wails of the damned. Grotesque outlines of giant cactus took on the menacing quality of fiendish arms clutching and clawing at horse and rider, seeking to pull them into barbed embrace. This land for which Range Templeton and I had felt such an affinity — where we had sought and found beyond spiked defenses those natural elements that were vigorous and challenging to a man — seemed to turn against us this night with an animate hostility. It was too vast a thing to curse, too fearsome to ignore. So I fought it, taking the punishment of poisonous jabs and bruises in order to stay close on the sound of the rider I followed and sometimes over stretches of prairie sight the dim outline of movement ahead of me.

As we rode on into the early morning hours and came ever nearer to the cabin at the springs, I fought another kind of fear — the fear for what I must do when we arrived there. In the madness that now ruled him, Range would kill Luke and Marina. I must protect them

372

— their lives contained something of Luvisa. I loved them through myself too. I knew intimately the generosity of mind, the depth of spirit that dwelt in Luke Templeton. His nature embodied the goodness of his mother, the fearlessness of his father, and all the understanding I could pour into him through good books and sound knowledge. Now love of Marina and prospects of fatherhood were the very core of his existence. I could not allow all this to be snuffed out, even if I had to kill Range Templeton to preserve it. Kill Range Templeton! That was not an entirely new thought to me, for the brutal element in his nature had goaded me to such consideration before; but now that it seemed inevitable, I felt that life was placing upon me the most agonizing assignment I had yet experienced.

It was at that hour just before dawn, when life seems weakest before it is strong again, that we arrived in the vicinity of the springs. When Range sighted the cabin against the reluctant light of the low moon, he stopped his horse and dismounted with careful quietness. Tall and gaunt, stiff from his long hours in the saddle, he moved like a sinister shadow toward the cabin. I was not far behind him, a gun waiting in my hand, a prayer pounding in my heart — a prayer for a miracle — in the fervent language of Spain, "Un milagro! O Jesucristo! Un milagro!" The cynic and the skeptic with a passionate petition — daring to reach out to a power undefined for a solution beyond myself.

Range paused, perhaps to consider the best way of invading the sanctuary of silence that enfolded the little cabin in the predawn.

Then the whole still, gray scene was broken by a high, thin, human sound, and the stooped shadow near the cabin jerked as if struck with a lash. It was the wail of a very young and very hungry child greeting the dawn . . . vigorous, lusty, and demanding, yet plaintive and appealing. The cry was intensified, indignant with delay, then slightly appeased, then quiet altogether.

Range Templeton's body sagged, his arms hung limply, and the gun in his hand dropped harmlessly onto the carpet of wild flowers at his feet. But the caution of twenty years on the frontier was strong

373

enough in him that he stooped to recover the gun. Slowly he returned it to the holster, turned his back on the cabin, and walked with the stiff effort of the doomed or mortally wounded back toward his horse.

I was almost directly in his path and he stopped very near me, admitting for the first time an awareness of my presence. He must have known that I comprehended the depth of misery and desolation in him. The only sound was his labored breathing that became a strangled sort of sobbing as he stood beside me, his anguish almost suffocating him, his tears in an acrid concentrate of pain falling on the grass where Miguel Sándivar's cow once grazed.

A Dr. Weideman jest was now a prophecy fulfilled: Range Templeton was grandfather to a child with Mexican blood coursing buoyantly through its veins, and in terms of the doctor's philosophy had thus become a father of the brood continental, making his particular contribution toward final attainment of the divine average somewhere down the corridor of centuries. But Range Templeton, the fire of his fury quenched by a baby's cry, had no comprehension of such a contribution and the bitter acceptance of his destiny was unrelieved by any compromise within himself. The compassion I felt for him was for all — both the innocent and the self-committed — who must be tortured on the rack of race prejudice and conflict.

A soft light glowed in the cabin. Had Luke, awakened by the baby, been disturbed by some sound or sense of intrusion? My anxiety that he might discover us brought on a coughing seizure.

He called out, "Who's there?"

I couldn't answer and Range was without voice or movement.

"Who's there?" he called again.

"Bryson," I managed to answer. "I'm early — don't get out — I'll tend to my horse."

Range and I went to our horses. No word passed between us. I led my horse to the springs. He rode off the way he had come: no solace of spring waters for him and his fagged mount, but rather some grudging refuge beside a still imprisoned pool in the tight seclusion of brush barricade.

374

I sought the far side of the springs, away from the cabin, delaying my meeting with Luke. I knew he'd be out before long. He'd always liked getting up early and absorbing the glories of sunrise as a spiritual stimulant.

My horse sank his muzzle deep in the cool water and drank in swift gratifying surges. I scooped up water in my shaking hands to slake my own feverish thirst, bathed my bruised and burning face, and sat down to rest.

The birds began fluttering and chirping in preparation for their full-throated morning songs. A cow, so white and sleek that she glistened with a silken sheen, lay by the sweet rippling waters chewing her cud. Was this cow ageless, I wondered, some sacred symbol of possession to the Sándivars who called their acres Regalo de la Vaca — Gift of the Cow? I had seen her for so many years on every visit to the springs, always near the waters, as if the area were her special domain. On this occasion she gave me the feeling of being in the company of ghosts.

Luke came, as I expected, and greeted me from a distance with a voice that revealed new dimensions of happiness. "Mr. Bryson! I have a son!"

"I'm glad you have a son, Luke," I answered.

"I call him Mike — Big Mike Templeton."

So Michael was the name of Range Templeton's grandson.

To Marina he'd be little Miguel — Miguelito.

"Mike Templeton is a name for a strong man, Luke," I said.

The grandeur of the sunrise caught him before he crossed over to me, and he stopped very still, hands on hips, watching the play of dark red, then copper and gold, on the fringes of the thin clouds in the east. He stood before me in the morning light as a youthful and exalted Range Templeton. Augmented by the elements in his mother's nature, the seed of nobility dormant in his father flourished mightily in him.

While he dwelt in a passion of joy at the revelations of fatherhood, I dwelt with wonder on the miracle that a baby's cry had done what I had thought my gun must do.

375

From our separate pinnacles of exaltation, we shared the spreading splendor of sunrise with vision magnified and idealized, spanning the great gulf of the future, glimpsing man's ultimate goal.

wwwwwwwwwwwwwwwwwwwwwwwwwwwwwwwwwwwwwwwwwwwwwwwwwwwwwwwwwwwwwwwwwwwwwww

A BOOK WAS MADE

wwwwwwwwwwwwwwwwwwwwwwwwwwwwwwwwwwwwwwwwwwwwwwwwwwwwwwwwwwwwwwwwwwwwwww

FROM IDEA to finished story the making of this book of fiction, fashioned from the realities of those violent years in Texas history 1838 to 1858, was a fifteen-year process. Focusing upon a borderland of continental significance, the dividing line between Latin and Anglo-American cultures, the author explored vast areas of recorded facts, sought human values and truths as revealed in legend, folk story, and ballad, and was ever sensitive to the more subtle influence of the artifacts of that period and the artistic expressions growing out of the life of the times . . . to become absorbed in the detail of a Charles M. Russell picture or stand before *The Seven Mustangs* by A. Phimister Proctor was to realize something of the heritage of the great Southwest, to sense something of the glory of the past.

Varied and too numerous for listing were the sources upon which the author drew to make this book: the teachers, the historians, the librarians; the recorders and map-makers, the researchers and note-takers; the writers of journals and diaries and letters and the pre-servers of all these; the begetters of the printed word in all its forms; the tellers of tall tales and the singers of heart songs.

There were main sources and basic references, however, as well as specific influences and inspirations, that are set down here as the keystones in the structure of *Divine Average*.

J. Frank Dobie — his publications (especially *The Longhorns* and *A Vaquero of the Brush Country*), his classroom instruction on "Life and Literature of the Southwest," and his private files on New

Orleans and California cattle drives . . . his friendly interest, guidance, and encouragement throughout the years of labor involved.

Mrs. Mary Adams Maverick — her *Memoirs,* an inspiring human-interest account of early times in San Antonio, contributing the historical documentation of Dr. Weideman, used by permission of the copyright owner, Mrs. Rena Maverick Green.

Walter Prescott Webb — his distinguished works *The Texas Rangers* and *The Great Plains* furnishing exhaustive detail and documentation of Indians, weapons, Rangers, and frontier warfare.

Texas Folklore Society Publications — a rich repository of songs and stories, tales and traditions. Permission granted by Mody C. Boatright, editor, to make general use of all published materials and specific use of the mockingbird story from "Folk-Lore of the Texas-Mexican Vaquero" by Jovita González published in *Texas and Southwestern Lore.* The publication *Mustangs and Cow Horses* was used as the basic source book on wild horses.

Files of *The Southwestern Historical Quarterly* — published by the Texas State Historical Association, the oldest learned society in Texas, H. Bailey Carroll, editor and director. In fifty-five years this publication has never missed an issue and its fifty-five volumes comprise the greatest single source of information about Texas in existence. Typical of its contributions to the structure of this book is the article "Laredo During the Texas Republic," by Seb. S. Wilcox, Vol. XLII; also the study of "The Free Negro in the Republic of Texas" by Harold Schoen, Vols. XXXIX, XL, and XLI, validating the creation of such a character as Victor Chenet.

The Eugene C. Barker Texas History Center of the University of Texas — where the author dug for buried treasure in the archives with Winnie Allen, archivist and bright-eyed enthusiast, directing the excavations . . . explored the fascinating walled kingdom of rare books in the inspiring company of Marcelle Lively Hamer, Texas zealot extraordinary . . . roamed the bookshelf corridors in the general Texas Collection examining hundreds of volumes, famous, obscure, erudite, picturesque, romantic, factual . . . reached often

377

for the Texas history volumes of H. Yoakum, Esq., and John Henry Brown . . . and learned the full magnitude of the works of Eugene C. Barker.

Historical Essay by Irene Ibarra — "The Founding of Los Ojuelos." This warm and simple story of La Brema, the cow, written by an orphaned Mexican schoolgirl, focused the author's attention on a historical implication that after intensive research became not only a keystone but a gracious archway in the structure of the book.

The Cattleman — monthly publication of the Texas and Southwestern Cattle Raisers Association, Inc. . . . its articles on cattle, horses, guns, and trail drivers . . . its fine regard for authentic Western art.

Colt's Manufacturing Company — its specific service to the author by photograph, letter, and bulletin on the history of the Colt revolver.

A History of Mexico by Henry Bamford Parkes (1938), and *The Texas Republic,* a social and economic history by William Ransom Hogan (1946) — high-quality material that went into the study forming the foundation of the structure.

Our Wild Indians by Colonel Richard Irving Dodge (1882), *Indian Depredations in Texas* by J. W. Wilbarger (1889), and *Three Years Among the Comanches* by Nelson Lee (1859) — stirring narratives, hair-raising episodes, and colorful description offering incredible truths for a fiction framework of startling design.

Hervey A. Adams Diary, *Expedition Against the South West in 1842 & 1843* — a rare documentation of the Somervell Expedition with careful description of San Antonio and the Laredo Road. Vivid and teeming with the life of the times, its detail mortared many a historical crevice in the structure of *Divine Average.*

Private Library of Mr. and Mrs. A. H. Viets — where the author learned in childhood that "Books are a substantial world, both pure and good" and absorbed through the Waverley Novels and Mulbach's Historical Romances an everlasting affinity for the historical novel.

ELITHE HAMILTON KIRKLAND